BOOK ONE OF
THE AWAKENED CHRONICLES

ABIGAIL BLACK

THE AWAKENED CHRONICLES
Book One: *The Awakened*
Third Edition

Published by Awakened Publishing
www.awakenedpublishing.com

Please note: This is a work of fiction, and any resemblance
of the characters therein to actual people is purely
coincidental. The ideas presented in this work-especially in
the ways of theology and history-are based largely on
speculation and imagination; not to be taken as fact.

Cover design by Brian Volckmann
www.vmandesign.com

Book design by Abigail Black
www.abigailblack.com

Printed in the United States of America

To The Sleeping Ones About To Wake:

THIS ONE'S FOR YOU

A Note from the Author:

It isn't easy giving up everything you are to something you're unsure of, only to come out on the other side so scathed and burned you don't even recognize yourself anymore. Just like it isn't easy to tell yourself you don't believe in something when you know you really do.

That's the frustrating thing about lying to yourself. No matter how convincing you are, you always know the truth, even if you're too afraid to speak the words out loud.

I think that's what *The Awakened* has proven to me more than anything; that sometimes a dream has to die before it can be brought back to life.

Even if you don't believe it. Even if you don't want it. Even if you run from it with everything you are. Some dreams are about a lot more than you, and you owe it to more than just yourself to let them come to pass.

Sometimes it's simply about a story. Sometimes it's about a whole lot more. But you never really know for sure until you reach the last page.

As much as you may want to skip forward and look at the ending, to do a thing like that would be to completely miss the point. Because the promise is in the pages, and if you don't follow them through from first to last, you won't see what you've been looking for from the start.

That's what this story is to me. That's what it has always been: *A promise that refused to die.*

ABIGAIL BLACK

Table of Contents

Be Warned:

This story has been known (in more than just a few cases) to dramatically alter the lives of those who read it; without intention, without provocation, and without any clear means of avoiding this result. Read at your own risk, and only if you are not afraid to see.

Because I really can't promise that you'll come away the same.

ABIGAIL BLACK

Prologue

Rachel Blake trembled as she held her son's hand. "Just a little farther," she whispered to him. She tried to sound optimistic, even flashed him a smile, but her efforts were wasted. Nathaniel could see right through her. He had always been able to see through her like that, or through anyone for that matter, to a measure that was sometimes unsettling.

Just one of the many things that made him different than other nine-year-old boys.

Clutching his mother's hand as she dragged him through the woods, Nathaniel tried not to be afraid. He didn't know how she managed to navigate her way so swiftly through the trees, but he had yet to question her on it. He may not have known why they were running or where they were going or why his mother was so frantic she was shaking, but he did know this: He trusted her with his life.

Nathaniel held his breath in the eerily still night, which was darker somehow than it should have been. Even if the clouds overhead hadn't veiled the stars, there was a depth to the dark he had never seen. Or maybe it only seemed that way. Maybe the darkness he felt pressing in on him came from someplace he couldn't see. Either way, he didn't like it.

Brushing limp blonde strands of hair from his eyes, Nathaniel pushed himself to run harder, determined that they would not slow down on his account. He could feel the urgency that pulled his mother forward, as if death itself were on her heels.

1

Rachel skidded to a halt in a move so abrupt that her feet kicked up dirt in Nathaniel's face. He immediately started coughing and she grabbed him in response, covering his mouth and whipping her head back and forth like she expected to see someone...or some*thing* leap out at them from the forest.

She wasn't breathing normally, Nathaniel noticed. He looked up at his mother while her hand was still clasped over his mouth. She was even more afraid than he had realized.

"Quick," she told him.

Rachel dragged him off the trail in an attempt to find cover, and as she pulled him with her into the woods, a jagged rock tore through the knee of Nathaniel's jeans. It sliced cleanly into his skin, but he didn't make a sound.

Another of the many distinctions between Nathaniel Blake and the others his age was his uncanny ability to ignore pain; something that proved quite beneficial in a situation like this.

Rachel directed him to the hollowed-out shell of a rotten tree. "In here," she said.

Nathaniel realized she didn't know he was bleeding. He also realized that this tree, though a very effective hiding place, was not big enough for the both of them.

Looking back at her, he told her flatly, "No."

Rachel looked down on him with a pained expression. "Baby, please," she begged. "I need you to hide...just for a little while. I'll...I'll come back to get you as soon as it's safe."

Nathaniel clenched his jaw stubbornly. "You are not leaving me here."

Running her long slender fingers through her strawberry blonde hair, Rachel tried not to cry. Nathaniel knew he was making this worse for her, but he wasn't about to give in to what he could see behind her eyes.

"Who are we running from?" he asked her point blank.

Rachel's eyes softened helplessly as she touched his face. "I can't explain that now," she choked out. "Nathaniel, please...tell me you trust me."

Her words stung deeper than the gash in his knee.

"Baby, look at me," she whispered when he avoided her eyes. She took his arms in her hands and rubbed them softly.

2

Nathaniel's face was tight as he met his mother's gaze, but still he couldn't force the words.

"It's going to be okay, sweetheart." She tried to hide from him that she was terrified and failed at it miserably. "I promise he is not going to hurt you."

Nathaniel's voice quivered as he spoke, out of anger as much as fear. "*Who* isn't going to hurt me?"

Rachel hesitated and looked behind her again, then quickly back to her son.

"Don't leave me, Mom," Nathaniel whispered, pleading with the sapphire eyes that were a mirror image of his own.

Grabbing him with shaking hands, Rachel held him so close that her tears spilled onto his face. Nathaniel couldn't move. He just stood there frozen as she kissed the top of his head, paralyzed by the truth he did not want to see.

"Mom…" he choked.

Rachel took his face in both of her hands. "I love you, Nathaniel," she told him. "More than I knew I could love anything."

Tears burned in his eyes, but he refused to let them fall.

"Be strong, baby. Be strong for me, please."

With his jaw still tensed, Nathaniel whispered in a shaken voice to the woman who gave him life, "I trust you."

Rachel swallowed hard and closed her eyes. "Forgive me," she whispered. Then she squeezed his hand and disappeared into the forest.

Nathaniel knew exactly what she was doing. He just wished that he didn't. Shaking as he hugged his knees to his chest, he pressed his back against the rough, rotted bark, attempting to stay as hidden as he could. It was dank and musky in the hollowed-out tree, the air so thick he could hardly even breathe. He could feel things crawling all around him on the inside of the wood, but there was no telling what they were…or what waited for him on the outside.

The forest was hauntingly still when his mother's footsteps faded, to a measure more disturbing than Nathaniel had ever felt. Waiting there in the dark for the fate he could feel pulling at the edge of his soul, he breathed hard and kept his eyes open. He had never known a fear like this. It constricted him in a way that his lungs weren't even able to fill with air.

But what he felt in that moment didn't compare to what he felt in the next.

A shrill scream sounded that split the silence, piercing the darkness that hung all around him. Nathaniel went rigid at the sound. Eyes wide. Heart frozen. The blood drained completely from his face. He felt a shock of fear and a wave of nausea, and an impulse to run despite what he had been told. But he didn't listen to his instincts; he listened to his mother, to the words she had spoken which he knew would save his life.

Nathaniel's breath was hollow and the night air was thick. Everything spun and twisted in different directions, distorting reality so he didn't even know what was happening anymore. He didn't know if he was still in the mountains or if somehow he had hallucinated all of this, but Nathaniel knew he wasn't dreaming. He only wished that he was so he could deny this now.

He only wished he could deny that unmistakable scream.

There was a shuffling in the distance, and low muffled noises that he couldn't make out. Nathaniel's blood stopped cold when the sound grew nearer. Someone was out there. They were looking for him…and with every step they took, they were getting closer.

Nathaniel sucked in his breath and held it fast, keeping his eyes open as he peered through the tree. His mother had known what she was doing in hiding him here. He was covered by the dark, kept safe in its bitter embrace, protected by the very thing that was his enemy.

Again, the forest fell silent. Nathaniel stopped breathing so he could listen for a sound, but all that reached his ears was the same empty nothing he felt ripping through his soul.

That was all it took for him to bolt from his hiding place. Springing from the tree, he tore through the forest, guided only by the light of a dimly lit moon. The clouds were breaking over it now, just enough to let its light reflect down on the trail, like a beacon to guide him to the place where hope died.

Nathaniel slammed to a halt and his whole body froze. His eyes grew wide in sickened horror. He knew it when he saw his mother's lifeless body lying broken on the trail. He knew it before he even touched her, before he checked her pulse or tried to see if she was still breathing.

He knew she was gone.

Nathaniel could feel it in the absence where he would have felt her spirit. It just wasn't there anymore; that permeating warmth, that depth of love, the promise of safety that only a mother could give. None of it was there. All that was left of Rachel Blake was a body...an empty shell of who she really was.

Collapsing to his knees, Nathaniel's hair hung down in his eyes. This couldn't be real. She couldn't be gone. This woman was the only thing he had in the world.

Brushing the strawberry-blonde curls away from his mother's face, Nathaniel jerked his hand back quickly when he saw the blood. The laceration was deep, at least several inches.

Someone had cut her throat.

He crawled backwards away from her in a knee-jerk reaction, frantic as he tried to distance himself from what he didn't want to see. But at the same time he couldn't look away from it.

That was when the silence of the forest broke away once more. They were footsteps Nathaniel heard, and they came from somewhere in front of him, but it was too dark for him to see a thing. The clouds that blanketed the moon made that completely impossible. But then the footsteps sounded again, slowly this time, and the white glowing orb in the sky broke past the clouds, opening up just enough light for Nathaniel to see.

He froze at the sight of the figure that emerged, paralyzed in fear at the man's approach. Nathaniel squinted hard into the dark, attempting to make out the newcomer's features, not that it would matter what this stranger looked like if he was there to kill him.

The man looked young, probably in his early twenties, but his presence was commanding; and there was something

5

Nathaniel felt from him that left him absolutely terrified. Not in the way he would have expected to be, though. The terror he felt came from something different than his obvious fear that this man might be the one who had killed his mother.

The stranger looked down at Rachel's body robotically, emotionlessly. Even though Nathaniel could see his eyes by the light of the moon, he couldn't tell what he was thinking; at least not enough to judge if he was the killer. Nathaniel couldn't understand his expression at all.

Suddenly, the stranger turned to face him. "Do not be afraid," the man said. "I am not here to harm you."

"Who are you?" Nathaniel asked in a shaky voice.

"My name is Seth."

Nathaniel swallowed hard. "What do you want from me?"

The stranger named Seth did not advance, just looked down knowingly on the frightened boy on the path. "I am here to protect you, Nathaniel."

Nathaniel's face went white. This man should not know his name.

Chapter 1

"...through gates forbidden."

Nathaniel Blake and Caleb Holcomb walked with measured steps along a winding cement path. The day was overcast, warm and muggy as a result of the sporadic rain, but nobody on campus seemed to mind. Not with it being the last day of the term.

The two of them hardly fit the image of the other Oxford students who couldn't contain their excitement over their just-completed finals, though even on a normal day, these two stood out in any crowd. At passing glance it was their height, their build, and the unnerving degree of their beauty that caused most people to double-take when they saw them, and the unnatural grace to their stature that held their gaze. But this day more than most, the contrast was stark between them and those around them. Especially in Nathaniel.

Taking in every detail with his piercing blue eyes, Nathaniel scanned the campus of the oldest surviving university in the English-speaking world. He carefully observed everyone around them, shutting off the impressions he was given by his physical sight and using another sense, a deeper sense to discern what was really going on.

He was frighteningly good at that.

Nathaniel looked past the skinny, awkward boy who was carrying ten haphazardly-stacked textbooks, the professor bee-lining for the parking lot and the overly confident lacrosse player attempting to make a move on an unimpressed brunette. These did not hold any interest to him.

"Anything?" Caleb asked him.

Nathaniel's tone was devoid of emotion when he answered him, "No."

Caleb frowned and Nathaniel knew exactly what he was thinking. "That doesn't mean the information was wrong," he told the boy he considered his brother. "We still keep on our guard."

Caleb looked uncomfortable as they walked. His steps were rigid and his shoulders were tight; something he always did when he was frustrated. It wouldn't have been so obvious either, had he not been next to Nathaniel. Anything would look awkward compared to that. Time after time, Caleb had tried to get him to "loosen up," saying he wasn't helping his cover by walking and moving and speaking the way he did. A tower of strength and commanding grace, Nathaniel had always been different than Caleb and the others. And while a thing like that was to his advantage in their world, it wasn't in this one.

Caleb nodded to a fellow classmate who had a book bag slung over his shoulder, a tall gangly boy with wiry red hair and pants that were at least three inches too short. Nathaniel didn't recognize him. The boy nodded back to Caleb, then tightened his grip on his bag and gave Nathaniel a quick glance as he passed them by. The boy tried to be inconspicuous about it, but failed at the attempt. Not an uncommon reaction by any means.

Needless to say, Nathaniel knew it wasn't Caleb that had scared the boy off.

Appearing nonchalant as they walked side by side, Nathaniel and Caleb continued on their way. Caleb acted as if his attention were set on nothing except the random acquaintances he passed as they made their way toward an undefined destination on campus, but Nathaniel knew he was aware of what they approached. Caleb was always aware, just not quite in the same way he was.

They were a lot alike, Nathaniel and Caleb, as much as if they had been brothers by blood. They even looked alike for the most part. Caleb wasn't as built as Nathaniel, the muscles in his arms and his chest not quite as defined, but it would surprise almost anyone to know how strong the boy truly was. His green eyes were soft and un-alarming, a stark contrast to Nathaniel's sapphire blue daggers, which was the reason most people didn't have a problem talking to him. And also one of the clearest distinctions between them.

Nathaniel kept his gaze slightly off from anyone passing them by and anyone off in the distance who might think he was making eye contact, but he was no less aware of the ones they approached. A familiar group of girls stood ahead of them on the cement path, eyeing him and Caleb from about twenty yards away.

"You're up," Nathaniel said.

Caleb nodded discreetly, his sign that he was ready; just not in a way that anyone else could tell what he was doing.

Nathaniel stopped walking a ways back from the group. He folded his arms across his chest and waited for Caleb, making an effort to look bored and uninterested in whoever it was that stood there. But his attention was carefully fixed. Out of his peripheral vision, he took note of which of the girls were there and which ones were missing. Then he saw the small pretty one with reddish-brown hair break away from the others to approach Caleb. Nathaniel recognized her immediately.

Her name was Samantha Ross. And he did not trust her.

"Hello, Caleb," the girl said sweetly in her soft British accent.

Caleb greeted her with a nod. "Samantha."

Nathaniel cringed internally. Continuing to analyze everyone's placement on the campus, he kept himself open to feel if the one they had been warned of, the one called Donovan had decided to show up here. But for Nathaniel, that was only a side focus at the moment. Even if Donovan had come here as they had been warned, that didn't hold his attention over this group of girls who had already taken more than enough notice of him.

One of the prettier ones from the group, a tall slender blonde with a degree of nerve the others didn't seem to possess gave Nathaniel the once-over and eyed him like the huntress he knew her to be. His focus remained unbroken as she slipped her hands into the back pockets of her designer jeans and sauntered coyly toward him. There was confidence in her movement, but it wasn't merely flirtation. Nathaniel knew she intended it to appear that way, but he also knew there was nothing about this girl that was like it seemed.

"You're Nathaniel, right?" she practically cooed, tilting her head to one side.

They had never met, but Nathaniel knew who she was, just as she knew him. Normally, he went out of his way to keep distance between himself and these sorority girls, but today things were different. He couldn't leave Caleb to this alone today; not under a warning like the one they had received.

"I'm Mara," the blonde told him. "Mara Whitlow."

Nathaniel grimaced internally, though his expression didn't show it. The feel of her spirit alone was enough to make him wretch. He was careful not to make eye contact with her, and careful to make sure the gesture appeared as disinterest more than caution. It didn't surprise him that Mara Whitlow would make an attempt like this. From what Caleb had told him, she'd been waiting for a while for the opportunity he had been careful not to give her. But Nathaniel wanted no part of this one; her or any of her kind.

Nathaniel smirked at the girl and spoke to her curtly. "Listen…*Mara Whitlow*. I am going to do you a favor and let you know right now that I'm not interested."

Mara blinked a few times, staring at him like she expected him to say he was joking, but when she realized he wasn't, her entire countenance changed. Her cheeks flushed first to a distinct shade of pink and there was a look on her face that Nathaniel guessed wasn't normal for her. Rejection was something she was obviously not familiar with, but it wasn't merely embarrassment he saw in her now.

Hurriedly grabbing two of the girls from out of the cluster that had formed, Mara dragged them both away with her when they were mid-conversation with their friends. Mara was definitely freaked out. From what Nathaniel could discern of it, she hadn't expected to have so little effect on him, so little control over him. She was used to that sort of thing, getting what she wanted when she wanted it, using her beauty to manipulate men and control those around her. Even if Nathaniel hadn't heard this about her from Caleb, he

10

would have seen it as clearly as if she had told him herself. He could always see a thing like that.

Making a face, he looked away from Mara and her friends as they scampered down the sidewalk. Caleb must have caught on that Nathaniel had upset someone, because he brought his conversation with Samantha to a quick close.

"I'll see you tonight, Sam," he told her. Then he took Nathaniel forcefully by the arm and steered him in the direction opposite of where Samantha and the few girls still waiting for her stood.

Caleb shook his head and laughed. "You're really something, you know that?"

Nathaniel chose to ignore the irony of the remark. "Is the plan set?" he asked.

Caleb rolled his eyes. "You're talking to *me*. Of course it's set."

Nathaniel ignored his brother's arrogance and gave the area one last look. "Campus is clear."

Caleb sighed. "Somehow 'I told you so' just really doesn't cut it."

"You know our protocol," Nathaniel responded flatly. "We have to adhere explicitly to the orders we are given."

The boy was frustrated. Nathaniel could feel that without even looking at him.

"But for how long?" Caleb challenged. "How much time are we gonna waste pursuing these dead-end leads and getting the same result? Face it, Nate. Donovan isn't here. He's never been here and he's never gonna be here because he doesn't know *we* are! Whoever is feeding us this information, they're wrong."

Nathaniel's tone was firm. "We do not know that."

"If they weren't, do you really think we wouldn't have found him…or at least found *something* by now? I'm telling you, we're wasting our time."

Nathaniel frowned at the suggestion. "That isn't our call to make."

"I just wish…" Caleb started.

Nathaniel stopped moving forward and turned to face him. "You wish what?" The gesture coming from him would have intimidated just about anyone, but not Caleb.

"I wish you would talk to Seth," he said.

Nathaniel didn't waste a second before he started walking again. "No."

"He won't listen to me," Caleb argued, scrambling to keep up with his brother's long stride. "He won't listen to anyone...except for you."

Nathaniel wasn't about to entertain this. "Seth is our superior. Our leader. And as such, I will not question his orders or his judgment. If we second guess him now, then we may as well forfeit this assignment."

Caleb was emphatic. "I *know* that! I am *not* suggesting we go against Seth here. You know I would never do that. I just think if you tell him..."

"No." Nathaniel's voice was firmer this time.

"Fine," Caleb said tightly.

"We continue as planned," Nathaniel said. "Is that understood?"

"Yeah, I get it," Caleb muttered.

Nathaniel didn't like the hesitation he felt coming from him. "Caleb..." he stopped again so his brother would turn and look at him. "I need to know you are with me on this."

When Caleb looked back at him, Nathaniel could see the respect he carried in his eyes. "I am always with you, Nathaniel."

Nathaniel placed a hand on Caleb's arm and Caleb placed one on his; the sign of the brotherhood. Then they nodded to each other once and went their separate ways.

Nathaniel frowned as he walked forward, suppressing his frustration.

He knew that Caleb was right.

*I*t was an eerie night in North London. Quiet and still, a feeling lingered in the air that was as difficult to place as it was to ignore. Caleb Holcomb took in a deep breath. Such a feeling was to be expected on a night like this; the anticipation, the caution, the conviction that none of them should be here at all. But as he and Nathaniel approached Highgate Cemetery enshrouded in the fog, that feeling wasn't what concerned him. Caleb knew that more than anything, he had to keep himself in check.

Submission had always taken effort for him, and tonight in particular, he knew it was going to be difficult. It helped that Nathaniel was at his side, since his presence more than any of the rest he called his "brothers" seemed to incite at least some level of obedience in him. But even with Nathaniel, Caleb still had his moments.

Walking through the massive stone tunnel at the entrance of the West Cemetery, Caleb took another deep breath and prepared himself for the meeting. The place was known as the Egyptian Avenue, and though the gates of its tunnel were locked this late at night, scaling them was effortless for him and his brother.

After passing quickly and soundlessly through the tunnel, they wound their way between the moss-covered headstones that filled the expansive cemetery grounds. Caleb looked up and saw two figures in the distance; both silhouetted by the moonlight that spilled through the trees overhead, both wearing the same long grey trench coats he and Nathaniel wore.

Ethan, the watcher, stood there like a statue, his dark hands folded behind him in his typical quiet dignity. He was the only one of the four of them that didn't look like he belonged. But although his African ancestry separated him from the likeness of Seth, Nathaniel and Caleb, he held the same degree of beauty that was strikingly peculiar, the sort that made people question if that should even be normal. Ethan was the most reserved of the brothers, similar to Nathaniel in his severely lacking emotion, but slightly less cold. Kind of like winters in London were slightly less cold than those of the Arctic Circle. But emotionally challenged, cold or not, Ethan was good at what he did. They all were, which was why they were here.

They called themselves the *Resitore*, the "Resistance"...this brotherhood with ties that ran deeper than human

13

comprehension. But they were not the only ones who went by that name. And they were not the only ones of their kind.

The London faction had only recently been formed, an action that in and of itself was vastly outside of protocol, but the circumstances the brotherhood had found itself in when this decision had been made required a drastic course of action. That was why the leaders of the Resitore, Samuel and Malachi, had appointed Seth as head over the newest faction. His training of the young ones had proven so effective that he was the only one they could trust to take charge of something so crucial. And they had sent his three best "students" along with him, knowing the bond he had with Caleb and Ethan and Nathaniel, and knowing the four of them could not easily be divided.

These were dark times for the Resitore, as a quickly encroaching threat hung over the cause they warred for. Not only the threat of the one called Donovan, but all who had taken an oath to serve him and bring an end to this brotherhood he stood so adamantly against.

As the scout of the London faction, Nathaniel had encountered several members of this...*alliance* when he was on assignment, moving along the perimeter of the city as discreetly as a shadow. It had always amazed Caleb the way Nathaniel could move, how he could navigate his way with such speed and accuracy, never to be seen by any he followed. It was why Nathaniel was so much more highly sought after than the rest of the brothers, be they of the London faction or otherwise. One of the reasons, anyway. His skills as a scout were unparalleled by any other member of the brotherhood, but it was his heightened discernment, the way he could feel things and see things in people or in situations that the rest of them could never hope to that truly set him apart. It was uncanny how precise it was, and something that invoked a great deal of fear from the others they used to train with. But it wasn't Nathaniel's discernment alone that brought on this fear.

It was the fact that he was never wrong.

For that reason, Samuel and Malachi had debated drawing him into one of the two standing factions; either Samuel's in

Athens or Malachi's in Rome. But observing Nathaniel's connection to Seth and Caleb, they decided against separating them, seeing the opportunity they had been presented with in the unlikely bond these three specifically had forged.

That was two years ago. Many things had changed since then, both in the structure of the Resitore and in their internal affairs. There were none except the leaders of each faction that even knew where the others were located anymore, and they only knew in a general sense. Holding specifics to a minimum was the only way to keep the brotherhood safe from those who hunted them...and the only thing that gave them the ability to hunt.

That was the way it was in their world. Everything had to be done covertly or they would be exposed for what they were. And the members of this brotherhood were *not* ready to be exposed for what they were.

Stepping up to where the others waited for them, Caleb nodded first to Ethan and then to Seth. Ethan returned the gesture, but their leader didn't acknowledge him.

There was even more intensity behind Seth's icy blue eyes than usual tonight. *Something has changed*, Caleb thought. Whether good or bad, he didn't know...just something.

"I have received word from our brothers in Rome," Seth told them in his typical detached tone. Caleb wondered sometimes if that was where Nathaniel got it. There was no biological relation between him and Seth, but if any were to judge by the way they looked and acted, they would immediately assume otherwise.

Caleb looked up curiously. If Seth wasn't even going to bother having them report on their status, this must be important.

"It seems there is a new development in our search to locate Donovan," Seth explained. He hesitated before adding, "And it would appear that the information we were recently fed about his finding us here was false."

Caleb exchanged a look with Nathaniel before he turned his attention back to their leader. "What new development?" he asked.

Seth looked frustrated when Caleb spoke out of turn. Not that there was anything unusual about that. "I'm not sure," he told him. "I am meeting with Samuel and Malachi tomorrow to find out."

Caleb's face dropped. "What?"

Seth ignored his surprise, as well as that of Nathaniel and Ethan. "Nathaniel..." he addressed the one who stood beside Caleb instead.

Nathaniel looked up.

"You are on watch with Ethan for the next two nights," Seth told him. "I do not want you scouting the perimeter until I have spoken with Samuel and Malachi and learned what is going on."

Nathaniel nodded, but he seemed uncertain.

As the weight of Seth's words sank into Caleb's mind, he could see it on his brother's face as well. No meeting between the leaders of the Resitore was ever instigated unless under the most dire of circumstances.

"You two are in Oxford tonight," Seth instructed Nathaniel and Ethan, "and not to leave your point of watch until morning."

They both nodded.

"And Caleb..." Seth paused, grimacing a little. "You just do what you do."

A smirk found its way onto the boy's face. "You got it, boss."

Seth's cringe was more apparent now, but he didn't bother rebuking him. He knew Caleb enough to realize that he wasn't being disrespectful. Not hardly. He was just different than the rest of his brothers. And while the tendencies that distinguished Caleb from the others often aggravated him, Seth recognized something in him that was unique enough and important enough that he tolerated those tendencies.

Ethan's watching and Nathaniel's scouting alone didn't accomplish their purpose; they needed Caleb for that. His abilities at what they referred to as "tracking" were invaluable to the Resitore, and enabled him to uncover a depth of information they could never attain otherwise. It was the way he was with people, the unnatural favor he held with them, the way he could pull at their emotions or alter their will that gave him access to the things the rest of them couldn't touch.

Things like Samantha Ross.

"We meet back here in forty-eight hours," Seth told them. Then he dismissed the meeting and slipped inconspicuously out of the cemetery.

Ethan dropped his head and followed after him, but Nathaniel didn't move.

"What do you feel?" Caleb asked his brother once they were alone.

Nathaniel frowned. "I'm not sure. Something is different."

Caleb gave him a look. "Well, obviously..."

Nathaniel shook his head. "That's not what I mean," he said. "*Everything* is different."

Caleb looked at his brother in question and Nathaniel met his eyes.

"Be careful tonight, Caleb."

The boy gave him a smirk. "You know I got this."

Nathaniel didn't look convinced.

*P*erched motionlessly on the ledge of Carfax Tower, Nathaniel and Ethan looked out over the city of Oxford. The night was still, thick with moisture and threatening to rain, but it held in spite of the building clouds. Neither of them spoke as they scanned the streets below them, their eyes moving back and forth in careful sweeps. Neither of them ever did.

Nathaniel wasn't able to connect with Ethan the way he could with Caleb. He wasn't able to connect with anyone like that. Caleb wasn't intimidated by him, for one, which was more than the rest of his brothers could say. Nathaniel had yet to even find a decent explanation for it, or for anything Caleb did. The boy was just a phenomenon, and Nathaniel wasn't convinced that his being raised in far different circumstances than the rest of them was the reason for that, either. He was just different. He was...special. And because Nathaniel had always taken it upon himself to protect him, he didn't enjoy nights like this where Caleb was on assignment alone away from him. Especially not this assignment.

Ethan could sense his anxiety; Nathaniel didn't have to use his discernment to know that.

"He's fine," his dark-skinned brother told him, breaking their long-held silence.

Nathaniel kept his gaze forward, nodding once in acknowledgment and allowing the controlled calm that was his driving force to take him over.

Sometimes being on assignment with Ethan did have its advantages.

The clouds that hung in the sky that night reflected the lights of the city back down to its streets, masking the stars they held behind them. Caleb hated not seeing the stars. Something in him didn't feel right unless he could, but tonight he knew it was probably for the best. He needed to stay focused, connected to where he was and what he was doing, and stargazing right now was not going to help him achieve this. Quite the opposite, actually.

As Caleb staggered out the entrance of the club he'd just spent the past two hours in, he slipped his hand around the waist of the girl he had come here with. Samantha's dress was short, red and tight, and the heels of her strappy sling-back pumps clicked against the sidewalk as she stumbled unsteadily forward. Caleb swung her away from the street in an effort to keep her from getting run over, and the two of them laughed together as he held her up against him one-handed.

Samantha found it hysterical. The five shots she'd thrown back probably had something to do with that. They also probably had something to do with her grabbing Caleb with force, slamming him up against the brick wall behind him and attacking his mouth.

Caleb felt his heart spike sharply then he quickly got it under control. *Easy there*, he told himself.

Holding Samantha's face, he was careful as he kissed her, though the force with which he pressed his hand against her back was enough to convince her otherwise. He pulled back from her slowly and whispered in her ear, "Not here."

Samantha objected adamantly. She usually did.

Luckily the girl was trashed enough not to become suspicious when he worked his way out of her grip. He maneuvered himself behind her, kissing her neck as he took her hand, and before she realized what was happening, the two of them were walking down the sidewalk in the direction of the sorority house she had recently taken up residence in.

Caleb toyed with her fingers as they walked, and in response she leaned against his arm. Samantha was over a foot shorter than he was, so her head only came to the middle of his chest, but tonight it seemed to be working for her, which meant it worked for him. The happier Caleb kept Samantha Ross, the more likely she was to start talking.

Samantha hummed lightly and nuzzled her face in his chest, running her free hand up and down his forearm as he continued to play with her fingers. Her hand stopped when she reached his brown woven-leather wristband that buckled at the back.

Toying with it, she unlatched the buckle and slipped it onto her own wrist, which was practically lost inside of it.

"I like it," Samantha said. "Can I have it?"

Caleb laughed when it almost slipped off of her hand. "You sure you can even wear it?" he asked.

Samantha looked down at her tiny wrist and pushed it up higher onto her forearm, satisfied when it finally stayed in place. She gave no regard to the fact that she looked ridiculous.

Caleb shook his head and looked out across the street away from her, internally deliberating over whether or not in would be wise to give any possession of his to a witch.

Then again, he hadn't determined that Samantha was a witch yet.

"Fine," Caleb said. "It's yours."

Samantha reached up to him on her tip-toes and kissed his cheek. "You're such a dear, Caleb," she told him.

His smile was only on the outside. *Oh, if you only knew...*

By the time they reached the front door of the house, she was already at his face again, kissing up his jaw line and running her fingers through his dirty blonde hair as he tried to wrestle the keys out of her hands. Caleb laughed drunkenly and intentionally stumbled to his right.

"The others aren't here, are they?" he asked as he slipped the key into the lock.

"Mmm mmm," she mumbled, her lips still pressed against his. "Party."

Caleb had the door open in no time. Tossing the keys to the table in the entryway, he slid both his hands up Samantha's sides, lifting her so she would jump up on him and wrap her legs around his waist.

Careful, he warned himself a second time. Caleb knew his orders enough to know that he had to keep this situation under control. Cross any lines here and Seth would have his head.

Shutting the door behind them, he tried taking her over to the couch.

"No," Samantha told him. "My room."

Caleb's heart spiked again, and again he steadied its beating.

Her bed wasn't made, but she didn't seem to mind. The billowing purple comforter was hanging halfway off the mattress and there were clothes strewn carelessly across the pillows at the head; several dresses, several shirts, and two different sets of lacy black lingerie. Probably the outfits she'd tried on for tonight and rejected in favor of the tight red number she was now eagerly trying to get out of.

Caleb set her down gently, but the moment her feet touched the ground, Samantha shoved him down on her bed onto his back and pinned him beneath her.

Caleb's breathing quickened again as she climbed on top of him, and this time he had to work harder at getting it right. He kept his hands on her hips as she moved back up to his mouth, knowing he didn't have much time. He had to make his move.

"Samantha…" he breathed softly.

She didn't answer him.

20

"*Samantha*," he said more firmly.

She moaned in response.

Caleb closed his eyes and took in a slow breath. He had to get a hold of this fast. Taking her by the waist, he flipped her onto her back, his hair hanging in his eyes as he looked down on her tiny, flawless body.

"Tell me something," he whispered to her, dropping to his lower register.

Samantha giggled and slipped her arms under his, sliding her hands up his back beneath his shirt. Apparently she liked that.

Caleb tensed his jaw and looked away from her, questioning if he had been too quick to assure Nathaniel he could handle this.

"What would you like to know?" she asked him coyly.

Caleb leaned down and started kissing her neck, knowing how it made her putty in his hands. "Tell me something you've never told anyone," he said. "Tell me a secret."

Samantha pulled his shirt over his head and tossed it to the floor. "What sort of secret?" she asked him in her sultry British voice.

Caleb's breathing became unsteady when she touched his chest.

Focus, he thought firmly. He knew the kind of restraint this was going to take.

Running his hand up her arm, he whispered to her again, "Tell me..." He slid his hand up her neck and moved it slowly back down to her chest, slipping his fingers through the 24-inch gold chain she had tucked into her low-cut dress.

Samantha opened her mouth in surprise, though Caleb couldn't determine if this came more from his fingering the medallion on the end of the chain or from the way he was touching her right now.

Suddenly he worried that his approach was too direct. He had to play it down. "Want me to help you get this off?" he asked her, acting as if the necklace were nothing more than a nuisance to him.

Even in her drunkenness, Caleb could see the fear come into Samantha's eyes. She grabbed his hand so he dropped the necklace.

"Leave it," she said.

He gave her a curious look. "Does it really mean enough that you can't part with it for ten minutes?"

Samantha clutched the necklace securely to her chest. "Yes," she told him.

Caleb let his frustration play on his face, wanting her to see it.

"What is it?" she asked him. "You look mad."

He sighed and rolled back on his knees, causing her to lift her head in concern. Propping herself up by her elbows, Samantha looked to him to see what was wrong.

"Who gave it to you?" Caleb asked her.

The question caused her to falter. "I...I don't know what you..."

He pressed his lips together and looked away from her, and as she studied his face she seemed to realize what he was getting at. Or at least what he wanted her to think he was getting at.

"Caleb, no..." she said. "It's not *from* anyone."

"No?" he asked tensely. He made sure to allow the perfect degree of inflection in his voice. "Then where's it from?"

She looked panicked now, afraid to tell him the truth and afraid to let him keep thinking it had been given to her by an old boyfriend, or at least something that would evoke an equal amount of jealousy in him.

"Samantha, please..."

Before Caleb could finish, the door to her room burst open and he jerked his head up to see three very angry-looking girls marching over to them.

They looked nothing alike by their height, their hair color or their skin tone, but the way they stood at the foot of the bed with their arms folded tightly, glaring at him with identical looks of malice, Caleb thought they almost did. Like some sort of robots or brainwashed Barbie dolls.

22

The Stepford Sorority Clones, he thought. Now there was an idea Hollywood could cash in on. Three different bodies all controlled by one mind.

And if he were to guess, he would say it was the one in the middle.

Her name was Mara Whitlow, and she absolutely despised him. Samantha had told him that the first time Caleb got her drunk; not that he wouldn't have figured it out on his own. Mara was not the kind of girl who kept her opinions to herself.

Caleb never could understand why she hated him so much. He had never given her a reason to. But from the first time they met, Mara had made it clear to Samantha that she did not approve of him; which he really couldn't have cared less about if it didn't make his job that much more difficult. Especially now.

Samantha worked her way out from under Caleb and crawled backwards toward her headboard, slipping the necklace into her dress again when she realized it was in view. She looked frightened. More frightened than he expected her to.

"I think it's time for you to leave, Caleb," Mara said firmly, though her eyes bore into Samantha when she said it. Her voice told him it was anything but a suggestion.

"What?" he asked sarcastically. "You still bent out of shape over my brother shooting you down today?"

Mara shot him a fierce glare, and at first he thought she might slap him. Instead, she gave the redhead to her a left a commanding look and the girl responded by walking around the bed and grabbing Samantha by the arm.

Oh, yes. Mara Whitlow was definitely the one who called the shots around here.

Caleb stood unsteadily to his feet and put his hands up to show Mara that he meant no harm. Then he continued to laugh like a drunken fool as he grabbed his shirt from where it lay on the floor and stumbled out of the room.

Once he rounded the corner, he dropped his smile and walked completely sober.

Seth was not going to be happy about this.

Chapter 2

"...some are made of stone."

Moving swiftly down a darkened alleyway, Seth could feel the sobering weight of the night on his shoulders. But it wasn't just this night, it was also this place...its history so deeply woven through every building and structure, every square inch of ground he set foot on as he walked. *The Capital of the World. The Eternal City.*

Rome.

Nearing the entrance of a cathedral-looking church, he hesitated before going inside. The building was old, like something out of a history book or a bedtime story...like everything in this city. Its walls were made of ancient stone whose edges had eroded beneath the wearing of time, and thick unkempt ivy grew up its sides. During the day, it might not have looked so intimidating, but standing in the dark before its jutting spires, Seth couldn't shake his unease. Not when he knew what was held within those walls.

Not when he knew what was beneath them.

Standing before the oversized wooden doors of the church, he took a deep breath and stepped inside. He moved down the aisle with inconspicuous strides and slid into the far back pew on the right, removing a tattered old Bible from the wooden slot it was tucked in at the back of the pew in front of him.

Seth turned the pages slowly, carefully, until he found the passage he was looking for. The passage he always looked for on nights like this. When his fingers turned the page to find Genesis 6:4, his eyes skimmed over the verse he'd read a thousand times; a thousand times and the words never ceased to fill him with awe. Beneath the text, there was a thin piece of parchment tucked neatly between its pages, and on it, a location written in a code that only he and two others could decipher.

Studying the code once, Seth slipped the parchment out of the leather-bound book, closed it again and returned it to its wooden holder. Then he stood and left the church with his hands shoved into the pockets of his long grey trench coat.

Making his way again through Rome's shadowed streets, he periodically glanced to his left and his right, and every once in a while behind him to make sure he wasn't followed. In the distance, *Ponte Sant Angelo* was illuminated by the light of its streetlamps. Spanning over the Tiber River, the bridge was faced with travertine marble, glowing yellow against the castle behind it, the *Mausoleum of Hadrian*. Even here, Seth could feel the history pulsating from this place; the legend that surrounded this *Bridge of Angels*...held by the ten stone guardians that stood at its sides.

They were all different, the statues that lined the bridge, sculpted in different centuries by different men, but still strikingly similar to one another even despite this. Each one was of a different angel that held a different message at its base. They stood there in somber glory, each on its perch as if watching over those who waited there, guarding a purpose that the wearing of time did not diminish. A mysterious purpose...a hidden purpose. Something only an angel would be able to see.

Walking step by measured step along the bridgeway, Seth glanced uncertainly to the ominous statue towering over his head. He hadn't meant to do it, but it was difficult for a thing like that to not draw his eyes. This of the ten stone angels carried a cross on its arm, the inscription beneath it reading: *Cuius principatus super humerum eius*. Latin for, "Dominion rests on His shoulders."

Seth felt a tremor through his body at the thought. The Romans certainly thought they had it figured out. But what would they do in a time like this if they knew what was astir in their city? How firmly would they cling to the faith that had carved these stones?

Turning his head away, he focused on the two living figures in the distance that stood waiting for him at the end of the bridge; one that was taller and stronger, one that had been worn by the passing of time. Both silhouetted by the light of the streetlamp they waited beside.

Seth cleared his mind so it wouldn't take him to conclusions he knew he shouldn't draw; at least not before he spoke to Samuel and Malachi. He bowed his head submissively as he stepped up to his superiors, his mentors, but most importantly, the two highest ranking leaders of the Brotherhood of the Resitore.

It was clear in their expressions (as it was in his) that they could all feel the sobriety of this night. Seth, along with Samuel, looked immediately to Malachi, who as the oldest member of the Resitore and the leader of the Roman faction had called this impromptu meeting.

The gesture from Samuel was slightly surprising. Seth thought he would have already been informed of what had taken place; but while Malachi's second-in-command was privy to information the rest of them weren't, there were some things even he wasn't told in advance. Apparently, this was one of them.

"Thank you both for coming on such short notice," Malachi spoke in a drawn voice.

"What is this about, Malachi?" Seth asked impatiently. "Have you found him?"

The lines in Malachi's face were tight, pulled back like his long white hair from his forehead. "Yes, we believe so."

Seth felt his pulse surge. "Where is he?"

Samuel held up a hand and looked at him sternly. "Calm yourself," he told him. "You must realize we are all as anxious to find Donovan as you are."

Seth snapped his head up. The way Samuel stood, commanding and firm like Malachi used to, he probably should have intimidated him. But right now, Seth was too mad to be intimidated.

"No," he told Samuel. "You are not."

Seth continued to receive a long hard glare from the younger of his superiors. "We understand that Donovan has

27

taken more from you than he has the rest of us," Samuel said, "but you must know that your pain is our pain. Your blood is our blood and ours is yours. Thus is the nature of the brotherhood."

Seth tried not to allow the bitter tinge of his resentment to rise in him further, though he thought Samuel a fool to assume he could possibly know his pain. He nodded in a way that would appear as understanding to appease them and then he and Samuel looked back to Malachi to continue.

Seth kept his voice much more controlled this time. "Where is he, Malachi?"

Malachi paused before answering him. "He's in the States."

That was not what Seth expected to hear, and judging by the look on Samuel's face, it seemed to catch him every bit as much by surprise.

"Where?" Seth asked. He was baffled by the thought.

"Colorado," Malachi answered him. "Manitou Springs."

Seth felt his blood grow cold. "Manitou..." he started to say, but his voice trailed off.

Scrambling to make sense of this, he tried to think of any way Donovan could have learned of that location. Surely he didn't know...

Samuel cut off the thought from Seth when he voiced a question of his own. "Who is your source, Malachi?" There was disbelief in his voice.

"His name is Eli," Malachi said. "He is...one of Donovan's."

Seth didn't blink as he stared at the ancient-looking man before him, this one whose greatness in their kind knew no limit, who used to hold his deepest respect. Looking at him now, Seth wondered if Malachi had completely lost his mind.

"You're serious?" he asked.

Malachi didn't appear to like his apprehension. "He is one who has defected from Donovan's alliance, though we still have yet to learn exactly what that alliance consists of."

"And you haven't thought to *ask* him?" Seth spoke through clenched teeth.

Malachi's eyes squinted tighter. "Eli was not in a position to have access to such knowledge."

28

Seth scoffed and shook his head. "You cannot trust this."

Pressing his thinning, wrinkled lips together, Malachi told him, "I have reason to believe I can."

Seth's fingers bore into his temples as he tried both to control himself and wrap his mind around the idea. "Then what *has* this Eli told you?"

Malachi pulled a sealed envelope out from beneath his coat with a shaking hand. "There isn't much, but it is enough for initial surveillance."

Seth took the envelope and looked at him in question. "Surveillance?"

"I assumed you would want one of yours to be tasked with the assignment."

Seth's face tightened. "You mean you want Nathaniel on it."

Samuel looked away from them and Malachi placed a withered hand on Seth's shoulder. "I understand how difficult this must be for you…"

No, Seth thought. *You don't.*

"…but we have all known this day would come."

Seth kept his jaw tight as he looked his leader in the eye. "Let me do it."

Malachi shook his head. "You know that isn't possible."

Seth looked away. He had to keep his gaze fixed on the light post behind him in an effort to control his emotion. "He isn't ready," he insisted.

Malachi and Samuel exchanged a glance that made him anything but comfortable.

"How else is he to be made ready?" Malachi asked. "How else is he supposed to fulfill his destiny?"

Seth tightened his grip on the envelope he held. "Nathaniel doesn't believe in destiny."

Samuel and Malachi exchanged another glance.

"No," Malachi agreed. "But he will."

*A*s Nathaniel made a steady approach toward Highgate Cemetery with Caleb at his side, the fog on the ground moved in wisps around their feet. Ethan was already inside waiting for them, and as they neared him, he looked up over the headstone he stood behind.

There was an intense sort of pressure that hung in the air. Nathaniel could feel it, how anxious they all were to hear from Seth; especially since he had not yet arrived.

Odd, Nathaniel thought. Seth was usually the first to show up.

Caleb was the first one Ethan looked to, partly because he was curious and partly because Nathaniel still intimidated him, even after all the years they had trained and hunted together.

"How are you holding up on assignment?" Ethan asked him.

Caleb was frustrated. Nathaniel would have seen that even if his brother wasn't completely transparent to him.

"There was an interference," he said. "But I still believe our suspicions to be true. There's something more to this sorority than what they want us to know, and if Donovan does have any sort of connection here, I really do think they're our best shot at finding him."

"And what leads you to believe that?" Ethan asked.

Caleb hesitated before he answered him, glancing halfway toward Nathaniel before he did. "A symbol I saw on Samantha's necklace."

Nathaniel looked up. Caleb hadn't mentioned that before.

"I didn't recognize it," Caleb said, "but it definitely didn't look like a sorority symbol to me."

Nathaniel tensed his jaw and his brother avoided his gaze.

"Did you secure the necklace?" Ethan asked him.

Caleb's expression was tight. "No. Like I said, there was…interference." He shot Nathaniel another nervous sideways glance before returning his gaze to Ethan.

Nathaniel wasn't happy about this, and judging by the tension he could feel in his brother, Caleb seemed to know it. It upset him to think of what Caleb had been tasked with, of how far he had to have taken this assignment to learn even that much. Nathaniel hated his brother continually being placed in such a vulnerable position, though Caleb hardly seemed to mind. Risk of any sort didn't cause him to bat an eye, even when it should have. He was absolutely fearless, to a fault sometimes, Nathaniel thought. And it was that fearless determination in Caleb that was currently fueling Nathaniel's own unease.

Caleb wasn't stupid; he just didn't realize in full how dangerous his behavior was to their kind. Granted, he had an uncanny ability to handle it, and did so far better than the others who had been tasked with similar assignments. But he was not infallible and Nathaniel wished he understood that.

Before any of them could speak again, they looked up as they felt their leader approach. Folding their hands behind their backs and standing at ready, all eyes looked to Seth.

He was worried, Nathaniel saw. Something was wrong.

Seth nodded as he stepped into their midst, but he didn't meet their eyes. He paused longer than they expected him to, and as was typically the case with him, he was emotionless as he spoke.

"It would appear that Donovan has been located," he told them.

He was met by silence and three baffled expressions.

"Where?" Caleb asked.

Seth looked uncomfortable. "A small mountain town in Colorado," he replied. "A place called Manitou Springs."

Nathaniel's face dropped. He questioned if he heard him right, but Seth wouldn't meet his eyes when he tried to verify this.

"Colorado?" Caleb asked. "You mean…in the States?"

"Yes," Seth confirmed. He didn't look happy about doing it.

Caleb shook his head. "Let me get this straight," he said. "We've been on assignment here for over two *years* trying to get to the bottom of this whole sorority-suspected-witch-coven thing, and now you're telling us Donovan hasn't been anywhere near us?"

Seth tensed his jaw and Nathaniel kept trying to read him.

"Whether the coven we have been seeking to uncover does or does not exist, it appears that our efforts in London have been in vain," Seth said. "We've been tracking the wrong one."

Caleb stared forward with a blank expression. "The wrong coven?"

"It would appear so," Seth answered him dryly.

"Permission to speak?" Nathaniel interjected.

Seth looked uncertain as to whether or not he should grant this request. Nathaniel could imagine why.

"Go ahead," Seth finally told him.

"Do you still believe our theory of the alliance to be true?" Nathaniel asked.

"I have no reason to believe otherwise at the moment," Seth responded. "There is still substantial evidence to support it, the strongest being Donovan's fixation with the occult. Whatever he is doing, he needs power to do it, and he needs a source from which to draw that power. Apparently, he has found a source in Manitou Springs."

Nathaniel was skeptical. "And you really think that is why he is there?"

Seth looked down and furrowed his brow, still not meeting his eyes. "I don't know," he admitted.

Nathaniel didn't like this.

"So what the hell have we been doing in London?" Caleb asked furiously.

Seth shot him a glare. "Do not question me on this as if it were my decision," he rebuked him. "You know we were ordered here by Malachi."

Caleb bit his tongue and Seth went on.

"We had no way of knowing; not when every lead we were given directed us here."

His attempt at justification fell somewhat short of convincing Caleb, and even Nathaniel found himself questioning their leader. The difference was that Nathaniel would never voice those questions out loud. Caleb would.

"So who is responsible for this?" Caleb all but demanded. There wasn't a trace of respect in his voice. "Who fed us the lead on this sorority that put us on a two-year waste of an assignment?"

Seth looked about three seconds away from hitting him. "I will not warn you again."

Nathaniel gave his brother a look and Caleb shut his mouth.

"I do not know who supplied the lead," Seth told all of them. "It is not in our protocol for me to know. I was simply instructed to set Caleb on this assignment. Samuel was the one who charged him with infiltrating the sorority in an attempt to uncover any tie they might have with Donovan. Not I."

Since the days they were younger and Seth was training them in the States, Nathaniel hadn't seen him look quite so unsure of what he was saying. After Malachi appointed him as the head over the London faction, Seth had been thrust into a place where his confidence was a necessity in every word he spoke, something they had all grown used to seeing in him in the past two years. Nathaniel didn't see that confidence in him now.

"Permission to speak?" Ethan asked suddenly.

All eyes turned to him and Seth nodded in his direction.

"What is it about Manitou Springs that you or Malachi or Samuel suspects to have drawn Donovan?"

Finally, Seth met Nathaniel's eyes. It wasn't an immediate gesture, and it might not have been deliberate, but Ethan's question made his gaze unavoidable. The answer hung thick between them like a heavy cloud that was threatening to break, much like the ones even now over their heads.

Nathaniel didn't want to be right about this.

"We don't know for sure," Seth answered Ethan, "but we have our theories."

Nathaniel dropped his eyes, not even sure he wanted to know what he was almost certain he already did.

"Nathaniel..." Seth addressed him.

He looked up at the sound of his name.

"You are going to Colorado on surveillance."

The assignment didn't surprise him, but the confirmation he received through it still left a sting.

"We will receive a replacement for Nathaniel while he is on assignment," Seth told the others. "A highly capable scout named Justin who was recently recruited to Samuel's faction."

Caleb and Ethan exchanged a look, appearing as confused by this as Nathaniel was. They had never had to replace a single of their members, temporarily or otherwise. Granted, this was the first assignment they'd been given that required any of them to leave the country unaided, but there was still something about it that alarmed them.

Seth didn't stop there. "I will be out of town for a few days," he told them. "Justin has been instructed to find you and outline the strategy laid forth to him by Samuel. I know this isn't normal protocol, but these are not normal circumstances, and it is imperative that you act as if nothing has changed while I am gone. Justin should arrive by morning. Caleb, I want you off your assignment and on watch with Ethan until I return and determine whether this alteration will be temporary or permanent. Is that clear?"

Caleb flinched. It was obvious he wanted to protest, but somehow he managed to restrain himself. "Yes," he grumbled.

Seth returned his focus to Nathaniel. "I will come to you in several days," he told him. "Until then, you are assigned with surveillance only." He pulled a sealed manila envelope out from inside his trench coat. "This should contain all the information our informant, Eli, left us with; photographs, addresses, and the notes he was able to take before he was supposedly forced to flee and find Malachi."

Nathaniel nodded in understanding. Normally he would question Seth about the development of a new informant, but he was distracted, waiting for the right time to ask if Donovan's relocating to Colorado could possibly be a coincidence.

"Do not attempt to locate Donovan," Seth warned him. "For now, you are only to follow the leads contained in this envelope, which is not to be opened until you reach Woodland Park."

Nathaniel tensed up at the name of the city, his theory proven true. Slowly, he took the envelope from Seth, meeting his eyes as it was transferred between them and seeing that his leader felt his same concern.

"There is an estate twenty minutes north of Manitou Springs owned by a man named Howard Blake," Seth spoke mechanically. "I believe you are familiar with it?"

"I should be," Nathaniel said tensely. "He *is* my uncle."

This was news to Caleb and Ethan.

"Whoa, whoa…" Caleb put his hands up in front of him. "Nate's uncle *lives* twenty minutes from where Donovan's holed himself up?"

"It's a summer home," Nathaniel corrected him. "He lives in Los Angeles."

"Nathaniel…" Seth rebuked him.

Nathaniel looked down and fell quiet, knowing he was wrong to disclose that information when Seth was obviously trying not to, but he was upset by the thought of his uncle being in danger, even if the man was almost a stranger to him.

Caleb looked back and forth between Nathaniel and Seth as Ethan took his typical passive stance and kept his eyes on the ground. "Am I the only one who has a little trouble writing this off as a coincidence?" Caleb asked.

"No," Seth replied. "You are not."

"Then why are you sending Nathaniel? I mean, doesn't this whole thing trigger any red flags to you?"

"It wasn't my call," Seth told him in an overly-controlled voice.

Nathaniel looked up again.

"Oh yeah?" Caleb asked. "Whose call was it?"

Seth looked downright mad now. "Malachi wants him on this."

That was enough to shut Caleb up. Even he knew that an order set directly by the leader over the Resitore was not a light matter, and was definitely not one to be questioned. But after a long enough silence, he finally broke and asked the question all of them were thinking.

"What reason could Malachi possibly have for wanting to send Nathaniel straight into Donovan's territory?"

Seth's eyebrows pulled together in frustration, and Nathaniel could see through it that he was holding something back. "Malachi's reasons are his own," Seth answered him. "Our only concern is following the orders we are given."

"Yeah, well, my concern is that my brother might be walking into a trap," Caleb retorted.

Seth had just about had it with him tonight. "Enough, Caleb."

The boy wrinkled his face and Seth turned his attention once more to Nathaniel.

"You are to proceed with the highest level of caution," he instructed him. "And yes, we assume at every moment that this is a trap."

Nathaniel gave him a single nod. "Understood."

"It is imperative that you do nothing to compromise this cover," Seth told him. "At all times, you are to remain as inconspicuous as possible. Do you understand?"

Nathaniel felt a tension in his chest when he realized what Seth was ordering him to do...or rather what not to do. He understood perfectly, he just didn't like it.

"That will not be a problem," Nathaniel assured him.

"Good," Seth said. "You leave tonight."

*I*t was uncharacteristically warm for an early June morning in London, but Caleb didn't mind the heat. Born and raised in San Francisco, he was actually partial to it, but it still felt odd to him. He had grown used to the persistent rainfall in the last two years he'd lived here, and somehow felt almost protected by it. So as he came up to Samantha Ross where she sat outside a café called *Apostrophe* that morning, he thought he could have used all the protection he could get, imaginary or otherwise.

The café was iconic, to say the least, with everything done in black and vibrant magenta. Samantha made a habit of stopping by here on the weekends she came into the city to visit her aunt. She liked the colors, he remembered her telling him the first time she'd ever brought him here. They made her feel happy and relaxed at the same time, and somehow she found that fascinating. Caleb wasn't sure why.

With a frothy cappuccino in hand and a book set on the small black table in front of her, Samantha appeared deeply engrossed in whatever she was reading. Good. That would make his approach easier, or so Caleb thought before he walked up from behind her.

"Hey, Sam," he greeted her with a kiss on the cheek.

The girl jerked away so hard she nearly sent her book flying, and her drink for that matter.

Caleb stepped back. "Whoa there. You alright?"

Samantha looked up at him and smiled tensely. "Sorry," she said. "You just caught me by surprise."

"Why so jittery?" he asked, pulling up a chair and sitting across from her.

She closed her book and pushed her hair nervously out of her face. "It's nothing. I suppose my nerves are a bit shot since I haven't slept much the past few days."

Caleb glanced down at the white ceramic cup she was running her index finger along the edge of. "Really think coffee's gonna help that out?" he asked her.

She smiled at him again, still nervous, but at least this time it was unforced. "It's decaf," she told him.

Caleb laughed, trying to play the situation off as lighthearted when he knew that it wasn't. "Let me buy you something to eat," he offered. "You need more than coffee if you're gonna buffer your nerves; decaf or not."

"Thanks," she said, "but I'm not hungry."

"C'mon, Sam, let me."

"I don't want anything."

"Why not?" he prodded her. Not that he could care less whether or not she ate; he was trying to find the source of her irritation.

"I just don't, alright?" she snapped.

Caleb put his hands up. "Fine, no food," he said. "Will you at least tell me what's going on?"

Samantha fidgeted, glancing around her like she was worried about being seen with him. "Nothing is going on," she lied.

Caleb paused for a moment, feigning contemplation. "Is this about last night?" He made sure to sound like the idea had just dawned on him.

Samantha flinched at the question and he wondered what happened to her when he left...what they might have done to her.

"Look, I'm sorry if I got you in trouble..." he tried to apologize.

"It was my fault," she told him quickly. "I shouldn't have brought you back there." Samantha paused and looked down. "They don't want me seeing you anymore, Caleb."

He tried to appear shocked. "*Why not?*"

"I just...I can't."

Caleb grabbed her hand. "Samantha..."

She jerked her hand out of his. "Please," she said. "You have to stay away from me."

Caleb looked hurt, when in truth he was frustrated. "Can't you at least tell me why?"

Samantha shook her head. "I have to go."

He wanted to fight it. He wanted to find out what had really happened and why he suddenly had these sorority girls so freaked, but he knew he couldn't. He may have questioned Seth's orders on an all but daily basis, but when push came to shove he knew he had to obey them. That still didn't mean he had to like it.

As Samantha hurried away from the table, Caleb rested his forehead against his fist, trying to force aside the temptation to follow her. That was when he saw someone watching him; a college-looking kid in his early twenties sitting at a table across from him. He looked like a student, nobody threatening by appearance, but the look he gave Caleb immediately made him cautious.

Caleb sat up when he caught the look and the stranger stood from his table, slinging the strap to his book bag across his chest as he walked over to him. He was tall and skinny with dark, slicked-back hair and wire-rimmed glasses. "Handsome nerd" was the best way Caleb could think to describe him.

"It's too bad about that girl," the stranger said. He put his hands in the pockets of his khakis and followed Samantha down the road with his eyes. "I wouldn't want a thing that looked like that to get away from me."

Caleb looked him square-on. "Can I help you?"

The nosey stranger waited until Samantha was out of sight before he turned back to answer him. "Actually, you can," he said. "My name is Justin, and I believe you are expecting me."

Caleb narrowed his eyes at the newcomer's arrogance. "Right," he said.

Justin didn't appear fazed by Caleb's disdain. Instead he glanced back in the direction Samantha left in. "I must say, seeing what you appear to have underway here, I am quite eager to work with you."

Caleb made a face as he stood from the table. "That makes one of us," he grumbled. Then he brushed past the skinny dark-haired twit that had been sent to replace his brother and left the café.

As far as he was concerned, Nathaniel couldn't finish his assignment and get back here fast enough. This was a joke.

*I*t was hot in Rome that night, humid and eerie as Seth ducked into a familiar church. Sitting in the far back pew, he wasn't looking in any Bibles this time. He wasn't seeking to uncover the location of a meet, but rather waiting for the one he had come here for. And he was beginning to lose his patience. Another five minutes passed before he heard the oversized doors of the church open, but even when they did, Seth didn't turn around. He kept looking forward as a young man with a pointed chin and a careful stride walked down the aisle and slipped into the pew behind him. Leaning forward and resting his elbows on his knees, the one called Shebna apologized for being late.

"What took you so long?" Seth asked him. He could feel that the boy was nervous, even beyond his compulsively looking to the right and left to make sure there was no one watching them.

Shebna was a recent inductee to the Roman faction, which provided Seth with both advantage and disadvantage in this situation. Advantage for his lack of indoctrination, disadvantage in how skittish he was over meeting with him here.

"I came as soon as I could get away," Shebna explained.

Seth didn't like what he heard in his voice. He knew the boy was a gamble, that asking one as young as he to go behind his leader's back went against everything the Resitore stood for. But it was a risk he had to take. He didn't know of another who could get him to Eli.

Shebna stopped looking around and finally settled his gaze on his feet beneath the pew. "I can't do it," he told him.

Seth tightened his jaw. "I just need a location. I am not going to harm him."

Shebna frowned and kept his eyes down, appearing legitimately remorseful. "It isn't that I don't believe you...it's Malachi."

More than just Seth's jaw tightened this time. "What *about* Malachi?"

Shebna cringed. "He has forbidden us from speaking to you of Eli...from helping you to find him."

Seth fought to keep back his anger as he stood from the pew, despising his leader's foresight. "Then you are of no use to me anymore," he said.

He left the church furious.

Chapter 3

"...the dangerous leadings of loose-leaf paper."

Nathaniel stood before the castle-like estate on Falcon's Rest, hesitating before he made his way to the front door. He remembered this place, though the image of it was vague in his mind. He had lived here with his uncle for years before the man bought a place in Los Angeles. But much like the rest of Nathaniel's childhood, the memories he had of that time were faded at best.

It wouldn't be accurate to say that Howard Blake had raised him. Shipping him off to boarding school the moment he stepped through his uncle's door would hardly qualify as that. Nathaniel's mother, Rachel, had taken care of him until he was nine years old, but then she died. He didn't remember a thing about her. Any "raising" that had been done from the point that Howard became his legal guardian had been done by Seth.

His uncle had still taken him in, though, and he *was* the only biological family Nathaniel had left; which was one of the predominant reasons he was the one here now and not someone else. Yes, his exceptional skills at scouting made him a prime candidate for this assignment, but his personal tie to it could prove to be of far greater value.

Malachi must have known that, even despite Seth's objections, which Nathaniel knew he only ever made out of a desire to protect him.

Nathaniel shook his head, still not having moved one step closer to the door. He didn't like to think about his life before Seth took him under his wing; the pieces of himself that tied him to his humanity. There were too many unanswered questions, too many things that would haunt him if he were to let himself remember. This was why he had given himself so fully to the brotherhood...so it could be as if his former life had never been.

Howard Blake didn't know anything about Nathaniel's life (much less his double-life) aside from the tuition check he sent him every semester to pay for his schooling at Oxford. Nathaniel doubted he even cared to, which made this situation a great deal more difficult than any typical nephew dropping by to visit his uncle.

Frowning at the sight of the stone-covered mansion, Nathaniel analyzed its face. The oversized urns on each side of the door spilled over with freshly planted flowers, leaving little chance in his mind that his uncle wasn't here. Unless, of course, Howard had kept some of his hired staff at this estate to tend to the grounds for a pending visit he might be making.

Squaring his shoulders and walking beneath the arch of the rotunda, Nathaniel knocked on the dark wooden door three times. He listened as the sound echoed through the entryway and held his breath, hoping no one would answer and relieved when no one did. But it did strike him as odd to find the place empty. He really had expected Howard, or at least someone to be here.

In under three seconds, Nathaniel had already picked the lock and moved inside, careful to get out of sight before any neighbors or nosey passers-by caught sight of him and called the police. Something told him the people in this neighborhood didn't think too fondly of breaking and entering.

Taking a deep breath when he shut the door behind him, Nathaniel glanced around the entryway, the sitting room and the oversized living area for any sign that the place had been recently lived in. Other than the flowers out front, he found nothing.

Slowly, he took in the interior of the mansion. From the spiraling maple banister to the marble-flooring that spilled off into the hallway, it was apparent that no expense had been spared in the furnishing of this home. But almost none of it was familiar. In all the time he had lived here, surely he should have remembered something about it?

Nathaniel didn't dwell on the thought.

The place was easily ten times bigger than his unmarried uncle needed. *So much useless, wasted space,* he thought.

Once he determined he was alone in there, Nathaniel moved into the kitchen and set his backpack at his feet, pulling the envelope Seth had given him out from his inner jacket pocket. He emptied its contents onto the marble-topped island, sifting through the papers that were scrawled with writing. He stopped when his hand fell on a stack of black and white photographs.

Picking them up off the counter, he looked through them one at a time, analyzing each with careful detail. Whatever Nathaniel expected to find, this certainly wasn't it.

The first of the photographs was of a small girl with light hair and strangely intense eyes. The next was the same girl and a boy who looked maybe nine or ten years older than her. Most likely her brother, judging by the similarities in their appearance and that fact that he had almost identical eyes. The third was another of the two of them with an older girl who had her back turned to the camera. That one looked closer to the age of the boy, Nathaniel thought, though it was hard to tell since her hair hung down over the side of her face. Her being in the picture at all was probably irrelevant. Chances were, it was taken for the other two.

When he flipped to the last photograph, Nathaniel rethought the assumption. He recognized the same girl by her long dark hair, but in this picture she was facing forward. Unfortunately it was blurred, and taken from too great a distance away to be useful.

Apparently Eli didn't own a telephoto lens.

Nathaniel set the pictures down, trying to find what Eli was even getting at. Scanning through his notes, Nathaniel looked for any mention of these three whom Eli deemed significant enough to watch. They looked normal enough to Nathaniel, but he was the first to know that looks could be deceiving.

Eli's writing was only partially legible, and most of it was completely irrelevant, but after looking through five sheets of paper that had been ripped from a notebook, Nathaniel finally found something of value:

The child is protected.
They are afraid of the boy.
The girl is no longer a threat.

Nathaniel reached for the pictures again, studying them even closer and trying to understand what these words might mean. Assuming "they" indicated Donovan and those in his charge, the second line was a weighted statement in itself. What was it about the boy in the photographs that could possibly have Donovan afraid? Eli wasn't giving him answers here, only more questions; and quite frankly, Nathaniel didn't need any more questions than he already had.

Turning the page over, he saw something else. It was an address to a location just outside the city, and there was something written beneath it:

Watch the child. She sees.

Nathaniel frowned. Folding the piece of paper, he slipped it back into his jacket pocket, returning everything he had spilled onto the counter to the envelope Seth had given him and sliding it into a drawer beneath a silverware tray. He reached for his cell phone and pulled up Mapquest as he headed for the door.

There had to be something at that address.

Nathaniel was still looking down when he stepped outside and onto his uncle's driveway, studying the image on his phone. He looked up when Seth's words resurfaced in his mind, bringing a tension along with them that he didn't care to feel. Nathaniel looked down the road and made a face. He had enough to worry about right now; having to figure out an acceptable means of transportation while "remaining as inconspicuous as possible" was not something he wanted to deal with.

Seth really hadn't thought this assignment through.

Glancing to his left at the attached three-car garage, Nathaniel frowned again and moved quickly back through the house and out to the garage. He grabbed the keys that were hanging on a hook by the door and was surprised at what he found out there. Immediately he wondered if his uncle might have recently suffered some sort of midlife crisis. Parked directly in front of him was an untouched Ducati 1198 S. Midnight black. Red frame. Only eighty-eight miles on the odometer.

Nathaniel narrowed his eyes at the sight of it.

*T*earing up Highway 24 pushing close to ninety, Nathaniel was more than irritated at how slow he was moving. The wind on his face mimicked the feeling he had known in coming to Woodland Park, but it was only enough to tease him. He was reminded as he sped up the road of what he wouldn't be able to know again until he left this place, and he knew he couldn't leave until he accomplished this assignment.

All the more reason not to fail, he thought.

Nathaniel didn't know how long he could take being held back like this. He had been tested in many things throughout his life, more than most would ever know, but he had never been tested quite in this way before, so directly forced into the existence he despised.

Following the directions Mapquest laid out for him, he took a left on Edlowe Road when he came just outside the city limits and wound his way through the aspens and evergreens that towered over him on both sides. The road took him a decent way up the mountain, all the way to Skyline Drive, where he ended up parking the Ducati. It took him about ten minutes to get there from his uncle's house, though it would have taken longer if he'd paid attention to the speed limit. Still, it felt like an eternity.

Nathaniel was careful as he walked up the dirt and gravel road, not sure what he would find there or what he should expect; but he knew his orders were to remain unnoticed, so he took his time.

When he neared a log home that sat on top of a hill, he felt a very distinct, sudden shift in the atmosphere. He wasn't sure what to make of it, but even before his eyes fell to the mailbox and he saw that the address was a match, he knew he'd found the place Eli was directing him to.

The name "Howell" was printed on the other side of the black metal mailbox, which was staked into the ground at the end of the driveway. There were lights on inside the house, and as Nathaniel came closer to it he saw figures through the window that were moving around; some large, some very small, but he couldn't get an accurate count on how many there were from the viewpoint he held.

Winding through the pine-spotted yard, he stayed at the edge of the woods so he wouldn't be seen. He circled around to the back of the house without making a sound and noticed a separate garage that had been converted into what looked like a bedroom. Some sort of guesthouse from the looks of it. Either way, it caught his attention enough to pull his gaze to the glass sliding door that served as its entrance; not because of what he saw, but rather what he felt.

The feeling Nathaniel discerned around this place was even stronger here, directly around the room, though it didn't look as if anyone were inside.

Turning away from the garage-converted-bedroom, he moved swiftly back beneath the cover of the trees and took in the rest of the picture before him. There was a deck coming off the house and a pool in the backyard surrounded by a flagstone patio, and also a blacktop with a basketball hoop and a tool shed that backed up to the tree-line at the edge of the property. There were toys floating in the pool and several pairs of flip-flops strewn carelessly along the edge of it, small enough that they had to belong to children. These people appeared to have a lot of them.

Nathaniel moved back into the woods and climbed quickly up to the center of a towering pine, which placed him at eye level with the main floor of the house. The oversized windows that covered the wall made it easy for him to see inside.

46

There were six of them; a pretty, slightly overweight blonde woman holding a baby, a tall lanky man with a mustache, two little ones with wildly curly hair that could have been twins and a small girl he immediately recognized.

That was the one, the child from the photographs.

It didn't take Nathaniel even a moment to realize she was different than the others. While the curly-haired boys ran around screaming and the baby cried and the blonde woman laughed with the man he assumed to be her husband, the girl sat motionless on a barstool at the kitchen counter. She had the same blonde hair as her mother and she didn't appear to be saying a word, just sitting far too still for any child her age, watching everyone around her.

She looked about seven or eight, but Nathaniel couldn't be sure, mostly because the expression on her face was completely unreadable. There was a maturity behind her eyes that a child her age simply should not possess, and as he watched her, he thought on Eli's words, trying to determine what this girl could possibly see.

Then something happened that he did not anticipate.

The girl turned her head sharply, looking directly across the yard in his direction. Not hesitating for a moment, her gaze was locked, and a chill fell over Nathaniel immediately. He had to be at least fifty yards away, hidden so carefully in the trees there was no way she could have seen him. But what he felt in her gaze contradicted this logic.

She knew he was there.

Nathaniel was both awed and disturbed by this new revelation. That was what Eli meant. His notation of the child's ability to see was not confined to the physical alone. Not hardly. What this girl could see defied the logic of reality itself.

Who was she that she could do such a thing? She was so small, so young...the youngest Nathaniel had ever seen with that gift. And what was she doing in this place?

As he continued looking at her, it all started to make sense to him; the reason she was protected, the reason she had been watched.

Suddenly, he made the connection. Looking in every direction, Nathaniel realized what it was that lingered around this place. That same chill hit him again, but it was different than before. Not something he'd never felt by any means, just something he'd never felt this strongly. He was speechless, fascinated, and at the same time unsettled. In quiet awe he stayed there, his eyes fixing in on the family inside.

Who were these people that they would draw such a heightened level of protection? Why was the activity here so strong and who was this child?

Remembering the shaggy-haired boy from the photographs, Nathaniel realized he didn't see him with the rest of the family. He compulsively scanned the perimeter again, and when his eyes fell on the makeshift guesthouse, he questioned if it might be the boy's. Judging by the feeling that lingered around the place, it was possible. This degree of supernatural activity wasn't found just anywhere. There had to be something specific, dangerous even, about a given location to draw that kind of attention, such as the level of guarding required by those who lived there.

If the girl was protected, Nathaniel had to assume that the boy would be as well, especially if he was the one "they" were afraid of.

Focusing in on the guesthouse with the glass sliding door, Nathaniel climbed down from his watch-point and made his way toward it. He looked behind him as he wound through the trees, making sure he wasn't spotted as he slipped into the room. Strangely, it was unlocked.

He felt it when he stepped inside, exactly what he expected; a stronger concentration of the presence he'd felt before. This seemed to be the center of it, or at least one of two central points, and though he didn't know why that was the case, he was determined to find out. That would tell him more than Eli's notes ever could.

The room was clean; almost too clean. It didn't look like anyone had lived in it for a while, which didn't do much to explain why it would still feel like this. The bed was made with hospital-style perfection and there was a guitar case in the corner of the room, but nothing on the floor. It had been recently vacuumed, or at least not occupied since the last time it was, and there were posters on the walls; band posters, by appearance.

The Devil Wears Prada. Sleeping Giant. For Today. In Fear and Faith. Demon Hunter.

Strange names, Nathaniel thought. Then again, he thought everything about music was strange.

When his eyes fell to the mirror over the dresser against the wall, he saw that there were pictures pressed into the cracks of the mirror, and ticket stubs, it seemed. Just as he suspected, the shaggy-haired boy from Eli's photographs was in almost every one.

Nathaniel was right. This was his room.

There were five pictures altogether and each one was different. One was of the boy standing with several strange-looking men, all who had long, stringy hair hanging down in their eyes, tattoos covering every inch of their arms and wild expressions marking their faces. Nathaniel glanced back to one of the posters behind him and recognized the same men at the center of it.

Concert photo, he concluded. Foolish teenagers and their obsession with fame.

Quickly scanning over the other photographs, his eyes fell to the one at the top and center of the mirror. Like the others, it was of the boy, but also of a long-haired girl he quickly recognized. She was holding onto his arm, her eyes squinted closed and her mouth open wide, and they were both soaking wet and laughing.

Nathaniel didn't understand the picture, nor did he care to. He glanced instead to the handwritten note beside it that read:

Caden, You're my favorite. Don't forget me when you're in Nashville or I will be forced to find a replacement best friend.

Love, Kyla

Nathaniel contemplated the words and remembered the mailbox outside. *Caden Howell*, he thought. That must be his name.

He had no way of knowing when this note had been written, but judging by the state of the bedroom, it was possible that the boy presumably named Caden was in Tennessee now. Which would be inconvenient at the very least.

Nathaniel reached to grab the picture down from the mirror so he could look at it more closely, but before he had the chance, he felt something shift. Snapping his head up, he moved to the door, then he positioned himself behind the curtain so he wouldn't be seen and quickly scanned the yard.

Nothing appeared out of the ordinary. The toys were still floating in the pool, the people he saw before were still inside the house and the flip-flops were still lying against the flagstone in the exact arrangement they had been before. But everything Nathaniel felt in him and around him screamed a different truth than his eyes could see.

Something was out there. He was not the only one watching.

Carefully slipping out the door, he made his way with impressive speed through the trees and back out to Winding Valley Road. He was methodical as he moved and able to keep his pulse and breathing and heart-rate perfectly even. Nathaniel didn't allow himself to doubt or second-guess a single decision he made, and within thirty seconds he was back out on the Ducati on Edlowe Road, racing toward Falcon's Rest.

He reached his uncle's estate in a little less than ten minutes. Returning the bike to the garage and putting the door down quickly, Nathaniel moved back into the house and pulled the envelope from its hiding place. Dumping its contents again onto the counter, he sifted through the papers and separated out the photographs.

First, he looked at the one of the long-haired girl, verifying that it was, in fact, her in the picture on the bedroom mirror. Nathaniel could see that it was, so he didn't waste time with it. Next, he pulled the close-up of the child. This one he spent more time on.

Studying her face, he was able to see in her eyes what he hadn't before, mostly because he didn't know to look for it. It was as clear to him as it would be if they were face to face: The child was a seer.

Nathaniel set the picture down and rested his elbows against the counter, not even sure what to think right now. This was more complicated than he had expected. Surely Seth had not accounted for this.

A thousand questions raced through his mind as he stared at the black marble countertop. Who was this child? What had she seen that caused her to look at him like that and why was she so protected? Why had the boy named Caden left and what reason did Donovan have to be afraid of him? That was, of course, assuming Eli's notes were even accurate…and that Nathaniel had interpreted them correctly.

He continued to wrestle with these thoughts, knowing someone had been out there tonight, watching the child like he was. He needed to know who they were. He needed to know what they were after. But most importantly, he needed to know what a creature as twisted and depraved as Donovan could possibly want with these humans.

Alexa Howell sat motionless by the pool in her backyard. Hugging her knees to her chest, she stared into the woods and focused forward with a level of concentration no eight-year-old should be able to attain. A breeze blew wisps of her soft blonde hair around her face, but she didn't move a muscle. She was determined to focus. Determined to see.

"Lex, honey…" Melissa Howell called sweetly from behind her in her thick Southern drawl. "You comin' inside?"

Alexa shook her head, not even turning to acknowledge her. She could feel her mother's nervousness and imagine how she must be looking at her.

"Alright," Melissa agreed, seeming to take the hint, "but not too long, okay?"

Alexa didn't respond.

Her mother waited for a moment before going back into the house to put Jackson and Jaime to bed. The twins had already been up an hour past their bedtime, but Melissa didn't seem half as concerned with that as she did with her daughter. That was how things always were between them. That was how things were with Alexa and anyone...except Caden.

Fixing her gaze and setting her mind, Alexa looked through the pine trees that edged the woods at the back of their yard. She knew something was out there; she just wasn't sure what it was, but she had been out here for the past half hour trying to figure it out.

When she saw it before, it was like a flash of light at first...the kind she knew didn't physically exist. The flash was what caught her attention, but when she looked to the trees, Alexa hadn't seen what she'd expected to. The truth was she hadn't seen anything, and that was what disturbed her.

Straining her eyes even though she knew the effort was wasted, she had narrowed in on the place where the flash had occurred. That was usually when she saw them, as soon as the light had faded...the guardians that always stood around this place. But this time was different.

It wasn't uncommon for Alexa to see these ones who supposedly watched over her, but it had been happening less frequently since Caden had left. They had been there since she was born, or at least that's what he had told her. Her brother knew a lot more about the guardians than she did, and he could always tell when they were there, but he couldn't see like she could see. He told her no one could.

Alexa didn't understand the way she was different. Caden always told her she was unique, that she had a gift, but everyone else just treated her like something was wrong with her. She wondered sometimes if Caden only said that to make her feel better, but she knew he wasn't a liar. Even if she didn't understand what he meant, she trusted him. And she trusted what he said of her, that there was a reason she could see angels.

Wrinkling her forehead, Alexa cast her gaze from the trees in frustration. Something was wrong about this. It felt off to her, even if only by a few degrees. Where her sight was usually clear, it was faded tonight, confused in a way that made her question what was really out there.

She had seen the initial light, but she hadn't seen the protector, as if one were there where a guardian should stand, disguised by light and hidden in the dark, making it impossible for her to see what it actually was.

She had never known this before. It had always been black and white to her. There had always been good and bad. But with whatever had been out there or whatever still was, she only saw gray. And Alexa Howell did not know what to do with gray. She needed her to brother to understand a thing like that.

After staying outside for another ten minutes, Melissa's voice came from behind her again. "Okay, honey, it's time to come inside."

Alexa frowned. Standing obediently to make her way back to the house, her bare feet padded against the flagstone as she walked, and she couldn't help but glance one more time to the woods.

"Mom?" she asked, her eyes still set in the opposite direction.

Melissa looked startled to hear her daughter speak. "Yes, sweetheart?"

Alexa was careful with her words as an idea formed in her head. "Is it okay if Matthew comes over?" she asked.

Her mother looked confused. "When, honey?"

"Tonight."

Melissa laughed a little, unsure of whether or not she was serious. She stopped at the back door when she realized she was. "I don't know, sweetheart. It's getting late."

Alexa didn't allow her mother's initial denial to sway her resolve. "What if Kyla brings him?" she suggested. "He could stay the night."

Melissa eyed her curiously, trying to figure out what she was after. "This is important to you, isn't it?" she asked.

Alexa nodded to let her know that it was. The girl so rarely ever asked for anything that Melissa couldn't write it off.

Alexa knew her mother didn't understand her, that she didn't understand her motives and she didn't understand her mind, but even in her lack of understanding, there was a level of trust Melissa had in her that most children never knew with their parents.

"Alright," she finally agreed. "You can invite him over. But no staying up till two in the morning this time, you hear?"

Alexa made a conscious effort to smile. "Thank you," she said. Then she made her way into the kitchen and reached for the phone.

*N*athaniel Blake sat precariously on a rocky ledge that was located about a mile from the Howell's home. He stared out across the canyon before him, watching the setting sun cast pink and orange arcs across the sky, silhouetting Pike's Peak to purple-hued perfection. A breeze blew past his face and he closed his eyes, breathing in deeply and taking in the sensation.

This was the closest to normal he had felt since he'd been here.

It was bad enough that he had to live like this day to day in London, but at least there he had the night. It was only then that he truly came alive; letting down the façade, the deception...the lie.

Nathaniel grimaced as he looked down at his hands, disgusted by their weakness. He felt bound, trapped as if in a cage and appearing as something he knew he would never be. He understood why Seth had ordered him to remain in human form. The repercussions that would result if Donovan or any of his followers discovered him here could be cataclysmic. Still, he wished there was another way.

Something peculiar happened as Nathaniel wrestled with the thought. A golden eagle caught his vision, soaring through the valley by the cover of the dark. He was struck by the sight, not only because of the magnificence of the bird, but because he knew it shouldn't be there at all...much as he shouldn't be able to see it. There were a lot of things Nathaniel Blake shouldn't be able to do.

It was a peculiar thing, watching this bird of prey speed through the air. Nathaniel knew that eagles were not nocturnal.

Staring forward in contemplation, he focused in on its outspread wings, shoving away the bitterness that met him at the sight.

You have to stop this, he told himself. There were more important things at hand than his envy over a bird's ability to fly. He wouldn't have seen it if there weren't.

In his world, coincidence did not exist.

Once the eagle flew out of his view, Nathaniel looked back curiously at the Howell's home. Something was moving tonight; he could feel it. Even as far away as he was, he could feel it as if he were right there. But still he didn't move.

He had already spent an hour here watching, waiting in the dark on the mountain. It was the only tangible lead he had, and with what little Eli had left for him, Nathaniel was lucky to have even that. Still, it frustrated him. If he could just see who it was that had been watching the little girl, he could track them back to wherever they came from. Questionable or not, he reasoned that such an action fell within the parameters of his assignment, that he would merely be following the leads that Eli had provided him with. Plus, he wasn't about to miss the opportunity to uncover a location, especially not one that might take him to Donovan.

Find the enemy before the enemy finds you. Nathaniel had always believed that.

Unfortunately, it wasn't always that easy. Nathaniel was an incredible scout, the best of his kind, but he wasn't used to assignments like this and he was not about to trust it. A defected member of Donovan's alliance suddenly approaches the leader of the Resitore and feeds him just enough information to intrigue him, just enough that one of them would be sent here to validate his claim? It was more than suspicious. And what was worse, Malachi had actually taken Eli in, inducted him as the newest member of the Roman faction, throwing away any trace of common sense he might otherwise have possessed.

Nathaniel would not be as naïve as the leader of the brotherhood. He would proceed from a distance, just as he had been trained by Seth to do, anticipating that any move or strategy that could be made against them would be made, and he would take every potential scenario into account.

It was what he did, and just as his brothers, Nathaniel was good at what he did. Possibly even better. His instincts were flawless, his intuition uncanny, and right now both were telling him there was more at work here than Malachi or Seth or any of them realized.

Closing his eyes again for a moment, Nathaniel breathed in deeply and allowed the cool mountain air to fill his lungs. It helped to keep him focused on what was at hand so he wouldn't become frustrated by his limitations on this assignment. Then quickly, his eyes shot open again.

Someone was coming.

Making his way effortlessly down from the rocky ledge, Nathaniel moved back to the trail with unnatural speed.

The Howell's were about to have a visitor.

Chapter 4

"...there are no shades to black and white."

Lying on her stomach in bed, Kyla James stared down at the drawing pad in front of her, making a face when she realized it was all wrong. She had been sketching like this for over two hours, moving black charcoal streaks across the paper in hopes of unveiling a masterpiece; a masterpiece that so far had only proven to be a waste of her time.

Just like the rest of this stupid week.

Glancing up at her bedroom walls, Kyla analyzed the hundreds of drawings framed in black that covered them. The arrangement of the drawings itself was a form of art, and one that she was quite proud of, considering that she'd only been at it for about four of the eighteen years she'd been alive. It was just unfortunate that almost anyone who ever set foot in there found it creepy beyond all reason. But nothing, in her opinion, could have been a more accurate reflection of her soul.

Returning her eyes to the charcoal mess in front of her that was supposed to pass for art, Kyla wrinkled her nose. No, this was definitely not right.

She tore out the page and crumpled it up, tossing it into the wastebasket beside her desk; then she flopped backwards onto her bed dramatically and covered her face with her arms. She was really getting tired of this.

Kyla turned over onto her side after a few seconds, unintentionally letting her eyes fall to the picture on her bed stand of her and her best friend. She scowled at the sight of it, knocking it over on its face so she wouldn't have to look at it anymore.

Caden Howell was the last thing she wanted to see right now. It was probably his fault that she hadn't been able to draw in a week anyway, and the last thing she needed to be reminded of was why.

Honestly, how hard would it be for him to pick up his phone and call her?

Kyla blinked at the sound of irony when the home line started ringing downstairs.

"Matty, can you get that?" she called down to her little brother.

He didn't respond, but the ringing stopped, so he must have picked it up. Kyla ran her fingers through her long auburn hair, pushing it away from her face. She was about to go downstairs to see who was calling, but then she heard the basement door open and rethought the idea.

"Awesome," she mumbled sarcastically.

As soon as she heard a shrill, condescending voice start screaming at her brother, Kyla swung her legs around to the side of her bed and bolted down the stairs.

"Hey!" she snapped once she marched into the kitchen.

Loni James spun around to face her and Kyla folded her arms staunchly. She could see the woman was drunk, wearing matted fuzzy slippers and the same grey sweatpants she'd worn for the past five days, her short dark hair in a tangled mess and tell-tale bags under her eyes. Nothing Kyla didn't expect.

"Do not talk to him like that," she threatened the woman.

Matthew's eyes were wide as he stared at his sister, and Kyla saw that he was still on the phone.

"Who is it, Matty?" she asked him.

He didn't blink once. "Alexa. She wants to know if you can take me over there."

"Absolutely not," Loni scoffed.

Kyla continued to stare her down. "Tell her you'll be right over," she said to Matthew. She kept her hands on her hips and her eyes on the woman who had the nerve to call herself her mother.

That was when Loni lost it.

Kyla probably should have paid attention to what she started screaming then, figuring it might aid her in understanding the rage on the woman's face, but her deductive reasoning was pretty good, so she decided against listening to it and tuned her out instead. She did, however, catch the tail end of her ranting.

"*I* am the mother here!" Loni shouted. "*Not* you!"

Kyla flinched when she said it. *Oh, no you didn't,* she thought. She thought several other things too, but decided against speaking them out loud since her ten-year-old brother was standing right in front of her.

"Actually, you gave up that right two years ago," Kyla said.

Loni was indignant. Her face was turning redder by the second and Kyla thought there had to be at least a hundred things she wanted to scream at her, every one of which she was far too drunk to articulate.

Matthew mumbled into the phone, "I'll be right over, Lex," obviously embarrassed and anxious to get off the line.

Loni took a step toward him when he tried to hang it up, and Kyla grabbed her arm instinctively to stop her, twisting it behind her back hard enough to force her to her knees. Kyla may have been half the woman's size (despite that they were both 5'8") but she was strong. And the fact that she was sober definitely played to her advantage.

"If you touch him," Kyla threatened her, "I swear I will break your arm."

Matthew hung up the phone quickly, his eyes even wider than before.

"Go get in the car, Matty," Kyla said. "I'll be right there."

Loni was swearing up a storm and obviously in pain, but Kyla didn't let go of her arm until her brother was safely outside. Once he was, she grabbed her purse and keys from where she'd left them on the kitchen table and sprinted to the front door before Loni had time to right herself. Thanks to the woman's present lack of coordination, she was able to pull it off successfully, too.

Kyla hopped into the silver Honda Civic that her mother hadn't driven in longer than she could remember; then she started the engine and cringed at the sound of the banshee-like screaming that was coming from inside the house.

"Buckle your seatbelt," she told Matthew. Kyla peeled out quickly, hoping to get far enough away from the battle zone and their ogre of a mother that they were out of range of any projectile lampshades or dinner forks that may or may not be launched in their direction.

Once they were out on the highway, Kyla was finally able to exhale. "You alright, kiddo?" she asked.

Matthew didn't answer her. He just stared out the passenger side window.

Kyla hated that her brother had to go through this. She hated that he had to be so afraid and that he always shut down this way. But more than anything, she hated that there was nothing she could do about it.

Clicking the back arrow of the ipod she had hooked up to the car speakers last month, she put on her Underoath playlist, took a deep breath and let the sound of Spencer Chamberlain's voice calm her down.

Now that was the kind of screaming she could handle.

Underoath was like an addiction for her, like a mind-altering drug that kept her from flinging herself off a cliff whenever she was so compelled with the urge. She had plenty of cliffs around here to choose from, too. One of the benefits (or disadvantages) of living in Colorado, depending on how you looked at it.

Kyla and Matthew had lived in Woodland Park their whole lives, the place that was known as "The City Above the Clouds." It was one of those places people dreamed about living and wanted to run away to; crazy people who didn't know any better.

She hated this town.

Pulling onto Edlowe Road, Kyla sighed as they wound their way up into the trees. In all of Woodland Park, in all of Teller County, in all of Colorado, this was the one place she felt even halfway sane. The road was hidden on the edge of Pike's Peak where hardly anyone even knew to look for it. Sheltered on both sides by an endless array of aspens and pine trees, it looked like something that belonged in a

60

fairytale; like the kind of road you would expect to lead to a house with seven dwarves or a cottage in the woods made of gingerbread.

Kyla used to love it up here. It had always been an escape for her, the place she would run to when she needed to get away from her stupid mother and that stupid town and the stupid people who lived there. Even if reality always did manage to catch up with her eventually, it was nice to be able to breathe every once in a while and forget momentarily how much she hated her life.

It wasn't like that for her up here anymore. It hadn't been in a really long time.

Kyla looked up and saw the road sign for Skyline Drive, and as soon as she did, a familiar sinking feeling found its way into the pit of her stomach; the same one that always did whenever she came up here like this.

She'd assumed that after eleven months and thirteen days, she would have stopped missing him this much, like maybe if enough time passed she wouldn't still feel so empty and lost. And maybe that would be the case with anyone else, but not with Caden. Definitely not with Caden. She was just too close to him, too connected to him for that. Or at least they used to be that close until he decided to ditch her a year ago and move to Nashville.

Kyla still didn't get it, how the person who introduced her to Underoath, who lived and breathed scream and metalcore could just run off and leave her to go record an *acoustic rock* album, of all things. She understood that it was a great opportunity for him, but seriously? Caden with a Takamine? Please.

She had questioned a time or two if Randy Howell, his country-singing musician father had persuaded him to do it, but knowing the man as well as she did, Kyla highly doubted it. Randy and Melissa Howell were not the kind of parents that pushed their kids to do something they didn't already have a heart for. Randy hadn't gotten him into this; he had merely opened the door. Caden was the one who had chosen to walk through it.

He was the one who had chosen to leave her.

Making a face to mask the ache in her heart, Kyla pulled into the Howell's driveway and parked the car. She turned to Matthew when they came to a stop and gave him a smile. "I'll pick you up when I get off work tomorrow, okay?"

He looked confused. "You're not coming in?"

Kyla tried not to let him see her frustration, knowing he would feel bad if he realized it was hurting her to be here. "No, not tonight," she told him. "I'd actually be surprised if anyone but Alexa's even still up."

Matthew frowned and looked toward the house. She could see that he was worried about something, and suddenly Kyla wasn't sure it even had to do with Loni.

"You okay, kiddo?" she asked him.

He nodded and opened the door. "I'm fine," he mumbled. "Thanks for the ride."

Kyla looked at him curiously, but he was careful not to meet her eyes. "No problem," she told him.

She watched him walk up onto the deck and go through the massive double doors of the Howell's log home, and as she fit the pieces together, she felt a little foolish for not picking up on this sooner. She should have questioned before why Alexa would call him so late, but at the time she was so mad at Loni for screaming at him about it that she'd completely forgotten logic in the whole scenario.

Not that logic ever played much into anything that involved Alexa Howell.

Biting her lip, Kyla reached down instinctively for her phone, pressed number one on her speed dial and held it to her ear. It was a compulsive action, and one she should have known would prove useless, but she couldn't stop herself from doing it.

When Caden's voicemail came on, she hung up without leaving him a message. Setting her elbows against the steering wheel, she put her forehead in her hands, trying to suppress the ache in her chest that served as an ever-present reminder of all that she'd lost.

Kyla had never been very good at that. The harder she worked to forget what she was desperate not to remember, the more it flooded into her against her will.

Sitting there like that with her head in her hands, she realized after about twenty seconds that couldn't breathe. Kyla threw open the door of the Civic and scrambled to get outside, her claustrophobia increasing to a point that was almost unbearable.

She had to get out of there.

*P*ositioning himself carefully in the trees, Nathaniel neared the edge of the Howell's property for the second time that night. He watched as a silver Honda Civic pulled into the driveway and saw a little boy with brownish-red hair and freckles get out of the passenger-side door. Nathaniel stayed focused on the boy until the front door of the house opened and he was welcomed inside.

Nathaniel's attention was diverted back to the Civic when the driver's side opened and the girl who had been behind the wheel scrambled out of it. She looked a good eight or nine years older than the boy. She also looked like she was gasping for air, though Nathaniel didn't know why. When he studied her more closely, he realized she wasn't frightened, just frustrated.

He also realized he had seen her before.

It was her auburn hair that first caught his attention, but he only made a positive identification when she turned and he saw her face. Immediately the image of Eli's photograph flashed through his mind. Nathaniel glanced back toward the garage-converted-bedroom behind him, remembering the picture on the mirror.

This girl's countenance and demeanor didn't remotely resemble what Nathaniel had seen in that picture, but she was quite clearly the same person. She had been laughing in the photograph, so much that her eyes were squinted closed, and certainly not in a forced kind of way; a detail that hadn't initially held his interest. He had been more focused on the boy than on her, but seeing the contrast in her now, he couldn't help but question the difference. Especially when he thought on Eli's words: *The girl is no longer a threat.*

Curious, Nathaniel moved closer, hoping to discern something about this girl that would help him understand. What he had seen of her in the photograph held no trace of false pretense. Her joy was legitimate, completely unforced. And what he saw in her now was about as stark a contrast to that as possible.

Nathaniel watched the girl (whose name he assumed to be Kyla) straighten the shirt she was wearing; a tight black one with the word "Thrice" scrawled on it in colorful letters. He remembered the name from a ticket stub on the boy's mirror.

The girl sighed and put her hands on her hips, looking up the road and then down at her flip-flops. Clearly, she was upset about something. Leaning her back against the driver's side door, she closed her eyes and took a deep breath.

Nathaniel analyzed every detail of her movement as he assessed the situation. He knew before anything else, he needed to verify her identity. His best guess at that point was that she was the one who had written the note on Caden Howell's mirror, but he realized there was a chance the note had been written by someone else and its placement next to her photograph merely a coincidence.

Either way, he needed her. There was a reason Eli had tracked her, and a reason he had written about her what he did. The thought of this girl ever having been a threat to Donovan or anyone in his charge was completely beyond Nathaniel, but he wasn't going to question the validity of the claim. Not yet.

Keeping his eyes on the auburn-haired girl, Nathaniel weighed his options. If he could get close enough to read her, he could see why she was marked, and possibly even use her to attain the information he needed about the boy and his sister; information he suspected she had. He needed to uncover Donovan's motive here, and while the other two from the photographs were obviously higher on his priority list, this girl was the only one of the three Nathaniel had access to. She was now the best lead he had...and a lead he was about to lose by the looks of things.

Nathaniel frowned when the girl got back in the silver Honda and started the engine. This wasn't good. If she left now, he wouldn't be able to follow her, at least not so long as he stayed within the boundaries of his orders.

He could hear music blaring through the speakers inside the vehicle when she started it, though the sound was muffled to him where he stood watching her from the trees. Nathaniel made a face as the screaming reached his ears, but as soon as it came on, the girl took a deep breath and smiled to herself, exhaling as if she were completely at peace.

There may have been a lot about humans that Nathaniel didn't understand, but even this didn't seem to fit the parameters of normal human behavior. There was something strange about this girl, he thought. Still, she was the best shot he had right now, and he knew he couldn't let the opportunity slip away from him. Not when he didn't know when or if he would get it back.

Feeling a tension in his chest, Nathaniel watched her drive away, his brow creasing as the Civic disappeared around the corner.

He was not ready to make a decision like this.

Alexa Howell stared toward the window at the front of the house, but it was too dark outside for her to see anything. She knew it was too dark; it had been too dark for hours. She still couldn't force herself to turn away.

Matthew James, her best and arguably only friend looked at her quietly where he sat beside her on the couch. His eyes were soft behind his lightly freckled face, and though they remained on her expectantly, she wasn't afraid. There was nothing frightening about Matthew's eyes. If it was true what people said about them being the windows to the soul, then he had the purest soul she'd ever seen.

That was why she trusted him.

Alexa had put a movie on when he'd gotten there, but they weren't watching it. They were both too distracted; she with staring out that window and Matthew with waiting for her to explain herself. When he saw that she wasn't going to, he decided to take the initiative.

"What's going on, Lex?" he finally asked her.

Alexa didn't answer him, just turned her gaze back to the television, though the images on the screen were the last thing she was concerned with.

"Come on," he tried again. "I know you didn't ask me over to watch a movie."

She glanced down the hall toward her parents' room.

"They can't hear us," Matthew assured her. "You can talk to me."

Alexa turned her head, but she didn't meet his eyes. She could feel him studying her anyway.

"You saw something, didn't you?" he prompted. It was hardly a question.

She nodded slowly, keeping her gaze on a pillow by her feet.

Matthew looked disturbed. "What was it?"

Finally, she spoke. "I don't know," she said. It was the truth, too. Alexa couldn't have had less of an idea what was going on tonight; she only knew that something was. She wouldn't feel like this if everything were normal.

To be honest, it surprised her to feel anything at all, because as much as she was able to see, this part of it wasn't typical for her. Caden was the one who always felt these things.

It had started earlier with a flash of light, and the knowledge that something was watching her…possibly more than one. But where she initially thought she knew what it was, Alexa wasn't sure anymore. It was hard for her to place it, with her sight so unclear and everything inside of her screaming of danger. That was why she had called Matthew. She didn't feel safe being alone right now.

Matthew leaned back on the couch and looked down in contemplation. Alexa knew he didn't understand, despite how he tried to, but she also knew he believed her.

"Did you tell Caden?" he asked.

Somehow the thought saddened her. "No," she answered quietly.

Matthew looked confused. "But you tell him everything," he said. "Especially stuff like this."

Alexa looked up at him to respond, but when she met his eyes, she saw something she couldn't believe she hadn't seen sooner. That was all it took to distract her from her focus, just one look into Matthew's eyes.

Her heart sank when she realized he had lied to her, but she did nothing to outwardly reveal the emotion.

"It was worse than you let me know," she told him.

She had heard it on the phone, his mother's enraged, yet muffled voice screaming at him in the background, and she knew what it did to him whenever that happened. But he had assured her it was fine.

Clearly, it wasn't fine.

If she had just been more conscious of him and less focused on the window at the front of her house, she would have seen that when he walked in the door.

Matthew turned away. "I thought Kyla was gonna break her arm," he said, laughing a little to try and make light of the situation. He always did that.

Alexa could hear the pain behind his voice, though she knew he wouldn't want her to. But before she could speak again, she felt a pang in her head, something comparable to an electric shock.

Wincing, she brought her hand to her temple, surprised by the unfamiliar feeling. When she pressed her lips together and closed her eyes, Matthew looked worried.

"What is it?" he asked her. He sat up and leaned forward.

"It's nothing," Alexa lied. She dropped her hand. "Just a headache." But even as she said it, she couldn't stop herself from glancing again toward the window at the front of the house.

Kyla's heartbeat quickened as she looked down Winding Valley Road. She was standing ten feet from the Civic, only twenty yards from the Howell's front porch, but suddenly (and without the slightest clue as to why) she felt completely unsafe.

She couldn't help but feel that someone was watching her.

Trying to shake the feeling, Kyla got back in the car and started the engine. At the turn of the key, Spencer's screaming hit her ears again, but rather than flinch, she closed her eyes and took it in, breathing slowly and letting the calm of the sound fill her.

She was more than anxious to get away from here, but she tried not to speed as she hurried down the road. At least not too much. When she came into town a full five minutes sooner than she should have, though, Kyla realized she probably hadn't paid the attention to her speedometer that she needed to.

By the time she reached the outskirts of Woodland Park, she was starting to feel normal again.

See? she told herself. *You were imagining it.*

Kyla looked at the clock on the dashboard and frowned. She was so not ready to face Loni again. God only knew how that would go down, and right now delaying the inevitable didn't seem too terrible an option to her. Maybe if she gave it long enough, the old hag might even sleep it off.

Just before she passed the next exit, Kyla cranked the steering wheel hard to the left. It wasn't a conscious decision, turning off where she did. It just happened to be the last exit before the one that would take her home.

She drove behind the buildings along the back of that road, nervously tapping her fingers against the steering wheel. Kyla didn't want to be back here, and she didn't know why she was. It felt more like she was being pulled by a magnetic force than moving forward on her own free will.

If it were up to her, she would never drive down this road.

She parked without thought, and in the same way got out of the car and walked forward, moving as if on autopilot up the embankment toward Woodland Cemetery. Kyla bit her lip as she neared the entrance. While she debated it a time or two, she didn't turn around, but it took her a full ten seconds to realize she wasn't breathing.

When she finally forced herself to take a breath and passed beneath the wrought-iron arch, a crow cawed to her left and made her jump. Kyla gasped out loud and instinctively

68

covered her mouth; then she dropped her hand again when she saw the stupid bird and scowled at her own foolishness.

"Get a grip," she told herself. She seriously needed to calm down.

Everything was quiet in the cemetery that night. The dusked shadows of the headstones stretched onto the ground, creating a haunting yet strangely artistic image that Kyla couldn't help but appreciate. Still, she would rather not have been here. She would rather that she never had a reason to come here at all.

Winding her way through the headstones until she reached an all too familiar slab of black marble, she knelt in the dirt and trembled as she slid to the ground. Choking back the emotion that was trying to take her, she unconsciously clutched at the bracelet on her wrist; but she didn't let herself cry. She never let herself cry anymore.

Kyla closed her eyes, trying to fight off the images that flashed through her mind that she had been trying for two years to erase.

She saw herself where she had stood in this place when she was sixteen years old, at the edge of a six-foot hole that had been dug into the ground. She saw herself staring down at the cherry-wood casket being lowered into the hole and feeling as if someone was stabbing her with knives. She couldn't breathe then and she couldn't breathe now; she could only stare forward at the black marble headstone and remind herself for the thousandth time that she was never going to wake up from this.

Kyla hadn't been able to move that day...or cry or blink or feel. She could only stand there covered head to toe in black with her little brother on her right and her mother on her left, clutching the bracelet on her wrist that she hadn't taken off since. The bracelet her father had given her eight years before. The bracelet she was still clutching now.

It had been a logging accident, whatever that was supposed to mean. Kyla hadn't even wanted to know. She didn't hear a word the pastor spoke that day or the condolences the people around her had to offer; all she could hear was a painfully loud ringing in her ears that she thought might deafen her.

When she had finally looked up over the casket, her eyes had fallen on Caden where he had stood with his family across from her, only to see that his eyes were already set on hers. They had been soft; softer than normal even, which said a lot...filled with compassion and love and grief.

The sight of them made her sick.

Kyla had cringed and looked away from him, feeling the pain it caused him when she did. She had always been able to feel Caden like that, and it really wasn't fair. None of it was fair. He had been hurting because she was hurting, which in turn made her hurt twice as much. Even now thinking back on it, she felt the same, knowing she should never have had to hurt like that...to hurt like *this*. No one should ever have to.

Swallowing hard as the memories filled her mind, Kyla traced the name on the headstone with her fingertips, feeling again what she felt when they lowered the casket into that hole, when she watched her heart die as they buried her father.

She had slipped away the moment it began, unable to bear the sight of it. But nobody had stopped her. She had moved quickly, desperate to get out of the cemetery and away from there as fast as she could, and when she'd come to the metal-gated entrance, she thought she was actually in the clear. But Caden came after her.

"Kyla!" she remembered the sound of his voice as he called her name.

Whipping around, she had looked at him, her eyes as hollow and dark as her soul now felt.

Caden had stopped suddenly, looking almost frightened when he saw what was in her eyes. "Where are you going?" he asked her nervously.

"I don't know," she told him. "I don't care."

He had been careful as he stepped toward her. "Can I come with you?"

Kyla thought about it longer than she would have under any other circumstance, then finally she gave him a nod.

She couldn't remember another time that Caden Howell had been so quiet. He had walked up cautiously beside her,

70

like he was afraid he might say or do something wrong. She had wanted to tell him to stop stressing over it, that it wasn't his fault and that he wasn't going to hurt her...that it meant more to her than anything that he was there with her then. But she didn't tell him anything. She just didn't have the strength.

They walked like that for a while, though she couldn't remember how long. Even at the time, Kyla didn't really know. Time that day had been somewhat irrelevant in her mind. It was always moving forward but never moving back, never giving her the opportunity to fix what had happened or to make anything right. Robbing her of the chance to say goodbye.

Caden had reached for her hand compulsively. She wasn't sure if he meant to or if he questioned how she would take it, she only knew that when his fingers slid around hers and he moved his thumb along the back of her hand, she had to choke back the surge of emotion that came over her at his touch.

Squeezing his hand back, Kyla shoved down the cry she felt rising inside of her, but she couldn't speak a word. She knew she wouldn't be able to handle it, that if she so much as let herself open her mouth, she wouldn't be able to fight back this torrent that was trying to crush her. So instead she pressed her lips together, determined not to let them open.

And Caden never once let go of her hand.

Walking up the hill that day, they made their way into the park. It was a small park, conjoined with the elementary school, and in all honesty it was pretty pathetic. But Kyla loved it. She and Caden had been going there together since the day they first met on that playground when they were seven years old. Every time one of them was upset or hurt or wanted to be alone, every time they just needed to get away, that was where they would go. Sometimes they talked, sometimes they didn't. Whether they spent five minutes swinging or three hours lying on the grass in the sun, it really didn't matter. All that ever mattered was that they were there.

Sitting on the swing in silence, Kyla had rocked back and forth slowly, staring at her feet, which she kept on the ground. She would never forget how tortured Caden looked in that moment, or the way his voice sounded when he finally tried to say something to her.

"Ky, you don't always have to be so brave, you know."

She looked up at him slowly, unable to say the words she wanted more than anything to say.

"Yes I do," she told him instead.

It was all she could force, and she hated herself for it. She knew he could see through her, how much more there was behind her eyes, but Caden didn't push it. He just nodded as he looked into her, understanding her in a way that no one had ever been able to.

It was then that she realized he was everything to her.

Kneeling in the dirt by her father's grave, remembering that moment against her will, Kyla shook her head and righted herself. She shoved away the memory and gave in to the anger that had been building in her for days, letting it shield her from what she had no desire to feel.

Fighting with Loni may not have been her favorite thing in the world, but putting herself through this just to avoid an inevitable confrontation wasn't worth it.

Kyla brushed the dirt off her knees as she stood to her feet. She started to turn to leave, but when something that felt like a cold breeze hit her skin, she looked up quickly in confusion.

The feeling didn't make sense. It was an unnaturally warm night tonight. Then she was hit with something else, something she had already felt earlier that evening. Just as she had in the Howell's driveway, she felt suddenly and distinctly as if she was being watched.

Shuddering slightly, Kyla shook her head and moved back toward the metal arch at the entrance of the cemetery.

You're being ridiculous, she told herself. *You don't believe in that stuff anymore.*

Chapter 5

Nathaniel was strangely intrigued as he followed the auburn-haired girl into the cemetery. Looking all around him to make sure no one was watching, he slipped soundlessly through the entrance, allowing his curiosity to overcome the anxiety he felt over what he'd just done.

Watching from a safe enough distance that he wouldn't be spotted, he saw the girl kneel carefully at a headstone. Her eyes were vacant in a way that made him think she was a thousand miles away, remembering something, perhaps, about the person who was buried there.

Glancing at the headstone, Nathaniel read the name carved into the marble: *Darrell James*.

He was curious who this man might have been, and more importantly, why the girl most likely named Kyla was kneeling at his grave. When the thought began to linger, Nathaniel realized he was being distracted from his intention in coming here. He focused himself again and realigned his mind to the task at hand, knowing he couldn't afford to be divided on this now. But even in his efforts to set his attention, it was caught even further when the girl stood to leave.

Nathaniel watched as she fought back emotion. He thought it strange that she would do this when there was no one else there...or at least no one she was aware of. Typically when humans were alone, they didn't attempt to hold back their emotions, and saved that for keeping up appearances in front of others.

Whatever this girl was doing, she appeared to be fighting with herself.

When she brushed the dirt from her legs, Nathaniel saw what looked like a bracelet slip from her wrist. His eyes focused in on it where it fell to the ground, but he waited for her to leave before he moved closer to see what it was.

Once she turned and walked past where he was hidden, he moved soundlessly over to the headstone, bending down on one knee to pick up the object that had fallen from her wrist.

He was right; it was a bracelet, strung together by a black leather chord with a name etched into its silver face: *Kyla*.

Apparently he had been right about that, too.

There was another inscription on the inside of the band, but before he had time to read it, he heard a voice shout from behind him, "Hey!"

Nathaniel spun around quickly, startled to see the girl who was supposed to have left the cemetery marching angrily toward him.

"What are you doing?" she demanded.

He was caught off guard by her bluntness, and by her anger. "I'm sorry," he said. "I wasn't aware that this was private property."

The girl folded her arms across her chest and glared at him. She looked so cold, so angry.

"That doesn't answer my question," she snapped.

Nathaniel studied her face. "You know, most girls would have sense enough not to talk to a strange man in the dark."

Kyla scoffed at him. "Most girls are stupid, impulsive and naïve," she argued. "And you're hardly a man. How old are you? Twenty?"

Nathaniel gaped at her. He didn't know why, but he had to fight off the urge to smile. "Twenty-one," he corrected her.

"Whatever," Kyla mumbled. "Can I have my bracelet back?"

Nathaniel looked down at the object he was still holding. "This is yours?"

She didn't answer him, just held out her hand for it.

"Yes, it certainly does look valuable enough to get bent out of shape over," he muttered.

When she ripped the bracelet out of his hands, he could see by her expression that the remark had hurt her, and he immediately regretted saying it.

"I'm sorry," he apologized again, this time sincerely. "I didn't mean to offend you."

Kyla ignored his apology. "You still haven't told me what you're doing here."

"No, I haven't," he said. "Nor do I feel a pressing need to."

Kyla's expression was still cold. "Fine," she said. Then she put her bracelet back on and walked away.

It was sudden and unexpected what Nathaniel did next, for her as well as for him. "Kyla, wait," he called after her.

She stopped moving forward and turned slowly back to face him. "How did you know my name?" she asked.

Nathaniel pointed to her bracelet and she clutched it compulsively to her chest. She looked afraid now; possibly even more afraid than she was upset. He couldn't pinpoint the sudden change in her, but it was distinct even though she was working to mask it.

Somehow Nathaniel felt that it was about more than his simply saying her name. It might not have had anything to do with that at all. Eying her curiously, he looked down into her face, and when Kyla hesitantly met his gaze, he was all but paralyzed.

It was in that moment that everything changed.

Aided by the moonlight, Nathaniel was able to see the depth of her eyes. He was gripped by them, captured to a degree that made him unable to move. Immediately, he was pulled in by their color, though he couldn't discern it, and not just because of the darkness around them. If he hadn't known any better, Nathaniel would have thought they were changing even as he looked at them. At first they appeared blue, but then no sooner than he had determined this, that blue began to shift to a vibrant green. It wasn't their color alone that fascinated him, though.

It was the way she was looking into him.

Nathaniel had never known anything like it. Completely mesmerized, he was held there in suspension, feeling as if this girl could see right through him…as if she knew what he really was.

"Who are you?" Kyla asked him. She didn't break her gaze for a moment.

Nathaniel swallowed hard and took a step backwards. He hadn't counted on this.

*T*he fog that clung to the winding mountain road spilled out before the darkened figure that moved through the trees. It was a full moon tonight, and the only light by which Donovan was able to see as he made his way toward the silhouette at the edge of the woods.

The one called Cerin was already waiting for him.

As Donovan approached him, he gave a slight nod to the small, gangly creature whose head was bowed low.

"My lord," Cerin greeted him soberly.

Donovan held up a hand. "No need for formalities tonight, Cerin."

The creature's black beady eyes darted back and forth like a lizard's as he nodded to his leader.

Of all of Donovan's informants, this was the one he was always least anxious to meet with, even if only for his awkward demeanor and complete inability to present himself as human. But despite the unpleasantness of such meetings, Cerin had proven on more than one occasion to be useful. Sometimes extremely useful.

Donovan looked out over the edge of the cliff on which they stood and spoke in a measured tone, "Tell me what you have learned."

The night air was cool, but beads of sweat were forming on Cerin's brow. Clearly he was nervous about something.

Donovan had to force himself to channel his distaste for this pathetic creature and wait to hear what he had to say, though he found it difficult when Cerin's attempt at articulating himself didn't produce a single intelligible word.

Donovan cut him off on his third attempt. "Speak plainly," he commanded.

Cerin swallowed hard. "It is Seth, my lord."

Donovan stared into him with slanted eyes. "What *about* Seth?"

Cerin looked terrified to speak another word, but even more terrified not to. "He...he knows you are here."

Feeling heat against his blood as it surged through his veins, Donovan clenched his fists. He knew there had to be fire in his eyes, judging by the way his informant was looking back at him.

"*Eli...*" Donovan breathed furiously.

Cerin spoke quickly in an attempt to calm his leader. "As of now, it appears only to be surveillance."

Donovan's eyes were still slanted. "Is Seth here?" he asked. He was unable to keep the tremble out of his voice.

Cerin shook his head vigorously. "No, my lord. He sent Nathaniel."

Donovan heard him speak, but it took a moment for this to register to him. When he finally found his voice, he was only capable of forming one word.

"*What?*"

Cerin unconsciously took a step backwards. "He...he sent Nathaniel," he reiterated, no doubt wondering if these words would be his last.

Donovan felt ice through his veins where the heat had coursed through him only seconds before. Could this really be possible? Would Seth really have let him come?

"How can you be certain of this?" Donovan asked.

"Because...because I saw him, my lord."

Donovan was shaking now. "*Where?*" he demanded.

Cerin stammered his answer. "In the cemetery...Woodland Park. I followed him there when I saw him watching the child."

Surely Donovan hadn't heard that right. "What?" he asked again through clenched teeth.

Cerin backed up further, his eyes darting around frantically. "Th...that was where I saw him. He was on the mountain...watching the little girl."

Aside from the fury he knew he should feel, there was another feeling that hit Donovan then. "There is something you are not telling me, Cerin."

The gangly creature trembled and looked up at him.

"Speak now," Donovan warned him, "or I will rip out your heart."

Cerin swallowed and answered him slowly. "When I saw Nathaniel in the cemetery, he...he wasn't alone. He was...with a human."

Donovan was held in tense curiosity. "What human?"

Cerin cringed away from him.

"*What* human, Cerin?" he asked more firmly.

"The girl..." he stammered. "Kyla James."

Donovan flinched at the name, his every fear spiking to the surface before he could control it enough to press it back. It was enough to break him past his control, to let that one last part of calm he held over himself completely snap.

With his blood boiling to the surface, Donovan snarled, "And how in the name of Lucifer did he find *her*?"

"I don't know," Cerin insisted. "I swear I don't know."

Pressing his fingers to his temple in an attempt to calm himself again, Donovan breathed through his nose.

"M...my lord?" Cerin prompted. But Donovan was quiet.

"Leave," he finally said. "I will handle this." Then he narrowed his eyes into the dark.

Alexa Howell sat in an oversized purple armchair in her living room, staring out the window she was still unable to see through. Matthew was crashed out on the couch, but she hadn't even noticed yet. She was too busy waiting, too busy watching, too busy trying to quiet everything inside of her so that she could see.

But that was the thing...she couldn't see. Something was blocking her vision and she didn't know what it was. She could feel something stirring, more powerfully than she ever had, but she couldn't see a thing.

Alexa had thought if she told Matthew about it he might understand, reasoning that it was possible since his heart was so willing. But she had been wrong. She knew he believed her, that he didn't question for a moment if she might be lying or crazy, but he wasn't going to be able to help her to make sense of this. There was only one person who could, and he wasn't here.

Alexa frowned at the thought of her brother. Then suddenly, as a shock of light to her unopened eyes, she was jolted by a vision.

It happened right when she'd determined it wasn't going to. At exactly that moment, her sight came back, only not in a way she had ever experienced.

She saw a grave…a familiar grave. It was dark all around, but there was a light coming from behind it that she didn't understand. Alexa couldn't see the source of it, but it left her uneasy…unsure. There was someone standing there, but it took her a moment for her to see who it was, and another to see that that they were not alone.

Alexa's eyes shot open.

She was in danger. Kyla was in danger.

*S*taring into the beautiful stranger, Kyla tried to calm her erratic pulse. She didn't understand it, the way it felt to look in his eyes, but it thrilled her and terrified her all at once. There was something behind them that she knew he didn't want her to see…something he didn't want anyone to see. She didn't mean to catch it, but the moment she did it became undeniable.

This chance meeting was no chance. And there was something that he wanted from her.

Even if Kyla had denied her ability to see into people like that and abandoned her belief in the reason she ever could, it wasn't something that had ever really left her. It was just easier to ignore with some people than others.

With this tall, blonde, disturbingly handsome stranger, it was nearly impossible.

As soon as she saw a trace of the motive behind his eyes, Kyla's defenses kicked into high gear. She was about to tear into him, insisting he tell her why he was there and who he was and what he really wanted with her; but before she could, he snapped his head up as if he'd heard something.

Kyla felt a tinge of fear at the sudden motion, but she didn't ask him what was wrong. Instead she watched his expression grow tense.

The gorgeous stranger turned back to her quickly. "You need to leave," he said.

Kyla blinked a few times, questioning if she'd heard him right. "What?"

"You need to go get in your car and drive back to wherever it is you came from," he told her. "Right now."

There was something about his tone that frightened her. "Why?" she asked him. Judging by his attitude thus far, she knew the question would only aggravate him, but at that point she really didn't care.

"Don't ask questions," he said. "Just do it."

Kyla wanted to protest. She wanted to lay into this guy and ask him who he thought he was to demand something of her like that. But as he looked at him and read him, she could see that he wasn't playing around.

Whatever this was about, he was dead serious.

Hardly aware of what she was doing, Kyla hurried back to Loni's car and peeled out of the parking lot below the cemetery. Her heart pounded as she drove back up the mountain, completely unable to make sense of why she was listening to a stranger whose name she didn't even know. She tried to snap herself out of the fear that was coming over her, but she couldn't shake it off.

She couldn't forget what she saw behind those impossibly blue eyes.

After Nathaniel watched the silver Honda drive out of view, he turned back to the cemetery and pulled a dagger from the sheath that was strapped to his back. His eyes fell immediately to the figure wearing black that stood in front of the grave that the girl named Kyla had been kneeling at. Whoever it was had his back turned, but Nathaniel didn't hesitate.

Marching forward, he spoke in a firm, threatening voice, "Turn around."

Slowly the man turned, and at the sight of him Nathaniel froze, not because he recognized him, but because of the feeling that hit him on the sight. Quicker than his shock set in, Nathaniel forced himself into control over it again so that this stranger wouldn't be able to read him. Something told him he did not want that to happen.

"Hello, Nathaniel," the man spoke as if they had already met.

His eyes were hollow with dark circles beneath them. Lined in black, they were set deeply into his chalky skin, and there was something wrong about them. His ears were gauged and his lips pierced, and Nathaniel could see through the cutoff leather gloves he wore that his nails were painted black. Whoever he was, this man certainly had a fixation with darkness.

Nathaniel stood at ready, clasping his silver dagger in a way that he could use it if necessary. But while he outwardly remained expressionless, his mind raced to discern who this stranger was. He couldn't feel anything, though. It was as if this man had a guard over himself that didn't allow Nathaniel to see into him. He had never experienced anything like it.

"There is no need for hostility," the man assured him. "If I wanted to harm you, you would already be dead."

Nathaniel's eyes narrowed at the insinuation. "Who are you?" he asked in a very controlled voice.

The man stepped casually to one side, not appearing to hold the slightest degree of fear in his presence. "I have done you a favor, Nathaniel. I knew you were looking for me, so I thought I would spare you the trouble of having to track me down."

Nathaniel's blood ran cold. He could feel it as if it had frozen in his face, in his chest, ceasing its movement entirely as his fear swept him under. Working to control it, he swallowed hard and clasped his dagger even harder.

"Donovan..." he breathed.

His long-held enemy, who until this moment had been faceless to him, looked extremely pleased with himself. Trying to read him, Nathaniel kept his gaze forward, disturbed when he realized he couldn't. There was so much deception that surrounded this one, so much manipulation that he couldn't navigate his way through it.

"We meet at last, Nathaniel Blake," Donovan greeted him with a mocking bow of his head.

Nathaniel glared at him in contempt. He had no intention of giving him a response.

"I have to admit, I'm a little curious, though," Donovan said, glancing in the direction Kyla had left. "Who is your new friend?"

It was fortunate that remaining unreadable to any who attempted to see into him was a talent of Nathaniel's. If it weren't, he would not have been able to keep the anger out of his eyes at the suggestion. "You know as well as I do," he lied.

Donovan gave him a condescending look. "I hardly believe that."

"Believe whatever you'd like," Nathaniel said blandly. "I have no idea who she is."

Donovan began circling him slowly, studying him as if he were a unique sort of specimen being viewed through the lens of a microscope. The deception was still thick over him. Even looking into his deep hollowed eyes, Nathaniel still couldn't see a thing. This didn't feel right to him at all. Going in alone was one thing, but going in blind was another.

"What are you doing here?" Nathaniel asked him. He followed him with his eyes as he continued to circle him. He wasn't about to let this one out of his sight.

Even if he couldn't see into Donovan's head, Nathaniel could tell by his movement, his mannerisms, by thinking of what he would do if their roles were reversed exactly what he was after.

"I have an offer to make you," Donovan told him.

Nathaniel didn't budge.

"Join me," Donovan said. "Abandon this pathetic little brotherhood of yours and I will give you access to a level of power Seth can't even touch on."

Nathaniel eyed him intently. "And why should this power of yours entice me?" he asked.

A chalky grin spread across Donovan's face. "Because I know what you fear, Nathaniel Blake."

Nathaniel leered at him. "You don't know anything about me," he said. But even through his denial, he couldn't help but question if that were true.

"On the contrary," Donovan insisted. "I know everything about you."

Nathaniel smirked at the audacity of the claim.

"I know of your…*disdain* for humankind," Donovan told him. "The way you blindly follow orders without feeling any conviction behind them. I know you don't believe what Malachi believes, that there is redemption for what we are."

"I am *not* what you are," Nathaniel snarled.

Donovan didn't miss a beat. "I also know you don't believe that."

Nathaniel had to hold himself back. *You cannot engage him*, he told himself. *No matter what he says, you cannot engage him.*

"It makes me question why you would ever give your life to a cause you don't even believe in," Donovan continued. "How you could willingly submit yourself to a leader you don't even know, who has hidden from you the very power that you hold."

Nathaniel didn't ask him what he was talking about, but he didn't have to. Donovan could see the question in his eyes.

"You are more than they are, Nathaniel. You always have been. They know it, too, and that's why they're afraid of you."

"Who is afraid of me?" Nathaniel asked. He wasn't about to trust what this liar was saying, but lie or not, he still needed to find out what Donovan was talking about.

"Malachi…Samuel…Seth. They all are."

Nathaniel sneered at him, but didn't respond.

"You don't believe me," Donovan said. "That is alright; you don't have to. Time will confirm what I have spoken to you."

Nathaniel was becoming agitated by his arrogance. "And why is it that you would tell me my leaders are afraid of me?" he asked. "What gain could you possibly find in that?"

Donovan was still looking into him. "Because I can change everything for you," he said. "I can teach you how to step fully into the power you have so that no one will ever be able to alter your will again. Not Seth…not Malachi. No one."

Yeah, no one except you, Nathaniel thought.

Donovan gave him a look as if he had seen into his mind. "Not even me," he added.

Nathaniel's eyes narrowed further as he studied this serpent before him. Surely Donovan couldn't see his thoughts.

"I can change your world, Nathaniel. I can set you free."

With a grip so firm on his dagger that his knuckles turned to white, Nathaniel started to step forward.

"I wouldn't do that if I were you," Donovan said calmly.

Nathaniel stopped, but he didn't ask why.

"I know you are here alone," Donovan told him. "I, however, am not. And when I leave this place, you are not going to follow me."

"You're sure about that?" Nathaniel taunted.

Donovan seemed confident enough. "Oh, I am sure. If you do, you'll be dead before you set foot outside this cemetery."

"Then why not just kill me now?" Nathaniel asked daringly.

Donovan's gaze was intent. "Because I need you."

It was becoming exceedingly difficult for Nathaniel to control himself, especially with that last comment. With each passing second, he found his urge to engage Donovan only to grow stronger.

"I understand that you may not be willing to listen to me yet," Donovan said, "but I have confidence that in time, this will change."

He walked past him to leave, but stopped when he came up beside him, glancing down at the dagger in Nathaniel's hand.

"*Ut reluctor atrum*," he read aloud the Latin inscription on the blade just below Nathaniel's name. "To resist the dark." Donovan grinned mockingly at the motto of the Resitore. "You cannot stop this, Nathaniel Blake. Seth cannot stop this. There are things that have been set into motion that you cannot hinder, that you can't even slow down. And I *will* have you."

84

Nathaniel wanted nothing more than to reach over to Donovan and smoothly snap his neck, especially on the last words he spoke. He envisioned several different ways he could accomplish this, too, as he stood not even three feet away from him.

"Leave," Nathaniel threatened. He needed Donovan gone before he did something he wasn't even sure he would regret.

Donovan kept his smile in place as he passed in front of him. "Certainly," he said, dipping his head in mock compliance. But he stopped as before and turned back to him again. "You know, I was thinking about paying your new friend a visit," he said as if the idea had just struck him. "You wouldn't happen to know where she lives?"

Nathaniel's jaw locked. "No," he answered flatly, "I don't. But you go right ahead and pay her a visit. I have no problem with you wasting your time on useless humans."

Donovan eyed him curiously again. "You could be right," he said, "or you could be lying. Either way, I will know tonight."

Nathaniel felt a tinge of anxiety, but his face remained expressionless. He made sure of it.

"And again," Donovan added, "unless you have a death wish, I would suggest you wait at least five minutes before you leave here."

Watching Donovan pass beneath the metal arch at the entrance of the cemetery, Nathaniel cursed under his breath. He waited another five and a half minutes that felt to draw on for hours, then he moved out cautiously and looked up toward the mountain, wondering if this was a trap. With Donovan, he knew it had to be; but what choice did he have? He couldn't allow the girl to be compromised. Seth would be furious with him if he were to cause that sort of collateral damage. And who knew what else would be affected or altered as a result? After all, she *had* been mentioned in Eli's notes. Perhaps they needed her.

It made sense in his mind, the logic and reason and rationality of it all, but even through his excuses, Nathaniel couldn't forget what he had seen in her eyes. He couldn't stop thinking of how the girl named Kyla had looked at him, how she had seen him in a way no human ever had. He was simply unwilling to admit how much his desire to understand this compelled him to go after her.

No, he told himself. *This has to be about protecting an asset.*

Making the decision, Nathaniel took off running down the embankment with steady, measured steps. Then he closed his eyes as a flash of light consumed him, careful to make sure that no human saw what happened next.

Chapter 6

"...behind sapphire eyes."

Donovan moved through the forest quickly, darting in and out of the trees as he approached his chosen point of watch; the point where he was supposed to be met by his second-in-command. Stepping out to the edge of the mountain, he cursed Balak's name when he found the clearing empty. That fool knew better than to keep him waiting on a night like this.

Donovan could feel his blood burning as he paced between the trees. He did not like to wait. And he did not have time for this. For everything to work tonight, it had to be perfect. They couldn't afford to miss one moment, and right now Balak was threatening exactly that...which was not putting Donovan in the most gracious mood.

A branch snapped in the distance and he growled beneath his breath Fixing his gaze forward where Balak approached, Donovan forced himself into a level of control that he wasn't sure he could maintain. Especially not when he caught sight of his subordinate's face.

Balak was breathless as he ran up to him, and it took a great deal to make this one breathless. His rocklike chest heaved beneath his darkened skin and beads of sweat had formed on his brow. Donovan couldn't imagine how fast he had to have been moving to work himself up like that.

"Forgive me, my lord," Balak spoke quickly. "I came as fast as I could."

Donovan could see by the fear in his eyes that Balak was questioning what might be done to him. He was wise to think such things.

"What took you so long?" Donovan snapped.

Balak tried to justify himself. "You called so suddenly, and I…was not in the area."

"Where *were* you?" Donovan demanded.

Balak faltered as he answered him. "Following a lead."

His eyes shifted in a way that caught Donovan's attention. By the inflection of his voice and the rapid beat of his pulse, it was clear that Balak was hiding something. And if there were not far more pressing issues currently at hand, Donovan would have looked deeper into his mind to find out exactly what that was.

"What happened?" Balak asked him, anxious to redirect his leader's attention.

Donovan grabbed him by his right shoulder and jerked him with force, facing him out over the mountain. "*That* is what happened!" he snarled.

Balak's face dropped at what he saw.

*N*athaniel positioned himself in the trees, watching as the auburn-haired girl named Kyla pulled up Winding Valley Road and parked the silver Civic below the Howell's driveway. She stepped out cautiously and looked all around her, then jogged up the driveway on her toes, obviously wanting to hurry but not wanting to be heard.

She slowed to a walk when she neared the deck, then stopped altogether and looked up at the front door. Nathaniel didn't know why she stopped, but it made him nervous.

Glancing around him in an attempt to spot Donovan, he found himself urging her to get inside. She pulled a cell phone from the pocket of her blue jean shorts instead and cringed when she looked at its face.

Probably checking the time, he thought.

Then he saw her glance to the side of the house and bite her lip before she cautiously made her way into the backyard.

Nathaniel had no idea what she was doing, but he followed her at a distance, staying hidden in the trees and watching as she moved toward the garage-converted guesthouse he had broken into earlier that same night.

What was she doing?

Opening the sliding door carefully as she glanced back up toward the house, Kyla slipped inside and locked it behind her. Nathaniel repositioned himself at a more optimal vantage point, but then just as he had found the perfect spot, she quickly pulled the curtain.

Nathaniel frowned, questioning if this would be enough. He had counted on her going inside, back into the house where the child was. Here, he wasn't certain she would be safe.

Then again, the concentration of angelic activity around that room had been unexplainably strong. Maybe it would be enough to protect her for the night.

Scanning the woods again, Nathaniel quieted his mind and tuned his senses, unsettled by the realization that hit him when he did.

Donovan wasn't here.

*W*atching from a place of cover, safety and careful distance, two dark figures waited in the trees. Donovan's eyes were fixed on the edge of the Howell's property line. Balak's were as well, and they had been since his attention had been forced there to the silhouette of a man…or what appeared like a man, hiding in the trees.

It was distant, indistinguishable to the human eye, but then nothing was distinguishable to the human eye from up here.

"What is he doing?" Balak asked.

Donovan didn't break his gaze. "He is watching her."

Looking back and forth between the figure in the distance and his leader who stood beside him, Balak was confused.

"But how…"

"I don't know," Donovan cut in. "I don't know how he found her. Cerin is the only reason we know even this much."

Balak made a face. "*Cerin?*"

"Yes…Cerin," Donovan confirmed with a grimace of his own. The thought obviously disgusted him, too.

Balak returned his gaze to where Nathaniel Blake waited in the woods below them, positioning himself in a way that led them both to believe he was stationed for the night. It irritated Balak, watching this one who to him seemed as nothing but a boy, knowing what Donovan had staked on him.

"What does this mean?" he asked.

Donovan didn't answer, just kept his eyes on Nathaniel, then a slow careful smile began to grow on his lips.

Balak tried not to become frustrated, knowing he could not afford in these circumstances to upset his leader. Something like that could result in a mental prodding he did not need from him, especially given where he'd spent the past hour he was supposed to be on watch. Still, it was hard not to let his frustration show.

Donovan was always doing that to him, ignoring questions as if answering them were an option, grinning like that and obviously withholding information he didn't deem necessary for him to know. And every time Balak questioned it, he was told to have patience. They all were told to, despite the fact that Donovan never did. He would keep them in limbo for months on end, put them on rigorous assignments to gather the information he needed, and then he wouldn't even explain what it was about once they'd gotten it for him.

Balak himself had found for him what he wanted to know about Caden and Alexa Howell, those brats that had almost stopped them from forging the alliance with the coven in Manitou, but he had never been told why they couldn't just kill them. Or why they were no longer an issue once the boy left the state...or what this Kyla James even had to do with them.

All he had ever seen from it was that the boy was borderline obsessed with her; that she drove every decision he made, including his most recent one to leave Colorado. But the way Donovan acted sometimes, he was almost more afraid of her than he was of Caden.

Or at least he used to be until her father died.

Balak still thought his solution was best. Once they uncovered that the child was a seer and her brother was...what he was, all they needed was to take them out into the woods and quietly snap their necks. But Donovan had forbidden him, not explaining why. He had simply told him they were not here to incite an even greater war.

Balak hadn't understood what he meant. He still didn't understand, but that was the way it went in their world. The one with the power called the shots, and here, Donovan was the one with the power.

"My lord?" he tried again.

Donovan turned his head, his gaze falling somewhere between the Howell's property and his subordinate who stood beside him. He was obviously in deep contemplation, but just when Balak thought he wasn't going to answer him, Donovan looked up.

"Wake the others," he told him. "I am calling a meeting."

Balak was confused. "Now?"

Donovan did not like repeating himself, and his tone did nothing to hide this fact. "*Now.*"

"But my lord, who will keep watch here?" he asked.

Donovan spoke as if he already had a plan. "There will be no need for that tonight. Nathaniel has already told us what we need to know."

Balak's smooth black skin creased together at his forehead. "And what is that?"

Donovan gave him a look, obviously having reached his quota of patience for the night. "Just do as you are told," he snapped. "You leave the thinking to me."

Balak wanted to retaliate, but instead he folded his hands behind his back and dropped his head. "Yes, my lord."

Donovan may have been only half his size, but Balak was wise enough to know he could never stand against him if he were engaged. None of them had the power Donovan had, and none of them dared to challenge it. There wasn't a single being that ever had and had lived to tell about it.

As Balak left their point of watch, he saw his leader turn back to watch the figure in the trees. He had never understood his obsession with Nathaniel Blake.

*K*yla turned after closing the curtain, standing uncomfortably at the entrance of Caden's bedroom. She unconsciously held her breath as she scanned the room, completely unprepared for the feeling that hit her when she did. She had expected the sting, that familiar nausea that met her whenever she thought about him, but she hadn't expected this.

Her heart was still racing as her mind scrambled to make sense of the stranger in the cemetery, of the fear she had felt at his warning and the overall creepiness of this screwed up night. But as she slowly inched forward and stepped further into the room, she was met with something else...a feeling she hadn't known since the last time she had been here with Caden over a year ago, just days before they were supposed to start their senior year of high school.

She had started the next week. He hadn't. Instead he took a course online to get the few credits he still needed to graduate, and that, he did in Nashville, leaving Kyla to fend for herself in those bleak, suffocating hallways the entire year without him.

He hadn't come home for Christmas, or her birthday, or to see everyone graduate. He hadn't even flown back when his parents adopted Sadie, the newest member of the Howell family whom Caden would adore. But no, not even for her. He hadn't even seen his new baby sister.

Breathing in slowly as she stepped into the room, Kyla realized in spite of these irritating thoughts that she could. She blinked in surprise, wondering what had changed. There was no explanation for it, not when she had been so unsettled only moments before, but she couldn't deny the peace that held her now, even if she didn't understand it.

Then her eyes fell against her will to the picture at the top of Caden's mirror.

Stepping forward slowly, she took it down and sat on the edge of his bed, which Melissa had obviously made judging by its hospital-style perfection. Staring at the picture, Kyla let her memory pull her back to the day it had been taken.

It was August. Late August. The sweltering kind of day that had the newscasters warning people to keep their pets and small children inside. She had spent the entire afternoon in the Howell's pool with Caden and the guys from his band, most of whom she had grown up with since grade school.

She didn't remember why they were there. It had probably been a spontaneous decision made on an afternoon when they hadn't been able to think of anything else to do, as was usually the case when they ended up at the Howell's. They usually didn't even bother giving Caden's parents forewarning, just showed up and jumped in the pool. Melissa loved it, though. There was nothing that excited her more than having people in their home so she could play mom and hostess and love on them until they got sick of it. Not that anyone could ever get sick of being spoiled by Melissa Howell.

Kyla was always the apologetic one of the group, though Cody Fletcher, the band's keyboardist joined her in that occasionally. Melissa told them both they were crazy.

Cody was an interesting one. He had always been more sensitive than the other guys, more awkward and out of place in just about any situation he ever found himself in. But the kid was a genius. One of those musical prodigy types who'd started playing keys when he was four and who made people's jaws drop when they listened to him. He was also one of her and Caden's closest friends.

Cody had always been more comfortable sitting at the kitchen counter talking to Melissa than hanging out back with the guys when they were playing basketball or wrestling in the grass or attempting to drown each other in the pool. They gave him hell for it, too.

He was the one who had taken the picture.

She and Caden had both been horribly sunburned by the time they'd gotten out of the pool that day, despite all the layers of block they'd put on. An inevitable side effect of the mountain sun. It was miserable and painful and Kyla ended up looking like a lobster for a solid week, but it had been completely worth it.

As the two of them had crawled out of the pool around four o'clock that afternoon, Caden had tackled her onto the grass and started tickling her until she squirmed and flailed and kicked at him in protest. Cody had snapped the picture just as she closed her eyes and screamed.

A slight smile crept up on Kyla's lips when she remembered the sound of Caden's laugh. That was the last day they were together before he told her he was going to Nashville.

Replacing the picture on the mirror, her smile faded quicker than it came. Kyla turned away with a grimace and reached impulsively for her phone. She again hit number one on her speed dial, then put her free hand in her pocket as she nervously held the thing to her ear.

Caden's voicemail came on for the second time in under an hour and Kyla felt even sicker than she already did before. It had been a week now since she'd heard from him. With anyone else, she wouldn't worry, but nothing could be less like her best friend. If that was even what he was anymore.

Kyla set her phone down on the table beside the bed. Walking over to Caden's closet, she took a black hoodie from a white plastic hanger and slipped it on over her shirt. Then she crawled across his queen-sized bed and curled up on the right edge of it in the fetal position. Pulling the sleeves of the hoodie over her hands, she closed her eyes when she breathed in.

It still smelled like him.

Kyla tried not to be afraid as she held her arms to her chest, but she couldn't stop seeing the beautiful stranger from the cemetery. What she had felt when he told her to leave, she felt it still. She couldn't shake it, despite how she tried, and as she lay there like that, clutching her arms to her chest and trying to breathe, she was only capable of thinking one thing.

Caden, where are you?

*I*t was dark in the Coven chambers. Buried deep underground between the ancient cliff dwellings of Manitou Springs and the cavern structure that ran for miles beneath those mountains, it was always dark in here. Torches hung along the adobe walls, guiding the thirteen figures cloaked in black that made their way into the ritual room.

Normally these meetings were planned. Tonight's was not. That was why every Coven member was currently uneasy, questioning what Donovan could want at a moment's notice, knowing that anything their lord ever wanted at a moment's notice usually cost them blood.

Balak stood along the wall with his arms folded across his dark, barreled chest. He didn't like this. Meetings in this place were tense enough as they were, but having to call this one himself (especially when he didn't know what it was that Donovan wanted) was enough to put even his nerves on edge.

He could see the fear in the eyes of every witch that filed into the cavern. The only eyes he didn't see fear in were the one that should have held it; the girl who stood at the edge of the wall, not yet allowed near the ceremonial fire at the center of the room, not yet inducted as an official member of the Coven. She was the thirteenth member in waiting, and one that Donovan was particularly fond of.

And right now, her eyes were set on Balak's.

Balak shifted uncomfortably beneath her gaze, not wanting his lord to notice. If he did, Donovan might be tipped off as to the reason for his tardiness earlier that evening when he was supposed to be on watch.

Fortunately, Donovan didn't notice. He was much too distracted as he entered the chamber to pay attention to the green-eyed beauty along the wall.

Everyone froze when he entered, clasping their hands in front of them and keeping their heads down. Their hoods were pulled in a way that their faces weren't shown, and they kept their eyes fixed on the fire, but when Donovan stepped up and addressed these that had made a covenant to serve him, it was apparent in every one that they feared the worst.

"Our plans have been altered," he told them. "It seems we have been met with resistance a bit earlier than expected."

The others didn't react, at least not outwardly.

Donovan went on. "We will need to realign our strategy to deal with this…issue. That is why I have called you here tonight, so that we can take care of this matter quickly." He looked up and directly to the girl who stood against the wall.

The gesture made Balak nervous.

"Step forward," Donovan commanded her.

Immediately the girl complied, walking gracefully across the stone-floored chamber to stand before him. Donovan lifted her chin with his fingertips, smiling as he looked into her porcelain face.

"I have an assignment for you, my dear."

Her emerald eyes glowed brighter in anticipation, illuminated by the light of the fire. She was excited. Even in her working to hide it, Balak could see that clearly. He knew what this one looked like when she was excited.

It always made him uncomfortable when Donovan touched her…when he looked at her like that. They were a lot alike, those two. Their eyes held the same hollow darkness, the same blackened fire that burned for the blood of the awakened ones. Still, as evil as this black beauty was, Balak knew she didn't compare to Donovan.

The bloodlust of a witch was one thing. The maniacal drive of the Nephilim was another.

*K*eeping watch outside the Howell's home, Nathaniel spent the entire night on edge. At every moment he expected Donovan to make another appearance. He refused to let his guard down for even a second, but Donovan never showed. And now as the sun began to spill through the pine branches above him, reality slowly sank into Nathaniel's mind.

It was a mind game. It was nothing but a mind game.

Seth had warned him of this. He had told Nathaniel of Donovan's ability to manipulate the mind. He had even told him it was what he lived for; but Nathaniel had fallen for it anyway.

Scowling to himself in anger, he resisted the urge to snap the pine tree he stood beneath into two separate halves. He should have listened to his instincts. He knew this, yet still he had fallen into Donovan's trap and done exactly what he wanted him to do.

Nathaniel looked up when he saw Kyla slip out through the glass sliding door across the yard. She was wearing an oversized black hoodie now, long enough that it came to the frayed edges of her cutoff jean shorts. She looked nervous. She was quiet and cautious and she kept her eyes fixed on the house as she moved.

Nathaniel didn't understand. He didn't know why she would come here in secret, why she didn't let the people who lived here know that she needed a place to stay. Perhaps she wasn't as close to them as he assumed, but by all appearances she was at least close to the boy. Or she used to be. Nathaniel didn't know how long he had been absent.

Watching as Kyla tiptoed across the backyard and down the driveway, Nathaniel debated his next move, trying to determine whether or not he should follow her.

She is just a girl, he told himself. *Just one little human girl.* Surely they couldn't compromise this entire mission for one human.

Nathaniel sighed, knowing Seth would not agree. Especially given the fact that she was being watched by Eli. Threat or no threat, there was a reason he had marked her, and if she held a key to any of this, he could not let anything happen to her. Even if Nathaniel had never shared Seth's sentiment toward humankind, or Caleb's for that matter, he knew that assets must be guarded. He was just not looking forward to informing Seth that he had placed a potential one in danger by his carelessness.

Nathaniel watched as Kyla moved closer to the street, ignoring the feeling in the pit of his stomach that told him this was not the only reason that he felt the need to protect her. He knew this curiosity in him was dangerous, that it could only deter him from his focus and that it could also become detrimental to all of them if he didn't find a way to quench it. But the more he let himself think on these things, the more it drew him to feel what he knew he shouldn't feel. This intrigue, this compulsion, these emotions that were almost...human.

He couldn't let it go, and the harder he tried, the more prevalent it became in his mind. He couldn't keep himself from questioning what it was that this girl was able to see in him. He couldn't stop himself from asking who she was that she could do a thing like that.

Suddenly, Nathaniel felt a shift in the atmosphere, enough that he turned to look behind him. When he did, he noticed something in the window of the massive log home.

It was the child.

The curtain was pulled back and she was watching Kyla as she scampered down the street, and when Nathaniel saw the faintest trace of a smile on her lips, he felt a sudden unease. He should have expected this. What he saw in the little girl's smile matched what he had seen in her before; both in the photographs Eli had taken and in the time he spent watching her from the woods. He had seen this coming from the moment she turned and looked in his direction. It made sense that she would know Kyla was here, but somehow it didn't leave him any less alarmed.

That must have been what Eli meant.

Remembering back on the peculiarity of the child, of the things Nathaniel had witnessed in her so far (however few they were) all of the pieces began to click into place and he started to see a bigger picture at work than he was prepared for. But then, just as he started to let that reality sink in, he was startled by a voice he did not expect to hear, speaking as clearly into his mind as if he were standing beside him.

"Cemetery. Now."

It was Seth. And he wanted a meeting.

It was a frustrating ability their leader had, being able to speak so clearly into their minds. Most of the time, Nathaniel and his brothers found this...*talent* of Seth's to be useful, even if they couldn't respond to him in a way that he would actually hear them. In situations where he needed them to gather on a moment's notice, or he needed to communicate in a way that would go completely unseen by those who may be watching them, this method was invaluable. Tonight, Nathaniel found himself wishing his leader could be slightly more normal.

Of course, he supposed Seth could always reach him on his cell phone if he really needed to (heaven forbid) but there was something more absolute about being given a command through his mind. It made it harder, if not impossible to deny him what he asked for.

It was the protocol of the Resitore to meet in cemeteries, even when on location for surveillance or any other sort of assignment. Normally this wouldn't have bothered Nathaniel, but given recent events, he questioned the intelligence of such a move. If he was honest with himself, he would have to admit that his unease might be tied more to leaving Kyla alone than to the potential security risk their chosen meeting place now presented. But Nathaniel wasn't honest with himself, so he forced the feeling aside.

This was not the time for him to worry with such things. Right now, he had been given an order from his superior and needed only to obey it. Still, as he watched the silver Honda Civic turn out of sight, he couldn't help but wonder if he was making the right decision.

As Kyla drove back down the mountain, she tried to get control over her needless anxiety. Shaking her head a little, she told herself that everything was okay, that she was going to go home and crawl into bed, avoid Loni like the plague and forget completely about the insanity of last night. She almost had herself convinced, too...at least until she came back into town and drove past the cemetery.

Kyla was jolted from the thought as her eyes were suddenly pulled to the left. Making a sharp turn off of Highway 24 that elicited a distinct feeling of déjà vu, she narrowly avoided being rear-ended by the Mack truck behind her and jerked the car to a halt once she got off the road.

Blinking hard and breathing heavily, she tried to convince herself she wasn't seeing things. Then she slowly let off the brake and wound her way cautiously back behind the buildings along the road she'd just turned onto. Sure enough, when she pulled into the back corner of the parking lot she'd just entered, her sight was proven accurate. She really had seen who she thought she saw, and he really was making his way once again into Woodland Cemetery.

Kyla squinted to make sure the heat wasn't playing tricks on her eyes. After all, people still had to be able to see mirages in the mountains, didn't they? She quickly got out of the car, making sure to stay at least twenty yards behind the tall handsome blonde who moved forward with apparent purpose. She kept to the far right of the street so he wouldn't see her if he turned around, but moving up the paved uphill road was a little trickier. The gravely dirt path that wound between the headstones was noisy, forcing Kyla to walk with soft, careful steps.

As if her nerves weren't already shot being back here again.

Kyla could see him up ahead of her, his eyes set forward like he knew exactly where he was going. She was struck by how quickly he moved, completely disinterested in the gravestones that surrounded him. Creeping down the sparsely grassed decline and ducking behind an oversized pine tree, she peeked around the side of it and watched him stop. He was standing down below, about thirty feet away from her on the path that cut through the cemetery in four different directions, staring off into nothing with his back turned.

This was her shot. Kyla sprinted on the balls of her feet to the largest headstone she could find, which as luck would have it was actually a stone wall with a cross set into a cutout circle at the top. Ducking behind the wall, she instinctively crouched down in the fetal position, trying to control her breathing and convince herself she wasn't crazy to be doing this.

Slowly, so slowly it took her a full minute, Kyla inched her way up and peered very carefully through the circle with the cross, which happened to give her a straight shot of the boy on the road. He was pacing now, running his hands through his perfect blonde hair, and it was then that she heard a second set of footsteps coming from behind him.

Kyla held her breath instinctively. It was a man, a blonde man who was taller and had a broader build than the boy. He looked like he could be his father, and acted like it too, though he didn't appear old enough. Maybe an older brother or an uncle.

100

Adjusting her footing as soundlessly as she could, Kyla watched them from where she was crouched behind the headstone. They talked for a while, low enough that she couldn't hear them, but what struck her more than anything was the boy's countenance. It was so stark a contrast from last night that Kyla almost didn't recognize him. He nodded to the man submissively, his eyes cast halfway to the ground, and something about it just looked off to her. Maybe she'd made the assumption before, but he hardly seemed like someone who was fond of taking orders.

Suddenly, the man raised his voice. "Nathaniel!" he said sharply.

Kyla held her breath. His name was Nathaniel. Somehow it seemed fitting for him, though she didn't know why, and without even realizing it, she thought the name to herself several times.

The boy turned away and ran his fingers back through his hair, which she assumed by that point to be a nervous habit. The two of them dropped their voices again before she could make out another word, just indistinguishable mumbling in deep, somber tones. Then the man walked away.

Kyla was thankful that he left in the same direction he had come, but curious when the boy didn't move. His gaze was still cast to the ground and his brow was furrowed like he was frustrated or listening for something, which didn't really make sense to her. But then, as she peered through the top of her makeshift peephole, his head suddenly snapped around and he looked straight at her.

Kyla gasped out loud and dropped to her knees. Scrambling to spin herself around, she pressed her back up against the stone wall behind her, trying not to panic and struggling to breathe.

He saw her. The boy named Nathaniel knew that she was there.

Chapter 7

"…when defiance is justified."

Nathaniel Blake moved cautiously into the cemetery and onto the path that cut through the trees. He paced back and forth as he waited for the Naphil that had summoned him to this impromptu meeting; then he stopped and looked up when he felt Seth approaching. Bowing his head, he waited for his leader to place a hand on his arm.

"Did you find Eli?" Nathaniel asked once he'd returned the sign of the brotherhood.

Seth didn't look happy. "It seems that Malachi has taken extra measures to conceal him. He must have discerned my intentions."

Nathaniel didn't hide his dissatisfaction with that answer. "Surely there is someone you could have persuaded to help you locate him?"

"Persuaded?" Seth asked.

Nathaniel gave him a look and Seth rebuked him sharply. "Nathaniel!"

He dropped his head at the sound of his own name.

"That is *not* an acceptable course of action," Seth corrected him. "I would expect you to know that I would never use measures of persuasion on another member of the brotherhood."

Seth seemed disturbed that Nathaniel would even suggest this; not only due to its being completely against the protocol of the Resitore, but because it wasn't at all like him.

"You're right," Nathaniel conceded, keeping his head down. "Forgive me for speaking out of place."

Get it together, he told himself.

Nathaniel knew their objective, their purpose. He knew the Resitore existed to stop those of their kind with an unquenchable thirst for power before they could bring the destruction to the earth that they planned to bring. And if in that process means of coercion became necessary, then so be it. But they did not torture their own.

"What is the status of the assignment?" Seth asked.

Nathaniel hesitated to answer him, not wanting to say what he knew that he had to. "I saw Donovan," he finally admitted.

Seth froze. "You found him? Already?"

Nathaniel wasn't looking forward to explaining this. "He found *me*."

Seth was more than agitated by this new development. Apparently he hadn't anticipated such a bold move. "Did he speak to you?" Seth asked.

Nathaniel shifted uncomfortably, this time unforced. "Yes."

Seth's voice was tight. "And what did he say?"

Nathaniel struggled with what he should disclose to him, and his silence lasted longer than Seth's patience.

"Nathaniel…" Seth started to say, but instead he looked up. Something struck him suddenly, and he scanned the area around them, taking in the setting as if discerning something about the place. "We shouldn't talk here," he told Nathaniel. "What is the status of your uncle? Is he in town?"

"No. I'm alone."

"Get back to the mansion then," Seth ordered him. "I will meet you there soon."

Nathaniel flinched, but remained unmoving. He thought Seth might have caught it, too, but he couldn't be sure.

"You are not to leave the estate until I arrive. Is that understood?"

"Understood," Nathaniel agreed robotically.

Seth gave him another look before turning to leave the cemetery the way he had entered.

Once he was gone, Nathaniel scowled and looked down at his feet. He wasn't comfortable with this, but he didn't have time to question what should be done before he discerned something clearly that he should have recognized sooner.

He was being watched.

Jerking his head up, Nathaniel saw a set of eyes peering at him through the hole of a headstone in the distance. He felt ice on his skin as the eyes disappeared, and the person behind them ducked down behind the headstone to avoid being seen.

Nathaniel felt his anger flare up when he realized that he and Seth had been compromised. Moving over to the headstone, he turned at an angle and stopped directly in front of the small, cowering girl who was crouched down on the ground with her back against the stone.

Slowly, her eyes rose inch by inch, and when their gaze finally met, his face completely dropped.

"You..." he said. Then quicker than his surprise came, his anger returned. "What are you doing here?"

Kyla scowled and righted herself. "What?" she asked as she brushed the dirt off her legs. "You're the only one with stalking rights?"

Nathaniel glared at her. "What are you *doing* here?" he reiterated.

"If anyone has the right to ask questions right now, it's me," she said. She folded her arms across her chest. "Starting with *who are you?*"

She was beginning to try his patience. "Who I am does not concern you," Nathaniel told her.

Kyla wasn't fazed by his threatening tone. "Oh, really?" she asked. "So you get to show up here in the middle of the night and scare me half to death, send me off thinking I'm in some kind of serious danger, and I don't even get to know who you are?"

"I don't have time for this," Nathaniel muttered. He turned away to leave, but she followed right behind him.

"It's not so fun when you're on the receiving end, is it?" she asked.

Nathaniel shook his head, not believing her audacity, but he didn't stop moving forward. Kyla sprinted to get in front of him and cut him off so he couldn't leave.

"What is wrong with you?" he asked her.

She was so confident now, so sure of herself...so unlike when he found her huddled up in a ball on the ground only a minute before.

"Just tell me who you are," Kyla said. "Tell me what you're doing here."

"I'm visiting my uncle," Nathaniel replied generically.

She didn't look convinced. "Is he dead?" she asked.

He looked at her, confused. "What?"

"Well, if you're visiting your uncle in a cemetery, I assume he's dead. Unless you're referring to the blonde man you were just talking to."

Nathaniel flinched when he realized she saw Seth. "I didn't mean that's why I'm here in this exact location," he clarified. "I meant that's why I'm here in Woodland Park."

Kyla's arms were still folded as she eyed him skeptically. "Still doesn't tell me why you like hanging out in graveyards."

Nathaniel didn't enjoy being interrogated like this. "Well, why do you?"

Kyla tightened her jaw and again he could see that his words had hurt her. She dropped her gaze angrily in an attempt to mask her emotion. "I don't come here out of pleasure if that's what you mean."

Nathaniel tried to read her, tried to understand what she was hiding, but no sooner than she started to show a trace of vulnerability, she looked up again in the same bitterness as before. "And you still didn't tell me who you are."

He was baffled by the rate at which her demeanor could shift. "Nathaniel," he told her. "Nathaniel Blake."

Kyla smirked at him. "That wasn't so hard, now was it?"

"I don't know," he retorted. "You seemed to have a difficult enough time with it last night."

The glare she gave him suggested that she was not amused. "So what are you really doing here?" she asked him. "And why the spontaneous need to freak me out last night?"

Nathaniel sighed. "Has anyone ever told you that you ask too many questions?"

Kyla looked at him straight on. "Yes."

106

Nathaniel gave her a look. "Has anyone ever told you that unguarded curiosity could get you into trouble?"

Kyla narrowed her eyes at him again, only this time it was different than before. She looked into him deeper than he wanted her to and asked him out of the blue, "What are you so afraid of?"

It wasn't the question he expected from her, and hearing it, Nathaniel was slightly offended. "I'm not afraid of anything," he answered a little too fast.

She continued to eye him skeptically, and Nathaniel began to feel the same unease he felt with her last night. He didn't know who this girl was that she could look at him like that and not even be afraid.

"No..." Kyla said thoughtfully. "You really are."

Nathaniel clenched his jaw, determined to stand guard against whatever it was that enabled her to do that.

"Who are you, Nathaniel Blake?"

He took a step back unconsciously. "What do you mean?"

Kyla stepped forward, completely fearless. "Who *are* you?" she asked him again.

Nathaniel didn't know how to answer her. For the first time in his life, he was completely at a loss.

"You were watching me, weren't you?" she said. It was more an accusation than a question, not that he would have been comfortable hearing it either way.

Kyla's eyes were still locked onto his, and he felt his breathing quicken beneath them.

"I want to know why," she told him.

Nathaniel scrambled to think of anything he could say to her, any way he could gain control over this situation, but he was entranced by her gaze, never having felt so vulnerable or weakened. As it happened, however, he didn't need to say a word. Nathaniel could tell by the look on her face that she saw the answer to her question in his eyes, and he watched as understanding fell over her.

"I wasn't the one you were after," she said in a quiet voice.

His heart continued to pound. "How do you know this?" he asked her.

Kyla blinked a few times and stepped back, shaking her head as if knocked from a trance. "I...I don't know."

He was speechless as he looked into her. In a matter of seconds her countenance and demeanor shifted again, more dramatically this time than it had at any other point. She didn't appear strong now, confident like before, but a lot more like she had when he had found her here, afraid and confused.

"Hey," he whispered softly. Without even thinking, he reached forward and touched her arm, overcome by the sudden desire to comfort her.

It appeared to catch her every bit as much by surprise as it did him, but Kyla didn't jerk away. Instead she looked up at him again, timidly this time.

Nathaniel was held there for an indefinable amount of time, awestruck in a way that he couldn't shake himself from. He was locked there, overtaken by this force, enrapt by this auburn-haired girl and her inescapable eyes, which he realized once again were changing color as he watched them.

"What do you want from me?" she asked him.

His face softened when he realized she was frightened. "I am not going to harm you, Kyla..."

She cut him off before he could finish. "That doesn't answer my question."

Nathaniel felt exposed. "You're the one who followed me here," he responded coldly. "I don't want anything with you."

Kyla blinked a few times, surprised by his bluntness and appearing confused. "Then why..." she started to ask.

Nathaniel let go of her arm. "I have to go," he told her suddenly.

"No, wait..." she said.

Kyla grabbed his hand to stop him from walking away, and at her touch, a shock of heat and electricity surged through his arm, so intense and sudden it froze him in his tracks.

Nathaniel turned back to look at her, frightened as she continued to hold onto his hand. He could see behind her eyes that she felt it, too.

"What *are* you?" she breathed to him in a whisper.

108

He broke away from her quickly, his heart pounding harder with every step.

Moving through the cemetery and slipping out of sight, Nathaniel wound through the buildings below the parking lot and leaned his back against a stucco-sided wall. After waiting there for a good five seconds to make sure Kyla hadn't followed him, he closed his eyes and forced himself to breathe.

It took him a while to get a grip on himself, and when he finally did, he looked back at the entrance of the cemetery just as Kyla walked out of it. She looked bewildered and disoriented; not far from what he felt himself. Debating whether or not he should follow her, Nathaniel again found himself pulled between what he knew he should do and what he felt that he had to do. He deliberated over it for another five seconds before he finally caved.

Seth cannot know about this, he determined. At all costs, he could not let him know.

*K*yla could hardly breathe as she watched the gorgeous blue-eyed boy leave the cemetery that morning. Paralyzed by this feeling, this torrent, this unexplainable heightening of every one of her senses, she stared forward blankly, unable to understand what had just happened.

Shaking her head, she stumbled out of there by the light of the sun that was barely beginning to peak over the mountains. Between what happened here last night, the lack of sleep she had gotten when she'd stayed in Caden's bedroom and the second freakish cemetery encounter she'd just managed, Kyla didn't know what to think.

Looking around quickly upon exiting the cemetery, she scanned the parking lot and the trees and the few buildings down below for Nathaniel Blake, disturbed to find that he was nowhere to be seen.

Even beneath Caden's oversized hoodie, she rubbed her arms to keep the chill off her skin. As hot as the summers were here, the mornings were a different story, though she knew the goose bumps on her arms had more to do with

Nathaniel's disappearing act and less to do with the air temperature than she wanted to admit.

This was all getting a bit too weird for her.

Scampering back down to the Civic, Kyla started the ignition as fast as she could, thinking she couldn't get home fast enough, which was a far cry from last night, to say the least. Funny how creepy encounters in a cemetery could change a person's perspective.

Slipping quietly through the front door of the condo, Kyla tiptoed upstairs to the bathroom she and Matthew shared and breathed in relief when she didn't wake Loni. As thankful as she was to be home right now, that was the last thing she could deal with.

Jumping in the shower and letting the warm steamy water wash over her skin, she closed her eyes and tried to steer her mind away from the boy named Nathaniel. But no matter how hard she tried to push it aside, her curiosity continued to pull at her, drawing her back to the beautiful stranger.

And so did her fear.

She tried to ignore the questions that kept resurfacing in her mind, but she couldn't push them far enough away, and the feeling they left her with had her so shaken up that even beneath the hot water, her arms were still covered with goose bumps...as if he were a ghost.

Kyla flinched at the thought; then she laughed nervously at her own foolishness.

That's ridiculous, she told herself. She didn't believe in ghosts or aliens or vampires. She didn't believe in anything but flesh and blood humans. At least not anymore.

Forcefully shutting off her mind, she told herself to get a grip and focus or she was going to be late for work. Her shift started in fifteen minutes at the coffee shop she had been working at since she graduated two months ago and escaped the evil clutches of high school, and the last thing she needed was to get bitched out by her co-worker Val Linley about showing up on time.

Kyla made a face when she remembered she was working with Val today.

Somebody please just kill me now, she thought.

110

Val Linley, as far as she was concerned, was the worst person alive and very possibly the daughter of Satan. Not to mention that the girl's entire purpose in life was to make Kyla's hell. They had known each other since they were in grade school, and even then Val couldn't stand her. One of the first interactions the two of them ever had involved an argument over a brand new eight-pack of Crayolas. Apparently Val never got over it, because she'd been harassing Kyla ever since.

And then there was that thing Val had with Caden back in junior high. Nothing ever came from it, but it was still one of the worst weeks of Kyla's life. Fortunately, Caden had wised up before he let anything stupid happen between them; or maybe he just realized how much it was hurting her and cut it off for Kyla's sake. Either way, Val never really got over that either.

Grumbling as she pulled a black, work-appropriate t-shirt over her head, Kyla glossed her lips in the mirror that hung on her wall by the door and then moved quietly down the stairs. She glanced toward the basement door on her way out of the house, making sure Loni wasn't awake yet and internally sighing as she passed it.

If she were to guess, Kyla would say her mother had the door locked and was sprawled out on the couch in the same hideous sweatpants-slipper combination she wore the night before with a bottle of vodka in one hand and a TV remote in the other. Hell, she might not even know that Kyla hadn't come home last night.

That was basically all the woman ever did anymore. She had gotten enough money from her husband's life insurance to extinguish any motivation she would otherwise have to get a job, which was beyond revolting in Kyla's opinion. It disgusted her, what Loni had become. It was bad enough that she had opted altogether out of being a mother, but when it came to way she treated Matthew, that was where Kyla lost it. It was also the entire reason she was even still here.

Kyla may have hated this town, her mother, and her life, but if there was anything she still loved, it was her little brother. She knew that aside from the Howell's, she was all

Matthew really had, and even if she had thought about it a thousand times, there was no way she could rationalize leaving him alone with the pathetic excuse for a human being who was passed out drunk downstairs.

Kyla grimaced as she looked away from the basement door. She would deal with Loni later.

As she drove the short distance up Highway 24 to the coffee shop, Kyla fixed her eyes stubbornly on the road, determined not to look to her right when she passed Woodland Cemetery. Somehow she managed to pull it off, too. When it really came down to it, she had impressive self-control; not that she was able to stop thinking about what compelled her to look there in the first place.

Stupid gorgeous stalker ghost.

Coming in through the back entrance of the coffee shop, she half-sighed, half-grimaced when she saw Val up front opening the register. Grumbling as she tied a purple apron around her waist, Kyla prepared herself for a very long day.

Since it was a weekday, the coffee shop wasn't extraordinarily crowded, a fact for which she was surprisingly grateful, despite the lack of tips she knew would result. She just couldn't keep her head straight for her life, and trying to tend to dozens of impatient, caffeine-addicted customers on top of all the duties she had to perform would be all but impossible under the circumstances. Normally she was amazing at it, but today, well…today was anything but normal.

"What are you doing?" Val snapped at her.

Kyla flinched and spilled the coffee beans she was attempting to pour into the grinder all over the floor. Mumbling under her breath, she reached for a broom to sweep them up. "What is your *problem*?" she snapped.

"You're grinding the wrong kind," Val answered smugly.

Kyla looked at the label on the bag, hating that she was right. "Sorry," she muttered. Then she closed the bag and replaced it on the storage shelf in the back.

Val continued reprimanding her long after she'd decided to tune her out and busy herself in the storage room, as was typically the case with them.

112

Get a grip, Kyla told herself for the second time that morning.

But no matter how she tried, she couldn't get the image of Nathaniel Blake's frustratingly perfect face out of her mind.

*N*athaniel paced in the entryway as he waited for Seth. He had been back at the mansion for ten minutes with no sign of him, and he was beginning to wonder if he should be concerned.

When the front door finally opened, Nathaniel stopped and looked up.

"I booked you a flight for this evening," Seth told him. He did not look happy.

Nathaniel stared at him blankly. There were so many reasons the words weren't computing for him. "A flight? What are you talking about?"

Seth spoke bluntly, "I am calling off the assignment."

Nathaniel had to work hard to stay emotionless. "May I ask why?"

"They know you are here, Nathaniel. You no longer hold the advantage." His voice was as emotionless as it had ever been.

Nathaniel forced himself not to show the opposition he felt to what he knew he was being ordered to do. "I understand," he said, "but is this really the best course of action we can take?"

Seth hardly looked willing to negotiate.

"I've been following several of Eli's leads," Nathaniel tried to explain. "If I could just see them through…"

Seth cut him off. "It is too dangerous."

Again Nathaniel held himself in check, though he was finding it increasingly difficult to do so.

"You do not know the power Donovan operates from," Seth told him. "You do not understand the way he thinks…the way he works."

Nathaniel was unbending. "Then explain it to me."

Seth shot him a look, but Nathaniel didn't stop there.

"And while you're at it," he added, "maybe you can tell me what he wants me for."

Seth's face became drawn and white. "Is that what he told you?"

Nathaniel pressed his lips together. He didn't know why he said that. It went against every logical thought in his mind to do so, but his questions over what Donovan had told him were still pounding in his head to the point that he couldn't let them go. Let them go or stop the words from spilling out of his mouth.

Seth could see the answer behind his eyes, even though Nathaniel didn't speak again. "Believe me when I tell you, you are *not* ready," he said.

Nathaniel couldn't hide his frustration now. "And I never will be if you don't stop sheltering me from the truth."

Seth was stunned, hearing this from him. He looked into him questioningly, as if trying to discern what had come over him. "What exactly did Donovan tell you?" he asked.

Nathaniel knew if he told him the truth, there was no way he could convince Seth to let him stay on this assignment.

"He gave me an offer to join him," he replied dryly. "Naturally, I turned him down."

Seth eyed him suspiciously. "And he just let you walk away?"

"Actually, he walked away from me."

Seth looked disturbed. "This doesn't make sense," he mumbled. "Why would Donovan do this?"

"I don't know," Nathaniel told him, "but I can find out if you let me stay."

Seth snapped back at him quickly, "That is *not* a risk I am willing to take. Not with you here alone."

He was close to desperate now. "Then stay with me or send someone else."

Seth tensed his jaw and immediately Nathaniel knew it was a mistake to push it.

"This assignment is no longer limited to surveillance," Seth told him, "which you know by our protocol means you cannot stay here any longer. Not without backup."

114

"I stand by my previous suggestion," Nathaniel said. There was an abrasive edge to his voice that he knew he should have worked harder to suppress.

Seth was starting to get angry. "*Suggestion*? Is that what you call it?"

Nathaniel's eyebrows pulled together. "There is something here; I can feel it. We can't just let this go."

"I have no intention of letting it go," Seth countered, "but I also have no intention of placing your life in danger."

"He isn't going to kill me if that's what you're worried about." Nathaniel heard the words leave his mouth before he could stop himself from speaking them.

Seth flinched visibly, turning and looking away from him. "You do not know Donovan," he spoke in a low voice. "You do not know what he is capable of."

"Nor do I have any intention of underestimating him."

Seth's face contorted bitterly. "You already have."

Nathaniel ignored the accusation. "Do you not realize that you have leverage here?" he asked. "You have something Donovan wants and you can use that against him."

Seth tensed even further. "And what is that?"

Nathaniel could tell by the tone of his voice that Seth was not going to take anything he had to say well, but he didn't let that stop him.

"Me."

Much as he suspected, Seth became furious at the suggestion. "You are going back to London *tonight*," he all but snarled. "That is an *order*!"

Nathaniel closed his eyes in an attempt to calm himself. "Is the flight really necessary?" he asked.

Seth gave him a look, then he turned without another word and left.

Nathaniel cursed under his breath when he heard the door close. This was not good. He couldn't leave Kyla here unprotected, not after Donovan had seen him with her. Whether she was or wasn't a threat to him before, and whether she was or not any longer was completely irrelevant now. After what had happened in the cemetery last night, Nathaniel may as well have painted a target on her back. But he couldn't explain this to Seth; not without admitting his own failure. Which left him here, stuck at this impasse, struggling between correcting that mistake and following his orders.

Nathaniel picked up the ticket Seth left for him on the counter and clutched it tightly in his hand, hating that it had to be this way.

This isn't right, he thought to himself. None of this was right.

Chapter 8

"...heroes don't always come with swords."

Somehow, (though she wasn't quite sure how) Kyla managed to survive through not only her own shift at the coffee shop that day, but half of another co-worker's who had called in frantically saying they were stuck in Denver traffic as well. Running on a collective three-and-a-half hours of loosely defined sleep and more caffeine than any person should ingest in a ten-hour period, Kyla was so relieved to get off work that evening that she hardly even let herself think of the unpleasantness involved in going home.

The clouds she saw building in the distance when she walked out into the parking lot helped with that. She smiled to herself when she saw them, thinking they looked dark enough that it might even storm. That would definitely get her spirits up after being forced into a confined space for half the day with Val "I'm-A-Little-Hoe-Bag" Linley.

Walking in through the front door, Kyla was surprised to see Matthew on the living room couch when she got home. She had thought she was going to have to drive up to the Howell's to pick him up, but Melissa must have dropped him off earlier. Kyla would have to remember to thank her for that.

"Hey buddy," she greeted her little brother with a hug from behind the couch.

He didn't exactly return her level of affection, but it didn't offend her. That just wasn't Matthew's style. "Hey," he said coolly.

"You and Lex have fun?" she asked as she kicked off her work shoes.

He hesitated. "Yeah," he said unsurely.

"Everything alright?" she asked.

Matthew shrugged a little. "Alexa's just acting kinda weird."

Kyla laughed at that. "When isn't Alexa acting weird?"

Matthew smiled in response, but the smile was tense. He was trying to play it off and hide from her what was really going on, but Kyla saw through him. Rather than call him out on it, though, she glanced toward the still-closed basement door.

"Has she come out yet?" she asked of their mother.

Matthew frowned and shook his head.

Probably for the best, Kyla thought. But she didn't voice it out loud. As much as she hated Loni, she tried not to be so verbal about it around her brother. It didn't always work out that way, but at least she tried.

Kyla gave Matthew a kiss on the back of his head and picked up the shoes she'd just kicked off so she could take them to her room. Her obsessive compulsive tendencies would never let her leave them down there.

Walking into her bedroom, she saw three envelopes on her desk that hadn't been there when she'd left that morning. Matthew must have left them there after he'd gotten the mail.

Frowning as she flipped through them, Kyla scanned over the names of the Universities that were stamped on each one.

New York. Texas. Colorado State.

Her art teachers were the ones who had pulled the strings to get her into these schools. They were the ones who wanted her to go on and pursue her talents, but she had no intention of leaving her little brother. Kyla knew eventually she would have to, but Matthew couldn't handle that right now and she couldn't either. Even when she did decide to leave, running off to some stupid University where she would be confined and conformed to the opinions of her professors was not Kyla's idea of being released into artistic freedom. When the right time came, she wanted to get as far away from that as she possibly could. She wanted to get as far away from *here* as she possibly could.

She wanted to be somewhere across the sea, someplace where history spilled from the ground and spoke to every

118

creative place inside of her. She wanted to be somewhere that could wake her again to color and light and sound and pull her from where she'd been living in a world of black and white...where all the vitality she had ever known had been sucked completely dry.

Kyla tossed the envelopes into the waste basket by her desk without opening a single one, irritated that they were ever there in the first place. When she turned away from her desk, her vision started to blur, and it was only then she realized that she hadn't eaten since breakfast (if grabbing a granola bar on her way out the door could qualify as breakfast.)

She went downstairs and found Matthew still on the couch. "Want some dinner, kiddo?" she asked him.

He shrugged unenthusiastically and she grabbed the remote from beside him. He looked up at her when she clicked off the TV and she playfully messed up his hair. "Come on," she said. "Help me cook something."

A typical ten-year-old boy might be upset over his big sister turning off whatever show he was watching and telling him to help her cook dinner, but Matthew didn't mind so much. He and Kyla had always had an interesting relationship. Not entirely abnormal, just deeper than what most siblings had, especially at their ages. It had been just the two of them for so long that they really kind of needed each other. That was why Matthew didn't resent it when she did things like that.

"What are we making?" he asked her.

Kyla smiled teasingly and told him, "Chicken Avocado Ranch Salad," knowing he would hate that. Matthew wrinkled his nose and she laughed. "Fine, for me then," she said. "What do you want?"

He settled on soft shell tacos.

Kyla sautéed the chicken she'd sprinkled with fajita seasoning while Matthew pulled two whole grain tortillas from the bread basket on the counter.

"Can't you at least buy me the white ones?" he asked her.

"Nope," she said, portioning off half of the chicken in her skillet onto the tacos he was assembling (or at least trying to assemble.) She had to help him when the things started to self-destruct.

Matthew may not have been into salads, but Kyla could usually get away with sneaking some lettuce and tomatoes in with the tacos she made him. Just one of her subtle attempts to keep him healthy in the midst of all the boxed macaroni and neon-colored cereal he insisted she keep in the house.

Once she got him cheese and sour cream and the trace amounts of fresh veggies he would let her stuff in there, she tossed the chicken she had left over onto some iceberg lettuce for herself. Half an avocado, a diced tomato and some homemade ranch dressing later, she had a picture-worthy salad in hand that she took to the counter where Matthew was already sitting, busily munching on his dinner.

"See? They're not bad, are they?" she said.

Matthew made a face at her, his mouth stuffed with chicken and whole wheat tortilla, and Kyla gave him a knowing smirk. He wasn't serious. If it tasted bad, he wouldn't be eating it.

Putting her right leg up on the barstool so she could hug her knee while she ate, Kyla stabbed at her salad with her fork, making sure she had equal parts chicken, lettuce, veggies and dressing in each bite.

The joys of OCD, she thought. She had gotten that from her dad.

Loni had never been the organized, methodical type, even back when she was still sane. She never obsessed over details or cared if things were perfect; that was all Kyla and her dad. They were the only obsessive compulsive ones in their family.

"The curse of the artist," he had always told her. "Perfectionism in its most frustrating form."

Her dad had been with painting the same way Kyla was with drawing. He was also like that with the motorcycles he used to work on. Both her and her father's obsessive tendencies would channel into the most random things at times, and the more stress they were under, the more pointless the things were that they would channel into. Like the salad-to-protein ratio on a dinner fork, for example.

Suddenly, there was something that tasted very wrong with the bite of avocado in Kyla's mouth. Setting down her fork, she told Matthew she'd be down later to finish her salad, that there was something she needed to take care of first. That was a lie. She just couldn't stomach it anymore.

Thinking about her dad had that effect on her.

Kyla felt queasy as she made her way upstairs and gagged down that last bite of salad, but all it took was her glancing out the window by her desk for the feeling to leave her. The sky had grown darker since she'd gotten off work, and not just because it was getting later. There was a storm building; quite nicely, in fact.

Kyla smiled at the sight of it.

Woodland Park was more prone to thunderstorms than all the rest of Colorado combined. Or at least it seemed that way. It was also the only reason she had been able to survive living here for the past eighteen years. Kyla loved it when it stormed, when ominous grey clouds filled the expanse of the sky and low muffled thunder rumbled in the distance. She loved feeling the rain pound against her body as she ran the hilly streets and completely shut out all thought and memory of her life as she knew it.

Yes, Kyla thought as she examined the sky, it was definitely going to rain. And there wasn't a chance she was going to miss it.

If Underoath was her drug, then running was her therapy; and in light of the strangeness of last night and the miserable hours she'd spent at the coffee shop that day, she could use a little therapy right now.

Walking into her closet, Kyla slipped on a strappy black sports bra, a tank top to match it and the bright blue running shorts she'd just bought to replace the ones she'd worn ragged in Cross Country last year. She laced her Mizunos and threw her hair up in a ponytail, and in no time flat she was out the door.

*P*eering through the sparsely needled branches of a pine tree by the road, Donovan's eyes locked on the girl who emerged from the last blue-roofed condo on Ponderosa Way. She had her auburn hair pulled back tonight, away from her face so it wouldn't bother her when she ran, and by it he could see the crease in her brow that suggested her frustration. Nothing unnatural there. This one was often frustrated.

He adjusted his position as she moved, careful to keep close to her and yet far enough away that his presence wouldn't be discerned. It was easier than it used to be, given the girl's refusal to engage in the sort of behavior she used to anymore. Convenient, truly, that her father had died. Kyla James was always such a headache for him before that.

Donovan grinned to himself at the memory. *Such a shame*, he thought as he watched her now. All those logs careening out of control, with no one there to stop them from crushing dear Daddy into the ground. It may as well have been a steamroller, but then that wouldn't have looked much like an accident.

And he needed it to look like an accident.

Watching Kyla run up the road with her long, evenly-paced strides, Donovan thought how much easier it would be if he'd been able to take care of her that way. Not nearly as fun as watching the agony it caused her, but if he'd been able to kill her back then, he wouldn't be here now watching her like this, trying to figure out how she ever found Nathaniel Blake.

Still, Donovan couldn't have killed her then and he knew it. She was too protected...just like the boy. It was that sickening joy Kyla used to have that made her all but untouchable to him, guarding what she possessed so he couldn't get to it. It had almost driven him mad.

But that was the brilliant thing about humans: Steal their joy and you had an open target to their heart. Take the shot and you'd strike them down. And when they were left there writhing in their own blood, in the broken pieces of what they used to have and who they used to be, it was in that moment that they made the choice; either get back up or lose their soul.

Kyla didn't get back up.

Donovan could have killed her after that if it hadn't been for the boy; his constant covering over her, his ceaselessly warring on her behalf, sending those to keep guard over her life that so continually guarded him. Caden must have known that something wanted her, even if he didn't know what it was. As far as Donovan knew, Caden didn't even know of their existence…of anything of the Coven or especially the Alliance. But he did know enough about the realm of the dark to be able to tell when something was wrong.

Donovan's inability to kill Kyla James after that was really more of an annoyance than anything since she was no longer moving in the power that threatened them. Still, it was an issue he wished could be resolved. The Howell kids were one thing, but Kyla wasn't like them. Before she had decided to abandon all she was and run from that power, she had posed a far greater threat to the Coven's purpose here. A greater threat even than the boy.

Fortunately, Caden Howell was gone now, and there was no other means by which Donovan suspected her capable of being re-awakened.

At least that was what he'd thought before he saw her with Nathaniel.

Glaring forward as Kyla pumped her long runner legs and charged up the hill, Donovan questioned again how she had found him. Suspicious didn't begin to describe one like Nathaniel Blake just so happening to come into her life. It had to be more than chance. It had to be more than Eli.

In the world of the Nephilim, coincidence did not exist.

It had been over a year since Donovan had watched her like this. Kyla had grown far more beautiful since he'd seen her last summer, and her soul had grown darker as well.

Donovan quivered at the thought of her.

To have access to one like this, with such raw power and such raw beauty, he would kill for such a thing.

He would kill for far less.

Kyla may not be moving in it anymore, but that power was still there. He could feel it as he drew nearer to her. It never really left the ones who were marked by it, this power that ran deep in their blood. Some of them just chose to deny it.

Dancing at the edge of his mind, a thought came back to Donovan that had been toying with him for the past twenty-four hours, daring him to trust in a scenario he knew was too perfect to believe. But if it were true (or if it could become true) that Nathaniel would have a reason to protect this one, then Donovan could use her for more than he had realized.

That was the theory he was operating under now. He had to think positively, too, or he would have to admit he'd been placed in a position of disadvantage with the Resitore. And that was simply not acceptable.

Donovan shuddered at the thought.

He would not let Seth win this. This was *his* war...or at least it would be before the end. The brotherhood was not going to stop what he had worked so hard for, shed so much blood for. They were not going to stop anything because he would stop them first. And he would do it by turning their own against them, the strongest among them to the dark they so avidly resisted.

He would do it by turning Nathaniel Blake, whom he could feel here even now, watching the girl.

A grin spread slowly across Donovan's face at his discernment of Nathaniel's presence. It seemed fortune, after all, had found him again. And he knew exactly what he was going to do with it.

Kyla breathed in deeply as she ran, the taste of the coming rain sweet on her tongue. She loved running the road up Majestic Parkway. There was hardly ever any traffic, for one, and the aspens and pines lining both of its sides were incredible. It was like another world up here, free from the stupid rich people who lived down below and the little women in pink jogging suits walking their toy-sized dogs that were so ugly they needed to be drop-kicked.

After about thirty minutes of running hills, Kyla slowed to a walk when she came back down into the neighborhood, into an oversized roundabout that the rich people needed for their fancy SUVs and enormous egos. She put her hands on her head and steadied her breathing, pacing back and forth so she could give her heart a chance to slow down. Apparently she'd been running harder than she had thought.

When she felt a drop of rain splash against her forehead, a smile broke out on her face. Looking up at the sky with her hands still on her head, she stared into the dark stormy clouds, urging them to break open as if her opinion on the matter might actually make a difference. It was dark enough that it looked like the sun had gone down, but she knew it was only hiding behind the clouds, and she was anxiously anticipating the lightning that would result.

What she wasn't anticipating, however, was the feeling that came over her as she stopped to stretch in the roundabout.

Kyla looked around her curiously. She didn't see anything at first, but then she heard something that stopped her in her tracks.

"Hello there," an unfamiliar voice sounded from behind her.

She spun around sharply and saw a strange man with jet black hair and hollow eyes step out from the trees and onto the road.

"Can I help you?" she asked. Her tone was anything but polite.

"Tell me your name," the man said.

Eyeing him carefully, she told him, "Sarah."

He was handsome...extremely handsome. But there was something about the grin he gave her that she found completely sickening.

"That isn't your name, is it?" he said.

The man took a step toward her and Kyla took one back to compensate.

"Who are you?" she asked him.

The man's response disturbed her. "I'd like to know the same about you." He looked her up and down slowly. "You don't look like anything special."

"Turn around and walk away," Kyla threatened, "or I will scream so loud every person on this mountain and ten miles out will hear me."

The man put his hands up innocently. "I apologize," he said. "I didn't mean to frighten you, Kyla."

Her blood froze at the sound of her name. "How did you..."

Before she could articulate the question, an icy hand was on her back. Kyla flinched away from him, not understanding how he had gotten over to her so quickly.

125

The man didn't let that stop him. "You have beautiful skin," he told her, tracing her shoulder with his fingertips.

Kyla whipped around to face him, ready to let him have it, but she was not prepared for what she saw when she did.

Her mouth hung open, but no words came out, and suddenly she forgot every threat she was about to breathe. It was in his eyes, in the intensity of his countenance and the beauty of his face... in that cold tingling chill that came over her when she felt him approach.

This man bore such a striking resemblance to Nathaniel Blake it made her head spin.

"Who are you?" she asked him again, but this time her voice shook.

Stepping back, she blinked her widened eyes, and the man moved his fingers down her arm, still not answering her question.

That was her cue.

Kyla jerked away from him suddenly and broke for the trees, but just as she did he sprang forward with a speed she couldn't wrap her mind around. Grabbing her by her arms, he slammed her against a wide-based pine tree with rough jagged bark jutting out from its trunk. She felt the wood impale her back, shooting a pain so sharp through her body that the wind was knocked out of her for a good ten seconds. A good ten seconds she could have been fighting this freak off of her.

Kyla saw it in the eyes of her attacker, a look of malice and hatred and lust so deep she couldn't understand it. He pinned her up against the tree with the full force of his body and slid his hands up her stomach.

They were cold...so cold. Kyla had never felt so sick in her life.

"What do...you want from...me?" she wheezed before her breath fully returned.

His teeth grit together angrily and he forced her head back, cracking it hard against the tree and holding both sides of her face only inches from his own. She thought he was going to crush her skull.

"You are not the one I want," he hissed. Then that repugnant grin reached his lips again. The man looked her up and down again slowly, nauseatingly. "But this game is going to be a lot more fun than I thought."

Kyla managed to suck in enough oxygen not to pass out. Now she was just pissed. She tried shoving the man off of her, which she knew was a pointless exertion of her energy, but the feel of his touch on her skin was intolerable. That was when he decided to bend down and press his cold, wet lips to her throat.

Kyla went rigid. Was he going to *bite* her?

The man didn't bite her, but when he opened his mouth and slid his tongue along the base of her neck, licking her from the top of her chest to the foremost part of her throat, she almost wished he had. Kyla thought she honestly would have preferred he draw blood than cover her in his saliva.

"Ugh!" she exclaimed. "*What* game, you pathetic emo freak?!"

She was still trying to break out of his hold, but she refused to be afraid of him. She didn't want to give him the satisfaction.

The man pulled back and studied her face, a smile growing on him again that left her more nauseated than his tongue had. "Cat and mouse, Kyla," he told her. "The oldest game there is."

She attempted to knee him hard where she knew she could at least faze him long enough to break out of his grip, but the man's reflexes were frighteningly fast. He grabbed her leg when she lifted it to strike him and pinned her back up against the tree, shoving her body into it even harder this time. As he slid his hand up her thigh, Kyla felt a cold sweat break out over her forehead.

Now she was afraid.

"So who's the mouse?" she whispered, breathing so hard she probably should have passed out.

The man didn't answer her. He just ran his free hand up her neck and whispered in her ear, "Five...four...three...two..."

He didn't get to one. He didn't get the chance. Something told Kyla he knew he wouldn't.

It all happened so fast that her mind couldn't keep up, which caused her to question if all this insanity might be part of an intricate nightmare she'd mistaken for reality.

She saw it first in the eyes of the dark, demented stranger who had her pinned against a tree. He looked thrilled beyond comprehension, as she was sure many serial killers and rapists were in the moments before they attacked. But there was something else behind his hollow amber eyes, which were so deep in hue they were almost red.

She noticed it at the last second, just as the word "one" was forming on his lips, and it so confused her that she was temporarily distracted from the terror she felt crushing her heart and constricting her lungs. Kyla had expected him to keep looking into her with that same ferocity that was intended to paralyze her with fear, but then his eyes shifted, so subtly she was sure he didn't expect her to catch it. Almost as if he anticipated…

Wham!

The body of her attacker was ripped from hers and hurled through the air like a rag doll. Kyla watched him fly ten feet backwards and crack his back against a boulder, gasping in shock and instinctively covering her mouth at the sight. The sound alone told her his spine had snapped, and somehow she was more fascinated by this than horrified.

Her eyes darted frantically between the lifeless body that lay in the street and the shadowed figure she saw moving toward it whose features were hidden by the dark of the storming sky. She heard the sound of feet hitting the pavement as the towering shadow sprinted toward the lifeless body on the ground.

Just as the figure leapt forward in an Olympic-worthy jump, the man who was supposed to be dead sprang up, colliding with him mid-air. Kyla screamed at the sight, her hand still over her mouth as she stared with gaping eyes that she couldn't pull away. Everything in her told her to run, bruised and bleeding or not, but there was a pull, a magnetism holding her there, fixing her eyes on the impossible sight before her.

"Damn it, Kyla!" a familiar voice shouted as the figure she still hadn't distinguished hurled her attacker to the ground. "Get out of here!"

She stepped forward unconsciously, not having blinked once since the man had been ripped away from her, unable to believe her eyes and ears...unable to believe any of this. She watched the two of them tumble onto the road, though she couldn't tell which was which anymore.

A fist came down on the face of the man wearing the black cut-off gloves as a peal of thunder sounded loudly in the distance. Plagued by fear and morbid curiosity, Kyla inched even closer despite the stupidity of such a move. And despite the fact that her blonde-haired, blue-eyed rescuer has ordered her to leave.

"I swear to you, Donovan, if you laid one hand on her..." Nathaniel snarled as he choked the man.

Before he could finish, the one he called Donovan whipped his legs around in a move Kyla was sure didn't even exist in professional wrestling. He kicked Nathaniel onto his back, bore his teeth and leapt on top of him in a way that made him appear more animal than human.

And that was the point that she was snapped back to reality.

It was a combination of primal instinct and reckless rage that pushed her then to the edge of the woods. Searching frantically, she found the largest rock she could hold in her fist and then ran at the man in black, planting her feet and throwing it fastball style the way Caden taught her three summers ago.

She nailed him right between the eyes.

It was enough to divert his attention for at least half a second, and apparently that was all Nathaniel needed. The man's head snapped up at the impact of the rock. His eyes locked onto Kyla's for only a fraction of a moment, but in that moment she was held in the arrest of evil...a darker, deeper evil than she even knew existed.

He flashed his teeth at her the way she would expect of a snake as a hiss escaped his lips, and when he did Nathaniel's arm reached up and smashed the rock she had thrown against the side of his skull. It hardly appeared to hurt him, though it did redirect his attention back to her defender. Not, however, before Nathaniel managed to scream at her again.

"Kyla, get *out* of here!"

Somehow she felt that he wasn't just trying to be noble now. Nathaniel Blake knew something she didn't know.

After knocking Donovan off of him again, he stood to his feet and tackled him back to the ground, and before they collided with the brick road beneath them, Kyla was already sprinting down the street.

She could feel the sting of the wind on her back, though the pain of her wide open gashes and the splintered bark inside them didn't even detract from the terror that compelled her forward.

Propelled by sheer adrenaline, Kyla was able to ignore that pain completely and run harder and faster than she ever had in her life.

Just keep running, she told herself. Whatever she did, she could not stop running.

Alexa Howell lay face down on her bed, her eyelids fluttering as visions and images flashed before her mind that she couldn't make sense of. Clashes of black and white, screams she could hear audibly in her head; familiar and unfamiliar faces colliding in a chaotic blur so that she couldn't distinguish who was who...what was human and what was not.

This had never happened to her before.

This wasn't like seeing angels.

It wasn't the same as feeling the battle that existed in another realm, warring in a place that remained unseen but affected the reality all around her. Whatever Alexa was seeing now, it was physical. No more or less real than the war of the risen and fallen ones, but so close she could almost touch it.

130

And right now, it was raging around Kyla.

It was her face that Alexa saw first in her mind. The sight of it hit her so suddenly that it rendered her incapacitated, and though she didn't understand it, somehow she knew that whatever she was seeing, these were not visions of the future or the past. They were happening right now, and moment by moment they were clenching the truth that her spirit was screaming at her, the one she still found too impossible to trust.

Alexa reached desperately for the worn black leather Bible by her bedside. Tracing its once silver-edged pages, she closed her eyes, her lips moving silently as she breathed a prayer. Carefully, she slid a finger between the pages, and the book fell open effortlessly.

Her eyes were drawn to a single line. It was the book of Matthew; Chapter Twenty-Four, Verse Six: *As it was in the days of Noah, so it will be at the coming of the son of Man.*

Alexa froze, then read it again. Reading the verse a third time, her heart started to pound.

Could that really be what this was about?

She felt dizzy, scrambling for a meaning or an explanation as if there actually was one. Her breathing quickened, but she didn't know what to do. Trying to make sense of it, she prayed again, hoping to learn that this was a mistake.

Alexa's head throbbed as the words echoed through her mind. The visions sped up and the fire in the eyes of these men she'd never seen burned hotter and deeper with each passing second.

As in the days of Noah…

Alexa knew of those days. She had learned of them from picture Bibles and felt boards in Sunday school, or at least the cute parts of the story about the animals being taken into the ark and the rainbows and doves and olive branches at the end that left her with a warm fuzzy feeling after God sent the flood to wipe out all of mankind.

But men were not the only ones on the earth in those days.

It was in Genesis; Chapter Six, Verse Four. She had read it for the first time a month ago when she'd decided to start reading her Bible from cover to cover: *The Nephilim were on the earth in those days-and also afterward-when the sons of God went to the daughters of men and had children by them. They were the heroes of old, men of renown.*

Something about the words had struck her the first time she'd read them. Alexa didn't know what they meant, only that they set her spirit on fire. Reading it last night had done the same.

These creatures who appeared as men and felt as angels, whose eyes were dark and souls were darker...she could hardly believe they would still exist.

Or maybe that they would exist again.

It was the *'and also afterward'* that disturbed her, like a promise that lingered over the end of days, that these ones who caused the flood in Noah's time had returned for a purpose of equal or greater destruction.

It was written there plainly in black and white (and sometimes red) that the flood was not the end of it. But what did that mean for now? What did that mean to her, to these visions that would not stop playing through her mind? Could the things she saw, these men who were either fighting over Kyla or at least fighting somewhere near her really be what she felt they were? Half-human...half-*angel*? Was something like that even *able* to happen again?

Normally Alexa would have thought no, at least not at this point in history. Not unless something were about to change.

"Oh, God..." she breathed, keeping her eyes slammed closed and her face buried in her pillow.

These were the ones who had been watching her. She knew it now so fully, yet she didn't know why; just like she didn't know how Kyla had been thrown into the middle of it.

No one was going to believe her...not about this. She wasn't even sure Caden would, and at this point she wouldn't have blamed him. She didn't even know if she believed it herself. But she did know there was a way she could find out for sure.

Glancing toward her bedroom door, Alexa bit her lip at the thought of calling Matthew.

She had to find out where Kyla was.

*N*athaniel backhanded Donovan as he stood, watching Kyla run down the street away from them. Neither of them shifted out of human form or used against each other any strengths or abilities they possessed that would mark them in the minds of others as anything but men. Even when the girl was out of sight, they didn't advance. They just faced each other, read each other, each of them waiting for the other to make a move.

But neither of them did.

Nathaniel knew Donovan wasn't going to. He waited for anything from him that might indicate otherwise, but no advance was made. Then with a taunting grin and a gleam in his eyes, Donovan spoke to him slowly, "Game on, Nathaniel Blake."

Then he opened his blackened wings and flew away.

*K*yla's feet pounded against the road in a frantic rhythm, matching with her heart and the throbbing in her head. She knew she'd lost too much blood. She could feel it dripping down her back as she ran, but she was determined to make it home before she lost enough to pass out.

Everything spun around her in a disoriented blur, and she was halfway convinced that nothing in the past five minutes had really happened the way her mind was telling her it had. Then, just as she ran past the green Falcon's Rest road sign, she was jolted at the sound of a voice shouting behind her.

"Kyla!"

She screamed and spun around in a panic, not knowing what she would find and not having the coherency to imagine it. But when she saw the blonde-haired boy tearing down the street toward her at full speed, Kyla instantly felt equal waves of terror and relief.

He sprinted over to her much quicker than she knew he should have been able to. Grabbing her just as her knees gave out, Kyla collapsed involuntarily into his arms, yelping in pain when her back fell against his chest. She saw Nathaniel's eyes grow wide when he pulled away from her carefully and turned her so he could look at it. By his silence, she could tell what he was thinking...and by the blood that was left on his shirt when he pulled away. But she wasn't concerned with that right now.

"Are you okay?" she blurted out frantically.

Her excessive bleeding obviously worried her, but at the moment it wasn't her primary concern. Her thoughts were still set on the nightmarish wrestling match she'd just witnessed on Majestic Parkway, and this mysterious boy who had thrown himself into harm's way in order to save her from that sick, demented man.

A man he appeared to know...

Without even knowing what she was doing, Kyla started to ramble out a string of questions she was far too dizzy and emotionally raw to articulate.

Nathaniel didn't answer a single one except the monotone, "I'm fine," he gave her before he lifted her in his arms.

It sent a shock of pain through her body when he held her like that, but Kyla was far too weak and confused to work her way out of his grip. He carried her up the street without a word, and though she wasn't conscious enough to see where they were going, she did take notice of the enormous castle-looking home that he brought her to the front door of at the top of Falcon's Rest.

"Where..." she tried to ask him.

Nathaniel didn't let her finish the question. "Shh...I have to get you inside. Try not to talk."

Kyla didn't understand where they were or what had happened or why she was being carried into this mansion of a home, but she didn't ask him again. Instead she clung to Nathaniel's chest and told herself this was all a dream. It had to be.

Things this crazy didn't happen to her anymore.

Chapter 9

"...playing doctor."

Carrying her quickly down the hallway, Nathaniel brought Kyla into the most lavish washroom she had ever seen. White marble countertops, gold-plated fixtures; even the painting that hung on the wall had to cost more than her entire house.

Nathaniel set her carefully on a red velvet settee that was propped against the wall, and it was only then that Kyla found her voice.

"Where are we?" she asked him confusedly. She didn't know what was happening or what had happened, or know why the boy from the cemetery had decided to play hero tonight. She wasn't entirely convinced she wasn't dreaming, either, because nothing felt real right now.

Nathaniel sat on the cushion beside her and turned Kyla's back so he could examine it. "My uncle's house," he told her.

She struggled to remember anything he had said to her before now. "The uncle you're staying with?" she asked him. Maybe if she kept her mind moving like that then she wouldn't have to think about the blood she could still feel trickling down her back.

Kyla saw Nathaniel's expression in the mirror that spanned the length of the wall. "Looks that good, huh?" she said sarcastically, failing at her efforts to laugh it off and sound brave.

Nathaniel didn't respond.

Ignoring the fact that she looked like she'd just gotten run over by a John Deere tractor, Kyla turned away from the mirror and cringed. She dug her nails into the velvet when he

135

gingerly touched the edge of her shoulders, biting her lip and trying not to scream as her heart pounded out of her chest.

The way it felt to be touched by him, to have that unexplainable heat flood through every inch of her body almost made the pain bearable. But her realization at that feeling terrified her enough that she shoved it back down again, rationing that it was safer to focus on the feeling of a dozen knives sticking into her back right now than the feeling Nathaniel's touch brought over her.

Kyla was probably in shock on some level, and she thought she even remembered him telling her something to that effect when he first brought her in here, because nothing was registering right in her mind. Like how she could trust this boy she didn't even know...who knew an attempted rapist that mysteriously knew her name. A boy whose behavior up to this point had been questionable at best.

Yet even though it went against everything that made sense in her head, she couldn't *not* trust Nathaniel Blake. Being this close to him was indescribably frustrating, if for no other reason than the way he made her feel, and she was convinced it was detrimental to her senses. Maybe she'd lost more blood than she thought or maybe her being in a relative state of shock has something to do with it, but Kyla was literally delirious in his presence.

"How are you with blood?" he asked her.

"I'm okay," she lied.

Nathaniel stood from the seat and moved to an immaculate maple cabinet. "Keep your eyes forward," he told her.

Kyla didn't listen. Instead, she watched him rummage around in the cabinet, and then in a drawer that was filled with enough gauze and tape and hydrogen peroxide to make her think she was in a doctor's office.

"Do this much?" she asked, steadying herself as best she could and telling herself in her head like a recording on repeat not to pass out. She saw him smile out of the corner of her eye.

"Kind of," he said. "I'm a first year med student at Oxford."

"Of course you are," she muttered under her breath. As if he weren't already intimidating enough.

136

It was impressive, the way they both avoided the elephant in the room, though the searing pain in Kyla's back made it somewhat easier for her not to jump headfirst into a game of twenty questions.

Pulling the velvet settee out from the wall and straddling it so his legs were on each side, Nathaniel sat down and arranged the liquids and gauzes and ointments that he had retrieved from the cabinet.

"You don't have to do this," Kyla told him. "I can go to the hospital."

"That won't be necessary," he said confidently. "I'll have you as good as new in no time."

Kyla hesitated for a moment, unsure whether or not she should ask the question that was hanging in front of her, daring her to voice it. Finally she caved.

"Nathaniel, who was that man?"

He froze at the question, then quickly continued whatever he was working with in an attempt to hide his discomfort.

"You said his name," she told him. "And...he *knew* mine. If you know who he is, please, tell me how that's even possible."

When Nathaniel didn't answer her, she glanced in the mirror again and saw his expression, set like stone and unwilling to budge.

"These punctures are relatively deep..." he tried to explain.

"Nathaniel..."

He kept his lips pressed together. "It's a long story," he told her.

Kyla gave him a look. "Do I really look like I'm going anywhere?"

That obviously wasn't what Nathaniel wanted to hear. "Look, Kyla, we'll get into that later, alright? I promise I will handle it. Right now, I just need you to focus on breathing."

That wasn't gonna fly with her and her guess was he knew it. "Where did he go?" she asked him.

Nathaniel sighed and dropped his hands. "I chased him off and lost him in the woods," he said, then he doused the rag he was holding with some strange blue liquid.

Kyla didn't know why, but she didn't believe him. Still, she decided to drop it, feeling far too lightheaded to argue right now.

Nathaniel pressed the rag with the evil blue liquid into her back and she grabbed his leg instinctually, digging her nails into his jeans as if somehow compensating for the pain he was currently inflicting upon her.

"You okay?" he asked.

Her teeth were clenched together. "Uh huh," she said, her nails still digging deep.

She cringed when he tried touching her back again and Nathaniel frowned. Standing up, he walked over to the cabinet and rummaged through a half-dozen pill bottles, then he took a paper cup from a ceramic dispenser next to the sink and filled it with water.

"Open your mouth," he told her.

Kyla looked at him, confused. "What?"

He knelt in front of her and demonstrated what he wanted her to do, dropping two large pills on her tongue when she followed his lead. Then he held the cup to her lips and gently poured the water down her throat until she gave him the signal to stop.

Kyla followed him with her eyes as he crossed the small room again and threw the cup into a shiny gold trash can. "So what'd you just drug me with, doctor?"

"Percocet," he told her. He moved back around behind her again and smiled a little. "Just don't tell anyone I gave them to you."

Kyla almost fell over again, only this time not from the blood loss. Well, not only from the blood loss. She blinked hard a few times, forcing herself to stay upright and conscious and not to think about how much she liked seeing Nathaniel Blake smile.

It became easier when she saw it drop by way of his reflection, but convenient or not, that probably wasn't a good sign.

"I hate to tell you this," he said, "but I'm going to have to cut your shirt off."

138

Kyla stared at him for a moment, knowing she couldn't have heard him right. "Excuse me?"

Nathaniel sighed. "Just your shirt. And pulling it over your head would be too painful. I need to cut it."

Kyla's heart started beating madly then, which upset her for more reasons than one. She had to get a grip here. He was a freakin' doctor, for crying out loud! Still, despite her mental scolding, she had quite a time slowing it down.

Nathaniel looked like he expected her to protest, and for a moment she thought about it. "Okay," she agreed instead, deciding against it. "I never liked this top anyway."

That was a lie. It was her favorite.

Nathaniel looked surprised when she conceded so easily. "I'm sorry," he apologized. "I hate asking you to do this, but I have to clean these wounds properly or they will…"

Kyla cut him off. "I said its fine, doc. Now hurry up and cut off my clothes before I change my mind."

Her attempt at joking made his cheeks flush pink, which she found impossibly adorable.

"Seriously, Nathaniel," she reassured him, "it's okay. I trust you."

He seemed almost as surprised by that as she was, and by the look on his face, confused.

Why *did* she trust him? Kyla didn't trust anyone.

Pulling some scissors from the drawer and carefully cutting the black cotton fabric up the center of her back, Nathaniel kept it pulled away from her skin as best he could, but it was still excruciating. Kyla tried to be brave as she felt the fabric braise against every cut, every bruise, every scrape and every gash, but she couldn't think of another time she had been in so much pain.

"I'm sorry," Nathaniel said remorsefully when she sucked in a sharp breath.

Her voice was strangled. "It's fine."

As soon as he cut through the top, Kyla exhaled for the first time in a minute. Nathaniel set the scissors down in front of him then very slowly, he moved both sides of the fabric away from her back and slid them carefully down her arms. She slipped her arms out of the holes to help him, instinctively holding the remains of her favorite black tank top to her chest.

Nathaniel paused before he touched her again, and when her eyes glanced discreetly to the mirror, she saw him swallow hard and shake his head a little, blinking a few times in an apparent attempt to focus.

Kyla bit her lip and tried not to smile, which became easier when he whipped out a pair of tweezers and used them to yank out a splintering piece of bark that was embedded in her skin. Kyla's eyes shot open wide and she went rigid at the pain, but she didn't make a sound. It hurt too much for her to remember how.

Nathaniel gave her a washrag to bite down on so she wouldn't scream, but that didn't stop the tears from streaming down her face. She was shaking under the intensity of the pain, and also the fire she felt coursing through her as his hands slid across her skin.

Kyla didn't understand it. She didn't know who this boy was that she should feel like that.

"I'm sorry," Nathaniel apologized for what felt like the hundredth time as he pulled an enormous piece of wood from her back. That one actually made her so woozy she started to lose her balance.

Nathaniel caught her just before she fell over. "Easy there," he said, holding her up and rubbing both of her arms with his hands. But even when he set her upright again, her vision began to blur.

"Kyla?" he said softly.

She could feel herself drifting away from consciousness, unable to answer him.

"Kyla?" he said again, only this time more firmly.

Had he said something about her having a concussion earlier? That stalker freak *had* slammed her head against that tree pretty dang hard.

After the third time Nathaniel said her name and she didn't respond, Kyla felt him take her by the shoulders and turn her body toward him, though the feeling was somewhat distant and difficult to distinguish. He slid one of his hands slowly up the back of her neck and pulled her carefully into him, and then suddenly she felt the warmth of his perfect lips on hers.

Kyla had never really given much thought to the expression "time stood still" before. Being the realist she was, she found it a little ridiculous, the idea of time and space slowing down at one specific time for one specific person. And even if no one ever meant it literally, it was the principle of the matter. Like, were they really arrogant enough to speculate that even being possible? But sitting there on that red velvet settee, confused out of her mind, seconds away from losing consciousness and immersed in an unnatural kind of delirium, Kyla James was convinced that time itself had, in fact, stopped moving.

Nathaniel's lips were warm, and softer than she expected them to be. He was careful not to touch her back as his hand cradled her head and careful not to move too suddenly, almost as if he realized he was placing her in danger of a heart attack. But with time slowing to a crawl and everything spinning around her in a diffused sort of haze, nothing had the chance to register in her mind before he pulled away from her again.

Her first instinct was to grab him and pull him back to her lips, but fortunately the shock that she was currently experiencing prevented her from doing anything quite so rash.

And people said going into shock was a bad thing.

Kyla stared at him in a daze, her eyes no doubt enormous, but Nathaniel's expression was completely unreadable. Then after what felt like an eternity of silence, she finally managed to find her voice.

"What...was *that*?"

A nervous half-smile crept up on Nathaniel's lips, but he forced it to drop by coughing once into his hand. "You can't fall asleep, Kyla," he told her in his detached doctor tone. "I'm sure you are aware of the dangers of a concussion."

She stared at him blankly, his words not computing in her mind. When he looked away after that and busied himself with the mess he'd made in cleaning her up, she gaped at him in awe.

"*What*?!" she finally exclaimed.

Again, Nathaniel almost smiled at her indignation, but again he managed to stop himself. "What do you mean what?" he asked innocently. He was almost as bad at playing dumb as she was.

Kyla was so angry she could feel her face starting to burn. "You...you can't let me fall asleep since you think I might have a concussion...so you *kiss* me?"

Nathaniel rolled his eyes. "Well I could have slapped you, but I thought I'd spare you the unnecessary pain."

Kyla was mortified. Standing up quickly (a little too quickly by her guess since the room started to spin when she did) she folded her arms across her chest and glared at him.

Nathaniel tried to hide his amusement, but he didn't try hard enough.

"You think this is *funny*?" she demanded.

"A little, yeah," he admitted. Then another kind of smile came on his face as he looked at her.

Kyla scowled and grabbed the Egyptian cotton towel hanging next to her on the wall, holding it in front of her chest and glaring at him harshly. But before she could let Nathaniel Blake know exactly what she thought of him, everything started to distort in her vision, almost like she was looking through some sort of freakish lens filter that made everything white and fuzzy.

And then she was down. Again.

Nathaniel grabbed her before she cracked her head against the countertop, probably figuring it would be counterproductive if he had to bandage up a head wound after all the trouble he'd just gone to.

"Let me go," Kyla demanded in a voice so weak it was pathetic.

Nathaniel scoffed. "You make it sound like I *wanted* to kiss you. I'm a doctor, sweetheart. I do everything in the name of science."

That was *it*. "Ooh, you have some nerve..."

She tried to break out of his hold, but he was much too strong and she was much too disoriented for the attempt to be successful.

"Would you please hold still?" he asked her calmly, looking down at her with his hypnotically gorgeous eyes.

Not fair.

Kyla ignored her throbbing back and stared up at him dizzily. "Put me down," she said. She had meant it to sound threatening, but her words came out in a whisper.

"Will you behave?" Nathaniel asked. "I don't need you getting all worked up and fainting on me again."

"I didn't faint!" she protested. Nathaniel gave her a look and she scowled. "Yes, Daddy, I'll behave," she sneered sarcastically.

He couldn't hide his smile on that one. "Good girl," he said, then he helped her sit back on the settee, which he had already cleared of all pain-inducing medical supplies.

Sighing in exasperation, Kyla leaned the back of her head against the wall and closed her eyes. It would be a lot easier for her to make her point if she weren't so dizzy.

"Eyes open," Nathaniel said, taking her hand in his and shaking it a little. A jolt of heat raced through her fingertips when he touched her, and this time quite frankly, it pissed her off.

What *was* that?

Kyla pulled her hand out of his. "I need to go home."

Nathaniel smiled at her patronizingly. "Oh, you think so? And just how do you plan to stay awake then?"

She narrowed her eyes at him. "By envisioning the thousand ways I'd like to inflict pain on you right now."

Nathaniel laughed. "You're funny."

"I'm serious."

"Either way, it doesn't matter," he said. "You can't go home right now. I didn't go through all this trouble just to let you slip into a coma and never wake up again."

He probably didn't mean to spark her curiosity, but whether intentional or not, he did.

"Would it really make that much of a difference to you if I never woke up?" she asked.

Nathaniel stared into her then in the last way she expected him to. "Yes," he told. "It really would."

Kyla felt her heart pound. "I have to go," she told him again. She wasn't asking his permission, she was trying to convince herself.

When she finally stood to her feet, she found that she was surprisingly able to retain her balance.

"Kyla…" Nathaniel started to say in a more serious tone. She cut him off quickly.

"Do you really want me to stay, Nathaniel? Are you really that anxious to answer all the questions I have?"

She was met by silence. "Yeah, that's what I thought," she mumbled.

"Fine," he said flatly. "Go."

Kyla squared her shoulders as she opened the door, telling herself she could make it home without dying or passing out.

"But first," Nathaniel said, standing up and stepping toward her, "I'll be needing this back."

He grabbed the towel she was still holding up in front of her and she gasped, covering herself with her arms as her mouth fell open. He didn't even try to hide his smile this time.

"You…you…" she started to say, but there was no word harsh enough. Then a familiar, hazy shade of white decided to take over her vision and everything around her fell to black.

*N*athaniel didn't know what had possessed him. He only knew there was no way he could have actually just done what he just did…and that he had never felt anything like it in his life.

Fortunately, his rationale kicked in and he'd managed to pull himself away from Kyla's lips before he did something even more asinine than that. It was harder for him than he expected. The feeling was more intense than he expected, too.

The moment it seized him, Nathaniel knew he'd made a mistake. He also knew he had to fix it, but when he gave Kyla the jackassed excuse that sounded like something Caleb might say and got her worked up to the point that she lost

144

consciousness again, he questioned if he might have taken it too far.

Lifting her in his arms, Nathaniel slipped into the hallway and carried her through his uncle's house, thinking he probably could have toned it down a notch. He felt guilty for provoking her and finding so much amusement in how red her face turned as she got madder and madder, but aside from his guilt, the apprehension he felt over this whole situation weighed down on him even more.

He didn't like taking Kyla away from here, where he knew he could protect her, but Nathaniel knew in order to keep things as uncomplicated as possible, he had to get her home.

As if any of this could be made less complicated.

Nathaniel knew it wouldn't be worth the risk involved to deliver her to her house the easy way. He had also broken the "no shifting into Naphil form" rule that Seth had explicitly laid out for him enough lately, so instead he resorted to carrying her. There was so much inconvenience involved in following the rules, but such was the nature of being human, he supposed. Or at least acting human, anyway.

Holding Kyla's limp, unconscious body in his arms, Nathaniel made his way toward the blue-roofed condo at the end of the street. Her head fell into his chest and she mumbled a little as he walked up Ponderosa Way, and for a moment he was worried that she might wake up. Luckily, she didn't, she just nuzzled against him and buried her face into his arm.

Nathaniel trembled when he felt her, then he quickly shook his head to try and shake away the feeling. Looking up at the second-story window to the left of the deck, he frowned when he realized he wouldn't be able to get her in there, at least not as long as he followed said rules. Then he realized there was a smaller window on a different wall that could very possibly lead into the same room.

That one was accessible by way of a lower-level roof.

Nathaniel was up on the deck in less than three seconds, keeping Kyla steady as he held her one-armed against his chest and grabbed the edge of the blue metal roof with his

145

free hand. Pulling himself up, along with the semi-unconscious girl he was still holding, he used his foot as leverage and moved soundlessly to the roof.

As it turned out, he was right. This other window did lead into Kyla's room. And fortunately for him, she had left it unlocked.

Donovan stood silently with Balak, hidden in the trees on Ponderosa Way. Both of their eyes were set on the road running horizontally in front of them, and they both kept human form as they took in the too perfect to be real picture of Nathaniel Blake sneaking the human girl through her second-story bedroom window.

Donovan grinned maliciously, though his subordinate hardly shared in his excitement. He knew Balak was frustrated by his obsession with Nathaniel Blake, as many of those were who did not know the power this one held. But Donovan couldn't care less about the frustrations of those beneath him. To him, they were merely means to an end.

Most things were with him, be they human…or otherwise.

Neither of them spoke a word to each other. They both knew absolute silence was the key to their advantage here, and that was something neither of them was willing to risk losing now that Nathaniel's carelessness had placed them in such an opportune position.

It surprised Donovan that Nathaniel hadn't discerned their presence when they first began to follow him tonight, but now it made sense. Now it all made sense, and as far as he was concerned, things could not have turned more in their favor.

Donovan motioned for Balak to leave with him and the two made their way out of earshot and of any discernable distance.

"Is this really necessary?" Balak asked when they were free to talk.

Donovan answered him with a flat, "Yes."

"And you're sure he's really worth all this effort?"

Shooting the fool a glaring look, Donovan was tempted to strike him across the face. "Without him, all we have labored for here will be for nothing. We *need* this one, Balak."

"And how do you propose on turning him?" Balak asked. "The boy has made it clear that he has no intention of joining us."

Donovan closed his eyes and took a breath, controlling himself before he answered him. "Do you remember the story of Adam and Eve?" he finally said.

Balak made a face. "Forgive me, my lord, but I do not find much use in reading Bible stories."

A patronizing smile moved onto Donovan's lips. "On the contrary, dear Balak. Such is the history of our existence, and it would do you well to know it."

His subordinate appeared irritated by this.

"When Eve gave in to the serpent," Donovan explained, "she was acting out of foolishness...as most women do. But it was not the same that caused Adam to fall."

He glanced up at the tree towering over his head, envisioning the serpent in its branches, shaking in the thrill of his own imagination.

"Adam made a choice," he said. "He knew full well what this choice would cost him, but he could not bear to be separated from her. He chose a woman over the God who created him, displaying for all to see the ultimate weakness of man."

Balak fidgeted nervously, avoiding his leader's gaze, and Donovan pretended not to catch it.

"It was a woman who incited the fall," he said, "and it will be a woman again who drives the purpose we labor for."

"And what is the purpose to which you refer?" Balak asked. "You draw us into many."

Donovan gave him a look with a warning behind it. "The purpose of destroying the Resitore, this pathetic resistance that believes they can stand against our power. The purpose of bringing a halt to the times that are said to be set for the destruction of our kind. Pick one, Balak. Pick any single purpose we have ever worked to achieve...Kyla James is going to accomplish it for us single-handedly."

Balak kept his arms folded across his bulging chest. "And you do not think that is too bold to say? She is just a girl."

Donovan smiled at his ignorance. "Not to Nathaniel."

He stopped to revel in the beauty of the moment. "She is a gift to us, Balak. I could see it in his eyes when I first spoke to him of her, when we watched him look after her the night he found her in the cemetery. I could see it as he fought me for her even tonight. This one is our way to Nathaniel Blake."

Balak was still agitated. "And how do you plan to use her against him? She is protected."

"Not the way she used to be," Donovan told him. "And let us not forget our greatest asset."

His mind was filled with the image of hope in the form of a dark-haired beauty. Her ruby lips...her delicious curves...her emerald eyes...

Balak's face contorted into a grimace. "Don't remind me," he grumbled.

*S*etting Kyla carefully on her bed, Nathaniel forced himself to look away from her the moment he felt the compulsion not to, and as a result his eyes fell on the black and white drawings adorning her walls. He was caught off guard at the sight of them, as it was hardly the image he expected to be met with, but there was something intriguing about them. There had to be a hundred black and white drawings up there, every one of which showed such darkness and pain, such a depth into the soul of this one little girl. He was fascinated by it.

Analyzing the drawings, Nathaniel began to see the same coldness he'd felt from the moment he'd first met her. The things he saw in her then, the anger that didn't match what he'd discerned of her heart, the evidence of this could be seen in every blackened stroke of charcoal. He just didn't understand why she was so angry.

That was when he saw a handful of envelopes in the waste basket beside her desk, large, unopened envelopes with University emblems stamped onto them. They were all addressed to Kyla James.

148

Immediately Nathaniel's mind flashed back to the name on the headstone he found her kneeling at in the cemetery. *Darrell James.*

"I don't come here out of pleasure if that's what you mean." He remembered her words and the pain behind her voice as she'd spoken them.

Nathaniel cringed, not believing he hadn't pieced this together sooner. He was her father. Darrell James was her father.

Looking again at the darkened drawings that hung from her walls, he saw in them what he couldn't before. A cry for help, cry for hope...and something else he was in no way prepared for.

He began to see himself.

Nathaniel dropped his eyes quickly, refusing to feel what he was starting to feel. But then he was distracted by the only trace of color anywhere in sight, a single framed picture next to the envelope from the university.

A picture of Kyla and a shaggy-haired boy he recognized immediately.

Nathaniel felt a tightness in his chest as he picked it up to look at it more closely. It struck him, the way she looked in this picture, and reminded him of the one he had found in the boy's room before. She looked so different...so happy.

Staring at the photograph, he felt uneasy, though he wasn't sure why. He didn't understand this feeling that had taken him over, but he knew at all costs that he must rid himself of it. Nathaniel knew he had made a mistake, that he never should have gotten this close. But as much as he knew he had to distance himself from her, he despised the very thought of it.

She weakened him, though he still had yet to understand how, and even as the thought came to him, he questioned if the blame really fell to her. Somewhere inside him, Nathaniel knew his own weakness had caused this. He just wasn't willing to admit it. Weakness was not a thing that was acceptable to him. Maybe to the others, but not to him.

Looking down on Kyla where she lay on her bed, Nathaniel brushed the hair out of her eyes softly and stared into her face. He didn't understand how he could be so taken, so drawn to and so mesmerized by this one little human girl, but as he touched her silken skin and felt the heat that rushed through his hands when he did, he was captivated.

"Goodbye, Kyla James," he whispered softly as he kissed her forehead. Then he left her quickly before he could change his mind, jumping out of her second-story window and landing soundly on his feet.

Chapter 10

"…phone call."

Kyla woke the next morning in searing pain. Her mouth opened wide as it tore through every inch of her body, causing her to question what point there was to prescription drugs if they didn't even work. Then again, who knew what Nathaniel Blake had drugged her with? The freak could have chloroformed her last night for all she knew.

Kyla felt nauseous at the thought. Everything in her mind was so jumbled and confused she hardly even remembered what happened to her. She would have thought she was hung-over, except that she didn't drink. Then all in one instant, she was flooded with a thousand different pictures and memories and feelings at once.

Suddenly she wished she had just been drinking.

Kyla's mind spun in intense circles, moving and twisting in so many directions it was difficult to lock in on any one image and impossible to determine which of the things she was seeing now had actually happened. She remembered the dark, creepy man. She remembered…*ugh*. She remembered him *licking* her neck. So gross.

And she remembered Nathaniel.

The way he had fought for her…the way he had moved. The way he had thrown the man he called Donovan against that rock as if he were weightless. As if he were…

Ow!

A piercing stab hit her side when she sat up too quickly. Looking down at her stomach (which was still bare since Nathaniel hacked up her tank top last night) she cringed at the sight of the purple and yellow baseball-sized bruise that had formed below her ribcage.

When had that even happened?

Kyla glanced quickly to the clock on her bed stand. She had an hour before she had to be at work. Just one hour to either hide every gash and scrape and bruise on her body or fabricate a believable cover story.

Yeah, good luck with that one.

That was when the thought hit her that she was in her bedroom. Looking around the room in confusion, Kyla realized she didn't know how she'd gotten here. She remembered being with Nathaniel at the place he told her was his uncle's house, but she couldn't remember how she had ended up here last night.

Surely he hadn't...

Kyla shook the thought away, not wanting to even entertain that. It wasn't safe, and right now she needed what was safe to her.

Grabbing her phone from her bed stand, she pressed number one on her speed dial before she gave herself time to think, but just as had been the case every time she'd done that lately, Caden didn't pick up.

Kyla's nausea hit her in full at the sound of his voicemail message. At first she thought about ending the call like she had every other time he hadn't answered her in the past week, but when the message was over and the obnoxious beeping noise sounded in her ear, she found herself talking before she realized what she was doing.

"You know, Caden," she spoke brashly into her phone, "usually when people call you, they have a reason for it. Just thought I'd let you know since you seem to have lost that knowledge somewhere in the back of that thick head of yours..."

Kyla stopped, hardly believing she was saying this out loud. She hung up quickly in hopes of preventing herself from making it any worse, which was probably what she should have done in the first place.

Breathing in deeply, (despite the fact that the intake of oxygen brought a sharp stabbing pain along with it) she forced herself to calm down and walked over to the full-length mirror in the corner of her room. She felt sick when she saw her reflection, both because she had never looked so awful and because everything she saw confirmed that she hadn't dreamed about what happened last night.

Kyla didn't have the courage (or the stomach) to turn around and look at her back; the bruises on her arms and her ribcage were atrocious enough. But how was it even possible that her head didn't hurt?

She touched her forehead as she tried to figure it out, then she shoved the thought aside and told herself she would deal with that later. Right now she needed to focus on getting a shower and figuring out how to fix this mess before Matthew or Loni saw her.

Showering ended up taking a lot more time than she wanted. It hurt a lot more than Kyla wanted, too, but that much was expected. She tried to find gauze and tape and anything sufficient for replacing the doctorish ointments and creams Nathaniel had used on her, but all she came up with were a bunch of knee-sized Band-Aids and a tube of Neosporin that looked about five years old.

She and Matthew didn't hurt themselves nearly enough.

It was pathetic and agonizing, the job she did on her back, but she didn't really have a choice. Going to the doctor meant explaining what had happened, which meant involving the police and Loni. So, yeah…no.

Wearing a black long-sleeved turtleneck on a ninety-degree day was not Kyla's idea of a good time, but despite her discomfort and the inconvenience of the situation as a whole, there was one thought in her mind that overrode over the rest.

What happened to Nathaniel Blake?

The phone rang once and Alexa bit her lip, twice and she started to get nervous. She shoved aside the feeling and told herself she had to do this.

Caden had to know.

When the phone rang a third time, Alexa frowned. She debated hanging up and trying again in a few hours, but then she talked herself into staying on the line until his voicemail picked up.

A second and a half later, a voice sounded on the other end instead. "Hello?"

Alexa opened her mouth to speak, but something stopped her.

"Hello?" Caden said again. Her mind scrambled to think of what to say to him, but she couldn't lock in on anything. "Lex?" he finally asked. "Is that you?"

She took a deep breath. "Yes."

"What's going on?"

She kept her eyes fixed on the windows at the back of the house. "I don't know," she said nervously.

Why was she so afraid to tell him the truth?

Caden paused for a moment, and she knew he was trying to feel out what was going on with her. "Talk to me, Lex," he said. "What happened?"

She took a deep breath and decided to get straight with him. "Have you been avoiding Kyla?"

Caden didn't expect the question. She could feel it when his heart sped up, and she imagined him looking side to side in anxious compulsion. He always did that when he felt cornered.

"I don't know what you…"

"Caden…" she cut him off.

He fell quiet. Obviously he knew lying to her wouldn't do him any good, and as he stayed on the line with his sister in silence, her suspicions were proven true.

Suddenly, Alexa felt nauseated. "I warned you," she said, making a face at the thought of what this could affect. "I told you not to push her away."

His voice was quiet. "I know…"

"Why would you do this?" she asked him, though she wasn't sure if she actually expected an answer or if she was just throwing the question out in her frustration. "Why would you do this now?"

That caught her brother's attention.

154

"What do you mean *now*?" he asked her cautiously. There was an edge of fear to his voice, and rightly so. "Alexa," he said, "what *happened*?"

She grimaced at the thought. "Just call her," she told him, then she started to hang up. Before she could do it, though, Caden stopped her.

"Lexa?" he asked in a small voice. "Is everything okay?"

She hesitated when she heard the fear in him, and she didn't respond for a full five seconds. "No," she finally told him. "I don't think it is."

*C*aden Howell could feel his heart beating at an abnormally fast pace when he pressed the "end" button on his phone after his little sister hung up on him. She didn't mean it to seem rude, that was just Alexa. Either way, he stood there in the apartment he'd been living in for the past year in Tennessee, running his fingers through his messy brown hair and staring intently at the wall without even realizing that he was.

Looking at the "new voicemail" icon at the bottom and center of the screen on his phone, he tried to find a reason why he didn't have to listen to it; the same as he had since it first appeared there that morning. But Caden was running out of excuses not to talk to his best friend, and it wasn't like he believed the ones he came up with anyway. He knew exactly why he wasn't listening to that voicemail, and it was the same reason he wasn't picking up those calls. The same reason he wasn't returning them.

He couldn't handle hearing Kyla's voice right now.

He had been sick from missing her...physically sick. And he knew if he talked to her for even a moment, he wouldn't be able to stop himself from telling her everything that had happened here. There was a good chance he wouldn't be able to stop himself from getting on a plane and flying back home to Colorado to see her, either, especially if he heard in her again what he'd been hearing in her voice for the past few months. He couldn't take hearing again how much she needed him.

Kyla didn't even realize how she talked to him, the way she would snap at him without reason and cut him with her words. He wasn't even sure she could hear herself do it. It had been like that for almost two years now, and while it was definitely wearing on Caden, it didn't hurt him for the reasons someone might expect it to. It just hurt him that he couldn't fix her.

For an entire year before he came out here, he had been in agony, watching her slowly slip away as she rejected everything that was even remotely comparable to love. Kyla didn't recognize it, how much she pushed him away in the year after her father died. It was almost like there was a three-way disconnect between her mind and her heart and her actions. She would say things...horrible things, and then have no memory of what she'd spoken even five seconds later.

And it killed him. Not because he took offense to the things she said, but because she wouldn't let him love her. She wouldn't share her pain when all Caden wanted was for her to fall into his arms and let him take it, or at least part of it so she wouldn't have to carry it alone. But the harder he tried, the more she lashed out, the harder she pushed; the angrier she became. Always deaf to her own words and blind to the knives she would cut him with.

Kyla didn't realize how clearly he could hear it, even when she tried to mask it and hold her tongue. Caden could always feel how angry she was at him for leaving her. And every time he did it made him sick.

It was painful, not being able to tell her why; letting her make assumptions that stole whatever trust she used to have in him, but knowing if he told her the truth he could lose a whole lot more than that. He couldn't tell her what he was doing out here, because she wouldn't understand until it was done. She wouldn't be able to see until she could actually hear it, which was why he couldn't talk to her right now. Before, it was bad enough, but with how badly he wanted to get out of here now after everything that had been happening to him, Caden didn't trust himself to hold back from her anymore. He was afraid that in his desire for her comfort, he

156

would tell her too much, and that she'd be scared off before he could even give this a chance to work.

With all the stress his producer had been putting on him, especially in the past few weeks, Caden had faced the temptation on more than one occasion to bail on this project altogether, this album he had been working on for what felt like his entire life. In reality it had only been eleven and a half months, but he could hardly remember a time when he wasn't completely consumed by it. And everything he did remember of his life before involved *her*, which only added to his desire to get out of Nashville as fast as he could pack his bags.

With that temptation already biting at his heels, Caden knew talking to Kyla right now would push him over the edge. It wouldn't matter if she was so excited to hear his voice she was giddy or so mad at him for avoiding her that she gave him a verbal thrashing. Either way, it would ruin him. He would be back by her side in the blink of an eye, and then everything he had sacrificed, all he had done…everything he had been through out here would be for absolutely nothing.

Caden felt ill, thinking of how he hadn't explained any of it; why he'd really left or what he was really doing out here…what this stupid album was even for. The excuse he'd given her was a cheap copout, and Kyla had to know that. At least he hoped she did. If she really thought he could leave her for something as trivial to him as a music career, that would break his heart. But the longer he'd been gone, the more Caden got the feeling that that was exactly what she thought, and even though he wanted to more than anything, he couldn't tell her otherwise. Not without telling her everything.

That was why he had to stay here and finish this, so that one day he would be able to.

Taking a deep breath, he dialed the number for his voicemail, knowing he couldn't put it off any longer. Whatever Alexa was talking about, something was obviously going on. He could feel that even without his sister telling him, and that feeling was only confirmed when he heard the anger in Kyla's voice as it came through the speaker of his phone. Caden cringed at the sound, feeling even sicker than before.

She was never going to forgive him for this.

*I*t was raining in Woodland Park. Watching the water stream down the glass as she stared out her bedroom window, Kyla James tried to distract herself from the pain at the center of her back. But even the rain didn't comfort her tonight.

After the knockdown drag-out of a fight she'd just had with Loni over her habit of randomly disappearing over the last few days, Kyla was not having a good day. Luckily the fight hadn't gotten physical or she knew she wouldn't have been able to keep her mangled back a secret, but it still wasn't pleasant by any means.

Part of her felt like she was making a mistake, that she should have gone to the police and reported the attack, but another part of her...a stronger part felt like that would be a mistake. Watching the raindrops slide down her window, she had to admit that her reason for the latter was wrapped up in her unexplainable desire to protect Nathaniel Blake, the mysterious boy she had no right to trust. And even though she hadn't seen him in over twenty-four hours, Kyla was no less capable of getting him out of her mind.

There was just something about him, even beyond the electricity she felt at his touch and the way he weakened her with every glance of his maddening sapphire eyes. There was something he wasn't telling her, something about this Donovan character that he knew and was intentionally keeping from her; which was probably the reason he'd gone missing in action.

Kyla wished it didn't bother her so much, but every hour that went by that she didn't see him, that Nathaniel didn't show up when she least expected him to and do something to leave her completely unhinged, she felt like she was going to go out of her mind. That was why she was here now at her window with her drawing pad in hand, sketching every detail she remembered of his angelic face. And those eyes...*gah*, those eyes.

She moved the charcoal carefully across the paper, searching her memory as she drew. Kyla felt torn, unable to make up her mind about what she was supposed to feel. One moment she would was glad she hadn't seen him, thinking of how arrogant and presumptuous Nathaniel had acted at their last encounter and how she had wanted nothing more than to haul off and slap him across the face. And the next moment she would become frustrated, realizing that even thinking about how angry he made her still meant that she was thinking about him.

Kyla hated it, too. That boy was the last kind of person she needed to have in her life, she knew that full well, but through all of her rationalizing and every logical thought, she still found herself at this window, obsessively drawing picture after picture of Nathaniel Blake, of the hideous man called Donovan...of everything that happened that night.

Wincing at another sharp pain in her back, Kyla made her way carefully downstairs and over to the medicine cabinet in the kitchen. Looking through it, all she could find was a bottle of Advil. Frowning and wishing she had something stronger, she threw a few pills into her mouth and swallowed them with water. Then she turned around and gasped when she saw Matthew standing in front of her.

Kyla jumped about a foot off the ground. "You scared me," she said, giving him a nervous smile. He didn't smile back.

"Kyla, what's going on?" her brother asked her point blank.

She wasn't used to him being so direct. "What are you talking about?" she asked.

"Alexa..." he started to say. Then he stopped as if questioning whether or not he should.

"Alexa what?" Kyla asked tensely.

Matthew frowned. "She said something happened."

That was not the answer she wanted to hear.

"She's worried about you," he told her.

Shifting uncomfortably and painfully, Kyla was careful as she responded to him. "Look Matty, whatever Alexa said, I wouldn't worry about it. There is nothing wrong."

He wrinkled his forehead, looking frustrated.

"I promise you don't have to worry about me," she reassured him. "I'm fine."

Matthew's eyes stayed fixed on the hardwood kitchen floor. "But she's never wrong," he said softly.

Kyla wasn't sure her little brother had ever said anything that worried her so much.

"What exactly did she say?" she asked him.

"That you're in danger," Matthew told her.

Kyla tried not to react to that.

"She said..." he stopped again.

"What, Matt?" she asked him. But before he could answer her, they both heard the basement door open.

And that was where the conversation ended.

Moving quickly back up to her bedroom, Kyla closed the door and locked it behind her, trying to explain away this inopportune reality she was now faced with.

Alexa didn't know...she couldn't. That just wasn't possible.

But through all of her reasoning, Kyla couldn't escape the familiar gnawing feeling in the pit of her stomach that told her she was wrong, the feeling that reminded her of the truth she'd been running from for almost two years.

Her eyes fell onto her bed and the drawings that lay there. Walking slowly over to them, Kyla lifted the most recent one into her hands. It was only halfway done, but even in its partial state of completion, it still managed to creep her out.

Did she really draw this?

She was struck by a thought as she stared at it, a memory from several years before. Moving across her room and over to her closet, she reached behind some boxes that were stacked in the far right corner beneath her winter coats. Kyla shoved them aside and pulled something out from behind them.

It was a leather-bound drawing folder, the brown one her father had given her for her sixteenth birthday. She'd never gotten the chance to use it before he died. And after...well...after, she'd shoved it to the back of her closet where it had been covered with dust ever since. She hadn't been willing to look at it before, not wanting to remember.

Kyla still didn't want to remember, but she needed it now.

Brushing off the dust that clung to the cover, she slipped the abstract drawings inside and tied the chord at its face. Then she slid her drawing supplies back under her bed and tucked the folder between her mattresses where she knew no one would find it.

A sharp pain shot through her back again and Kyla looked instinctively back out through her window. It was raining harder now.

And she still couldn't get Nathaniel's face out of her mind.

By seven o'clock on a Friday evening, Kyla had just about had it. She was sick of obsessing over that stupid boy and wondering where he'd gone, and also completely unable to stop herself from continuing in this obsession. She had tried to get her mind off of it, but so far nothing had worked. Anything she attempted only ended in failure.

At the moment, she was standing over her bed again, staring at the dark impressionistic drawings she had slipped into her father's drawing folder, telling herself to shove it back under her mattress and forget about it. It did her a whole lot of no good, too.

But then something did distract her enough to pull her attention away. The sound of a car pulling up the street.

Making her way curiously to the window, Kyla looked out to see who was there, but even though it had stopped raining, it was too dark for her to tell. She scampered down the stairs and out the door, anxious for the distraction. At that point she wouldn't have cared if it was a Jehovah's Witness.

When she leaned over the railing to see who it was, Kyla was surprised by what she saw. Squinting into the dark, she saw a rail thin boy with messy black hair and glasses making his way toward her.

"Cody?" she asked.

"Hey, Kyla," he greeted her nervously.

She tried to come up with any reason why he would be here, but quickly gave up the effort. "What are you doing here?" she asked him.

He gave her a classic Cody Fletcher smile. "Just wanted to stop by and say hi," he said.

161

Kyla knew there was more to it than that. "For real," she said, "what are you doing here?"

Cody shoved his hands into the pockets of his black skinny jeans. "Alright, so maybe I was a little worried about you."

Kyla looked at him curiously. "Why?"

He shrugged a little. "I don't know. I haven't seen you in a while and I wanted to make sure you were okay." He paused for a moment when she didn't respond. "Plus, Caden wanted me to check up on you."

The words stabbed her and immediately Kyla tensed up. Her instinctive reaction was a knee-jerk, *why the hell would he care*? Then a sinking feeling hit her heart that she really didn't want to feel right now. It messed with her more than she wanted to let it, but she tried to play it off so that Cody wouldn't catch on.

It was pretty obvious that he did, though. The boy had a 153 IQ; what did she expect? Cody eyed her skeptically and she knew he saw the change in her countenance. He looked worried about it, too.

"I'm headed to Trace's," he told her. "You wanna come with me?"

She raised an eyebrow. "Trace's?"

"For practice," he said. "The guys are already there."

Kyla hesitated. "I don't know…"

Trace McGallagher was one of the last people she wanted to see right now. Or ever, for that matter. Sure, they had maintained an arguable level of friendship for the past several years, but frankly, the guy was an ass.

"Come on, Kyla, the guys really want to see you," Cody tried to persuade her. "Plus, we have some new stuff we haven't played for anyone and we need an expert opinion."

She gave him a playful smirk. "Oh really? An expert opinion, huh?"

"Yep," he said. "Really."

She could see even through his playfulness that Cody was worried about her. He'd done this before since Caden had been gone, coming up with any excuse he could to get her out of the house and around other people, which was a bit ironic considering that for half his life, Cody Fletcher had been the definition of a recluse. She also knew he only did it when Caden asked him to.

Kyla rolled her eyes at him. Normally she would have stayed guarded and given Cody an excuse, but glancing up the road in the direction of Falcon's Rest, she realized she needed to get away…to do anything right now that would get her mind off Nathaniel Blake.

"You know what," she told him, "maybe I should."

Cody grinned excitedly and she walked with him out to his Toyota, not even bothering to tell Loni or Matthew where she was going. Matthew could always call her, and Loni…well, Loni didn't deserve to know.

Either way, Kyla was in his car in a matter of seconds.

She didn't talk much as he drove her up the road toward the McGallagher's massive estate. Too many thoughts and questions moving through her mind that threatened the nice little guard she'd put up over her heart, the one that was created out of her telling herself he didn't care about her anymore. Ineffective as it may have been, she was growing fond of that guard, and now what? He suddenly gets worried about her again? What was that?

Kyla frowned when she realized how close Trace's house was to Falcon's Rest. It was a few blocks over, sure, but still near enough to the place she didn't want to be thinking about that it got her thinking about it again.

"What's wrong?" Cody asked when he saw her expression.

She kept looking out the window. "Just wondering if it's gonna start raining again," Kyla told him.

"Right, because that sort of thing always concerns you so much," he laughed.

She forced herself to turn back to him and give him a smile. "I'm fine," she said. "Really."

He didn't buy it, but he didn't say anything else, either. That was one of the great things about Cody Fletcher. He was such a pacifist that he never pushed anything.

Kyla could hear the music coming from the basement as they drove down the McGallagher's driveway. The entire thing was laid with stone, and it wound around for nearly a hundred feet before it reached their five-car garage. But that was the case with most of the homes up here.

Ridiculous.

When Cody rang the doorbell, a woman with a stern expression (whom Kyla had never seen before) answered it quickly, one of Mrs. McGallagher's maids. Knowing Trace's mother, she'd already been through half a dozen maids since the last time Kyla was here over a year ago with Caden. This one obviously was one of the less-friendly ones.

It was awkward following the woman down to the basement, and somehow Kyla almost felt like she and Cody were inconveniencing her; which was really stupid considering that it was the woman's job to tend to visitors. Kyla was probably just nervous.

Trace looked up from his bass when the maid opened the door to the basement, and Kyla thought it a little rude that she wouldn't knock first. If she were to guess, this one wasn't going to have a job for very long.

Trace and Zeke, the drummer of the band with the wild red hair and a severe case of ADHD, both stopped playing when they saw the door open, but PJ was a little less observant. He kept hammering away at his guitar a good ten seconds after Cody stepped through the doorway.

"Bout time you got here," Trace scoffed. "What took you so long, Skippy?"

Kyla frowned at the nickname. She'd always hated that one. He'd been using it on Cody since they were in second grade, though in the past ten years she'd forgotten why.

"Sorry," Cody told him. "I had to make a detour."

He stepped out of the way so Kyla could walk through the door, leaving her with no choice but to face them.

As soon as Trace saw her, he gave PJ a good hard smack in the head and the boy immediately went off on him in a string of unintelligible Korean. Not that intelligible Korean would have been any easier for them to understand.

Walking cautiously though the doorway, Kyla forced a smile. "Sorry to crash the party," she apologized. "I was practically threatened."

A smile grew on Trace's face, and much as she expected, he eyed her not so subtly up and down. "Nice work, Skippy," he told Cody as the boy worked his way through the set-up to get behind his keyboard.

Kyla sneered at him and PJ gave her a nod. "S'up, Kyla," he said.

She smiled at the newest addition to the band, the Korean once-exchange student who had recently found his calling in life to involve guitar thrashing and metal breakdowns. He'd moved here permanently three months ago. None of the guys had the heart to tell him that just because he was in a band in America, that didn't instantly guarantee him fame.

"I hear you're working on a new song?" Kyla asked him.

PJ was about to answer her when Trace interrupted. "Easy, tiger," he said. He still hadn't looked away from her. "We'll get to that in a minute. I'm not done lookin' at you yet."

Kyla didn't have time to threaten him or dismember any part of his body before PJ stepped in valiantly to defend her.

"Yeah well, maybe you shouldn't look at her like that," he said in his thick Korean accent.

Zeke knocked the beanie off his head and a game of keep-away immediately ensued. Kyla sighed and shook her head. Some things never changed.

When Zeke finally threw the beanie back at PJ, she told him with a sympathetic smile, "You really need to stop letting them pick on you, Peej."

PJ was disgruntled as he put the thing back on his head. "Just wait," he said in as threatening a voice as a five-foot, four-inch Korean boy could muster. "One these days I show you my martial arts."

Kyla smiled at his broken English. He still had a hard time with contractions.

Trace and Zeke about lost it at that, and Kyla couldn't help but laugh with them, despite how serious she knew PJ was. She had seen him in competition before, and personally she was eager for the day the kid finally snapped and let those two idiots have it. Judging by the gleam in Cody's eyes, she was pretty sure his thought process was somewhere in line with hers, too.

After another five minutes of bickering, the guys got it together enough to play the song Cody had told her about. Kyla was still laughing at them when she went to sit on a stool at the mini bar to watch them. It was always like this when they practiced. Over a year since she'd been here and everything was exactly the same, minus one very obvious factor that she was trying not to think about.

She tried to keep her focus on Cody where he stood behind his keyboard and sang into the microphone, hoping that would be enough of a distraction. The boy was musically insane, a literal prodigy, but watching him sing in place of Caden just felt...*wrong* to her. Kyla didn't want to think of it that way, but she couldn't help it. And as she sat on that barstool listening to him, all she could see in her mind was how Caden used to stand there with them.

It was so vivid she could almost hear his voice instead of Cody's.

Kyla felt a sharp pang in her chest that came on her so fast it actually cut off her breath. The guys were still in the middle of the song, but she couldn't wait for them to finish.

"I'm sorry," she mumbled to no one in particular. Then she slipped off the barstool and bolted for the door.

"Kyla!" Cody called after her.

She didn't slow down.

Making her way out to the walkout back porch just off of the McGallagher's basement, she finally stopped and put her hands on her hips.

Cody ran up to her. "Are you okay?" he asked worriedly.

Kyla immediately felt guilty. "I'm sorry, Cody," she said. "I just can't do this right now."

"Can't do what?" he asked her. He didn't get it at all.

She didn't want to have to explain herself, but Kyla couldn't figure a way around it at that point. "Caden..." she said. "He hasn't been answering my calls." She tried to keep her voice even. "I never went a day without talking to him before, and all of a sudden out of nowhere it's like, he up and leaves for Nashville. And I get it, you know? I get that he

166

needed to do this. But at least before, he kept in touch with me. It's been over a week, Cody...and I've *really* needed him."

She was full-on ranting before she caught herself. Kyla was trying to sound as detached as she could, but the emotion still spilled through her voice.

Cody stared at her for a moment, and she watched as understanding came into his eyes. "We should get inside," he told her in an obvious attempt to change the subject.

She looked at him curiously, wondering why he suddenly seemed so nervous.

"What's wrong?" she asked him. "Why did you do that just now?"

"Do what?" he asked.

He was definitely nervous...and terrible at playing dumb.

"Get all shut down and weird," Kyla told him. "I saw your eyes change, Cody. Don't even try to deny it." She would have thought he'd known her long enough to realize she would catch a thing like that.

Cody had always been the kid in class who couldn't lie to a teacher or cheat on a test, and he'd been known on more than one occasion to break down in tears at an accusation of either one. All he ended up giving her, though was, "Kyla, it's not what you think."

She didn't understand what he meant. "What is it then?"

The boy pushed his glasses up on his nose, one of his more unfortunate nervous habits. "It really isn't my place to say."

Kyla gave him a look. "What's *that* supposed to mean?" she snapped. She wasn't about to let him off that easy.

"Look, we really should get back inside," Cody said.

She wanted to push him again, but she saw something in his eyes that she didn't expect; something that told her to drop it. "Fine," she said. Then she reluctantly followed him back into the McGallagher's basement.

Chapter 11

"...thicker than blood."

Nathaniel was nervous as he walked the streets of Oxford; far more nervous than he usually was in this city. Not because of the enemies that may be watching him, but because of his brothers...because of Seth.

His guilt weighed down on him as he moved through the streets, though he didn't regret what he'd done. If he hadn't done it, there was no telling what might have happened to Kyla James. But going so blatantly against an order from his leader, especially in a way that Seth would soon know it, was not something Nathaniel thought himself capable of before. It was something he had never considered before she came into his life.

Just as he reached the flat he and Caleb shared, a voice sounded distinctly in Nathaniel's mind, causing him to freeze with his hand on the key that he'd slipped into the lock.

"Get to the cemetery," Seth's voice spoke to him clearly. "You have some explaining to do."

Nathaniel cursed under his breath.

Turning the key, he shoved the door open and threw down his bag. The place was empty, which told him Caleb was already with the others. Nathaniel swore again.

This was not going to be a pleasant meeting.

The air was cool that night, thick and humid in true London fashion, and something about it only added to his nervousness. Nathaniel kept his hands in the pockets of his long grey trench coat, looking down at his feet as he came in through the tunnel at the entrance of the Egyptian Avenue. Focusing was abnormally difficult for him tonight, but he had to get his mind straight. He knew what he was about to face and he knew he couldn't let anyone see the evidence behind his eyes of his second encounter with Donovan; he just didn't know how he was going to pull it off.

Caleb's face was the first Nathaniel saw, though even he kept his eyes to the ground as he approached. Ethan did as well, but the skinny, dark-haired one beside him that Nathaniel didn't recognize just looked irritated. That must be Justin. Nathaniel didn't know a thing about him yet, but he was sure by the end of this meeting, he would at least know something.

Since the last thing Nathaniel could afford tonight was to be seen through, be it by his brothers or this awkward-looking newcomer, he went to extra measures to keep himself unreadable. If any of them were to catch on that something had happened, there would be hell to pay, and he could not let that happen; not when he knew what was at stake.

"You missed your flight," Seth told him, though it felt more like an accusation. "I would like to know why."

Nathaniel's pulse quickened, but his expression remained calm. And he did something then that he had never done before: He lied to Seth.

"I was being followed," he told him flatly. "I couldn't take the flight or our location would have been compromised. I had to wait until I lost the tracker to leave."

Seth looked into him with intent. Nathaniel couldn't tell whether or not he believed him, but he saw by his eyes that he'd already drawn his own conclusions of what had happened, which were probably closer to the truth than the story he'd just fed him.

"Who was following you?" Seth asked.

Nathaniel kept his voice monotone. "I don't know. I never saw him."

Caleb shifted uncomfortably and glanced up at him before Seth saw him do it, then he quickly dropped his eyes again. The look didn't even last half a second, but Nathaniel saw in it that his brother was worried.

Whether Seth chose to trust him or realized he was lying, Nathaniel wasn't sure, but for the time he decided to let it go. As was dictated by their protocol, he stepped up instead and presented the brotherhood with a formal deposition of their mission status, or at least their status from London. It didn't take much time for him to explain that they'd been in a holding pattern, that Justin had taken up Nathaniel's scouting position, Caleb had been kept on watch with Ethan, and that other than these changes, everything was as normal.

"We have had no sign of suspicious activity," Seth stated, wrapping up his deposition.

Caleb scoffed in response. "We've never had any signs of suspicious activity here," he muttered. "Not since you shut down my orders to track those sorority witches."

Seth shot him a glare and Caleb looked down immediately. He was obviously still bitter about being stripped of his assignment and stuck on watch with Ethan. Nothing drove Caleb Holcomb more insane than being on watch.

In typical fashion, Seth ignored his commentary and moved the meeting along, this time opening it up for Nathaniel to give them the status in Colorado. For once, Nathaniel would have preferred that Seth be more upset with his brother; anything that would buy him more time. Subtly taking in a breath, he tried to prepare himself. This was the part he was not looking forward to.

"While Eli left us with several leads," Nathaniel told them, "I wasn't able to follow them through before I was met with…interference."

Seth's face tightened and Caleb looked up curiously, as did Ethan and their newest recruit. Obviously, Seth hadn't taken the liberty of telling them that Donovan had already approached him. Fantastic.

"Whatever the reason Donovan has chosen this location," Nathaniel said, "it seems his resources are vaster and his intentions more complex than we anticipated. It took no time at all for him to locate me; and in doing so, he made it quite clear that he intends to turn me from the brotherhood and join him in whatever asinine endeavor has landed him in Colorado."

Caleb looked unsettled by this new bit of information. "Does he know about your uncle's house?" he asked. "Is that why he's there?"

The thought disturbed Nathaniel, too. "He has to," he said, furrowing his brow in contemplation. "I mean, he didn't mention it specifically, but the chance of that being coincidence..."

"Slim to none," Caleb finished the thought. "Got it." But instead of dropping it there, he eyed Seth in silent question, and Nathaniel couldn't help but follow his gaze.

Seth *had* grown very suddenly uncomfortable, but even if he did know more than he was letting on, Nathaniel wasn't about to call him out on it. Right now it was everything he could do to keep himself under the radar.

"I still don't get why we'd put Nate up in his uncle's place, knowing Donovan probably knows where it is. I mean, hasn't anyone ever heard of a Comfort Inn?"

"Nathaniel is there to ensure his uncle's protection," Seth responded. "On the chance that Howard Blake might become a target, we must ensure his safety from those who would attempt to harm him."

"Okay, I get that," Caleb agreed, "but I still don't get what his uncle has to do with any of this in the first place."

Nathaniel answered that for him. "He has nothing to do with it. He isn't even *in* Woodland Park."

Again, he noticed Seth's discomfort, and again, he narrowed in on the look; but just as before, Nathaniel didn't mention it, though it was clear he was not the only one with secrets tonight.

It burned in him, the lie he hid behind the truth, and kept him from questioning Seth on what he knew about his uncle. Nathaniel knew it was his responsibility to report everything that had happened while he was on assignment, including Donovan's using the human girl he hadn't even mentioned to them yet to bait him. But he couldn't let them know about that. If Seth learned what had really happened, he was sure to pull him off this assignment, and that was something Nathaniel simply could not risk.

He had messed this up without their knowledge, and he would fix it in the same way. Telling them now would do nothing except hinder his ability to make it right; or at least that was what he told himself.

"In following Eli's leads," Nathaniel explained, "I did come across a human Donovan has been watching; a little girl, probably around eight years old."

Seth looked concerned, as if questioning why Nathaniel hadn't spoken to him of this before. "What would Donovan want with a child?" he asked.

Nathaniel paused. "The best I can tell...she is a seer."

That caused even Ethan's and Justin's expressions to change.

"A seer?" Caleb asked. "An eight-year-old girl who's a *seer?*"

Nathaniel didn't react to his brother's disbelief. "Considering the level of activity and...*protection* around her, and considering the degree to which Donovan seems to have taken interest in her, my guess is that there is more to this child than meets the eye."

"Do you think..." Caleb started to ask.

Nathaniel finished the thought for him. "Yes, I do believe she is one of the awakened."

Caleb was confused. "What does this mean?"

Nathaniel shifted his weight, his discomfort moment by moment growing worse. "Whatever Donovan is doing with this coven he has supposedly forged an alliance with, they are threatened by this girl," he explained. "There is something that exists in Woodland Park, something surrounding her that might be able to stop them; something we need to utilize in order to draw this coven out and keep them from succeeding in their mission."

That was where he lost Seth. "Absolutely not," his leader responded staunchly.

Nathaniel tried not to let this faze him. "It could be our only shot..."

Seth did not look happy about this new attitude Nathaniel had taken on. "Either way," he said sternly, "it is not our call to make. I will meet with Malachi tomorrow and debrief him on the information you have given us. *He* the one who will determine our next move."

Nathaniel squared his jaw in frustration. "We may not have the luxury of going through protocol with this. By the time we jump through all the hoops Malachi has set up, it could be too late. Donovan could already have done something to harm or compromise this girl…"

"*Nathaniel…*" Before Seth could finish, someone else spoke up. And it was not the one Nathaniel expected to.

"Actually," Justin interjected, "I think he's right."

Nathaniel and Seth both turned to the newcomer.

"I'm sorry," Seth spoke to him with tension, "but I do not recall asking for your opinion."

Justin ignored the rebuke. "Think about it, Seth. In a situation like this, even a single wasted day could mean the success or failure of a mission. Is that really something you are willing to risk?"

Seth was livid. "Do not speak again," he warned him. Then he turned and glared at Nathaniel. "I will *not* go behind Malachi's back with this, and if I were permitted to make this call myself, I would call off the assignment now."

"But Seth…"

He cut Nathaniel off. "You do not know the power Donovan has behind him," he said.

Nathaniel threw back at him, "*You* have not seen this little girl."

Seth wore a frustrated look, as if he felt his authority being undermined. "One child," he said, "no matter how significant, would *not* be enough to merit such a dangerous course of action."

Nathaniel looked down, debating whether or not to voice his next thought. Then finally, even knowing it might be a mistake, he gave into it.

"What if there is more than one?"

*S*taring out over the city lights of Oxford, Nathaniel sat unmoving on the ledge of Carfax Tower. He wasn't on watch; he wasn't on assignment of any sort. None of them were until Seth returned from Rome with his orders from Malachi.

This was unbelievable.

Nathaniel was right and Seth knew it. He had seen the look in his leader's eyes as he told them what they needed to do; Nathaniel saw that he agreed with him. But Seth was blinded by their protocol, by these rules that only ever set them up to fail so long as they obeyed them, if for no other reason than that they wasted valuable time they could be using to make an advance.

This would all be so much easier if Seth would just trust him.

Nathaniel felt someone land on the edge of the tower, but he didn't turn around. He didn't have to use his eyes to know that it was Caleb.

Crouching beside him as he clung to the stone battlement, Caleb looked out over the city, his wings shimmering like a canopy over his head. It was fascinating to Nathaniel how something that could look and act so human could also appear the way Caleb appeared now; no longer as a boy, but a warrior of light, a guardian to mankind...an angel among men.

"Thought I'd find you here," Caleb said.

Nathaniel frowned.

Shifting out of this glorified form and back into the appearance of a man, Caleb sat beside him and hung his legs over the edge of the tower. "So you gonna tell me what's going on?"

Nathaniel tried to play the "I don't know what you're talking about" card, but the boy just rolled his eyes.

"Give it up," he said. "You might be able to fool Ethan, the cocky new guy, and even Seth, but you can't fool me. Actually, I'm a little hurt that you'd even try."

Nathaniel kept his gaze on the city. "I wasn't trying to hide anything from you, Caleb."

His brother wasn't convinced. "You can cut the act, Nate. There's nobody here but you and me."

Nathaniel sighed, knowing Caleb was right and thinking he was wrong at the same time. It was true that he'd never kept anything from him, and he knew if there were ever a time he needed to talk to him, it was now; but this was hardly an issue he had faced before.

Finally, he gave in.

Sighing, he pressed his fingers to his temple and told him before he thought better of it, "I didn't just *see* Donovan."

Caleb didn't understand. "What do you mean?"

Nathaniel glanced out over the ledge of the watchtower, hoping to find a way he could avoid this and knowing he wasn't going to be able to. "There was more to what happened than I let Seth know," he admitted after a drawn out silence, trying to be careful with his words. "Someone...a potential asset, was compromised."

Caleb's eyebrows pulled together and Nathaniel could immediately feel his concern. "How?" he asked.

Nathaniel didn't know how he was going to explain this, but he gave it his best shot. "I was following a lead," he told him, "trying to attain the necessary information about the child I spoke of, and Donovan...he saw me with her."

"With the child?" Caleb asked.

Nathaniel paused. "No," he corrected him, cringing internally. "With the asset."

It took a moment for that to sink in, but when it finally did, Caleb's countenance did a quick one-eighty. "*Her?*"

Nathaniel shot him a look and the shock dropped quickly from Caleb's face.

"You have to understand," Nathaniel told him, suddenly feeling the need to justify himself, "I had to do something. This girl...Kyla," he was careful as he said her name, "there is something about her. I don't know how to explain it, she just...she *saw* me, Caleb."

Caleb was dumbfounded as he stared at him. "What happened?"

Nathaniel cringed again, only this time he let it show. "I fought him."

Caleb's eyes about fell out of his head. "You *what*?"

Nathaniel shot him another look, hoping to keep him quiet, but it was completely ineffective.

"So let me get this straight," Caleb said, pressing his fingers to his temple. "You *fought* Donovan? *Donovan*? As in, the most dangerous, evil Naphil in existence, who is hell-bent on not only our destruction, but the destruction of mankind...to protect a *girl*? You, who are completely immune to the female species?"

Nathaniel looked away from him. "It isn't like that."

"Oh really? Then what's it like, Nate? Because I'm having a hard time understanding this one."

Nathaniel felt sick, wishing he knew the answer to that question himself. "I don't know," he admitted.

Caleb stared into him, reading him for a long time, and then as understanding settled over him, his bewilderment returned.

"Oh my gosh…"

"What?" Nathaniel asked him. His voice was tense.

"You *like* her," Caleb said.

Nathaniel became agitated, resenting the accusation without fully knowing why. As infantile as it sounded, it was different with him than it was with his brothers. His whole life, he had been so detached from anything human that it felt as weakness to him to feel anything that would place him in those parameters. And the way Caleb said it just sounded awful to him.

Before he had time to respond, however, someone unexpected interrupted them.

"Meeting. Ten minutes."

It was Seth. And Nathaniel had never been happier to hear his voice.

The sound startled him, as he didn't expect their leader to return so quickly from Rome, and judging by his brother's expression, Caleb didn't expect it either. But he welcomed it, given the alternative.

The two of them looked at each other. "We should go," Nathaniel said.

Caleb put a hand on his arm to stop him. "Nate, look," he told him, "I get that you're confused right now, but I want you to know that it's okay."

Nathaniel was still agitated. "What is okay?"

Caleb looked like he was trying to be careful not to say the wrong thing. "I know you expect a lot more of yourself than any of the rest of us do," he told him, "but whatever's going on here, I just don't want you to be freaked out about it."

Nathaniel felt vulnerable now, and he didn't like it. "What if it isn't okay?" he asked him. "What if she compromises my judgment?"

Caleb smiled, and there was more understanding behind it than Nathaniel expected. "That doesn't mean it's wrong," he said. "It just means you're human."

Nathaniel gave him a look.

"Alright," Caleb corrected himself, "*half* human."

Nathaniel smirked at the boy and the two of them exchanged a knowing glance. Then they dropped off the ledge in the dark and fell out of sight.

*A*s Nathaniel and Caleb entered the cemetery ten minutes after their departure from the tower, they saw that everyone else was already there waiting. It was obvious that they were all eager to hear what news Seth had brought them from Rome. Not one of them spoke, but instead they looked to their leader in question and waited for him to address them.

Nathaniel found himself nervous about more than just what Seth had to say. Though that obviously concerned him, he was also apprehensive about the conversation he'd just had with his brother that had ended so abruptly. He didn't like what Caleb knew, not because he didn't trust him, but because he didn't want any of the others to see that he was aware of something they weren't.

However, Ethan was the most perceptive in that respect, and also the least likely to pry or attempt to draw out any such information. Especially not tonight. It didn't take long for Nathaniel to realize they were all so anxious to hear Seth's decision that none of them were even paying attention to Caleb. Not even Justin, who apparently made arguing against him a habit.

Nathaniel had never witnessed this, but he took his brother's word for it, even if Justin *had* backed him up against Seth. It would take a lot more than that for him or anyone to supersede his trust in Caleb.

Seth spoke formally as he addressed them. "I have official word from Rome. After taking Nathaniel's proposal into consideration, Malachi has determined that we *will* move on this opportunity immediately."

Nathaniel and Caleb looked at each other, both of them surprised.

"Your assignment," Seth told Nathaniel, "is to return to Woodland Park. You are being tasked to verify this speculation, this theory that there may be more than one of the awakened." He paused. "But you will not be going back alone."

Nathaniel looked to his leader in question, and out of the corner of his eye, he saw Caleb smile.

"Ethan..." Seth said.

Caleb's smile dropped.

Ethan squared his shoulders. "Yes?" he answered, keeping his hands behind his back as he waited for his orders.

"You will go to Woodland Park with Nathaniel and keep watch for him," Seth explained.

Ethan nodded, and that was when Caleb's uncharacteristic silence came to an end. "Hold up," he said.

Seth sighed and Nathaniel could feel his irritation. Even without his heightened emotional perception, he could see that Caleb was testing their leader's already stretched patience.

"Why can't I go?" Caleb asked.

Seth remained calm as he explained himself. "I need someone on watch for this, Caleb. Not a tracker. We are not even remotely ready to get up-close and personal yet. I need Ethan on this."

Caleb scowled, "As much as you've had me on watch lately, I should be able to replace him."

Seth gave him a warning look. "You *will* be replacing Ethan," he told him, "here in London."

Caleb made a bitter face.

"Is that understood?" Seth asked him.

The disappointment was obvious in Caleb's voice. "Understood."

"Nathaniel..." his leader addressed him again.

Nathaniel met his gaze.

"You are to get close enough to these you have identified to determine whether or not they are who you believe them to be, but not so close that it compromises the mission. If you discover at any point that your theories are incorrect, you are to abort immediately. It is imperative that neither you nor Ethan is seen by Donovan or any member of this supposed coven. Do I make myself clear?"

He and Ethan both nodded and Nathaniel could see that Caleb was still upset.

Seth continued giving them their assignments. "Justin..." he said.

Justin looked to his new leader, waiting for the orders he had to know to expect by that point.

"There will be no variation in your assignment," Seth told him. "You are to hold the perimeter until Nathaniel and Ethan return, is that clear?"

Justin nodded, Caleb sneered and Seth turned back to Nathaniel.

"You leave first thing in the morning."

*I*t was almost five AM in Oxford. There was no light in the flat other than a floor lamp in the corner, but Nathaniel didn't mind the dark. He was much too preoccupied watching Caleb pace the length of the room.

"This isn't right," his brother ranted. "There isn't one stupid thing about any of this that's right!"

"Caleb..."

The boy didn't stop, just kept talking over him. "Putting me on *watch*? Seriously, what's the point of that when there's nothing even here for me to watch?! Why do I have to be stuck up in that stupid tower while that obnoxious little twit runs around and..."

"Caleb!" Nathaniel cut him off.

Caleb stopped pacing and looked up at his brother.

"It will be okay," Nathaniel assured him. "And what is it, exactly, that you have against Justin?"

Caleb made a face, and Nathaniel knew by looking at it that if he let him open his mouth again, things were going to get ugly.

"You know what?" Nathaniel said, "Nevermind. Why don't you stop with the aimless ranting and tell me what this is really about?"

Caleb scowled and looked away from him, putting his hands on his hips as he stared at the bookshelf against the wall. "I was so close, Nate. If you could have seen Samantha the last time I was with her…"

Nathaniel gave him a skeptical look. "*That's* what you're so upset over?"

"Seth is being an idiot to let that assignment go," Caleb snapped defensively. "I swear to you, those girls are hiding something."

"Yes, they probably are," Nathaniel agreed. "But there is no reason for you to get further involved in it. All we needed to know about them was whether or not they were connected to Donovan, which they aren't. Anything beyond that is completely irrelevant."

Caleb resumed his pacing. "But see, I don't know," he said. "What if it isn't? What if there is something else there and our ignoring it actually places us further in danger?"

Nathaniel didn't like where this was going. "Caleb, why are you bringing this up? Why now?"

Caleb sighed tensely. "I'm just sick of it," he said. "All these stupid assignments that always end up in dead ends. I'm sick of working so hard and having it come to nothing. I'm sick of nothing I ever do even *mattering*!"

Nathaniel put a hand on Caleb's shoulder to stop him from pacing. When Caleb turned to look at him and Nathaniel saw his face, he discerned the fear behind his outward expression.

Finally he understood.

"Caleb, this is going to be okay. All of it."

Caleb dropped his head in frustration. "I just don't trust it," he said. "I think your marching straight back to Donovan is the dumbest idea you or Seth have ever come up with."

"Caleb…"

"No, listen to me! I've got a bad feeling about this, Nate. I'm not kidding."

"I'll be fine," Nathaniel told him.

Caleb scoffed. "Right, because you're *Nathaniel Blake*. Completely untouchable, is that it? Is that what you believe? Because I gotta tell you, I don't buy it. I don't care how bad Donovan wants you or how much Seth trusts you or how different you think you are from the rest of us. You are *not* invincible."

Nathaniel pressed his lips together. "Trust me," he said. "I *know* that."

Caleb looked at him curiously as Nathaniel grabbed his backpack and the black Italian leather jacket his uncle had given him on his twentieth birthday.

"I'll be back when the assignment is accomplished," Nathaniel said, slinging the backpack over his shoulder and making his way to the door.

He could feel Caleb's gaze still on him.

"Why are you really doing this?" Caleb asked him when he reached for the handle.

Nathaniel paused, frowning and looking down. "I'll see you when I get back," he said. Then he slipped through the door and left his brother standing there, unanswered and frustrated in the middle of their flat.

Chapter 12

"…lying isn't always the easiest thing."

Nathaniel and Ethan sat on a strategic mountain ledge under the cover of dark, overlooking the Catamount Trail and the entire valley beneath them. Ethan took in the setting and established himself for watch as Nathaniel explained their strategy.

First, he showed him the Howell's home. Then he explained where Kyla lived and where his uncle's estate was located, making sure he was in control enough to appear as though everything were normal. It was far less easy than he'd hoped. The slightest thought of Kyla James and his voice started to shake, but he was able to cover it up.

"I am going to make contact with the girl tonight," Nathaniel said, forcing himself into a tone that was borderline-robotic.

"She is the one you suspect?" Ethan verified.

"Yes," he told him flatly. "She is."

Ethan seemed convinced enough.

"If you need to reach me," Nathaniel told him, "you will need to do so in discretion. My uncle may be out of town now, but he could show up at any time. I have no way of knowing for sure, so it would probably be best for you to stay up here."

"I understand," Ethan said.

Nathaniel's guess was that Ethan had already been planning on it. Given his assignment, Ethan was allowed to stay in Naphil form, as this was what enabled him to see and to feel to the measure that he could. His strongest ability was the way he could discern whether or not one of his brothers was in immediate danger, but Ethan's senses, his sight and his hearing particularly, were heightened above what the rest of them could engage in, making him a near-perfect watcher for a night like this. To some measure, those abilities still marked him whether he took the form of an angel or the form of a man, but remaining in Naphil form enabled him to go without sleep and to endure extreme circumstances with half the strain. His gifts were simply heightened when he shed his humanity. That was the case with all of them.

Nathaniel gave his brother the sign of the Resitore, then he jumped down from the ledge and made his way back out to the trail. Walking away from their point of watch, he took a deep breath to prepare himself and tried to convince himself that he could do this.

*A*fter taking another painful shower and attempting once again to bandage herself up, Kyla threw on some black drawstring shorts and a white scoop-backed tank top. The less fabric to rub against her skin, the better, she figured. But lying in bed, even on her stomach was so unbearably painful she eventually got up.

Not knowing what else to do, she slipped on some flip-flops, grabbed her sketchpad and charcoals and sat outside on the front deck. It was like a default to her; when all else failed, she drew. She had been defaulting to this a lot more than usual lately, too.

Kyla poised her hand above the paper, moving it back and forth in a mental practice run before she brought the charcoal in her hand to the paper beneath it. But then just before she was able to, a flicker of light like a street lamp about to burn out caught her eye. Kyla's head shot up.

There were no street lamps on Ponderosa Way.

She looked down to the street, then flinched and dropped her charcoal when she saw a figure standing there watching her; someone she did not expect to see.

"You've got to be kidding me," she muttered.

Tip-toeing quickly down the stairs, Kyla walked out to the street to meet the tall, gorgeous blonde who stood nonchalantly on the side of the road with a smile on his face.

She could have hit him.

"What are you doing here?" she snapped, folding her arms across her chest.

"Good evening to you, too," the visitor answered sarcastically. Then he looked out at the moonlit silhouette of the mountains as if they were of more interest to him than she was.

"I'm serious, Nathaniel. What are you doing here?"

He glanced back at her casually, feigning innocence. "I was just going for a walk..."

Kyla gave him a look.

"...and there's a chance I may have hoped I'd run into you," he admitted.

She felt her heart flutter and then quickly forced away the feeling. "How did you know where I live?"

Nathaniel's eyes were suspiciously wide. "I told you, Kyla, I was just going for a walk. The fact that you live on this street is news to me."

She didn't buy it for a second. "And I suppose you had nothing to do with me mysteriously waking up in my room the other night, either?"

Nathaniel gave her a look like she was crazy. "I have no idea what you're talking about."

She glared at him when she saw that he was holding back laughter.

"Who is he?" Kyla snapped suddenly.

Nathaniel obviously wasn't expecting that. "Who is who?" he asked her, the rising smile fading slowly from his face.

"Don't play dumb with me," she said. "You told me we'd get into it later, and guess what? It's later. So who is he, Nathaniel? Who is *Donovan*?"

She could see she'd struck a nerve, though he was trying incredibly hard to hide it. "Kyla..." he said, but she cut him off again.

"I want the truth, Nathaniel...if you're even capable of it."

"It doesn't matter who he is," he told her, "because you don't have to worry about him anymore. I took care of it."

Everything about the sincerity in his voice, his devastating charm and his confident, assured gaze should have quenched her skepticism, but Kyla felt something in her that was stronger than whatever might convince her on the surface.

"I don't believe you," she said.

Nathaniel stared at her, looking somewhat stunned. Something told her he wasn't used to people questioning him. Rather than address her comment, however, he made a face and circled her slowly, touching one of the makeshift bandages on her back.

"Good lord," he said. "What did you do?"

She scowled at him angrily. "Do *not* change the subject."

Nathaniel shook his head. "I'm sorry, but if I don't fix this job you massacred, it could get infected. You're coming with me."

Kyla didn't budge. "Like hell I am."

A coy, teasing smile played on his lips again. "I'll give you more painkillers."

Damn it.

Kyla walked down the street and told him grudgingly as she passed, "You don't play fair, Nathaniel Blake." *In more ways than you know.*

Glowering as they trekked the road up to Falcon's Rest in the dark, Kyla found herself unnaturally irritated by Nathaniel's perfect voice and his perfect body and his perfect face. And then there *she* was, walking next to him looking like road kill.

She grumbled under her breath as they walked, and Nathaniel smiled at her in that sickeningly adorable, boyish way that made her knees feel like they'd just gotten shot up with Jell-O.

Why did he have to do that?

"You know, I'm perfectly aware that you're miserable," he told her. "You don't have to go to all the effort of making your face look that hideous."

"Maybe I'm just ugly," she sneered.

Nathaniel laughed. "Well, naturally I accounted for that. I was referring more to the spiteful, bitter scowl you seem to be trying to perfect."

Kyla thought very seriously about tripping him.

186

"Is that why you brought me out here?" she asked. "To insult me? Because honestly, I could have stayed on my porch for that."

Nathaniel rolled his eyes. "Yes, Kyla, I came all the way down here to insult you. I had absolutely nothing better to do with my time than to pick a fight."

"Oh yeah? If you had so much else to do with your time then why are you here?"

Nathaniel tried to act irritated by the question even though clearly, he wasn't. "It is my obligation as a doctor in training to do follow-up on my patients," he told her. "I had to make sure you were still alive, first of all, and that you didn't ruin all the effort I went to the other night by doing something like *that*." He pointed at her back and she gave him a smirk.

"I thought it was a coincidence that you ran into me?"

Nathaniel didn't respond, just looked away from her and smiled out of the corner of his mouth.

Gah. Freaking heart.

Kyla turned away from him, too, refusing to speak another word the rest of the walk up to Falcon's Rest, mostly because she didn't trust herself to stay angry with him if she did. But when they reached the mansion, she found a reason to break her silence.

"Is your uncle home?" she asked him.

"No," Nathaniel told her, "I don't believe he is. But we might want to keep quiet just to be safe."

He creaked the door open carefully, just enough for them to slip through, and as they moved through the foyer, Kyla was able to see what she hadn't the other night, probably due to the loss of blood she had experienced and her theorized concussion.

The house was absolutely unreal.

"This way," Nathaniel whispered. Then he guided her down a familiar marble hallway.

When she stepped into the washroom, Kyla sat carefully on the edge of the velvet settee. "Ever had déjà vu?" she mumbled.

Nathaniel was already pulling his supplies out of the drawer when she bit her lip and frowned. Suddenly, she was

187

flooded with the same emotions she felt the last time she was in there, and seriously questioning her judgment in coming back here with him. Maybe she did have a concussion after all.

"I'm not taking my shirt off," Kyla told him.

Nathaniel set down his collection of supplies. "No need to," he said. "The back on that one is low enough for me to navigate around, I'm pretty sure."

Kyla glanced up at the medicine cabinet. "What about your promise, doc?" she asked. "Where are my drugs?"

"I'll get them for you," he said. "Better you take them now before I go to work on you, anyway."

Kyla raised an eyebrow and Nathaniel put his hands up. "Totally innocent comment, I swear."

It took a lot for her not to crack a smile at that, but she handled it like a pro.

"How did those work for you, anyway?" he asked her, pulling a prescription bottle down from the cabinet.

"Great until I mysteriously woke up in my bed the next morning," Kyla told him. Then she paused and smirked a little. "You know, which you had nothing to do with..."

Nathaniel worked to hide his smile from her, but Kyla saw it anyway. "Right," he said, holding the pills out for her to take.

"It *was* you, wasn't it?" she said.

Nathaniel gave her a look. "No, you sleepwalked home," he scoffed. "Do you want these or not?"

Kyla frowned, but didn't take them. "Nathaniel, seriously, how did you know where I live?"

"What?" he asked her teasingly. "You're the only one with stalking rights?"

She narrowed her eyes at him and he held out his hand again for her to take the pills.

"Let me wash the charcoal off my hands first," she told him, moving over to the sink. Kyla saw his confused expression in the mirror.

"Charcoal?"

She kept her gaze fixed on her hands. "I was drawing before you showed up," she said. "Guess I was wrong to peg you as observant."

Nathaniel nodded in understanding. "Of course, because you don't already have enough dark twisted drawings on your bedroom walls."

Kyla glared at him. "You had no right being in my room."

"I suppose you would rather I dropped you off on your porch then?" he challenged.

She didn't respond, just held her hand out for the pills.

Nathaniel filled another paper cup with water and gave them to her, and as she was swallowing them he asked her, "So while we are being honest, who is the boy in the picture?"

Kyla choked on the water and put the back of her hand up to her mouth as she forced herself to swallow. *Excuse me?*"

Nathaniel gave her a patronizing look. "I'm certain you know which picture I am referring to."

"Of course I know the picture," she said. "What were you doing looking at it?"

Nathaniel shrugged. "I just found it curious."

"Why?" Kyla asked defensively.

He guided her back over to the settee and sat her down.

"That picture is about the only trace of color in your entire bedroom," he said, "which I'm assuming isn't a coincidence. It just seems a little implicit, that's all."

Kyla looked at him skeptically. "Implicit of what?"

Nathaniel pulled the seat out from the wall again, straddled it and turned her back toward him like he had the other night. Removing her Band-Aids carefully, he answered her, "That he means something to you."

Kyla cringed as he pulled one of them a little too roughly away from her skin. "He does mean something to me," she told him. "He's my best friend."

Nathaniel tried to act intently focused on her back. "Isn't that a little weird?" he asked.

Kyla wasn't sure what he meant. "Isn't what a little weird?"

"Having a best friend of the opposite sex."

She smiled and shook her head. "Not hardly. I don't get along with other women at all."

Nathaniel gave her a teasing smile. "You're hardly a woman," he said mockingly. "What are you, eighteen?"

Kyla glared at him indirectly by way of the mirror and the gesture made him laugh.

"Nineteen in September," she said. "And you're not as funny as you think you are."

"I don't know," Nathaniel he said. "I thought that was pretty funny."

Kyla rolled her eyes. "My point exactly."

"So why don't you get along with other women?" he asked her.

She tensed up as he removed another bandage. "Cause they're stupid," she said.

Nathaniel laughed, then nodded thoughtfully. "Valid point," he agreed, but she could tell by his tone that he was still mocking her.

"Well, obviously there are exceptions to every rule," Kyla corrected herself. "Like Melissa Howell, for example."

She thought she saw something change in Nathaniel's face when she said the name, but she couldn't be sure.

"Who is Melissa Howell?" he asked her coolly.

She looked at him, trying to figure it out. "Caden's mom."

"Caden being the best friend?" he verified.

Kyla nodded thoughtfully as she traced her fingers along the edge of the seat. "She's more of a mother to me than my own has ever been," she admitted. She didn't know why she told him that.

Nathaniel opened the cap to the bottle of evil blue liquid he used on her the last time they were here, dousing a rag with the substance. "The Howell's," he said, "they're good people?"

Kyla frowned. "They're the best people I know," she told him, "and the closest thing to family my brother Matthew and I have had since…"

Nathaniel was frozen, holding the rag and waiting for her to finish. "Since what?" he asked her when she trailed off. But she didn't get the chance to answer him.

190

They both heard it at the same time, the sound of the garage door raising and lowering again, and then the door that led from the garage into the main house opening and closing behind whoever had just arrived; but it was Nathaniel's reaction to this that surprised her more than the sound itself. His face went completely white.

"What is it?" Kyla asked him.

Nathaniel's eyes were fixed on the door, but then they darted back to her abruptly. "Stay here," he told her. He set the rag down on the edge of the counter and moved out of the washroom, leaving her sitting on that velvet settee without a clue what was going on.

Nathaniel slipped quickly out into the hallway, his pulse moving faster as he prepared himself for the worst, which in this case would be the uncle he hadn't seen in almost four years walking through the front door of the home he had every right to walk into.

As it turned out, it was slightly less than worst-case scenario, but still far from ideal.

The man standing in the entryway was not Howard Blake. He was young, for one, probably around thirty, Hispanic, and far better-looking than Nathaniel's balding fifty-year-old uncle. His name was Miguel, and he was one of Howard's full-time estate caretakers. He'd been hired about two years before Nathaniel left his uncle's house in L.A., and he hadn't seen him since. Apparently in the last four years, Nathaniel had changed quite a bit, too, because Miguel didn't recognize him.

Reaching for a Baccarat candlestick on the glass-topped table in the entryway, the startled caretaker held it up like a baseball bat and told him not to move.

Nathaniel put his hands up quickly. "Whoa, whoa...Miguel, it's me."

Miguel didn't drop the candlestick, but he looked a little perplexed that the would-be burglar knew his name. Flipping on the light switch behind him, he got a second look at

191

Nathaniel, but it took a moment before the recognition hit him. Finally, he dropped the candlestick to his side.

"Nathaniel?" he asked confusedly.

Nathaniel sighed and dropped his hands, glancing nervously back toward the washroom to see if Kyla had seen that. She hadn't.

"What are you doing here, man?" Miguel asked him, shaking his head and replacing the makeshift weapon to its rightful place on the entryway table. "You nearly scared me to death."

"I'm really sorry," Nathaniel apologized, keeping his voice low. "This isn't how I meant for this to go down at all."

Miguel didn't look like he was buying it. "Start talking," he said.

Nathaniel glanced back down the hall to buy him some time, trying to figure out what to say to him. And this was where he had to start lying through his teeth.

"Look man," Nathaniel said, shifting his stance to what he thought a normal twenty-year-old guy might look like, "I'm on break from school right now. I came down here a few days ago to see my uncle, and when I saw that he wasn't here I was about to head to L.A." Nathaniel paused and looked behind him again, and when he did it this time it finally caught Miguel's attention enough that he followed his gaze.

Luckily there wasn't anything for him to see, though. At least not yet.

"So why didn't you?" Miguel asked him.

Nathaniel shifted his stance again and lowered his voice even further. Then he motioned with his fingers for Miguel to move closer so he could hear him. "I met a girl," Nathaniel told him.

Miguel looked at him skeptically and Nathaniel went on.

"I needed a place to bring her," he said, giving him a look he'd seen men often give each other behind a woman's back. This, Miguel seemed to understand, but it still didn't mean he was okay with it.

"Nathaniel..." he started to argue with him, but before he could finish, Nathaniel shot him a look when he heard a sound behind them.

192

Turning quickly, Nathaniel saw Kyla marching down the hallway toward them, her hair let down from her ponytail so it covered her back. She looked irritated.

Apparently she was done waiting.

Stopping beside Nathaniel and looking up at him impatiently, she folded her arms across her chest and asked him, "What's going on?"

Instead of answering her, he looked back at Miguel and gave him about as pleading a look as he he'd ever given anyone, and as he watched the man study Kyla, Nathaniel knew he was going to cover for him. He could see the look in his face that told him he would, a look he imagined was common for just about any man who had ever laid eyes on her, whether or not she ever realized it. His guess was she didn't.

Kyla was the type that was completely unaware of her own beauty, which only made her that much more intriguing. Nathaniel had suspected that much about her the first time he looked into her eyes, but watching her reaction now as Miguel stared at her in anything but a subtle way, seeing how oblivious she was to what he was really thinking, he realized it was true.

As if he needed this to be any harder on him than it already was.

He saw Miguel's expression change when he first caught sight of Kyla, and while Nathaniel was thankful for the discretion of this particular member of his uncle's staff, he suddenly felt protective in a way he wasn't used to feeling, almost wanting to grab her and hold her away from this man's view so he wouldn't even be able to think the things about her that he was thinking. Nathaniel may not have been able to see into this man's head, but he could see into his eyes, and they told him enough.

Nathaniel looked condescendingly at the girl beside him. "You really are incapable of following instructions, aren't you?"

"I never agreed to anything," she said. "Just because you assume I'm gonna listen to you doesn't make me rebellious when I don't. It just makes you either arrogant or stupid for thinking I actually will."

Nathaniel narrowed his eyes, unable to determine whether he wanted to kiss her or slap her. Fortunately, he managed to refrain from both.

"Get back in the room," he told her.

Kyla scoffed at him and Nathaniel gave her another look, only this time it was one that made her comply. She scowled and headed back down the hallway, muttering under her breath as she walked, and Miguel's eyes stayed on her the whole way.

"Damn," he said once she was out of earshot.

"Yeah," Nathaniel mumbled, "you're tellin' me."

Miguel just shook his head.

"Thank you, Miguel," Nathaniel said, trying to get the man to meet his eyes again so he would stop staring after Kyla.

When he looked back at Nathaniel, Miguel frowned warily. "Your uncle flies in in four days," he told him. "I want you out in three, aight?"

That was why he was here. He must have been here before too, planting the flowers in the urns out front.

Nathaniel put his hands up and started walking backwards down the hall again toward Kyla. "Three days," he agreed.

"I'm serious, Nathaniel. You wanna stay longer, you gotta take it up with him, but I never saw you, you got it?"

"I got it," Nathaniel said. He turned and walked straight again, his smile dropping as soon as he was out of sight.

This was going to be a problem.

Kyla glowered as she sat along the wall. She was hugging her knees to her chest when Nathaniel came back into the washroom, and when she saw him she gave him a look like a child might give their mother after being heavily reprimanded.

Kyla didn't like being reprimanded, and she did not like being lied to.

"Who was that?" she asked as soon as Nathaniel stepped through the door.

194

He didn't look thrilled about answering her. Or maybe it was something else he wasn't thrilled about.

"Miguel," he told her. "He's one of the caretakers of my uncle's estates."

Her eyebrows raised a little. "Estates?"

Nathaniel looked uncomfortable as he grabbed the rag from the counter again and sat back behind her. "My uncle lives in Los Angeles," Nathaniel told her. "This is his summer home."

"Of course it is," she mumbled. "So basically, the guy's loaded?"

"Something like that," Nathaniel said. "He's been in Southern California real estate for over thirty years, so what do you expect?"

"That, I guess," Kyla replied.

When Nathaniel fell silent, she glanced up at the mirror and saw a look of deep concentration on his face.

"What is it?" she asked him.

He held up the liquid-doused rag and kept his brow furrowed. "Nothing," he said. "This just might sting a little."

"Great," Kyla grumbled. She clenched the sides of the seat to prepare herself, but as Nathaniel pressed the rag to her back, she realized his definition of "stinging a little" was comparable to being burned alive. She started to scream, but as soon as she did, he clasped his free hand over her mouth and held her still by pulling her up against his chest.

And by that point, even if she wanted to scream, she had forgotten how.

Nathaniel was so close she could feel his breath on her neck. Pulling her head back against his shoulder, he whispered softly in her ear, "I'm sorry, Kyla. I know it hurts, but just breathe and it will feel better in a second."

Gah...that voice.

Kyla trembled as a shock rushed through her body, which she hoped Nathaniel would assume to be a reaction to the pain this chemical was supposed to cause her. But she couldn't feel the pain anymore; she couldn't feel anything. It had all slipped to the back of her awareness so that everything she knew and breathed and felt around her screamed Nathaniel's name.

His hand hadn't moved from where it was pressed against her back, and she swore she could feel his other hand tremble as he slid it slowly off of her mouth and down her neck. Kyla closed her eyes, breathing harder to compensate for the frantic beating of her heart.

"Nathaniel..." her voice shook as she said his name.

His hand slid up the side of her face and she felt his breath grow hotter on her neck.

"Yeah?" he whispered.

Her heart beat out of rhythm again, terrified at what it was starting to feel. Frantically, she scrambled to ask him the only question she could think that would stop this torrent from taking her over.

"What did Donovan want with me?"

Kyla didn't breathe as she waited in the silence that descended on them both. Slowly, Nathaniel pulled his face away from her neck and moved his hands subtly to her back to resume what he had begun.

Kyla's nails dug so deeply into the red velvet she was sure there would be marks left in the fabric when she pulled them away.

Breathe, she told herself. She had to breathe. *In...out...repeat.*

Nathaniel was quiet as he drenched the rag again in the blue liquid of death and Kyla braced herself as best she could, knowing he probably wouldn't be as gentle with her after what she'd just pulled. When he pressed the rag against another cut, she had to bite down hard on her lip to keep from screaming this time.

"He wasn't after you," Nathaniel answered her.

That was when Donovan's words resurfaced in her mind. *You're not the one I want.* That was what he'd said. The game...*cat and mouse.*

Suddenly it clicked.

"He wanted *you*," she said quietly.

Kyla's eyes were wide as it all sank in, but Nathaniel didn't respond. Somehow she felt that he wanted her to connect the dots on her own.

"But why?" she asked him. The question scared her so much she wasn't even sure she wanted the answer.

Nathaniel taped a piece of gauze over the gash on her right shoulder blade. "I can't explain that to you now," he told her, his voice low and reassuring. "I can only ask you to trust me."

That was hardly something Kyla would willingly go along with, but though there were at least a hundred questions racing through her mind, she didn't voice a single one. Somehow the silence was more comforting to her now than the truth she wasn't even sure she wanted to know.

Nathaniel worked on her back in silence for a full five minutes, but it wasn't uncomfortable. It was heavy, the weight on both of them as he left her question to linger there, but strangely peaceful, too. Even if Kyla didn't have answers right now, there was one undeniable factor that made her feel safe: Nathaniel was taking care of her.

Sliding his hand down her arm to let her know he was finished, Nathaniel was careful as he touched her. Kyla closed her eyes at the feel of it, hating how much she loved it when he did that. When she opened them again, she turned slowly to face him, staring into his sapphire eyes as he slipped his hand off her arm. Suddenly, breathing became a labored effort. Staring back at Nathaniel, she felt dizzy and detached, lost in some kind of dream she had no desire to wake from.

"It's getting late," she said. "I should probably...umm...home. Yeah, I need to go there."

Ugh, you sound like an idiot. Stop saying words.

Apparently Nathaniel found some sort of amusement in it, because when he turned away from her, he smiled. "Let me take you," he offered.

"I'll be fine," she insisted, trying to refocus. "Besides, that would probably wake...whatever his name is."

Articulate thoughts were not coming to her in vast supply at the moment, and try as she did, she really couldn't remember a thing about the man she'd just met.

"I'll walk you then," Nathaniel said. He obviously wasn't going to let up that easy.

Kyla eyed him curiously. "I thought I wasn't in danger anymore?"

He looked at her in a way that made her even more nervous than she already was. "Who said anything about danger?"

Kyla felt her heart skip another beat, probably the tenth time it had done that in the last five minutes.

Nathaniel's voice was soft. "Maybe I'm just not ready to let you go."

He touched her face carefully and she thought she might fall over. Staring into his inhumanly perfect eyes, Kyla was caught up in the unreal kind of ecstasy that was becoming definitive of his presence in her life. Or maybe the feeling had something to do with the drugs he had given her. Either way, it caused her to momentarily detach from herself.

"You're like an angel," she whispered, giving no regard to whether or not she should actually say something like that.

Nathaniel's smile tightened. "Yeah," he said. "Almost."

Chapter 13

"...in the name of science."

Nathaniel stood with Kyla at the bottom of the stairs that led to her front door. He looked into her curiously in the same way she looked back at him, reading her and trying to understand what was going through her head.

He had been careful to avoid every one of the questions she had for him as he walked her home that night, be they about Donovan, Miguel, or his conveniently absent uncle, but she hadn't made it easy. Kyla James was not the kind of person to just let things go. However, with enough prodding on his part for her to tell him about her life, Nathaniel had avoided it successfully.

But as she told him about her hatred of this town, her plans to move to Europe someday to study art, her love for music and drawing and running, and even her hideous excuse for a mother that she couldn't wait to get away from, Nathaniel found himself so engrossed in what she was saying that he almost forgot he was asking for the purpose of diversion. He was fascinated by every word she spoke, and by the fact that anything so trivial could fascinate him at all.

Or maybe it was the sound of her voice that did it. Nathaniel didn't know for sure, because as he stood over Kyla below her deck and looked intently into her now blue-green eyes, none of that seemed to matter anymore.

"What are you doing?" he asked her after a full ten seconds of silence.

Kyla wrinkled her nose. "Trying to figure you out."

That amused him. "Yeah?" he asked. "And what have you figured so far?"

She tilted her head to one side. "I'm not sure yet," she admitted. "You might be the most confusing person I have ever met."

He thought of the irony in her statement, but didn't comment on it. "You like being able to understand people, don't you?" he said.

She looked at him knowingly. "Well, don't you?"

Nathaniel smirked a little; then he asked her in complete nonchalance, "So is *he* easier for you to understand?"

Kyla's expression tightened when he said it. "Is who easier for me to understand?"

She was trying to act ignorant, but she was no good at it. She knew exactly whom he was talking about and both of them knew it.

"Caden," he answered her.

Kyla looked away from him. "I thought so," she said after pausing for a moment, "but I'm not really sure anymore."

Nathaniel was surprised she was actually being real with him. Maybe he should drug her more often.

"Why is that?" he asked her, keeping his voice unthreatening.

Kyla looked sad. "He's just the one person in my life I could always depend on," she told him. "The one person I thought would always be there."

"And now he's not?" Nathaniel asked.

She looked even sadder when she answered him. "No, he's not."

Nathaniel frowned, feeling almost guilty. Somehow he felt responsible for bringing this sadness over her, and even though he knew it was foolish to think that, he still didn't like it. "I'm sorry, Kyla. I didn't mean to upset you."

"It's okay," she told him. "It's just kind of a sore subject right now."

She seemed eager to stop talking about it, and while Nathaniel wished he could give her that, he knew it was more important that he find out about the boy. "So where is he?" he asked her. He watched her face tighten even further.

"Nashville," she said sourly. She waited there for a moment with a bitter expression on her face, but then some sort of understanding came over her and she looked up at him again. "I know how it seems..." she said, sounding almost like she was trying to justify herself.

Nathaniel wasn't sure what she meant, but he let her keep going.

"I'm really not that girl, you know? Music is Caden's life and I would never hold him back from that. It just hurts that he left when he did."

Nathaniel watched her intently, realizing as he listened to her that his assignment was about the furthest thing from his mind. Asking these questions, he had completely lost sight of the ones he should be asking, and he was having trouble caring enough to redirect the conversation.

"When was it that he left?" he asked her.

Kyla looked up at him, surprised by the sincerity in his voice. "I don't talk to people like this," she told him.

Nathaniel didn't break his gaze from her for a second. "Why not?" he asked.

"Because I don't trust them."

He stared into her for a long time without saying a word, held once again in Kyla's eyes. And just as before, Nathaniel couldn't help but think there was some part of himself he could see within them.

"That, I don't blame you for," he told her understandingly.

Kyla blinked and looked away from him. "I should go," she said anxiously. He could see that she was frightened, but he didn't know why.

"Don't," Nathaniel told her, taking her fingers in his hand on impulse.

She trembled when he touched her and looked up at him in frustrated awe. "How do you do that?" she whispered.

"Do what?" he whispered back.

Kyla was almost breathless. "How do you make me feel like that?"

Nathaniel felt his heart pound against his chest as her hand remained in his. "I don't know," he told her. "What does it feel like?"

Kyla's lips started to tremble and he found himself overwhelmed with the urge to touch them again...to feel them like he had before.

She didn't answer his question, but asked him one instead that he didn't want to hear, if for no other reason than that he didn't know the answer, himself.

"Who are you, Nathaniel Blake?"

Looking out from the trees edging Ponderosa Way, Donovan's mind reeled as he stared forward into the night, his eyes locking in on Nathaniel Blake. Standing here like this, hidden in the place that had become quite the advantageous point of watch for these two, he couldn't help but feel a distinct sense of déjà vu...minus the fact that Kyla James was conscious this time.

Donovan really didn't think it was true, and he was having trouble believing what his eyes were showing him. Cerin's track record as of late hadn't given him a reason to doubt this, but the idea of Nathaniel coming back to Woodland Park after what had happened only days before was far from what he expected.

When they had seen Nathaniel leave, he had been certain their strategy would have to change, that they would have to find another way to lure him back here. But this...this was almost too easy.

"I do not understand," Balak spoke from beside him in his deep throaty voice. "Why would Seth send him back alone?"

Donovan continued to glare in Nathaniel's direction, watching as he moved closer to the girl that he least wanted him to get close to. "He wouldn't," he answered him. "But Malachi would."

Balak sneered at the name and Donovan went on.

"Malachi doesn't have as much to lose if something were to happen to Nathaniel Blake. His motivations are...different from Seth's."

"And what are Seth's motivations?" Balak asked him. "What does *he* have to lose?"

Donovan sneered as he watched Nathaniel touch the girl. "Everything," he told his second-in-command. "His drive, his purpose…his very soul."

Balak seemed aggravated. That was becoming more and more frequent with him as Nathaniel's significance was further drawn out.

"Why?" Balak asked tensely.

Donovan kept his eyes forward. "Because he made a promise to Nathaniel's mother," he told him. "The same as I did."

Balak's aggravation gave way to his confusion. He had never heard of this before. "And what promise is that?" he questioned.

Donovan breathed tensely, and the sound came out as somewhat of a growl. "He promised he would keep her and Nathaniel safe," he explained. "But only if she betrayed me."

Balak turned nervously back to his leader. "And what promise did *you* make her?" he asked.

Donovan stared forward at Nathaniel in deep contemplation, his voice empty of emotion as he spoke. "That if she did, I would kill her."

*N*athaniel was confused as he looked into the face of the girl standing staunchly before him, this girl who was proving far braver and more difficult than he wanted her to be.

Again, Kyla asked him, "Who are you?"

"I'm not sure how you want me to answer that," he admitted.

She didn't back off. "There's something you're not telling me," she said. She was doing it again, staring into him in that same unnerving way that made him feel completely transparent. "There's something about you…something I can't figure out."

Nathaniel dropped his hand from hers. "I don't know what you mean."

Kyla paused again. "Why did you follow me?" she asked him suddenly. "In the cemetery…why were you following me?"

Nathaniel tried to deny it. "I wasn't following you…" he started to tell her, but she cut him off.

"Damn it, Nathaniel. Would you please just tell me the truth?"

He tightened his jaw unconsciously. "The truth isn't always the easiest explanation," he said.

Kyla looked straight into him. "Who said I wanted easy?"

Nathaniel was mesmerized by her, far more mesmerized than he knew he should be. He knew he should turn away, that he should stop staring into this maddeningly beautiful auburn-haired girl and go back to where he came from before he placed this mission in any more danger than he already had. But for his life, he could not look away from her.

"I was trying to protect you," he told her. Nathaniel struggled to retain his composure, but she wasn't making it easy.

Kyla looked confused. "Why?"

"What do you mean, why?" he asked her.

"I mean why would you protect me? Who was I to you?" Kyla stopped and looked down, then she said more softly, "Who *am* I to you?"

Nathaniel felt his pulse surge before it crashed back down again. "I don't know," he told her honestly. His eyes were vulnerable as he looked down on this one who already held over him such a frightening power.

Kyla sighed, looking tired. "I wish you would tell me the truth."

"I am telling you the truth," he said. "I haven't lied to you, Kyla."

She gave him a look. "You've never lied to me?"

Nathaniel paused for a moment as he thought about it, and when he realized what he'd said, a knowing smile came to his face. "Well, maybe I did lie to you once."

"And when was that?" she asked defensively.

Nathaniel smirked a little. "The first time I time I took you back to my uncle's house," he told her. He could see that she was curious. "The truth is, I do nothing in the name of science."

Kyla looked into him long and hard, this time flustered as she tried to read him again; and when she finally understood what he was saying, he could see that she was trying to fight off a smile. "Nothing?" she asked.

Nathaniel took a step closer to her. "Nothing."

"Kinda strange for someone aspiring to be a doctor," she said. Then she nervously glanced toward the front door of the condo.

"Perhaps," he said softly, still not looking away from her eyes.

"I really...umm...I need to get inside," she told him.

Nathaniel's heart screamed at the thought of her leaving him now. "Don't go," he said. His voice was edging on desperation, and the sound of it surprised her.

Kyla's breathing staggered. "Why not?"

He was trying to fight it, trying to resist this urge that was threatening to overpower him. "Kyla, I..."

Nathaniel moved close enough to her that he could feel her breath against his face, which quite possibly made him more nervous than he had ever been in his life.

"You what?" she whispered.

Her eyes looked up into his and Nathaniel felt his heart pound. The closer she moved to him, inch by inch, the quicker and more unsteady his breathing became.

And then it came to a crashing halt when the front door of the condo was thrown open.

Kyla flinched and jumped back from him, her head shooting up toward the disgruntled-looking woman who stood in the doorway. Nathaniel could only assume it was her mother.

"I'm sorry," Kyla told him quickly.

Before he could say another word to her, she let her hair down from her ponytail so that it covered her back, then she scampered up the stairs, leaving Nathaniel standing there breathless as he stared after her.

"Who is he?" Loni demanded. Kyla could see that her mother was furious. And drunk. Real shocker there.

She tried to push past her and into the living room. "He's nobody," she said coldly.

Loni grabbed her arm and she spun around to face her.

"Do not touch me," Kyla threatened, jerking her arm out of the woman's grip.

Moving up the stairs before she could grab her again, Kyla locked her bedroom door behind her. She looked out her window for Nathaniel, but she didn't see him anywhere. Sighing and leaning her head against the wooden pane, Kyla closed her eyes and attempted to control her breathing.

She was so in over her head.

The sudden banging on her bedroom door caused her eyes to shoot open again. Scowling angrily, she moved across the room and jerked it open. "What is your problem?!" she shouted.

"Who is he?" Loni demanded.

Kyla wasn't about to tell her the truth. "Who is who?"

"The boy you were standing with in the street," she snarled. "Who is he?"

Kyla didn't hide her disgust. "I really don't see how that's any of your business," she said. She thought she might hit her for it, too. "Seriously, what makes you think you have the right to know anything about my life?"

And that incited the screaming.

She didn't pay much attention to it when her mother's face turned all red and puffy like that. Everything around her slowed down, almost like a slow motion sequence in a movie. Even though Kyla knew she was shouting, the sound became muffled to her and faded somehow to the back of her consciousness.

Still, she would have done just about anything to shut her up, if only for the sake of their neighbors that Kyla was pretty sure even ten houses down, could hear this. But if her mother shutting up was too much to ask, then at least she could get away from her.

Pushing past her again, Kyla tried to move back down the hallway, but just as she did she saw Matthew step out of his bedroom.

"Do not walk away from me when I am talking to you!" Loni barked. Grabbing Kyla by the shoulder, she swung her around and slammed her back up against the wall behind her.

Kyla's eyes shot open.

Her body went rigid as the pain of the impact caught her breath, which caused her mother's eyes to burn into her fiercely. Loni jerked her from the wall with force after that and pushed her hair away from her back, exposing her gauze-covered skin.

Kyla was frozen and still not breathing when she caught sight of Matthew's terrified expression.

"What is *this*?" Loni asked.

Kyla jerked herself out of her grip and dropped her hair again, but she didn't answer.

In a complete tirade, Loni began freaking out and demanded at an even higher decibel level than before to know what had happened, though Kyla couldn't distinguish individual syllables enough to tell what exactly the woman was screaming.

"Nothing happened!" she lied adamantly.

That obviously didn't sit well with her mother.

After Loni screamed at her some more, Kyla told her forcefully to "drop it," which went over about as well as the number four reactor in the Chernobyl power plant. But Kyla waited it out this time. She let her mother scream and shout and throw her little temper tantrum, the whole time biting her lip to keep herself from doing something she would later regret; such as anything that would keep Loni yelling at her longer.

Matthew still hadn't moved from where he stood in front of his bedroom. He stayed there even after Loni stormed back downstairs in a huff, and when Kyla was left to face him, she sighed in response to his expression.

"It's late, Matty," she told him. "You need to get to bed."

He didn't budge. "You lied to me," he said, still staring forward.

Kyla fidgeted uncomfortably. "I told you everything was fine," she said, "and it is. That wasn't a lie."

He was still in disbelief. "She was right," Matthew said quietly.

Kyla hugged her elbows to her chest. "Alexa wasn't right," she insisted, though somehow she felt as if she were more trying to convince herself than him. "I'm not in danger, Matt. I promise."

Her brother looked up at her sharply. "Who is he?"

Kyla was surprised at his forwardness. "I don't know what you're talking about," she said.

He didn't believe her. "Who had Mom so freaked out tonight, Kyla?"

She shifted her weight. "He's nobody. Just a friend."

Matthew looked more worried than he should have. "What is his name?" he asked her slowly.

"Why does it matter?" She was starting to feel defensive now, protective even.

He didn't answer her, but asked her a question instead that about made her heart stop. "Is it Nathaniel?"

Kyla felt her own blood freeze. "How did you..."

"It is, isn't it?" he said.

Her head was starting to spin as she looked at him. "Look, Matty, I don't know what this is about..."

"He isn't safe, Kyla," he spoke over her.

Somehow, in addition to the intensity of her confusion, Kyla almost felt pain at his words. "Alexa..." she said, "did she tell you that?"

"Yes."

"How..." Kyla started to ask another question, but she couldn't find the words.

"I don't know how she sees the things she does," Matthew told her, "but she's never wrong. She's *never* wrong, Kyla."

The air felt like it was being constricted from Kyla's lungs as a familiar, long-suppressed feeling inside of her tried to resurface. "What did she say about him?" she asked Matthew tensely.

"She said you can't trust him," he told her. "That he isn't what he seems."

Kyla felt distinctly like she'd gotten nailed in the stomach with a croquet mallet. "I have to go to bed," she mumbled.

208

Then she turned away from Matthew before he could say another word and walked unsteadily down the hallway back to her room.

*N*athaniel approached the ledge on the mountain where Ethan remained at his post, but Ethan didn't turn to look at him.

"Are you aware that you were watched tonight?" he asked Nathaniel.

"I would certainly hope so," Nathaniel said sarcastically. "That *is* your assignment."

Ethan didn't appear amused. "Not by me. By Donovan."

Nathaniel felt a lead weight drop in his stomach at the words, but he didn't respond.

Ethan's brow was creased in frustration. "He was with the dark one. I do not yet know his name, but I have heard of him. He is Donovan's second-in-command."

Nathaniel felt a fire burning in his chest. How was it even possible that he was blinded to this? But he knew exactly how it was possible, despite his unwillingness to admit it.

"So tell me," Ethan said, finally turning to face him, "how is it that they were they able to track you and stake out a watch tonight without the slightest bit of awareness on your part?"

Nathaniel turned away. "I don't know."

Ethan was worried. "This isn't like you, Nathaniel. This is *nothing* like you."

Nathaniel didn't look back at him.

"I need to know what is going on," Ethan told him, "and I need to know now."

"Nothing is going on," Nathaniel insisted a little too quickly. "This is part of my assignment. I have to do this in order to obtain the information I have been sent here to find."

Ethan didn't buy it, and Nathaniel didn't blame him. The excuse was weak at best and hardly convincing.

"Do not treat me as if I am ignorant," Ethan said harshly. "As your appointed watch, you are placing me in danger by lying to me, and aside from the obvious reasons, *that* concerns me."

Nathaniel squared his jaw and tried to remain calm. "I will take care of it."

"Nathaniel…"

He raised his voice. "I said I will take care of it," he told him.

Ethan's face was tight.

"You need to get back to your watch," Nathaniel told him. Then he turned away and headed back down the trail.

He could feel Ethan's uncertainty as he left him, and he also felt his own. Knowing that he was followed, knowing Donovan had seen him made him sick with anger and regret.

How could he have let this happen?

But in spite of how furious he was with himself and angered by his own negligence, the only thing that mattered to him now was an auburn-haired girl that he had placed once again in the gravest of danger.

Shoving his frustration aside, Nathaniel set his focus before him, determining to get down to Ponderosa Way as quickly as he could. It didn't bother him as much as before, defying his orders to remain in human form. Even if Ethan saw him…even if he reported him to Seth. Breaking the rules seemed a small price to pay when the alternative could mean Kyla getting hurt.

He would break every rule if it meant keeping her from that.

Nathaniel knew full well what he was compromising and he knew where his priorities were meant to lie, but he also knew there was nothing more important to him now than protecting this girl…this seemingly insignificant human girl who had taken more of a hold over him than anything ever had. And though this realization frightened him, nothing frightened him more than the thought of Donovan finding her again.

No, he would not let that happen.

Chapter 14

"...what wakens in you when you least expect."

Kyla was all but incoherent at work the next day, dizzy when she thought of Nathaniel and nauseated when she remembered what Matthew had told her about him. His warning from Alexa and the fear that hit her along with it were enough to make her sick, but even despite this, she couldn't force her mind away from the blonde-haired boy who had so suddenly and forcefully crashed into her life.

And who apparently wasn't safe.

Taking a hot soapy rag to the counters, Kyla heard Val snap her name for probably the third or fourth time. Nothing was registering right in her mind today, so it took her longer than it should have to respond.

"Yes Val?" Kyla asked calmly. She was a little surprised when she didn't get the stainless steel steaming pitcher Val was washing chucked at her head, too. Judging by the girl's expression, she obviously thought about it.

"Get the register," Val snapped.

In place of the darts Kyla would have normally thrown at her with her eyes, she simply nodded to her once and headed to the front of the shop. Val seemed surprised by her compliance, but the last thing Kyla cared about right now was confusing her catty bitch of a co-worker.

Kyla greeted the woman who had come up to order with a sweet "hello" and got her a blueberry muffin and a decaf chai latte to go. Then, as soon as the woman left, Kyla rested her elbows against the counter and sighed, holding her head in her hands. It wasn't even ten yet and she already wanted this day to be over.

The thought didn't linger, though. It wasn't able to, as Kyla was jolted from it quickly when she heard a loud clang from behind her. Jerking her head up, she saw that Val had dropped the stack of blenders she was attempting to take back to the sink and shot her a look to see what her problem was.

Val's eyes were wide and fixed forward, and when Kyla saw this she followed her gaze...all the way to where a gorgeous blonde-haired boy stood at the counter with his hands in the pockets of his jeans.

Nathaniel Blake looked up at the menu as if his attention were completely focused on determining which beverage he wanted to order, but the smile pulling at the corner of his lips suggested otherwise.

Kyla's heart jumped up in her throat when she saw him and then proceeded to pound uncontrollably when she caught sight of the smile he was trying to hide. Forcing herself to exhale, she stepped forward with her shoulders squared and stood behind the register.

"Hello there," she greeted Nathaniel with as much professionalism as she could muster. "How are you today?"

He gave her a look that made retaining her composure extremely difficult. "Amazing," he said.

Kyla melted at the sound of his voice, to a pathetic degree that made her feel like she'd just turned to mush. And she was pretty sure Val was still frozen in place behind the pastry case and not breathing.

"Yeah?" Kyla asked him softly. So much for professionalism.

Nathaniel laughed a little. "Yeah," he said.

Was it just her or was the room starting to spin?

Kyla shook her head and forced herself to focus. "What can I get for you?" she asked him.

The way Nathaniel looked at her then was completely unnerving, as was the piercing gaze of the vulture behind her.

"A phone number," he told her.

Kyla laughed nervously. "What?"

Nathaniel glanced back up at the menu above her head. "A small hot tea to go, please," he said coolly.

Kyla's heart was racing, but she did her best to hide it. "What kind?" she struggled to ask him in an unshaken voice. "We have over two dozen flavors."

Gah, what was her problem? She never let anyone get to her like this.

Nathaniel looked into her with teasing ferocity. "Well, which one is the best?" he asked.

Kyla had to grip the edge of the counter to keep her hands from shaking. "It depends what you want," she said.

His smile changed subtly, as did his voice, just enough for her to catch it. "I think you know what I want..." he told her.

Kyla could have died.

She could feel her cheeks burning and she forced her gaze away from him. "How do you feel about blueberry?" she asked him, scrambling in her mind to remember how to breathe.

"I feel good about blueberry," Nathaniel said, sitting up a little straighter and letting his eyes move somewhere other than her face.

Kyla pressed her lips together, but it didn't help to ward off her smile. "Val, can you get me a small hot..."

"I heard him," Val snapped, moving past her and grabbing a white paper cup. Kyla had to bite her lip to keep from laughing.

She glanced coyly at Nathaniel again as Val murmured unpleasant things under her breath behind them. His eyes were unbelievably blue today, at least two shades darker than they'd been the night before. And hypnotizing did not begin to describe the effect they had on her.

When Val set the cup of blueberry tea on the counter, Kyla grabbed it up and scribbled ten digits onto its side with a pen.

A beam of amusement broke out on Nathaniel's face, but he didn't say a word about it. "Thank you," he told her politely instead. Then as he took the cup, he left a small folded piece of paper on the counter and gave her a look that told her to pick it up.

"Ladies," he said, nodding to her and Val and sipping his tea on his way out the door.

Kyla slipped the paper into the pocket of her apron before Val could see it, and when she turned around she was met by a cold leering glare. Once again, she found herself struggling not to laugh.

Val didn't say anything, thank God, but the malice in her fiercely green eyes said more than enough.

Oh, if jealousy had a face.

Making her way casually to the backroom, Kyla slipped out of sight and eagerly pulled the note out of the pocket of her apron. Unfolding it frantically, she stared unblinking at the words written at the center: *Outside. Now.*

Whatever her heart had been doing before, that was nothing compared to what it was doing now. "Val, I'm taking five," Kyla called out as she came out from the back and raced over to the door.

"*What?*" Val snapped, but Kyla ignored her.

There was only one thing on her mind right now.

Kyla didn't take three full steps outside or even have time to look up before she felt Nathaniel grab her from behind and pull her up against the side of the building. She screamed in surprise, but he already had his hand over her mouth before the sound could come out.

Holding her by the waist and turning her around, he pulled her so close to him that her entire body was pressed against his. Slowly, Nathaniel let his hand drop from her mouth and he whispered into her ear, "Ever had déjà vu?"

Kyla's heart was beating frantically by the time she turned to face him. "What are you *doing?*" she hissed at him nervously, but the smile plastered on her face made it hard for her to convince him she was mad about it. It was mesmerizing, being this near to him, and she only hoped he couldn't tell.

Nathaniel brushed her hair back from her forehead and looked into her in a way that made her whole body weak. "I wanted to see how you were feeling."

Staring breathlessly into his face, which was only inches from her own, Kyla whispered, "Amazing."

214

That made him smile.

"Nathaniel?" she said.

Kyla felt him toying with the edge of her shirt as he slowly moved his hands up underneath it.

"Yeah?" he asked softly.

She opened her mouth to say something else, but was jolted from the thought when his hands slid against her skin. Kyla looked up at him breathlessly, not understanding the shock of heat that burned into her beneath his fingertips, or what had possessed him to make such a bold move at all. But even more shocking was what she realized after he did.

It didn't hurt anymore.

"How...?" she started to ask him, but she was so surprised she didn't know how to form the question.

Nathaniel looked confused. "What is it?"

"The pain," Kyla said. "It's...gone."

Nathaniel froze for a moment, looking into her intently as if he were trying to gauge her sincerity. Slowly, he slid his hand back out from underneath her shirt. "What do you mean, it's gone?" he asked her. He seemed worried.

"I mean it's *gone*," she told him emphatically. "The second you touched me..."

Nathaniel turned her around and pulled the neck of her shirt down far enough that it started to choke her. Realizing this was an ineffective method of examination, he let go of her collar and told her, "I need to see your back."

Kyla looked at him, trying to understand. "Why?" she asked.

Nathaniel didn't look like he was going to be patient about this. Pulling her to the side of the building he told her, "Turn around."

Kyla blinked a few times as she looked at him, but she didn't do what he said.

Nathaniel sighed. "Kyla, please just turn around."

She kept her eyes on him as she turned slowly and faced the wall, skeptical of what he was trying to do. Kyla flinched when he pulled her shirt up from the bottom, high enough that he could see her back, and as an instinct reaction, clutched the front of it to her chest. She kept glancing over her shoulder to make sure no one was walking by, terrified that a customer, or even worse, her boss, would see her getting felt up from behind by some random blonde dude. That would just be the icing on the cake to this ridiculous week.

Nathaniel pulled her shirt back down again and took a step backwards.

"What is it?" Kyla asked, turning again to face him.

He stared forward, unblinking. "You should get back to work," he told her.

That was not going to work for her. "Nathaniel..." she tried to say, but he didn't let her finish.

"Kyla, really," he said. "Get back to work."

She didn't want to listen to him, but something in his eyes told her she should. She also knew if she didn't get back inside, Val would probably throw a fit that would make a five-year-old look mature.

"Fine," Kyla said, crossing her arms and walking back out to the front of the building. Nathaniel didn't follow her.

She turned back to look at him before she went around the corner, wishing she didn't have to leave things like that. Nathaniel looked disturbed. Really disturbed. His head was down and his hands were on his hips, and by the looks of things, he was brooding over something.

Kyla ducked back inside and frowned, wishing she knew what he was thinking. She didn't have long to wonder, though, before she came face to face with a black-haired girl who at the moment bore a striking resemblance to her mother.

Kyla had a hard time determining which of them was more malicious. Her mother took the cake when it came to unparalleled rage, but Val had the whole "I hate you and want to murder you with my hands" thing going on.

She eventually concluded that it was a toss-up.

Hurrying to the bathroom in the back right corner of the shop, Kyla got away from Val before she could rip her throat out with her fangs. She shut the door quickly behind her and flipped the lock, then pulled her shirt hurriedly over her head as she turned to face the bathroom mirror.

216

Slowly pulling a bandage away from the deepest cut on her right shoulder blade, Kyla felt dizzy when she saw what was beneath it. The gash that had been there only that morning was no longer there, but although the bruises around it remained, what was left in its place was something that looked like a three-inch scar. The way it appeared, she would have thought it had already had a week to heal, and the rest of them were the same.

Suddenly, Kyla couldn't breathe. Leaning against the sink and dropping her head, her mind scrambled to catch up with reality. This wasn't possible. People's backs didn't just heal like that...not just because somebody touched them.

She struggled to calm her breathing, telling herself it was okay. Looking up and into the mirror again, Kyla was met by the reflection of her own darkened eyes, but behind the hollow that had taken them, there was a truth that still was kept in there...a truth that told that was a lie. She *had* known things before exactly like that, and she knew refusing to believe them now couldn't make them not exist.

That was the thing about the supernatural. Just because you didn't choose to believe in it didn't mean it wasn't there. Just because you ran from it, because you held your breath and closed your eyes, it didn't lessen the reality of the things unseen, of the world that existed around all that was known.

Kyla used to know that. She still knew that, even if she tried to convince herself she didn't. And right now, all that stared back at her through the eyes in the mirror that had taken on a sudden tinge of green was the truth she couldn't run from any longer, and the realization that somehow, in some twisted sort of way, Nathaniel Blake had something to do with it.

*A*s soon as Kyla was back inside, Nathaniel left quickly, looking at his hands as he made his way up the street and into the woods behind the buildings. His heart was beating faster than normal, and despite his effort to calm himself, he couldn't shake the feeling that was over him.

Taking a sharp rock from off the ground, Nathaniel slashed his own forearm without a moment's hesitation, not even wincing at the pain. He held his breath as he stared at the gash, waiting to see something happen...but nothing did.

Nathaniel furrowed his brow and looked down at the blood that seeped out from his skin. Then carefully, he placed his other hand on top of the wound. He waited a few seconds, still holding his breath, but again, nothing changed.

Frowning in confusion, Nathaniel started to move his hand away, and it was then that something finally did.

Slowly, very slowly, he watched his skin pull together, staring in disbelief as the wound healed itself beneath his hand. His eyes grew wide at the sight of it, but he didn't know how to trust what they showed him.

Seth had never said anything to him about Nephilim having healing powers.

Nathaniel dropped his hand quickly and stared at his arm. The blood was dried and the skin was closed, and all that was left in its place was a scar. And while something like this should not be a bad thing, somehow it only frightened him now, mostly because he didn't understand it.

Thinking back on the night of the attack, Nathaniel remembered Kyla telling him the throbbing had left once he touched her head. Maybe there was a connection. He had assumed at the time that it was just a coincidence, but now he didn't know what to assume anymore.

Dropping the bloodied rock he held, Nathaniel cast his gaze to the dirt at his feet.

This was not possible. It couldn't be.

He glanced back up through the trees to the coffee shop, and his mind sped to make sense of what had just happened. But there was just no sense to a thing like this, only more questions than he knew how to answer. Through all of them, however, there was only one he really cared about.

Who was this girl that she could rise something out of him like this? Who was Kyla James?

There had to be a reason Donovan was threatened by her, and Nathaniel used to think he knew what that reason was. But this was about more than her just being one of the awakened. Even the awakened didn't possess a power like this.

Looking up the road in the direction of the estate, Nathaniel frowned when he thought of his uncle. Howard would be here tomorrow, and Nathaniel was supposed to be out of there tonight...which meant he had only one more shot at this. Tonight was the last chance he had to find out the truth about this girl, be it for the brotherhood or only for himself. And he would find that truth, no matter what it took.

Nathaniel was not going to let anything stop him tonight.

*K*yla was shaking as she came out of the bathroom again, not knowing what to make of what had happened to her back. It defied possibility...just as the man who attacked her had defied possibility when Nathaniel hurled him into a rock that should have broken his back.

What was going on here?

"Real cute stunt there," Val told her once she was back behind the counter. "Pull that again and you're fired."

Kyla didn't respond.

"Who was that?" Val snapped.

Recapping the pen she'd used to write her number on Nathaniel's cup, Kyla didn't move her eyes from the register. Somehow she felt like she was moving in slow motion.

"His name's Nathaniel," she told her. "Why?"

She could feel Val's eyes burning into her without even seeing them.

"No reason," Val said a little too tensely. "Just wondering if Caden knows about him."

That was enough to shake her from her daze. "And what is *that* supposed to mean?" Kyla asked, not even bothering to hide her glare.

Val acted like she was busy when they both knew she wasn't, re-stacking the already perfectly stacked cups behind them. "I don't know," she shrugged. "I was just thinking if you've moved past everything with him..."

"Moved past *what*?" Kyla interrupted her. "Caden's my best friend."

"Right," Val said. Kyla resented the sarcasm in her voice. "Well if that's really the case, then I guess you wouldn't mind giving me his number?"

Kyla folded her arms across her chest, forcing herself to remain calm under her rising anger. "I would rather ram a pencil in my eye than let you anywhere near him."

Val slapped her forehead mockingly. "I'm sorry. I must have forgotten who I was talking to for a minute there."

Kyla sneered at her and Val gave her a smirk, one of the only looks her face was capable of holding, as far as Kyla could tell.

"So what about you?" Val asked.

"What *about* me?"

Val looked at her condescendingly. "When was the last time you heard from your *best friend*?"

The question stung. "I don't see how that's any of your business," Kyla muttered.

"Been that long, huh?"

Kyla glared at her warningly and Val took the hint.

Unbelievable.

Reminding herself as the girl walked away that hitting her would undoubtedly get her fired, Kyla resisted the urge. She did debate it, though, thinking at that point that it might be worth it.

Kyla was more than anxious to leave work that night. It frustrated her that she didn't have the answers she wanted, and as a result she thought about Nathaniel the entire drive home, replaying over in her mind every move and gesture he had made, every word he had spoken; the way he had looked at her, the way he had smiled at her...the way it had felt to have his hands slide up her back.

Stop it! Kyla scolded herself. She couldn't do this again. She hardly even *knew* this boy. But despite her effort to convince herself that that should matter to her, she couldn't believe how little it actually did.

Even knowing he could be dangerous, she couldn't make herself want to stay away from him; and not because she was foolish enough to rationalize trusting a perfect stranger. There was just something about him... something that made

220

him different than anyone she had ever known. She couldn't explain it, she could only feel it. And she felt it every time Nathaniel looked at her.

Walking into her room, Kyla sat on the edge of her bed and took her shoes off. She knew there were about a thousand and three questions she should be asking herself right now, a thousand and three things she should probably be thinking, but the only thought in her mind was a blonde-haired, blue-eyed boy who was already more important to her than she ever should have let him become.

Glancing at her cell phone for the sixth time since she'd left work, Kyla frowned when she saw that she had no missed calls. This was ridiculous. She was driving herself nuts here and she needed to stop. But even though she knew she shouldn't be, she was so anxious to hear from Nathaniel she was about to go out of her mind.

Setting the phone on her desk, Kyla walked into her closet. She pulled the turtleneck over her head, slipped out of her work pants and tossed them to the floor. Then she threw on a pair of long black running pants, a matching sports bra and a tight white tank top that offset it to perfection. Not that it mattered since she wasn't going anyway; that was just her OCD coming into play.

As she was putting her hair up in a ponytail, her cell phone rang and made her jump about a foot off the ground. Kyla darted out of her closet and across her room, her face breaking out in an anxious smile. Her heart fluttered as she imagined the sound of Nathaniel's devastatingly perfect voice on the other end of the line, and even though she knew her excitement was unmerited given the way they had left things, it was all she could do not to squeal like a twelve-year-old girl when she answered.

Grabbing the phone from off her desk, she hurriedly answered it and gave him a teasing, "Hello?"

Kyla waited for a second, hearing only silence at first, and then someone spoke on the other end of the line. "Kyla?"

Her smile dropped at the sound of Caden Howell's voice.

"*K*yla?" The second time Caden said her name she realized she needed to answer him.

"Hey," she finally responded.

He was quiet for a second before he said, "Hey," back to her.

Something about the inflection of his voice caught her off guard. There was a softness to his tone that she didn't expect, a gentleness that made it hard for her to keep herself detached and cold and angry with him. But naturally, as soon as she felt the slightest tinge of emotion, Kyla closed herself off again.

"Why are you calling me?" she snapped. She didn't mean for it to sound as harsh as it did; it just came out that way.

"What do you mean?" Caden asked her nervously. Hearing the familiar roughness of his voice made her heart hurt.

"You haven't answered my calls in days, Caden. Why now?"

What was wrong with her? He freaking called her back and she was trying to push him away? *Gah*, why couldn't she just shut up and let the boy talk?

"Kyla, listen," he said. "I'm sorry. I've been so busy with this project and…and this one song I'm working on that I just…I haven't had time to call anyone."

Why was he stumbling over his words? Caden never stumbled over his words. He was the most articulate person she knew.

"You haven't had *time*?" She couldn't believe he was really going with that excuse.

Caden sighed in the way he always did when he knew she was right. "I'm just sorry, okay?"

It was obvious that something was making him feel uncomfortable, and there was a good chance that her biting his head off had something to do with it. Still, it took all the willpower Kyla possessed for her not to break down right then and tell him how badly she really missed him.

"Kyla?"

She clenched her jaw, knowing if she answered him now, she would never be able to hold herself together. "I have to go," she told him flatly, feeling sick as she said it.

"Oh," Caden said. "Okay…" She could hear the disappointment in his voice. After hesitating for a few seconds he started to tell her, "Kyla, this song…" but she didn't let him finish. The truth was she didn't want to hear it.

It hurt her more than he knew, his fixation with this new music…with this "project" that had taken her place in his life.

"Bye, Caden," she said quickly. Then she pressed "end" on her phone with a shaking hand.

Staring down at its shiny plastic face, Kyla watched the screen go black and felt a familiar stabbing in her chest; only this time it was stronger. With each passing second the pain grew more intense, more defined, and before a fraction of a minute had passed, her chest was throbbing.

She couldn't be here anymore.

Unwilling to take the time to lace up any shoes, Kyla slipped on a pair of flip-flops as she ran out the door. Breathing didn't come easy for her despite the unnatural coolness to the air; but she tried, nonetheless, as she clamored down the steps and out to the street in the dark.

Kyla didn't know where she was going; she only knew that she couldn't get there fast enough. Feeling distinctly as if she was suffocating, she moved further down Ponderosa, hoping that if she got far enough away, she wouldn't feel this fear at her throat that was choking her anymore. But distance didn't seem to matter.

Taking in oxygen in short, uncomfortable gasps, Kyla sat on the edge of the curb and put her head between her knees. She felt like the ground was turning sideways on itself and that somehow the pine trees towering over her head were about to collapse on top of her. Everything was spinning in the wrong direction. Her heart, her lungs, her mind…they were all wrong. Just like this night was all wrong.

Kyla's hands shook where they were pressed against her forehead, but no matter how hard she tried, she couldn't make the ground stop moving.

Why did you do that? she screamed at herself in her mind.

Maybe she had deluded herself into thinking Caden deserved it, or maybe she was so hurt by his abandoning her that she wanted him to hurt, too...but she knew that wasn't it. She had never wanted Caden to hurt a day in her life. No matter what he did or what he said, no matter where he was or how he treated her, whether or not he even chose to remember her name, he was still Caden.

Kyla dropped her hands to her stomach and doubled over. She wanted to tell him everything, to the point that it was almost a need. Maybe that's what was really wrecking her right now, the fact that she couldn't tell him what had happened...that she couldn't be weak and broken and vulnerable with the boy who had been there for her through every weak, broken and vulnerable moment of her life.

Kyla wasn't angry with him and she knew it. Chances were, Caden knew it too. But anger was always an easier emotion for her to give into than fear. What she was afraid of, she didn't even know. She only knew that it hurt like hell and she wanted it to stop.

Just before Kyla forced herself to stand up again, a motorcycle came tearing around the corner of Paradise and Ponderosa, close enough that she thought it was going to hit her. She jumped up and screamed, and the bike was spun around in a maneuver that would give Steve McQueen a run for his money as it was brought to a screeching halt. When the rider hit the brakes, the rear tire locked as he shifted his weight, and he flipped the bike around again to face her.

Snapping her head up to see who this maniac was that had just tried to kill her, Kyla's mouth hung open when she saw his face.

"What is *wrong* with you?!" she screamed at him.

Nathaniel gripped the clutch on the bike and brought it to an idle. "Nothing I'm aware of," he said. He looked surprised to see her on the side of the road, but he didn't ask her about it.

Staring at the pristine Ducati (and the black and grey Italian leather jacket he wore) Kyla scowled at him bitterly. As if it wasn't enough that Nathaniel was gorgeous, he had to have money too.

224

Kyla wasn't sure what upset her more, the pristine black and red Ducati Nathaniel was sitting on, the Belstaff label he was sporting on his arm or the fact that he looked so damn good doing both. His almost running her over hadn't done much to evoke warm, happy feelings from her either, so all in all, he had quite a few strikes against him.

Kyla grumbled as she eyed the bike. "As if I don't have enough reasons to hate you already."

"Look," Nathaniel said, "are you getting on or do I have to sit here all night and watch you drool?"

Kyla made a face at him, which only made him laugh, then she questioned for a moment whether or not it would be wise for her to go along with this. She knew the answer was no, but the gleam from the midnight black paint and the carbon fiber pipes held her spellbound as she stared at them.

"Yes, I'm getting on," she grumbled, wishing she had the willpower to deny Nathaniel and his stupid sexy bike.

Kyla put on the helmet that he handed her, then she grabbed his waist and held on for her life.

Chapter 15

"...if the stars could talk."

Nathaniel didn't waste his breath with any safety precautions. It was ridiculous of him to assume that Kyla knew how to ride (even though she did) and she was not beyond letting him know it.

"Thanks for the crash course," she said sarcastically.

"No problem," Nathaniel replied. He was clearly amused with himself.

Kyla scowled at his arrogance. If it weren't for her growing up around bikes the way she had, she would have been left back there on the street. Just one more reason for her to be thankful for her dad.

Kyla couldn't remember a time in her childhood that her father hadn't had a bike in their garage that he was working on. He loved them all; Harley's, Triumph's, Kawasaki's. He had never owned a Ducati, but she was sure he would be envious of this one. That was putting it mildly.

Loni used to hate it when he'd take Kyla out riding, and always complained about how unsafe it was. That was back when her mother actually gave a damn about her. Either way, the knowledge those experiences had given Kyla proved to be invaluable tonight, and she was grateful her dad hadn't caved to Loni's complaining.

As she and Nathaniel tore up Highway 24, Kyla was surprised at how quickly she was able to forget about the phone call that left her sickened only minutes before. But that was just the effect Nathaniel Blake had on her. Being in his presence was intoxicating, and it honestly scared her how little control she possessed over herself when she was with him like this…which was pretty evident considering she was on the back of his Ducati right now.

Kyla made a strenuous effort to keep calm as she clung to his rock-hard torso, but internally she was screaming. The feeling dropped like a lead weight in her stomach, though, when he pulled them onto Edlowe Road.

She tensed up involuntarily. "Where are we going?" she asked him, making sure to raise her voice enough that he could hear her over the exhaust.

Nathaniel didn't answer, even though she knew he had heard her.

"You're a very aggravating person, you know that?" she called up to him even louder.

"Right," Nathaniel replied, "because you would know nothing about being aggravating."

Kyla narrowed her eyes, and even though he didn't see her do it, somehow he seemed to know.

"Stop acting insulted," he told her. "I happen to find your stubbornness extremely appealing."

Gah…stupid heart. How did he *do* that?

Kyla turned away from him, wishing he didn't have the power to make her feel like that. It was dangerous in so many more ways than one. Matthew's words kept ringing through her mind as she and Nathaniel tore up Edlowe Road: *He isn't safe. He isn't what he seems. Alexa's never wrong…*

She didn't want to think on these things, but they prodded her, pulled at her mind like it was Silly Putty, pliable and shapeable to whatever they wanted…these things that compelled her to look away from him and drew her to look *to* him at the very same time. She could feel it inside her, the truth to what Matthew claimed, but Kyla failed to let this dictate what she actually did.

She knew she should stay away from Nathaniel Blake, and yet here she was. She knew he was lying to her, (or at least keeping her from the truth) and yet for all of the common sense she used to possess, she was still clinging to him now, feeling her heart beat against his back at a pace nothing else had ever driven it to.

And she felt like she was losing her mind.

228

Looking out at the trees and the stars that hung over their heads, Kyla hoped that the sight could distract her from her own stupid mind, which at the moment wouldn't shut up no matter how she tried to make it. The beauty of this road was unsurpassed in the moonlight, except possibly by the silhouette of the boy that she clung to. But she wasn't supposed to be thinking about that right now. She was supposed to be distracting herself.

Focus on the road, Kyla told herself. She just had to focus.

That proved to be a mistake, however, when they passed by Skyline Drive. Glancing down the long dirt road, Kyla suddenly felt queasy, though by it she'd discovered the solution to her problem. Just kick her in the stomach and remind her of Caden, then add a nice dose of nausea to the mix and that should do the trick.

"You okay?" Nathaniel asked her.

"Yeah," she lied.

How did he know to ask her that?

When Nathaniel pulled into the dirt and gravel parking lot at the base of the Catamount Trail, he locked the bike and popped the kickstand; then he helped Kyla down and took her helmet from her when she handed it to him.

"So may I ask why you were sitting on the side of the road tonight?" Nathaniel inquired.

"No," she said. "Not really."

"Fair enough," he replied. She was surprised when he dropped it so quickly.

Glancing up toward the trail, she squinted in the dark. "What are we doing here?" she asked him.

Nathaniel looked like he expected her to protest, especially when he pulled out a couple of flashlights from his inner jacket pocket. But Kyla didn't protest. She just held out her hand expectantly, despite that he hadn't even answered her with words.

Nathaniel gave her a curious look that she discerned by the nearly-full moon overhead. He tossed her the flashlight and smiled when she caught it one-handed.

"Where to, captain?" she asked.

Nathaniel shook his head. "You're unbelievable, you know that?"

"Yes, I do," she replied matter-of-factly. Then she motioned for him to lead the way.

Nathaniel shone his flashlight on the trail and Kyla stayed close behind him, trying not to let on that it scared her being up in the woods in the dark like this. But even still, she was far less afraid than she expected herself to be.

She felt protected with Nathaniel in a way that made her question what Alexa had said; and it wasn't only because he had potentially saved her life. It was something she felt deeper than what was based upon circumstance, though she really wasn't willing to admit that right now. For the moment, she would rather just follow Nathaniel through the trees and pretend that she couldn't feel anything at all.

After all, that was her favorite game.

Kyla listened to the steady crunching of Nathaniel's footsteps in front of her, comforted by the sound and somehow reassured. But then he decided to play with her again.

"Are you sure you trust a perfect stranger enough to follow him through the woods in the dark?" Nathaniel asked her. "I mean, you don't even know why I brought you here."

Kyla gave him back a quick, "Well, I'm following you, aren't I?"

Nathaniel laughed a little. "Yes, you are," he said, "and I'll admit I'm a little surprised. I expected more of a fight from you about it."

"Did you ever think that maybe I was just bored?" she asked sarcastically.

Nathaniel paused for a moment and then said, "Actually, yes."

"And?" Kyla prompted.

She could tell he was smiling when he answered her. "I don't buy it."

Kyla's heart did that obnoxious fluttering thing again, and she stumbled as she walked, which unfortunately resulted in her tripping over a tree root that was protruding from the trail.

"Ow!" she cried out. She instinctively grabbed her foot and winced in pain.

Nathaniel spun around sharply, looking far more afraid than she expected him to.

"Are you okay?" he asked her quickly, kneeling in the dirt and putting a hand on her knee.

She tried to laugh it off. "You could have mentioned I should put on something a little more substantial than flip-flops," she told him.

Nathaniel's face was level with hers. "I'm sorry," he said as he looked at her, "but I wasn't exactly paying attention to your feet."

Kyla felt her cheeks heat up, and she was immediately thankful it was too dark for him to notice.

"Okay, I'll tell you what," Nathaniel said. "We're not far, so get on my back and I'll take you the rest of the way."

Kyla laughed at him. "What?"

He spun around since he was already kneeling in front of her and told her again, "Get on my back."

Kyla gave him a look he couldn't see. "You want to give me a piggyback ride?"

"Yes, I want to give you a piggyback ride," Nathaniel sighed in mock exasperation. "Now hurry up and get on my back before I change my mind and make you trip over more rocks."

Kyla climbed nervously up onto Nathaniel and put her arms around his neck. It made her heart go insane when she touched him like that, but he only made it worse when he grabbed her by her legs and hiked her up around his waist.

"That's better," he said.

"You're ridiculous," she told him, trying not to giggle as she said it. Why did he always have to make her sound like such a damn girl?

"Take my flashlight," Nathaniel told her. "And hold them both up so I can see."

She held them both over his head and shone them on the trail. "Like this?" she asked.

He started walking and told her, "Perfect."

As Nathaniel carried her like that through the woods, relying on the flashlights she held to guide them, Kyla was amazed at how well he was able to navigate through the trail. If she didn't know any better, she would have thought he was moving faster than he had moved when she wasn't on his back.

Strange.

When the two of them broke through the trees into a clearing, they were met by a deep blue image of Pike's Peak in the distance. Silhouetted by the moonlight, it looked as though it had been painted across the sky in a way that it almost glowed. Kyla stared forward at the picture, awed that the mountain she had spent her whole life looking at could ever be so beautiful. She hopped down from Nathaniel's back and stepped slowly into the clearing, breathing in deeply the air that she loved.

"Beautiful, isn't it?" he asked her.

Kyla shook her head. "Unreal." She took a few more steps forward; then she frowned a little when she was hit with a thought. Turning back to Nathaniel, she asked him, "Why did you bring me here?"

He seemed a little unsure of how to answer that as he stepped up beside her and looked at the sky. After a few seconds of silence, he finally told her, "Because there's no other point on the earth where the stars look exactly like this."

Kyla laughed a little and gave him a skeptical look. "Couldn't you say that about anywhere?" she asked.

Nathaniel dropped his head and she immediately felt bad for laughing. It surprised her, but he was actually serious. "Well, yes," he admitted, "I guess you could. But there's something different about here."

Kyla felt dizzy as she looked at him, like she was caught up somehow in dream. "Different how?" she asked softly.

Nathaniel turned back to her for a moment; then he returned his gaze to the stars. "When I'm in this place," he told her, "I don't feel quite as close to them as I used to. I feel more like I belong…here."

Kyla was staring at him now, and she hadn't even realized she'd forgotten to breathe. She didn't understand what he meant, but she felt the conviction in Nathaniel's words, almost as if he had never been more honest with anyone.

"I've never felt like I belong here," she whispered. She didn't know why she told him that.

Nathaniel slowly met her gaze. The way he looked at her, like he was completely caught up in what she was about to say, she didn't understand it.

"How could you feel like that?" he asked her. His voice was so intent.

Kyla looked down nervously. "Have you ever felt...different?" she asked, "from everyone around you? Like you can be standing in a crowd of people and it's just the same as if none of them are there?"

Nathaniel laughed once. "Yeah, you could say that."

Kyla tried to keep the emotion out of her voice. "That's the way I've felt my whole life," she said. "Except when..."

The thought came on her against her will and immediately she regretted saying it.

"Except when what?" he prompted.

She bit her lip and shook her head. "Never mind. It doesn't matter."

Nathaniel's expression grew tight. "Except when you're with Caden," he answered for her.

Kyla tensed up, but she didn't respond.

"You were upset tonight when I found you," Nathaniel said. "It was about him, wasn't it?"

She kept her eyes on the ground. "Yes."

"What did he do?" Nathaniel asked.

She cringed at the memory. "It wasn't what he did, it was what I did. He called me and I pretty much hung up on him."

Nathaniel looked confused. "If you hung up on him, then why are you the one who is upset?"

Kyla groaned. "Because that's the *last* thing I wanted to do!" She held her arms to her chest nervously and started to pace, and Nathaniel didn't appear to understand at all.

"Then why did you?" he asked her.

"I don't *know*!" she insisted. "I never do or say what I want and I hate it. It's like that verse in fricken Romans," she told him. "*I do not understand what I do. For what I want to do, I do not do, but what I hate, I do.* I'm bloody Paul!"

"Paul?" Nathaniel asked her. He looked at her like she was nuts, and when she realized what she was saying, she suddenly didn't blame him.

Kyla sighed and stopped pacing. "I'm sorry," she said. "I'm not making any sense. I just hate that I'm always so against myself."

"Why *are* you?" Nathaniel asked her.

Kyla shook her head. "I don't know," she told him honestly. "I really don't. It's like I've been programmed to think I'm gonna lose every person I get close to and anyone I even start to care about, so I put up these stupid defenses before I ever give them a chance to get anywhere near me..."

Nathaniel interrupted her. "Because of your dad..." he said.

Kyla's mouth was still open, but no words came out. She was startled by his bluntness and unconsciously clutching at the bracelet on her wrist. "How do you know about my dad?" she asked him.

Nathaniel hesitated before he answered her. "I didn't at first, but I put it together after our last run-in in the cemetery."

Kyla looked down at her bracelet and Nathaniel motioned toward her wrist. "Can I see that?" he asked her.

Kyla was unsure. She eyed him skeptically, but then she slipped the bracelet off and handed it to him.

Nathaniel held the black leather chord with the silver face carefully. He held it up to try and see the inscription on the inside by the light of the moon, but he couldn't catch it at the right angle.

"It says, *Daddy's angel*," she told him coldly. Forcing the emotion out of her words wasn't easy, but she had gotten good at it over the years, enough that she didn't even have to feel it when she told him.

"What happened to him?" Nathaniel asked her with an unusual softness to his voice.

That was where she drew the line. Shrugging and looking away from him, she said simply, "Some stupid accident. You know how it goes."

"I'm sorry, Kyla," Nathaniel told her. He examined the bracelet one last time and then carefully tied it back on her wrist.

At the feel of his touch, she slowly looked back to him again. He wasn't making it easy for her to stay guarded.

Kyla tried to shrug it off again. "Yeah well, that's life, right?"

Nathaniel frowned. "I guess so," he said. "I never knew either of my parents, so I don't really know what it's like to lose one."

She stared at him, surprised. "You didn't know your parents?"

Nathaniel looked uncomfortable now. "My mother died when I was nine," he told her, "but I don't remember her. And I never knew my father."

Kyla felt an ache in her heart when she imagined Nathaniel as a little boy, when she thought about the kind of pain he must be suppressing even now to care so little about something that should break him. Suddenly, she didn't feel all that different from him anymore.

"What happened to your mom?" she asked him.

His face changed then, tightened even further, and she could tell that he didn't want to answer the question. "She was killed," he told her emotionlessly. "I never knew why."

Kyla gaped at him. "Killed?" she asked. "As in…murdered?"

Nathaniel looked away from her, but he didn't give her an answer, and this time, Kyla didn't want to press him.

"Your uncle," she said, "the one you're staying with…did he raise you?"

"I guess you could say that," he mumbled.

"How does that work?" she asked him. "I mean, either he raised you or he didn't."

It didn't take much discernment on her part to see that he was nervous, and in a matter of seconds, his entire countenance shifted.

"What is it?" she asked him.

Nathaniel looked at her again. "What do you mean?" he asked unassumingly.

Kyla stared at him, amazed that he was actually trying to play dumb. "Well to start," she said, "you were actually opening up to me for once and then for no reason at all you threw your guard up in my face."

"I'm not being guarded," Nathaniel told her. "You're imagining things."

Kyla scoffed at him. "Please," she said. "You're not even good at hiding it anymore."

She saw that same uneasiness in his eyes that she had seen before, but he turned away from her before she could look into him long enough to figure it out.

"Nathaniel, what aren't you telling me?" she asked him. "I mean, aside from the questions I've asked you that you refuse to answer."

"I don't know what you're talking about," he mumbled.

Kyla put her hands on her hips. "You know, I'm really getting sick of you acting like I'm stupid enough to believe that."

Nathaniel looked like he was trying not to get upset.

"I want the truth, Nathaniel. I want to know who you are...why you just showed up out of nowhere and came into my life like this. I want to know how you learned to fight the way you do and how you can make physical pain disappear by just touching me."

Nathaniel stopped trying to hide the fact that he was upset. "Why do you have to be so stubborn?" he asked her tensely.

"Why can't you just be honest with me?" Kyla challenged.

It was then that he finally slipped up, and in the last way she expected him to. "Did you ever think maybe I'm afraid?" he said.

Kyla didn't understand. "Afraid of what?"

Nathaniel looked back at her intently, and as he did she could see the fear behind his eyes. "Afraid of *you*."

He looked so scared, so vulnerable, and possibly for the first time since she'd known him, completely honest.

236

Kyla stared into him, trying to read behind the veil that he held over his eyes. "Why would you be afraid of me?" she asked him. The thought baffled her.

Nathaniel was breathing hard...hard enough that she could see it in his chest, and his voice trembled as he answered her. "When you look at me like that...you don't know what it does to me."

Kyla's face was on fire as she stared at him. Had she really just heard him right? Laughing nervously, she told him, "You probably say that to all the girls."

Nathaniel looked at her, confused. "I've never said that to anyone."

Kyla stopped laughing when she saw that he was serious. Looking into his eyes again, she was incapable of finding her breath. "Tell me who you are," she whispered.

Nathaniel swallowed hard, his hand trembling as it gently touched her face. She felt a familiar warmth rush over her at his touch, which didn't aid her in her current effort to take in oxygen. Kyla closed her eyes as his fingers traced her skin.

"Please..." she said.

Nathaniel stepped closer to her, pulling her toward him and pressing his lips softly to her forehead. Kyla trembled and put her hand on top of his.

"Damn it, Nathaniel," she said softly, her voice shaking as she spoke. "You can't just do that when you don't want to answer..."

He didn't let her finish. She had a suspicion he might not and she had to struggle to appear angry about it. But when Nathaniel pulled her face up to his and kissed her fiercely on the mouth, she lost that struggle in epic defeat.

Kyla's heart crashed against her chest when his lips locked with hers, and despite how she wished she could fight it, she failed at that, too. Swept up in an unnatural kind of ecstasy, she suddenly lost every doubt, every warning, and every suspicion she had ever had about this boy. They became irrelevant in her mind, to the point that it probably should have concerned her; but she was far too gone to be concerned with anything so trivial anymore.

If this was what it felt like to be in danger, then Kyla never wanted to be safe again.

*E*than looked down in silence on Nathaniel from his point of watch on the mountain. Speechless. Furious. Completely incapable of believing the sight before him.

His curiosity had been aroused when he saw Nathaniel hiking through the dark with the auburn-haired girl, but despite his unease, Ethan had chosen to trust that he was keeping his word…that this was somehow necessary for him to elicit the information he needed from this girl.

Still, Ethan was growing tired of these games. It had never taken Nathaniel so long to uncover anything, and that alone made him nervous. Luckily, Donovan and the dark one whose name he still did not know were nowhere in sight, so even if Nathaniel were being reckless, which had yet to be determined, he wasn't doing so in as much of a risk of danger as before.

But that was before he kissed her.

When Ethan watched Nathaniel pull the girl toward him, his eyes had almost fallen out of his head. Stunned, he moved down the mountain and got closer, despite his perfect vision, completely unable to believe what he was seeing.

When the sight had finally registered, his shock subsided, and an anger he'd never felt toward Nathaniel before quickly took its place. With all of his strength, Ethan had to restrain himself from moving down there and grabbing his brother by the throat.

Clenching his fists, he spoke furiously under his breath, "I should have known."

This was why Nathaniel's judgment had been compromised. This was why he couldn't see.

Ethan forced aside his anger and set his focus instead on the issue at hand. He knew what he had to do, even if he hated doing it. But his personal convictions didn't have any say when it came to following protocol.

238

Ethan narrowed his eyes as he looked at his brother one last time. Damn Nathaniel for placing him in this position. He had brought this on himself.

He had brought this all on himself.

*N*athaniel's heart pounded as he took Kyla's mouth onto his. His lungs felt constricted, like they were expanding and contracting at a faster rate than they should, and he questioned distantly in his mind if he should be worried about that.

Granted, there were about a hundred other things he knew he should be worried about right now, such as the fact that his impulsiveness and complete lack of self-control could very well cost them this entire mission. But with the heat of Kyla's breath pushing hard against his own, with the feel of her lips and the unnatural current of electricity that pulsed through him as he kissed her, Nathaniel couldn't force himself to care.

Then she did something that made him care. She started to kiss him back.

Nathaniel's eyes shot open in surprise as he was slammed forcefully back to reality. His heart took a sharp spike and he pulled himself back, holding Kyla by her shoulders and making himself inhale.

Her eyes were huge when she looked up at him, and Nathaniel could see that she was lost as to why he'd just done that.

"I need to get you home," he told her, making as strenuous an effort to control his voice as he'd ever had to.

Kyla continued staring at him for a moment without blinking; then very much like the first time he had kissed her in his uncle's washroom, a look of complete mortification came onto her face.

"*What?!*"

Nathaniel clenched his jaw and she looked at him as if expecting him to tell her he was joking. When he didn't, she pushed his hands off her shoulders.

"Fine," she snapped.

Jerking away from him, she clicked her flashlight back on and started down the trail again.

"Do you want me to…" Nathaniel started to ask, but she cut him off.

"I got it," she said. Then she moved back down the mountain with impressive speed, flip-flops and all.

As they rode back down to Woodland Park in silence, Nathaniel couldn't think of a time he'd felt sicker. Everything about this night had gone wrong. He had been hoping to get closer to her, to understand who Kyla James was in a way that he could make some part of this twisted reality make sense to him. He was hoping he could get her to trust him…to determine if she was one of the awakened.

But now that plan was shot to hell.

Nathaniel scowled to himself as he pushed forward on the bike. He was lying to himself and he knew it. He was no more concerned with her being one of the awakened than he was concerned about that foolish boy named Caden Howell. There was only one thing that mattered to him now, despite what he had tried to convince Ethan, despite what he tried to convince Seth, despite what he was trying even now to convince himself.

Even if he had to let Seth believe they needed this girl for whatever strategic advance could be made in the city, it wasn't about that for him anymore. Nathaniel needed more than that. He needed to know what Kyla had to do with any of this; to silence this voice in his head that kept telling him it wasn't a mistake that he had found her.

But even if that were true, what did that have to do with her being one of *them*? Assuming she even was, of course. It would seem that she would have to be if she had ever been a target of Donovan's in the first place, but Nathaniel didn't know. He didn't know anything anymore.

When he pulled up in front of the condo, Kyla got off the bike without breaking her silence, forcing him to make the next move.

"Kyla, wait…" he said.

240

She turned to him coldly, almost daringly.

"You're mad," Nathaniel told her.

"You *think*?"

"Why?" he asked. Granted, he had his ideas, but he couldn't think of anything else to say that would keep her there.

"Are you *serious*? First you grab me and kiss me like you have no intention of letting me breathe, and then you push me away like I repulse you! Honestly Nathaniel, what am I supposed to think?"

He gaped at her in disbelief. "You think that's why I pushed you away?"

Kyla folded her arms. "You wanna tell me I'm wrong?"

Nathaniel was practically twitching. He hated that she could draw a conclusion like that, but he hated not being able to explain himself even more.

"Fine," she snapped, shoving her helmet into his chest. "You don't want to be honest with me? Then you can just stay away from me."

Nathaniel watched her march angrily up the stairs to her front door and go into her house without even turning back to look at him. It took a moment for it to hit him, that she actually said that and actually meant it, and when it finally sank in he didn't quite know what to do with it.

Nathaniel had not been prepared for that blow.

Somehow, Kyla managed to get up to her bedroom and shut the door behind her completely undetected by her brother and Loni. To say she was furious didn't cut it, but she couldn't determine whether she was more upset with Nathaniel for the stunt he'd just pulled or at herself for falling for it again.

Grumbling under her breath, she started ranting to herself about who he thought he was and how anyone could be so impetuous and arrogant. Yet in all of her anger at Nathaniel Blake, Kyla couldn't help but detest her own impulsiveness over the way she had left him. Sitting on the edge of her bed, she groaned in frustration, feeling completely bipolar and borderline schizophrenic.

Why did she have to say that?

Even if she *had* meant it in the moment, the thought of never seeing Nathaniel again made her sick. Her guilt started messing with her head, enough that she actually debated running outside and taking it back; but then she spotted her cell phone where she'd left it on her bed and remembered what had started this train wreck of an evening.

Scowling, Kyla stood from the bed and walked over to her desk. She picked up her phone angrily and felt another stab of nausea when she saw that Caden had tried calling her back.

He left her a voicemail. This couldn't be good.

Even if it *was* good, Kyla was so upset when she saw the blinking voicemail icon that she gave serious thought to chucking the stupid thing out the window instead of listening to it. Fortunately for her phone, her curiosity got the best of her.

Dialing her mailbox, she pressed in the numbers to her password and glanced back at the window when Caden's voice came on, questioning if she'd really abandoned the phone-launching option.

"Kyla…"

She kept her gaze fixed on the window just in case.

"I know you're mad and I get it," he said. He paused for a long time. "You know what, never mind…" he mumbled.

The phone clicked off.

Kyla scowled, furious at Caden for not finishing his message and furious at herself for the sudden compulsion she felt to call him back and apologize.

Stupid Caden. Stupid Nathaniel. Stupid everything.

She shoved her phone into the top drawer of her desk so she didn't have to look at it anymore, wishing she could shove aside her memory of everything that had happened tonight so easily. But even thinking this, Kyla remembered it all, and despite how much she wanted to hate it, she didn't.

She really, really didn't.

Flopping backwards onto her bed, she sighed and put her hands on her face.

How did I get myself into this?

Chapter 16

"…to risk the sight of those who see."

Nathaniel was on the mountain again after riding the Ducati furiously up the highway as soon as he left Kyla at the condo. Making his way quickly through the trail, he came to Ethan's point of watch faster than any human feet would have been able to move him. But when he reached the ledge and found that it had been abandoned, he was more than slightly alarmed.

Ethan wasn't there.

Realizing this, Nathaniel felt a heavy sinking feeling in the pit of his stomach. He paced nervously back and forth and tried to wrap his mind around what might have happened. Obviously Ethan had seen him. Nathaniel had known that much since the moment he'd grabbed Kyla and kissed her. They would have been in plain view from this point, which had been Nathaniel's intention in bringing her there in the first place. He had wanted to make sure she was safe, knowing Ethan would be able to spot any oncoming danger. He just hadn't meant for it to happen the way it did.

And he definitely hadn't meant to kiss her.

Sitting on a half-rotten tree, Nathaniel put his head in his hands. How could he have let this happen?

He was sickened when he realized that in all of his efforts to gain Kyla James's trust, he still didn't have the information he needed from her, and he was the one who had ended up compromised as a result. Then he remembered her words, her voice as she'd told him to stay away from her, and the sharp knifelike pain he'd felt when he heard them returned.

Nathaniel's breath was starting to get choked off. How anyone...how anything could make him feel like this, he didn't understand. Nor did he understand how he could make it right. But before he could let himself think about that, he knew he had to find Ethan and make sure his own foolishness hadn't placed his brother in danger.

That wasn't the feeling Nathaniel was left with, but he needed to make sure. He didn't feel that Ethan had been compromised by Donovan or by this supposed coven that was protecting him and fueling his power here. More likely than not, this had become an issue of protocol.

If Ethan had seen him, if he had taken Nathaniel's actions as willful disobedience...*oh, God*.

Nathaniel moved down from the ledge where he was perched and through the woods more quickly than he even had in coming here. He was breathing too fast as his mind scrambled to think of anything he could do to make this right.

That was when it hit him.

The child, he thought. *I must go to the child*.

Even the thought of it left a bitter taste in Nathaniel's mouth, but he knew he had to do it. Moving down the trail with supernatural speed, he blazed past Edlowe Road and broke through the woods, coming to the edge of the Howell's property line. He approached it with caution, and again he was hit with what he'd felt before, the same presence he discerned the first night that he'd been here...only this time it was easily twice as strong. It disturbed him that it had gotten stronger, and even more that he didn't know why it had.

Circling around to the back of the massive log home, Nathaniel stayed in the trees and examined the yard. There weren't any shoes around the pool anymore and the toys that had been floating in the water before were now stacked neatly below the deck. But these insignificant facts did nothing to draw his attention, not when he saw the small blonde girl who sat alone at the edge of the water.

She was staring out at the tree-line intently, as if she were waiting...as if she had known he was going to come.

246

Nathaniel moved carefully out of the trees, approaching the girl with the highest level of caution. Her reaction to this move, however, was not what he anticipated.

"Hello, Nathaniel," she spoke in an unsettlingly calm voice.

Nathaniel stopped moving forward and met her eyes. She didn't appear frightened or even alarmed; she didn't appear anything. Nathaniel had never known anyone to be more difficult for him to read.

"You know who I am?" he asked her.

The girl remained expressionless. "No," she replied. "Not yet."

He didn't understand, but still he moved closer. "How is it then that you know my name?"

She met his gaze square-on. "I saw you," she told him.

Nathaniel pressed his lips together. It was just as he suspected. "You *saw* me?" he verified.

She nodded once and he could see in the gesture that the girl was unnaturally sure of herself.

"How?" he asked her. He was almost certain now that he knew the answer, but Nathaniel needed to be sure.

The girl looked at him knowingly.

"You're a seer," he said.

She didn't respond, but her silence spoke volumes.

"And what is it, exactly, that you saw?" Nathaniel asked her.

"You," she told him simply. "And another named Donovan."

Nathaniel's face dropped as he stared at her. He had stopped moving about ten feet from where she sat and stood now with his arms folded, mesmerized by the depth of sight this child possessed. "Go on," he said.

The girl turned away from him, casting her gaze once again to the water. "I don't usually see your kind," she told him. "That never happened until you came here."

His body tensed up when she mentioned his "kind."

"The things I see…" she tried to explain, "…they aren't the things that exist…here."

Nathaniel wasn't sure why she didn't answer him directly. It didn't seem in her character to dance around the truth.

"Meaning…you see angels," he clarified for her.

She looked up at him again. "Yes."

He was starting to become uncomfortable now.

"I don't know why I do," she admitted. "I've just seen them my whole life. But I've never seen…what you are."

Her saying this disturbed Nathaniel for more reasons than one. "Never?" he asked her. It surprised him that she hadn't seen Donovan before, given how long he appeared to have been here.

"Never," she said.

"And how is it that you are able to see us?" he asked her.

Shaking her head again, she told him, "I don't know. It has to be something about you being half-angel."

Nathaniel felt a cold heat rush over him when she said the words. It was one thing to speculate that she knew the truth, but to hear her confirm it was more than he knew what to do with.

Feeling exposed, he asked her tensely, "Have you told anyone?"

The girl stayed calm as she answered him. "No," she told him. "It isn't time for that yet."

Nathaniel wished he didn't know what she meant. "How do you *know* this?" he demanded, forcing himself to stay calm. It threatened him, somehow, having her possess this much awareness.

That was when he first saw a hint of frustration come onto the child's face. "Like I said," she told him, "it's been…different since you got here."

"Different how?" Nathaniel asked her.

The girl hesitated. "My brother," she said, "he used to be the only one who could feel things about what I saw."

Nathaniel realized she didn't know yet that this was called discernment, and it sent his mind racing when she unintentionally revealed to him that the boy named Caden had that gift.

"I only used to be able to see them," she said, "but now…I've started feeling…and hearing things too."

"Like what?" Nathaniel asked her.

The girl bit her lip as if debating whether or not to answer him. "Like how I heard your name," she told him, "and how I can feel danger." She paused. "I thought you were going to hurt her."

Nathaniel felt a tension in his chest. "Who did you think I was going to hurt?"

She looked up at him again. "You *know* who," the girl told him. Then she looked again to the water. "But you didn't," she said. "You protected her."

Nathaniel was fascinated. Never had he known any of the awakened to see to this measure, and especially not one who was so small.

The girl paused for a moment, appearing frustrated now.

"What is it?" he asked her.

She waited another moment before speaking again. "Why *did* you?"

Nathaniel didn't know what to think of the question. "Did you expect me not to?" he asked.

The child pressed her lips together and wrinkled her forehead. "I'm not sure," she said. "I still don't understand everything I see."

Nathaniel wasn't convinced of that. "I think you understand more than you realize if you are able to know what I am."

Her forehead was still wrinkled, and she appeared to be deep in contemplation. "I think I know something else, too," she told him slowly.

Nathaniel was concerned by her tone. "And what is that?" he asked her.

Slowly, the girl's countenance began to change. "She is still in danger."

Nathaniel felt the blood leave his face at her words, even though he should have expected that truth to still be in play. Nathaniel struggled to sound detached when he spoke again, but the thought of Kyla being in danger pierced him in a way that made that close to impossible.

"I need to know something…" he told her. She looked at him questioningly and Nathaniel took a deep breath. "I need to know if she is…like you."

249

The girl turned away from him. "No," she answered him plainly.

Nathaniel's confusion bled through his voice. "No?" he asked her. "But I was almost certain…" He was cut off before he could finish.

"She used to be," she explained. "Just…not anymore."

Nathaniel let this sink in. "Her father…" he said softly.

The girl gave him a single nod as his voice trailed off.

Nathaniel closed his eyes for a moment, trying once again to control himself. He was staggering beneath the weight that this new reality pressed into him. Remembering Seth's words, how he had charged him to abort this mission the moment Nathaniel's theories were disproven, he felt the crushing blow of failure boring into the place where his soul should exist.

But in spite of the assignment, in spite of this mission and his desire to stop Donovan from whatever destruction he was attempting to draw out in this place, Nathaniel couldn't convince himself to accept this.

"Help me," he begged the child in a quiet voice. "Help me to make her safe."

The girl's expression shifted slightly as she continued to read him, but not enough for him to see what she was thinking. "I'm not the one who can do that," she told him.

Nathaniel swallowed hard, emotion choking him again. "Then who can?" he asked her, unable to keep the desperation out of his voice this time.

When she looked into him again, Nathaniel saw the answer to his question behind her eyes, but before she could say another word, they both heard a voice from inside the house.

"Alexa, honey," the blonde woman called to her, "it's time to come inside."

Alexa. Her name was Alexa.

By the time her mother made her way to the back deck, Nathaniel was already gone. Watching from the trees, he saw the girl stand obediently and turn to go back into the house, and the whole time he was trying to wrap his mind around what he'd just seen.

250

If it was true what he had read in her, there was nothing this did not affect.

*N*athaniel was back on the mountain again. Whether he should be or not, he wasn't certain, but going back to the mansion after seeing the young girl just didn't feel right to him; right or wise. Miguel was still there, and Nathaniel knew as soon as the man saw him again he was going to tell him he had to leave. Even if he did have another night, he knew the fear his uncle instilled in those who worked for him, and he knew Miguel would try to push it.

And while Nathaniel thought there could be worse things in the world than him fleeing Woodland Park, he also knew that was not an option yet, and it wouldn't be until his assignment was accomplished. He didn't know what his next effective move was, though; not after what Alexa had said.

Surely, he had to have misunderstood her. Caden Howell couldn't have anything to do with keeping her safe. But the more he thought about it, the more he realized it was his resentment that drove him to think these things. It wasn't that he didn't believe it; it was that he didn't want to. Nathaniel didn't want anyone protecting her but him.

Grimacing at the thought, it hit him how deep he was getting in. So many things he never would have done before coming here, and they had all been effortless for him. So many ways he never thought he would fail, and yet here he was, at the point of watch that Ethan had held, with that particular of his brothers nowhere in sight. And it was because of him. It was because of Nathaniel.

Nathaniel had already reasoned at that point that Ethan wasn't and hadn't ever been in danger, but that he had simply aborted the mission. And while Nathaniel knew this would result in some drastic repercussions that obviously concerned him, he also knew that he could deal with that issue when it arose. For now, whether it was justified or not, Nathaniel was only concerned with one very confused and angry auburn-haired girl whom he knew at all costs that he had to keep safe.

251

It made him sick when he thought again of what Kyla said to him that night. He tried to convince himself that something as petty as the human girl being upset with him couldn't matter less right now. Nathaniel knew the only thing that truly mattered was keeping her from Donovan, with or without her consent. Still, he hated the thought of her hating him.

Leaning his head back against the rocky wall behind him, Nathaniel closed his eyes, though it did about as much good as if he'd kept them open, considering how dark it was out here; not that he couldn't see into it if he tried. It was foreboding in feeling, confusing in thought, and difficult for him to navigate through; everything about this night felt dark to him. Nathaniel didn't know what was going to happen and he didn't know when it was going to, he could only feel that something was coming and that whatever it was, he had to be ready for it. Which meant that he needed Kyla on his side again.

If he couldn't get her to trust him, she was as good as dead, and that only left him with one real option. Whatever it took, Nathaniel knew he had to make this right. He just didn't know how he was going to accomplish that.

Opening his eyes again, Nathaniel remembered something Caleb had told him once about a fight he'd had with Samantha. Caleb had had to apologize to her, Nathaniel recalled. According to his brother, that was the key with any woman.

"You always have to be willing to apologize," Caleb had told him, "even if you didn't do anything wrong."

Nathaniel had given him a look, which had in turn caused Caleb to correct himself. "Well maybe not *you*," he'd said. "But anyone normal."

Nathaniel smirked at the memory, finding the whole thing a bit ironic now. Then his smirk faded to a grimace when he realized he still wouldn't be able to explain a thing to Kyla.

This was never going to work.

Kyla was in a horrible mood at work the next night. After all that had gone down with Nathaniel, she had tried everything she could not to think about him, but Val had very conveniently decided to make that impossible for her.

First, when she was trying to refill the bean hopper, Val decided to ask her if she'd seen her "hot new friend" again since his drop-in yesterday. Kyla tried not to gag at the question and then proceeded to ignore her, and for a reason she still had yet to figure out, Val let it go. At least for an hour.

Their steady flow of customers had thinned out by the afternoon, and Kyla was clearing off tables and carrying a stack of dishes back to the sink when Val posed a seemingly innocent question that Kyla knew better than to trust.

"So how did you meet him?" she asked.

Kyla looked at her skeptically. "Why so curious?"

Val sighed as she toyed with the plastic handle of one of the blenders on the drying rack. "I'm not really curious so much as bored."

"Maybe you should try working," Kyla mumbled.

Val gave her a look and Kyla walked away before she said or did something that she knew she would regret.

Later that evening when Val brought it up a third time, Kyla had finally had enough.

"Okay," she said, setting the rag in her hand down firmly on the counter. "Let's get something straight here. I have no intention of telling you a single thing about my personal life. Ever. So do us both a favor and stop asking."

Val muttered something unpleasant under her breath that Kyla didn't bother paying attention to and they both got back to tending to their customers and avoiding each other. Which was best, really, for both of them.

In all the years that she had known the girl, Kyla had grown used to Val's coldness, her selfishness and just about every one of her infuriating tendencies. But she couldn't help thinking as she watched her that afternoon that something was different about the way she was acting; something that was strange even for Val.

Oh well, Kyla thought, resuming her scrub-down of the counters. *Not my problem.*

After she got off work that night and was finally able to take a much-needed shower, Kyla slipped on a pair of tight black, calf-length workout pants and turned around to examine her back in the mirror. She was still baffled at how awful it didn't look, and as she traced the scars with her fingertips, she couldn't help but remember Nathaniel sliding his hand up her back and how immediately the pain had left her when he had...and his blatant refusal to tell her how that was possible.

Shaking off the thought, Kyla slipped on a red sports bra with thick soft straps that crossed at the back, grabbed her drawing pad and charcoals and went outside to sit on her front porch. It was warmer tonight than it had been all week, almost to the point of discomfort, but right now there were so many thoughts racing through her mind that she could hardly bring herself to care. She just had to draw and disassociate herself from all of this before it drove her mad.

The minutes slipped by until she had been out there for almost an hour, though Kyla hardly even realized it. But then something hit her that she didn't expect to feel. Jerking her head up, she expected to see someone standing there, but she didn't see a thing. Still, she knew better than to trust her eyes right now. That feeling was undeniable.

Setting down her drawing pad and marching down the stairs, she imagined seeing that frustrating blonde boy she'd been aching to see all day either walking up the middle of the road or waiting for her in the trees, or acting nonchalant and pretending he was going for a late-night stroll. It was all the same to her, so long as she saw him.

Kyla knew she was supposed to be mad at him and that after what she'd told him he had every right to be mad at her, but that was the last thing she was able to care about right now. Her need for Nathaniel Blake superseded her irritation with him at any given time, and her desire to be near him left her helpless to resist his maddening charm.

As many times as she had tried to forget it, she couldn't shake her memory of their kiss on the mountain…and she couldn't keep herself from wishing he would finish what he'd started.

Even in her anger at him, her heart pounded as she looked up to see Nathaniel's face, but she slammed to a halt and froze in her tracks when she locked eyes with the last person she could have imagined she would see there.

Kyla's heart smashed into her ribcage at the sight of the shaggy-haired boy who was standing in front of her. Her breath caught in her throat and her eyes grew huge when she saw him, but she hardly had the coherency to notice.

Finally, she managed by some miracle to find her voice. *"Caden?"*

The fear in his eyes matched what she felt in herself, as did his complete inability to speak. Kyla blinked a few times, slowly at first and then hard as she tried to determine whether or not she might be hallucinating.

He looked taller, different…stronger even than he had been before. Caden had to have grown at least three inches since the last time she'd seen him, putting him at about 6'1" if she were to guess. She could see the definition in his chest and his arms through the black v-necked shirt he wore, and his olive skin was still flawless to a frustrating degree. It had always been incredible, the way it offset his deep brown eyes to perfection. She could see he'd grown his hair out too, and by the looks of it, had it styled. It hung down in his eyes the way it always had, but this time with intention. It was darker in some places and lighter in others, but even through the highlights that chestnut brown shone through like gold.

He looked good. Really good.

Somehow she felt safer analyzing every detail of his physical appearance rather than questioning the obvious, because the obvious hadn't sunk into her as reality yet, and she wasn't even sure she wanted it to.

"Hey," Caden said nervously.

At the sound of his voice, Kyla realized she wasn't seeing things…that he really was there.

And everything just got a whole lot more complicated.

*S*taring at the girl who'd stepped out of the shadows, Caden Howell could hardly breathe. The moment Kyla came into his view, he literally forgot the meaning of the term "lung function," and debated for a moment if he was going to be able to handle this. Seeing his best friend for the first time in over a year was enough in itself to wreak havoc on his nerves, but seeing her like *this*...well, that was just too much for him.

He had to think fast to hide his surprise at what she was wearing; or rather what she wasn't. "Forget your clothes?" he asked, laughing a little in an attempt to play it off.

Kyla folded her arms across her chest. "I wasn't exactly expecting visitors," she snapped. She pressed her lips together in the way she always did when she was mad.

As if this weren't already hard enough.

"What are you doing here?" she asked tensely.

Caden blinked a few times. "Uhh...I'm sorry?" He knew he should have expected a reaction like that, or at least something close to it, but her curtness still managed to catch him off guard.

"I'm serious. What are you doing here, Caden?"

He tried to stay calm, knowing the worst thing he could do right now would be to get defensive. It wasn't easy, though. He was way too much like her.

"I came to see you," he said. "I thought that might be a little obvious judging by the fact that I, you know...showed up."

Kyla narrowed her eyes at his sarcasm. "Don't be cute with me. I want an explanation."

Unbelievable. He had been with her for less than a minute and she was already pissing him off.

"An explanation?" he asked. "An explanation for what? Wanting to see my best friend?"

"Oh, so I'm back to being your best friend now?" she scoffed.

Caden stared at her, trying to appear confused and like he didn't know why she was angry. He'd been playing that card a lot lately. "What are you talking about?" he asked her.

Kyla didn't answer him; she just glared at him in a way that made him feel defeated and left him thinking this had been a serious mistake.

"You know what, I'm sorry I came by," he told her. "Next time I'll wait for a formal invitation before I make an attempt to see you."

She retorted a little too quickly, "Yeah, maybe you should."

Caden tried not to let it get to him, but his efforts to close off to her didn't stop the sudden pang he felt in his chest. Not that he didn't understand her acting like this...not that he even blamed her. But as he turned away from Kyla and started walking back to his Jeep, he couldn't help but feel as if he'd just been stabbed.

Caden clenched his jaw as he reached to open the driver's side door, angrier with himself than he was with the furious, half-clothed girl behind him. It was his fault she was acting this way and he was mad because he didn't know how to fix it. After all this time, after everything that had happened, he couldn't believe she was really going to shove him away again and let him leave like this. Pulling the door open, he felt sick with disappointment, but then just when he was sure he was going home, he heard Kyla's voice from behind him.

"Caden!" she called out.

He snapped his head around in frustration. "*What?*"

He didn't want to get defensive like that with her, but he couldn't help it. They'd been doing this for years, and apparently spending a year apart hadn't changed that. Kyla would get hurt and lash out, he'd close off and throw up walls, and they'd dance around like that sometimes for days until one of them finally broke. That was what he expected now, to see that staunch, lock-jawed expression on her face that Kyla had perfected over the years.

But what he saw instead, Caden was in no way prepared for. All at once in an unexpected rush, all of Kyla's coldness, her defensiveness and all that had been pushing him to leave and leave quickly completely fell away. And all he could see in its place was everything he had ever wanted from her.

She ran to him then...literally ran. And when she threw herself into his arms without holding herself back, it shocked

Caden to the point that at first he couldn't move. But then it started to sink in and he choked back the emotion that hit him at the collision, slipping his arms carefully around her waist.

Kyla was shaking now, and the more unsteady she became, the stronger he forced himself to be. He held her tightly and made sure she knew that she was safe with him, just like he'd been doing since they were ten years old.

Caden sighed as he held her. "I miss you too."

She laughed a little and nuzzled her head against his chest and Caden closed his eyes.

Breathe, he told himself. He didn't get the chance to try, though, before he felt her go rigid in his arms.

The feeling alarmed him. "What's wrong?" he asked her, pulling back so he could see her face.

When Kyla didn't answer him, he followed her gaze down the road…to the tall blonde stranger that stood before them motionless, glaring at him coldly from the middle of the street.

Caden tried not to appear alarmed when he saw him, but after his initial surprise, his protective instinct flared up and all he could think of was how to keep Kyla away from him. He didn't know who this guy was, but he did not like the way he was looking at her.

Almost as much as he didn't like the way she was looking at him.

Chapter 17

Kyla froze when she saw Nathaniel walking toward them... and when she saw the look in Caden's eyes as he did. It was already enough of a shock to her nerves being in her best friend's arms again, but this was more than she could deal with right now.

Caden kept his hand on her waist. "Can I help you?" he asked Nathaniel tensely.

Kyla knew she should probably run some sort of interference here, but she wasn't even remotely capable of it. Her complete paralysis at the moment was hindering her mediating abilities.

Nathaniel gave her a look that both worried and weakened her, but Kyla couldn't force a single word from her mouth. She slipped out of Caden's grip (which he really didn't seem to like) and tried not to let on that in spite of her surprise, the sight of the blonde-haired boy in front of her left her gasping for breath.

On any given day, Nathaniel was always a ridiculous kind of handsome, but right now he looked so gorgeous Kyla could have jumped him just for standing there and looking at her like that.

Nathaniel held out a hand politely to Caden. "Nathaniel Blake," he introduced himself. "And you are?"

Caden wasn't sure how to respond to that at first, but eventually he shook his hand. "Caden Howell."

Kyla didn't know how Caden was able to match up to Nathaniel's level of cool, but somehow he pulled it off. He also managed to avoid diving into a full-on interrogation, which was more than she expected from him.

They were polite with each other, Nathaniel and Caden, but it was tense to say the least. There was something about the way they looked at each other, too; something that left Kyla unsettled. She wasn't sure what it was exactly, but as she watched them, she felt like she was missing something. She didn't have long to think on it, however, before Nathaniel brought an abrupt end to their formalities.

"I need to talk to you," he told her.

Kyla looked at him like he wasn't serious. "Kinda busy," she said.

She could feel Caden reading them both, and whatever he was seeing, he appeared to be uncomfortable about it.

Instead of taking the hint, Nathaniel turned to Caden instead. "Would you mind if I stole Kyla from you?" he asked.

Kyla's mouth dropped open.

"Just for a moment," Nathaniel added smoothly.

Caden didn't look happy. "Not my call to make, bro," he said.

Kyla could not believe Nathaniel's audacity, and she was about to let him know it, too. But then he looked at her in a way that she knew was meant to disarm her, and as much as she hated that he would try that, she hated it even more that it worked.

"Please," Nathaniel said. "It will only take a minute."

Kyla wanted to tell him how little right he had to show up here like this and act so rude and demanding. She wanted to tell him to get lost, but she had only to look into those big blue eyes of his and her will turned to mush.

Looking away from him, she scowled. *Stupid, perfect, impossible boy.*

Caden seemed to notice when her countenance changed, and when Nathaniel broke through her guard. He looked confused by it, frustrated as he glanced back and forth between them; like he couldn't believe she was giving into this.

Kyla cringed as she turned back to the boy she hadn't seen in over a year, not believing she was actually going to ask him what she asked him next. "Can you give us a minute, Cade?"

Caden tensed up. "Actually, I need to get back to the house anyway," he told her.

Kyla's heart sank at the thought of him leaving. "No...don't," she said quickly.

Tension came into Nathaniel's face at her protest, but Caden just smiled at her in the way she had so desperately missed. And it was only when he did that she realized how much.

"It's okay," Caden assured her. Then he grabbed her in a hug and kissed the top of her head. "I'll see you soon."

Kyla closed her eyes, forcing back her emotion, and when she opened them again Nathaniel was shifting uncomfortably on his feet. Making an effort to act like none of this bothered him, he told Caden, "Thank you," in a voice thick with frustration.

Caden's smile dropped. "Yeah," he said flatly.

Kyla frowned as she watched him walk back to his Jeep.

*N*athaniel kept his anger controlled as the boy named Caden left them on the road. He didn't want Kyla to see what he was feeling, what it was doing to him even now. He didn't want her to recognize the jealousy behind his eyes that was burning in him at the thought, because he didn't want her to know she had taken hold of him like that. And yet what was possibly even worse, Nathaniel couldn't ignore what he had seen in the boy, or the opportunity that had been brought to him with it.

One thing was for certain; Nathaniel was up against more here than he could have imagined. They all were, in ways that none of them had anticipated...except maybe Donovan. Nathaniel knew Donovan had gotten enough insight into this to at least be afraid of the boy, which led him to believe that once again, Donovan was one step ahead of the Resitore.

He hated that thought.

Nathaniel had seen clearly in Caden's eyes, the truth in what Alexa had told him. He saw what he didn't want to be

261

true, that Caden Howell possessed a power Nathaniel himself didn't even know; a power to which he could never have access.

But then he might have been seeing this wrong, failing to find the silver lining that existed over this shadow of truth. Maybe Nathaniel's search to find another like the child hadn't gone as he'd expected, but it still wasn't lost. They might not be able to use Kyla James in the way he had originally thought they would...she might not be one of *them* anymore at all. But in this unexpected twist of fate, Nathaniel had been brought another who was. Someone he would mind placing in potential danger far less than he would Kyla.

Fortunate twist of fate, indeed.

Nathaniel frowned at the thought, still not convinced. Perhaps this had always been about Caden, that from the beginning (whenever the "beginning" might have been) Kyla had merely been a side issue for Donovan. Judging by what Nathaniel saw in the boy's eyes tonight, and by the angelic guard around his bedroom that remained there even when he wasn't, Nathaniel wouldn't doubt this. It wasn't hard to believe that Eli had been right, that Caden was the one Donovan feared. Nathaniel just hated that it was like that.

The last thing he wanted was another reason to feel threatened by Caden Howell.

Kyla turned around angrily to face Nathaniel once the Jeep drove out of sight. "What is wrong with you?" she snapped at him.

Nathaniel eyed her up and down in blatant judgment of what she was wearing. "What's wrong with *me*?" he scoffed.

The gesture made her self-conscious, which was very much his intention, and she folded her arms even tighter across her chest. "Don't look at me like that," Kyla scowled. But Nathaniel had to question if she really wanted him to. Something about the nervous inflection in her voice would suggest otherwise. "What about 'stay away from me' do you not understand?"

"Forgive me," Nathaniel said, "but I chose not to listen to you."

Kyla glared at him.

"You know, that won't help your case," he told her. "Giving me that look will do anything but convince me to stay away from you."

He didn't know why he said that. He didn't know why he was acting like this with her. The weight of the urgency he felt was completely opposite this tense, boyish flirting he was engaging her in now. But beyond everything that should worry him about all that just happened, Nathaniel could only feel one thing inside of him screaming in the rhythm of his already pounding heart.

"Don't give me that," Kyla sneered at him. "I don't want lines from you, Nathaniel."

He could feel an unexplainable smile teasing his lips. "And what *do* you want from me?"

Kyla wasn't about to give in to that. Nathaniel knew it, too, but again he couldn't stop himself from asking the question.

"I already told you what I want," she answered him. "I want you to leave me alone."

Nathaniel stepped closer, not allowing himself the luxury of hesitation. Looking down into the girl deeply, who by all appearances looked to be trembling, he told her in a low drawn voice, "I don't believe you."

Kyla faltered for a moment, but when she recovered, she looked at him even more angrily than before.

"You don't have to believe me," she said. "Doesn't make it any less true."

Nathaniel could see that she was lying.

"So you really want me to stay away from you?" he asked her. Even without meaning it, he hated posing the question.

Kyla's face was still tight. "I wanted you to tell me the truth," she said, "but I realize that isn't gonna happen, so honestly I don't see the point."

Nathaniel couldn't keep up these games anymore, and not just because they weren't working. He physically ached, having to hold back from her like this. He didn't want to hold back anymore; he was tired of holding back. But even in his wanting desperately to tell her the truth, he still knew he couldn't. And the thought of it tortured him.

"Why did you come here tonight, Nathaniel? What was so direly urgent that you had to pull me away from Caden?"

His confidence faltered when she said the boy's name.

"I would apologize for interrupting your little reunion," he replied before he could stop himself, "but I'd be lying if I said I was sorry."

Kyla gaped at him. "What is *that* supposed to mean?"

"I just find it strange," he shrugged. "For someone so capable of holding a grudge, you seemed awfully quick to forgive him."

Now she was furious. "Who do you think you *are*?" she demanded.

"He left you, Kyla," Nathaniel spilled the words before he could talk himself out of it. Then he began to question his grasp on the concept of digging himself deeper. "He left you for over a year, and now he gets an open-armed welcome?"

"What is your point?" she asked him through gritted teeth.

"My point is that if you can find it in you to trust *Caden Howell*," he sneered the name, "then shouldn't you be able to do the same for me?"

Kyla was indignant. "I don't even *know* you!"

Nathaniel took the blow and threw one back at her. "And what makes you so sure you know him?" he challenged. "Did you ever think the reason he stopped talking to you might be because he has something to hide?"

That was all it took to push her over the edge.

"You arrogant, presumptuous..."

Nathaniel put his hands up as if to surrender. "I'm not trying to upset you, Kyla. I'm just calling it like I see it."

She scowled furiously and pushed past him, trying to walk back up to her house, but before she made it to the stairs, Nathaniel grabbed her arm. She spun around to face him and looked about ready to rip his head off. Then just before she could attempt it, they both heard her phone ring from where she'd left it on the deck.

Jerking her arm from his grip, Kyla moved up the stairs two at a time and looked down at the screen. "Hey," she answered in a tense voice.

Nathaniel was uncomfortable as he watched her, knowing full well who was on the other end of the line.

"Why do you ask?" she said. Her voice held a sharper edge to it than he knew she probably intended.

Kyla looked down at him where he waited below the deck, and he didn't like what he saw in her face. She kept her eyes on him as she spoke into the phone. "Yeah," she said. "Pick me up."

Nathaniel felt a wave of heat hit his face as a new anger surged through him. He had to get out of here. He had to get out of here fast.

*K*yla was amazed that he knew, that Caden could feel even after all this time how she needed him tonight. He could always do that with her, to freaky measures even, and thinking about it now, she questioned if things really were as different as she'd thought.

After watching Nathaniel storm angrily up the road after she'd hung up the phone, she was now in Caden's Jeep with him, driving away from her house quickly and trying to forget what had just happened. She hated fighting with Nathaniel, even if that was what they ended up doing ninety-five percent of the time they were ever together.

Her train of thought was jolted when Caden reached to the backseat and tossed her a jacket. Kyla smiled and slipped it on.

"Want to tell me about it?" he asked her.

She made a face. "Not really, no."

Caden didn't press her. "So where are we going?" he asked.

"Anywhere," she told him. She meant it, too. Anywhere that would get her away from Nathaniel Blake.

She saw him smile out of the corner of her eye and wondered what idea had come into his head. Then, when he pulled the Jeep into the parking lot outside the elementary school, she sighed and shook her head.

Kyla walked with him over to the swing set without a word. They sat in the flimsy plastic swings so they were facing each other, and both of them were nervous. It wasn't uncomfortable, though. Surreal, maybe that they were finally together again, but definitely not uncomfortable.

"Do you remember the first day we met here?" Caden asked her, smiling as he stared at the sand beneath his feet.

Kyla didn't think he could be serious. "You really think I'd ever forget that?" she laughed.

Caden kept smiling. "Your hair was in braids," he said. "I don't think I've ever seen you wear them since."

"You haven't," Kyla assured him. "Loni and I had a standoff about it after that day. I told her they made me look too girly."

It was strange, remembering back to it. Had she really had a mother that used to braid her hair?

"Ahh...yes," Caden cooed nostalgically. "Because heaven forbid you take my telling you I liked them as a compliment."

Kyla gave him a look. "You told me they were pretty," she said. "Made me feel like a sissy."

"Thus the challenge that landed us in Principal Ware's office for the first time," Caden added. "Thank you for that, by the way."

"For what?" Kyla asked. She was still laughing at his tone.

"For making me a seven-year-old delinquent," he answered. "You know, I was very well-mannered before you came along with your pretty little braids and challenged me to that race to the edge of the football field."

A flash of the memory came to her mind; the image of the schoolyard, of the overweight, grey-haired Mrs. Schwartz blowing her whistle behind them, of the two of them being carted off to that little office, dragged by their ears after Kyla beat him to the goal post. He had complained it was only by inches, but she'd been quick to tell him that didn't matter, that a win was a win.

It was a simple misdemeanor, made by two very convincingly unassuming first-graders, but the way Mrs. Schwartz told it, (what was it...evading school property? Obstructing the system?) you'd have thought the two of them attempted to pull off a heist.

That was Caden's first day of school in Woodland Park. His father had just ditched his music career in Nashville and moved his family out to his favorite place on earth. They probably expected things to be more peaceful here, at least compared to the city. Maybe they expected Caden to make some nice friends on his first day, too, but instead he'd gotten her. And from that point forward, well-mannered was out the window.

Kyla rolled her eyes at him. "Please. It never would have lasted."

He raised his eyebrows innocently and looked at her in question. "Oh, you don't think so?"

"Save the look," she told him, looking back to meet his eyes. "I know you too well to trust it."

Caden didn't look away from her. "You think so, huh?"

Staring into him then, the situation finally became real to her. Where they were, what they were doing...the fact that she was sitting here now on the swing set where she met him, talking to him again like they hadn't spent the last year apart.

Kyla broke her gaze away and furrowed her brow. It was only natural at that point for her to look down at her feet, and for Caden to mimic the gesture. They both fell quiet; both continued to stare at their feet. Then Kyla broke the silence.

"Why didn't you tell me you were coming home?"

Caden was hesitant. "It was kind of a last minute thing," he said, "and you didn't seem too thrilled with me the last time we talked, so I wasn't really sure how well you would take it."

She cringed at her memory of their last conversation. "About that..." she told him. "I was kind of having a bad day."

"Kinda figured," Caden said with a smile. "And don't worry about it. I've grown used to your mood swings in the last ten years."

Kyla punched him in the arm and he laughed.

"So why did you?" she asked. "Come home, I mean?"

Caden's smile faded a little and he looked out across the park. "It was just time," he said.

She gave him a look. "Do you really think I'm gonna let you off the hook that easy?"

"No," he said, "but I was kind of hoping."

She dropped her head. "It was Alexa, wasn't it?"

Caden was slow to answer her, but he must have known it would be pointless to deny it. "Yeah," he admitted. "It was."

Kyla wrinkled her nose. "What did she tell you?"

"Not much," he said. "Not yet, anyway."

She thought about that for a minute. "But enough to get you to fly out here?"

Caden looked like he was trying to be careful with whatever he said. "She had me pretty worried, I'm not gonna lie."

Kyla sighed and shook her head. "I'm sorry," she apologized. "I have no idea what she told you, but you shouldn't have believed her."

Caden looked at her curiously.

"Alexa's been acting really strange lately," she explained. "I don't know what her deal is but she's been freaking Matthew out, too."

Caden looked like he was thinking about something. "So you're telling me it's unfounded, whatever she said?"

"Yes," Kyla affirmed. "That's exactly what I'm saying."

He gave her a look. "Don't lie to me."

She should have known he would be able to see through her like that.

"Look, Cade..." she tried to explain, but she realized there was nothing she could tell him.

He frowned. "What is going on, Kyla?"

She pressed her lips together and shook her head. "You don't have to worry about me," she told him. Then she said so quietly under her breath she was almost talking to herself, "I've been doing just fine without you."

She could see it in his face when she said it, the way that it hurt him, but he wasn't the only one. Even speaking the words, she felt sick.

They were both quiet again after that, but neither of them wanted to break the silence this time. Kyla thought if one of them didn't soon, though, she might lose it.

"I'm sorry," Caden finally told her.

She was tense as she asked him, "For what?" She knew exactly what he meant.

Caden sighed and rested his elbows on his legs. "You know I didn't *want* to leave you, right?"

Kyla forced back the emotion that hit her when he said it. "No?" she asked. She tried a little too hard to keep her voice even and it came out shaky anyway.

Caden's eyes softened when he looked at her again, and somehow he looked almost like he was in pain. "No, I didn't."

She wished she could drop it, but Kyla couldn't force herself to let it go. "Then why did you?"

Caden was obviously struggling to keep his composure, but she didn't understand what was so hard for him about this.

"That's not what matters right now," he told her. "What matters is that you're lying to me and I want to know why."

She resented the accusation, even if it was true.

"Who is he, Kyla?" he asked her. "Who is Nathaniel Blake?"

She cringed and looked away from him. "He's nobody."

"Please," Caden scoffed.

She was getting agitated now. "Look, I really need to get home before Loni freaks out."

Caden gave her a look. "Since when have you ever cared about freaking Loni out?"

Kyla frowned and looked away from him, frustrated that he knew her too well for excuses like that to work on him. "I just need to get home, alright?"

It was obvious that he didn't want to, but Caden gave in anyway. "Alright," he said, "I can take a hint."

Kyla smiled at him gratefully and they walked back to his Jeep, but when they pulled up out front of the condo again, she flinched at the sight that met her and debated whether or not she should have just stayed at the park.

It angered her that Nathaniel was there waiting for her, partially because she wasn't expecting him to be and partially because seeing him anywhere, in any circumstance and at any point in time always had that effect on her.

He was leaning against a tree by the road with his head down, and he didn't even look up when Caden pulled the

Jeep up to the house. Kyla didn't know what he was doing or what he might be thinking, but on both accounts she was wary.

Caden was too, and he looked even less happy about the situation than she did. He narrowed his eyes when he saw Nathaniel, and seeing this, Kyla touched his hand so he would look at her.

"Don't worry about him," she said.

Caden kept his eyes fixed on the boy at the side of the road. "How can I not worry about him?" he asked her. "You won't even tell me who he is."

Kyla tilted her head a little and gave him a look.

He sighed. "Alright," he said, "I get it. I have my phone, so call me if you need me, okay? For whatever."

Kyla smiled at him gratefully. "Thanks, Cade."

He looked into her for a long time before his lips turned up in a teasing smile. "No problem, kid."

Kyla smirked at him as she got out of his Jeep, wishing she didn't have to leave him. And she only felt the emotion stronger when she turned around to face Nathaniel, who was still leaning against the tree with eyes cast to the ground.

Her smile dropped when she turned to him.

*V*al Linley was not in a good mood. Working any miserably long shift at the coffee shop with the girl she despised more than life itself tended to have that effect on her, but it wasn't her merely working with Kyla James that had her so upset tonight. It wasn't what had happened that day, but rather what hadn't that was worrying her...and what she hadn't been able to find out as a result.

As Val made her way down a long dark alley in Manitou Springs, her lace-up black stilettos clicked against the pavement. She had made sure to put on her tightest black dress before leaving her apartment, to pin her dark silken hair up in dramatic swoops and to don an unnaturally red shade of lipstick. She was not going to take any chances tonight.

270

Checking her phone, she saw that she was three minutes early, which was far better in this situation than being three minutes late. Her nerves were on edge as she waited at the end of the alleyway, and she had to remind herself for about the tenth time to calm down. Val knew anxiety was not going to help her right now.

Suddenly, she felt a hand slip around her waist. Turning slowly, she looked up at Donovan and smiled deviously, trying not to let it show on her face what she was really feeling.

"Hey there," she greeted him in a low sultry voice.

Donovan slipped his arms further around her waist and pulled her close to him, a gesture with which Val immediately complied.

Breathing quietly into her ear, he whispered, "Did everything go as planned?"

She tried to keep her composure, knowing how easy it was for him to discern any change in her emotions. "She's being stubborn," Val pouted.

Donovan loosened his grip on her waist. He didn't look happy.

"Meaning what?" he asked tensely.

She had to keep him calm.

Val knew the last thing she needed was for Donovan to lose his temper. Tilting her head to one side and sliding her hand up his arm, she told him softly, "Don't worry. I can handle Kyla James."

He eyed her suspiciously. "And how exactly are you handling her?"

Val moved closer to him again, close enough that she was breathing onto his neck. "Trust me," she whispered. Then she pressed her lips gently to his throat.

Donovan faltered slightly, but not nearly enough. It troubled her, the extent to which he was able to resist her tonight.

"And for what reason, exactly, should I do that?" he asked.

Val knew she had to lay it on thick if she was going to successfully divert his attention right now. "I have something for you," she whispered.

He looked into her suspiciously again. "And what is that?"

She smiled as she kissed the side of his face. "You're gonna like it."

Sliding her hand up his stomach beneath the black trench coat he wore, she could see by the look in his eyes that she was getting to him.

"Tell me," Donovan said.

Val looked into him with her emerald green eyes. "I'd rather show you," she spoke to him softly.

She bit his lower lip as she kissed him on the mouth, and it was when she did this that Donovan finally broke. Grabbing her by the waist with both of his hands, he picked her up so she could wrap her legs around him and slammed her up against the brick wall behind her.

Val became ravenous, breathing heavily as he kissed her, knowing full well what it did to him when she did that.

Every time, she thought to herself as his hand slid up her leg.

He could have beaten her. He could have killed her...or at the very least denied her the standing in the coven she had been promised.

Such depth of power, such impenetrable evil...and yet the Nephilim were still so impossibly easy to manipulate.

*N*athaniel kept his head down as Kyla walked up to him. She didn't say a word, just stood there glaring at him with her arms folded across her chest. That was when he knew he had to speak up.

"I'm sorry," he told her.

She responded with a tense, "Okay," and Nathaniel lifted his eyes so he could look at her.

"I mean it, Kyla. I really am sorry."

She wrinkled her forehead. "What do you want me to say? That I forgive you?"

He thought about that for a moment. "Well, yes that would be nice, actually."

Kyla sighed and walked halfway past him. "This isn't working, Nathaniel."

"What isn't working?" he asked her.

She turned to face him again. "Whatever *this* is," she said, motioning back and forth between them. "I can't do it anymore. I can't keep playing these stupid games."

He felt his chest tighten when he realized what she was saying. "Kyla, I'm not playing games with you."

He knew she didn't believe him.

"Oh really?" she said. "Then I guess that means you're ready to tell me who you are? Who this Donovan freak is and why you like to hang out in cemeteries?"

Nathaniel searched for something...anything he could say that would help her understand, but he knew there was nothing. Apparently Caleb's theories on women didn't apply to someone as stubborn as Kyla James.

"You didn't know he was coming home, did you?"

Even as Nathaniel asked the question, he felt divided against himself, knowing there was nothing better and nothing worse that could happen than Caden Howell returning to Woodland Park.

Kyla didn't appear to like that. "Don't," she said firmly.

"Don't what?" he asked.

She glared at him again. "I am *not* talking to you about Caden."

He knew he'd struck a nerve, and he knew why, but it still concerned him.

"Why not?" he asked her.

"Because I don't *trust* you!" she shouted at him.

He'd never given her a reason to feel otherwise, but something about hearing her say it still stung.

"And you trust *him*?" Nathaniel threw back at her.

He wasn't even sure what he had to gain from the question, but before he had time to stop himself, he heard it leaving his mouth. Apparently this was a night for that kind of thing.

She scowled and walked away from him. "I'm not doing this again, Nathaniel."

"Kyla..." he started to say.

He had hoped he could stop her, but he didn't get the chance. Before he could speak another word, a voice sounded sharply in his mind.

"Cemetery. Now."

Nathaniel froze, struggling to keep a straight face when he heard Seth's voice, but his efforts were not successful. Kyla could tell that something was wrong.

"What is it?" she asked him.

"Nothing," he told her quickly. "I just...need to go."

She stared at him blankly in disbelief. "Are you serious?"

"Do I look like I'm joking?" he snapped back at her. It got him another glare, too. Nathaniel sighed. "Get inside, Kyla. Deal with your mother."

Her mouth hung open at his remark, but she didn't throw anything back at him the way he expected her to. After eyeing him curiously again, she mumbled, "If you say so," and turned to go inside.

Peculiar, yes, but Nathaniel didn't have time to analyze her unpredictable behavior.

He didn't waste any time making his way down the street in the direction of the cemetery. Clearing his mind as he walked, he tried to prepare himself for a meeting that he knew was not going to be pleasant. Nathaniel thought over the details he needed to present to Seth and forced himself to stop thinking about Kyla and his tension over their argument. He could deal with her later. Right now he had to do whatever it took to ensure that he would still be able to.

Damage control, he thought. Then he grimaced when he realized what he was up against here.

Nathaniel never thought it would come to this. He never thought he would reach a point where he would be forced to lie to his leader, where he would make the willful choice to deceive Seth like this. But there was nothing he wasn't willing to do in order to keep her safe...to keep her in his life.

And that realization frightened him more than anything ever had.

Chapter 18

"...some truth looks better from a distance."

Kyla saw it the moment something shifted in Nathaniel's countenance. She didn't know what it was, but she was far too curious to let it go and determined not to let him know it.

He turned away from her quickly and walked down the street again, not even turning back around to look at her once.

Obviously something had him spooked.

Kyla walked up to the front deck of the condo and pretended like she was going inside, but by the time she was at her door, Nathaniel was already halfway down the block. He didn't even bother to wait until she had gotten inside before he left. Upset or not, that didn't seem like him.

After opening and shutting the door carefully in case he was listening for the sound, Kyla tiptoed quietly down the stairs and crouched behind the Civic in the driveway. She peered over the hood just in time to see Nathaniel turn the corner onto Paradise Circle.

He was certainly making time.

Opening the back door of the car, she threw the flip-flops she was wearing onto the seat and slipped into the spare pair of running shoes she kept back there for emergencies like this. Well, maybe not exactly like this, but emergencies, nonetheless.

Once they were laced, she zipped up the jacket Caden had thrown at her when she'd gotten in his Jeep that night and sprinted down the road, keeping her weight on the balls of her feet so she hardly made a sound. Kyla slowed to a walk and crouched down low behind a bush when she neared the corner, looking to see where Nathaniel was now. He was already another hundred yards away from her.

How was he walking so fast?

Kyla crept along slowly behind him, then stopped and waited until a house blocked her from view before she resumed her stealthily mapped-out sprinting.

She followed him like that all the way down to Woodland Cemetery.

When she realized his destination, Kyla's heart sped up nervously. Why was he coming back here again? It made her anxious, to say the least, and it was only at that point that she was certain something wasn't right.

For a moment she debated turning around and walking away, but her relentless curiosity pulled her to keep moving after him. Keeping an even greater distance from Nathaniel than she had as she was tracking him down the road, Kyla knew she could never explain herself if he were to find her stalking him a second time. Which really begged the question, why was she doing this?

She was more skittish this time than she had been the first. The fact that she had been attacked and nearly raped since then by a psychopathic stalker probably had something to do with it, but either way, her nerves were on edge as she made her way slowly up the hill and into the graveyard.

Nathaniel looked intent. He was focused and cold, closed off to a greater measure than he even normally was. Since he didn't go down to the same place on the path that he had before, Kyla had to scope out another headstone she could hide behind. She found one similar in size and shape to the other, only this one would be more difficult for her to see from since it didn't have a cutout with a cross.

Figures, she thought. The person buried here *would* be an atheist.

Kyla waited there with her heart pounding madly, telling herself over and over that Nathaniel wasn't going to see her. But though this obviously concerned her, the thought quickly left when she saw him approach the same blonde man he had met here before. The man whose name he had never told her, whose relation to him he had never explained.

276

Kyla held her breath so she could attempt to hear what they were saying.

Nathaniel bowed his head in submission, though the gesture appeared slightly more forced than it had the last time she saw him do this. The man glared at him coldly, staring into him hard, and the silence between them was long enough that it should have been uncomfortable. But Nathaniel didn't seem fazed by it.

"I did what I had to do," Nathaniel said, his voice completely emotionless.

Had the man asked him a question?

His words appeared to anger the man, but still he didn't speak.

"I am not placing the mission in danger," Nathaniel told him. "And you can speak plainly. I'm standing right here."

Mission? What was he talking about?

"Oh, really?" the man asked. The sound of his voice startled her. "Where is he then?" he challenged. "Tell me, Nathaniel, where is Donovan?"

Kyla went rigid, the blood rushing out of her face at the name.

"I don't know," Nathaniel said, his voice still monotone, "but I have the information you need."

The man fell quiet before he asked him, "What?" He sounded surprised.

"There is another," Nathaniel told him. It looked painful for him to say it, too. "We have a hold in the city."

Kyla didn't know what he was talking about, and she wasn't sure she wanted to.

The man stepped back a little, eyeing Nathaniel skeptically. "How can you be certain?"

"Ethan was wrong in what he reported to you," Nathaniel said.

Kyla was getting more confused by the second. Who was Ethan?

"I haven't compromised anything," Nathaniel told him. "Everything I have done, I have had to do in order to attain the information you charged me with finding. I have not disobeyed you, Seth."

Kyla's heart pounded. *Seth*, she thought to herself. Why did that name frighten her?

"What is my assignment?" Nathaniel asked.

The man named Seth continued to look disturbed. "You will wait here in discretion until I return with the others." He paused and looked hard at Nathaniel. "Until then," he said, "stay away from the human girl."

Kyla stopped breathing. The *human* girl?

Her world froze on her in that moment and everything she was conscious of slipped away from her with those words. As soon as it found its pulse again, her heart started beating in frantic, rapid surges and her breathing became so quick she was afraid she might black out.

Whipping around so that her back was pressed up against the headstone, she stared with widened eyes toward the entrance of the cemetery.

The *human* girl?

Kyla held her breath, paralyzed in the fear that had her gripped in a stranglehold. She couldn't wrap her mind around what she'd just heard or rationalize it away to misunderstanding. Her instinct was screaming at her to get out of there fast, but she didn't know how to do that without being spotted.

As she crouched there in a terrified sort of shock, she heard the man called Seth tell Nathaniel he had to "get back," though she didn't have any idea what it was that "back" referred to. Then, when Kyla looked over to them again cautiously, she saw that the man was gone.

That was the point at which hyperventilation started to set in. Fortunately, by some miracle she managed to shut her mouth and breathe through her nose so that Nathaniel wouldn't hear her. Kyla could never have imagined that he would hurt her before now, but if he found her here like this and realized she'd heard that man blatantly state that he wasn't... she couldn't even bring herself to *think* the word "human," there was no telling what he would be forced to do.

Nathaniel continued to pace back and forth in frustration, and she thought he seemed distracted enough that she might be able to make a break for it. Kyla got up warily, using slow careful movements as she slipped out of the cemetery and moved as soundlessly as she could. But right when she neared the exit gate, she glanced compulsively behind her one last time, and when she did, Nathaniel snapped his head up.

That was her cue.

She bolted out of there as fast as she could, hearing him call out, "Hey!" as he ran after her.

Even though she was an incredible runner, Kyla was no match for Nathaniel's speed. He caught up to her in a matter of seconds and grabbed her from behind, spinning her around firmly to face him.

She screamed in fear and squinted her eyes closed, wincing like he was going to hurt her.

"Kyla?" he asked her in alarm.

Her eyes opened again slowly. She was completely tensed as she held her hands up in front of her. Her breathing was labored and she could see the surprise and confusion in his face.

"I'm sorry," she blurted out quickly. Her lips quivered as she spoke.

Nathaniel didn't appear to understand. "What are you talking about?"

Kyla's heart was working overtime to get blood through her body, and somehow no matter how hard it pushed itself, it didn't seem to be doing its job. She opened her mouth to respond to him, but she literally had no words.

Nathaniel looked into her, reading behind her eyes what she could only assume he knew she'd witnessed...what he knew she had heard. And as that understanding settled over him, she saw his fear rise to the surface.

"No..." he whispered.

The sound of his voice terrified her. "Nathaniel, please," she begged. "I'm sorry. I'll do whatever you want, just please don't hurt me."

A look more painful than she had ever seen came over Nathaniel's face.

"Kyla..." he choked. His voice was strained. "Do you really think that I would *ever* hurt you?"

She was shaking uncontrollably and she hated herself for it. Kyla hated how frightened and weak and vulnerable she was, but she didn't know how to be strong right now. Still, looking at the boy in front of her and searching him for truth, she allowed his words to penetrate her heart and a familiar torrent of emotion to flood through her, though it was far more confusing now than it had been at any time before.

"No," she told him in a strangled voice. "I don't."

Nathaniel swallowed again and brushed the hair out of her face, trembling as he touched her. "I am sorry," he told her. "I am so sorry." He looked tortured as he said it. "I never wanted to hurt you, Kyla. I never meant to place you in danger. This is my fault...all of it. I wanted to tell you the truth. I wanted to tell you everything, but I couldn't..."

She knew he had to be talking about the man named Donovan, if he even *was* a man, but she couldn't wrap her mind around what he was trying to say. Right now, that was not what concerned her.

"Nathaniel," she asked him in a broken voice, "what *are* you?"

*I*t was dark in Val's apartment. Lying on her back on the silken sheets beneath her, she stared at the ceiling with hands behind her head, and absolute satisfaction on her face. Val loved the dark. And she loved being able to control it. It did something to her, shaping and manipulating that level of power, knowing she had the ability to tame even the deepest kind of evil.

Donovan was a fool to think her subject to him. His uncontrollable ego and unquenchable lust had placed him in a state of weakness he would never admit...that he couldn't even see.

They never saw it, and that was what made them so easy to control.

Slipping out from under the billowing silk comforter, Val made her way to the bathroom and turned on the shower. She could feel Donovan watching her as she moved across the room. It excited her, knowing the power she held over him even now as he lay in her bed.

Stepping into the shower, she counted down the seconds until he was with her beneath the steaming water. Val closed her eyes and ran her fingers through her short black hair, but when eight seconds passed, she opened them again, slightly miffed when she realized he hadn't followed her. It made her nervous whenever men showed resistance of any sort...men or anything remotely comparable to them.

She heard a sound she didn't expect to hear and immediately shut off the water. There were voices coming from her bedroom. Wrapping a towel around her ivory curves, Val slipped back out into the room, surprised to see Balak standing over her bed. He was talking angrily to Donovan, who didn't appear to have any intention of getting up, but he stopped as soon as he saw her.

Balak always stopped talking when he saw her.

A devious smile played on Val's lips as she eyed Donovan's dark-skinned lackey from the doorway. "Balak," she greeted. Her voice was dripping with sarcasm.

Balak didn't say another word, just glared at her and left in the way he had come in. Apparently he didn't like that, or maybe he still hadn't forgiven her for the incident that almost got him in trouble with their leader. The night Val had...*distracted* him while he was supposed to be on watch.

She tried not to let her amusement show on her face, knowing how Donovan disproved of her toying with the others.

"What did he want?" she asked once Balak was gone.

Donovan frowned and furrowed his brow, obviously not liking whatever he had just been informed of. "Get dressed," he told her. "We have work to do."

*C*aden walked into his parents' house feeling sick. He hated leaving Kyla back there alone with a stranger...with that *Nathaniel Blake*, but he didn't have a choice. Not really. Still, Caden didn't like him, and if he had his way right now, Kyla wouldn't be with the guy at all. But after everything that had happened, Caden knew he couldn't push her too hard, too fast. That wasn't the way Kyla worked. If he wanted her to open up to him again, he needed to take it slow and he needed to be patient.

Yeah. Easier said than done.

Caden sighed as he stepped into the living room, wishing it never had to be like this. He wished he had never been stupid enough to go to Nashville and leave her in the first place, no matter how justifiable his intentions. If he hadn't, he wouldn't have to be working right now to get his best friend to trust him again.

Alexa was sitting in the oversized armchair by the fireplace. She was staring forward blankly, looking very near catatonic, and the moment Caden saw her, his frustrations over Kyla and the blonde guy and his own relentless stupidity left him.

"Lex?" he said, moving quickly to his sister's side.

She didn't even flinch.

Caden was hit by a sharp wave of fear as he knelt in front of his sister. Setting a hand on her knee, he asked her, "Lex, what is it? What's wrong?"

She didn't answer him.

She had to be seeing something. He knew that look well, and judging by the intensity of her expression, he also knew that whatever it was, it wasn't good.

"Alexa," he said more firmly.

She took a sharp breath, blinked once and turned to face him.

"Caden..." she said softly. Then she trailed off and continued to stare forward.

"What is it?" he asked her. "What did you see?"

He tried not to let the intensity behind her hazel eyes frighten him.

This is normal, he told himself. He just hadn't been around her in so long he'd almost forgotten.

Finally, Alexa answered him. "She knows," the girl said quietly. Caden didn't understand.

Moving his hand to her shoulder so she would look him in the eye, he redirected her focus and asked, "Who, Alexa?"

282

Despite the gesture she still didn't meet his eyes. "She's gonna run."

When he heard this, Caden was struck by a shock of fear that channeled suddenly through his body. It stabbed into him fast enough and hard enough that he struggled to make sense of it, and to make sense of what she was saying.

"Are you talking about Kyla?" he asked her. Even the thought of it nauseated him.

That same distant look came over Alexa's face again that let him know she was seeing beyond what was physically there.

Something was wrong...he could feel it. Something was very, very wrong.

Caden knew he shouldn't have left her. He should have trusted his instinct, but he had chosen not to listen to that prodding voice he had learned so well in the past year to ignore.

"I'm going to find her," he said as he stood back to his feet. "I need you to pray. Can you do that for me?"

The girl nodded without moving her gaze and Caden kissed the top of her head. Then he sprinted out the door, shaking as he pulled his keys from his pocket.

*S*taring into the face of the petrified girl that he held by the arms, Nathaniel was afraid...more afraid than he could ever remember being. But nothing compared to the fear he saw behind Kyla's now-hazy green eyes.

He didn't know how to answer her.

"Kyla," he said, scrambling to think of anything he could say that would help her to understand.

"Is it true?" she asked him. "What that man said...is it true?"

Nathaniel couldn't breathe. He knew he couldn't lie to her anymore. Not after this.

"It's true," he said.

Horror filled Kyla's eyes as he spoke the words. Every part of it moved in slow motion for him, the way she held her breath, hoping against hope that he would tell her "no," the way her face twisted in fear and mortification when he didn't.

Nathaniel felt like he was being stabbed.

Working herself forcefully out of his grip, Kyla broke away from him, leaving Nathaniel with a weight on his chest so heavy and unyielding he thought it might crush his lungs.

"Wait," he begged her, choking out the words.

Kyla's expression didn't change. "No," she told him. She shook her head and backed up from him slowly, and with every step she took, the suffocation Nathaniel felt grew only that much stronger.

"Kyla please..." he tried again, but before he could utter another syllable she cut him off.

"Stay away from me," her voice quivered.

Nathaniel froze. He felt his heart stop beating as he stared at her speechless, as he watched her turn away from him and run up the road. And that was all he could do, both then and even after that; stare forward in the shock that had fallen on him, watching as his reason ran away.

*I*t was pitch-black on Ponderosa Way, save for the light of the condo at the end of the block. Val drove slowly, as inconspicuously as she could, up the street. Then she parked a block up the road and crept on foot across the yard. No one was out here, but she could see that someone had been.

It was a cell phone she spotted at the top of the deck, and she recognized it immediately. Looking all around to make sure she wouldn't be seen, Val moved up the steps quickly and picked it up. It was Kyla's.

Hitting the button at the top so the screen lit up, Val saw that she had three missed calls. All from Caden.

Feeling far too exposed beneath the light on the deck, Val slipped to the side of the driveway that was hidden by the darkness of the night. Opening the phone again, she checked the call times and realized they were made only minutes ago. Caden was obviously freaked about something.

Then, as she held it, the phone blinged once with a text message. Val didn't flinch. Instead she opened the message Caden had just sent which simply read, "I'm coming over."

Her face went white.

He's here… The thought hit her slowly. *Balak was right.*

Suddenly her heart started beating faster. Erasing the text message and all three missed calls, she returned the phone to where she had found it and made her way quickly back to her car. Slipping her own cell phone out of her pocket as she moved through the dark, she dialed a number from memory.

When the other end picked up after the first ring, Val didn't waste any time with formalities.

"He was right," she told Donovan. "Caden is here. So what's my next move?" And although she tried, she couldn't keep the excitement out of her voice.

*K*yla couldn't remember a time she'd ever run as fast as she ran from the cemetery that night. She couldn't remember a time she'd ever had to. Cross Country races were one thing, where she competed for a cheap piece of ribbon with some silver scrawled writing on it, or maybe just the pride of knowing she could beat everyone in her division. But running in a race, even a race where she gave it all she had didn't compare to what this was. A desperation for escape, a flight for survival. The vain hope of evading the reality on her heels.

It was fear that propelled her, that pushed Kyla's legs to move harder and faster than she even knew they could. Like a jolt of adrenaline being shot through her veins, released by the thing she hated most in this life. But if fear could be used now to put distance between her and Nathaniel Blake…this liar behind her who wasn't even a man, Kyla was going to take it, and take as much of it as she could. Whatever it required for her to get away from him, that was exactly what she was willing to do.

Running down the road away from Donovan that night…the night that had since become blurred in her memory, Kyla thought she knew then what it was like to feel a blur take her vision, to be disoriented and confused, but to keep pushing forward in spite of this. Whatever she had felt on Majestic Parkway, it wasn't at all what she felt right now. This was worse. Much worse. Not because Nathaniel had tried to hurt her like Donovan had, but because her fear was no longer founded on speculation.

It wasn't just an idea in her head or a prodding question at the back of her spirit telling her something wasn't right. Nathaniel's own words had confirmed her fear. He was the one who told her he wasn't human.

It was a surreal feeling when the condo came into view, but at the same time it caused a hollow suspicion to rise in her. Kyla knew that Nathaniel could have easily caught her by now. If he'd wanted to, he could have had her by the arms again in a matter of seconds. She had seen the way he could move, and something told her that what little she had witnessed didn't do justice to what he was really capable of.

Kyla shoved the thought from her mind and picked up her knees to push the last fifty meters up the inclined road. She usually despised the last fifty meters of a race, but tonight, she didn't mind. She didn't waste time going inside, realizing as she neared the condo that there was nothing Loni or Matthew could do to protect her. The last thing Kyla needed was to be somewhere she could be found, because logic told her (despite how senseless logic seemed at the moment) that no shoddily-built structure could keep her safe from Nathaniel Blake. She doubted even prison bars could do that if he really wanted her.

No, her family couldn't help her right now. There was only one person who could.

Kyla raced to the driveway and jumped into the Civic before she let herself breathe. Pulling the spare key down from the visor, she attempted to start the engine, but it took her four tries to get the key into the ignition. When she finally got it, she threw the thing in reverse, slammed her foot down on the pedal and tore out of the driveway.

It wasn't until she'd passed Paradise Circle that she realized she left her phone on the deck, but there wasn't a chance she was going back for it now. She just had to get to Caden. She had to get where she would be safe.

Trying to shake the thought away of what she knew she couldn't deny (but wished with everything that she could) Kyla trembled as she gunned the accelerator and sped up the

286

road. She tried to calm her breathing, but the full mile of sprinting she'd just pulled off coupled with the fact that Nathaniel Blake apparently wasn't human made that completely impossible.

It had never taken her so long to drive up to Edlowe Road, and that was even with her pushing twenty over the speed limit. Or at least it felt that way. Thankfully the cops that kept the highway patrolled at night didn't catch her, which was oddly fortunate in itself, considering that they were usually all over the place.

Couldn't make this situation much worse if they were, Kyla thought. She wasn't sure anything could.

But then something happened that reminded her why it was a bad idea to think something like that, even if she didn't actually say the words out loud. As Kyla wove her way swiftly through the canopy of trees and drew nearer to Skyline Drive, she had a brief moment where relief filled the place where her fear had been kept, like oxygen in the lungs of a suffocating man. She was close now, so close she could almost feel him. Even as she saw the road up ahead, she could imagine the safety of Caden's arms.

And then it happened.

Suddenly, so suddenly she couldn't make sense of what she was even seeing, a dark, black...*thing* flew at the Civic and crashed against the windshield. It flashed in her mind like a picture from a nightmare, a hideous creature with jet-black wings; red eyes, fangs bared...no trace of humanity in it despite that it held the face of a man.

It didn't click in Kyla's mind that what she was seeing was real. This whole night felt unreal to her; now more than ever. It seemed to move in slow-motion, like time had slowed down so the image could be deciphered, so her terror could be felt as it seeped into her heart...so the horror of the real could bring death to the relief she had almost felt, crushing in one final blow whatever might have remained.

Eternity couldn't capture the length that it felt, though she knew it all happened in the blink of an eye. There was nothing about time that was right anymore; nothing about logic or the hope of escape. There was nothing but a shattered windshield, a monster with black wings and a sheer, unadulterated terror that clutched like death itself at Kyla's throat.

Shrieking at a higher decibel than her voice had ever reached, she swerved off the side of the road, plunging the Civic into an embankment beneath the trees. She cracked her head against the steering wheel at the collision, hard enough that she was momentarily disoriented. Blood dripped down her face from a gash over her left eyebrow; Kyla felt it as she struggled to right herself. Pulling her hand away, she saw red on her fingers, and as she locked in on the image, all she could remember were those red glowing eyes.

Jerking away from the door, she tried desperately to work her way to the other side of the car. She just couldn't do it fast enough.

Right when Kyla reached it, the driver's side door was ripped open. A hand grabbed her first by her arm and then by her throat, yanking her out of the car.

Kyla tried to fight it off...whatever that thing was, but her vision was too blurred and her senses too confused for the attempt to be effective.

She could feel the sharp gravel scraping up her legs as she was mercilessly dragged by this creature up the road. She screamed in pain and struggled to free herself from its grip, but it was no use. It wasn't about to let her go.

In a matter of seconds, the pain reached an intensity her body couldn't bear, and Kyla began slipping in and out of consciousness. This went on for longer than she could determine, and even in the few brief times she would finally come to, she still couldn't lock in on what was happening to her.

The next thing she was distinctly aware of was her body being thrown to forest floor and the wind being knocked out of her on the impact. It was so painful Kyla thought she might suffocate; and when she considered what was being done to her (or what was about to be done to her soon) she couldn't help but question if that was really such a bad idea.

Her eyes shot open when she hit the ground and she gasped for breath, becoming frantic when she couldn't catch

288

it. She wanted to look around her and see where she was, but when the air wouldn't come, Kyla knew her current location was far less important than her ability to get oxygen to her lungs. It took thirty-five of the most terrifying seconds of her life, but finally the air began to trickle in.

She remembered something Caden told her when she was nine years old, after she'd fallen out of a tree and she couldn't catch her breath. "Take slow, small breaths," he'd said, reassuring her the whole time that she was going to be okay. "Don't try to get the air. Don't be afraid. If you calm down, your breath will come back."

Kyla remembered that now as she struggled in a panic just the way he'd said not to, and it was when she listened to the words he had told her all those years ago that it started to work; at least enough to enable her to figure out where she was.

Jerking her head back and forth and all around her, Kyla tried to take in the scene. She could tell she was somewhere on the mountain, but that was about it. She had no idea how long it had been since she was pulled from her car or how far her attacker had dragged her into the trees. All she could see was the black…threatening and thick, closing in around her moment by moment and cutting off any chance of escape she might have otherwise had.

It was the darkest night she had ever seen, the darkest feeling she had ever felt, and as she lay there petrified on the forest floor, all she could think was that this had to be a nightmare.

Slowing her confusion and ignoring the pain, she looked deeper into the dark and her vision began to adjust. It was clear she'd been dropped in the thick of the forest, just as she'd suspected, but that didn't mean she knew where she was. All the woods looked the same around here; the towering pines, the moss-caked remains of dead, fallen trees. And they all smelled of pungent evergreen, which didn't do much to help her navigate her way.

She could have been anywhere, and though that thought certainly concerned her, it wasn't what drove her raging pulse right now.

Slowly, her vision began to adjust further. She squinted into the dark to look for a way out, but just as it started to come clear, a tall looming figure appeared in her sight. Screaming, Kyla crawled backwards away from it...away from this man who was cloaked in shadow.

And it was then that she knew who had brought her here.

"Donovan..." she breathed in a furious whisper. Recognizing his cold twisted grin, Kyla felt like she was going to throw up.

Donovan's grin widened at the sound of his own name. Taking a step forward, he pulled a black, jagged blade from beneath the trench coat he wore. "Hello, Kyla James."

His eyes held her in arrest through their horror and beauty, spellbound by a force she was unable to comprehend. She was captured by them...by the flame that existed beyond the windows of his blackened soul. And it was then that she realized, then that she knew what she should already have known:

Those eyes were not human.

Chapter 19

"...cat and mouse."

Caden was speeding as he peeled around the corner and onto Ponderosa Way, not even caring about waking anyone up who lived on the street. There was only one thing that concerned him right now, and the James' high-strung neighbors were not it.

When he saw the empty driveway and realized the Civic was missing, he racked his brain trying to think of anywhere Kyla might have gone. Parking quickly and getting out of the Jeep, he ran up the stairs, determining that he had a better shot at finding her if he asked Matthew where she went.

Caden frowned when he spotted her cell phone on the top step and realized why she wasn't returning his calls. He'd figured she had left it behind even though it wasn't like her to do that; he was just hoping he was wrong.

Caden hesitated before he walked up to the door, hardly thrilled with the prospect of seeing Loni right now.

It doesn't matter, he told himself. *You have to find her.*

But then, right when he worked up the courage to knock on the door, he heard someone from below him say his name.

"Caden?"

Spinning around quickly, he squinted into the dark to see who was standing in the James' driveway.

His face fell to confusion. "Val?"

Before he could make sense of what he was seeing, Val Linley stepped into the light from the deck and looked up at him with a smile.

"Wow," she said, giving him the up-down. "You look incredible."

Caden blinked a few times, surprised by the tight black dress and heels she was wearing, finding it an odd choice of attire at the least. Or maybe he was more surprised by seeing her at all. Either way, he glanced nervously around him. "You don't look half bad yourself," he mumbled.

He could feel the tension in his chest, both in being there with Val and in knowing he didn't have time to be polite right now. Even under normal circumstances, Caden felt guilty talking to Val. He knew how much it upset Kyla when he did; but these circumstances were hardly normal, and they easily made that feeling ten times worse.

"What are you doing here?" Val asked him.

He kept his response short, hoping she'd take the hint. "Looking for Kyla."

Val's smile hadn't dropped yet. "That makes two of us."

Caden didn't understand. "You're looking for her, too?" That didn't seem right.

"It's a work thing," Val told him. "I tried calling her, but she wasn't picking up, so I thought I'd just swing by."

It was hard for Caden to believe that in the time he'd been gone, Val and Kyla had formed enough of a bond that Kyla would let her know where she lived. And by bond, he meant anything short of them wanting to kill each other.

Caden nodded to her once and looked down the road, hoping in vain that he might see the Civic pulling up Ponderosa. When he didn't, the pressure in his chest started to increase and his eyes fell onto the wooden boards of the deck.

"You okay?" Val asked him.

Caden was short with her. "I'm fine," he said. "I just really need to find her."

Val paused thoughtfully. "You know, she's probably with Nathaniel."

Caden tensed up. "You know him?"

"Of course I know him," Val said. She made it sound like that should be obvious. "He comes by work all the time to see her. It's actually kind of irritating, really. They can't keep their hands off each other."

Caden clenched his jaw and Val studied his face.

"Did she not tell you they were…"

Caden didn't let her finish, partly because he didn't have the time to waste and partly because he didn't want to hear it.

"Where does he live?" he cut her off.

"I'm not sure," Val said, "but I wouldn't wait up if I were you."

He gave her a look and she suddenly got uncomfortable.

"I mean, not that I would know or anything," she said. "They just seem pretty intense when they're together, that's all."

Caden's head was starting to spin. Val's words weren't registering to him right, and even when they started to, he wished that they wouldn't.

"You know, I actually think I remember Kyla saying something about going up to Catamount with him tonight," Val added.

She had to be able to see the disgust on his face.

"I need to go," Caden said quickly.

"Look, I'm sorry," Val apologized. "I didn't mean to drop it on you like that."

"It's fine," he said flatly. Then he mumbled something like "it was good to see you" or "I'm sorry I have to run" under his breath as he pushed his way past her.

"Don't worry about it," Val told him. She gave him a teasing look as he left and Caden responded with a smile so tense it almost hurt his face.

It fell the moment he turned his back on her.

He was so angry he could kill something.

Kyla was rigid on the forest floor, her eyes darting back and forth between the face of her captor and the blade in his hand. This could not be happening. Whatever she was seeing, whatever this was about, there was no way that she was really here in the dark like this with Donovan, alone on this mountain where nobody knew to find her…where no one even knew to look.

Fear seeped into her like venom as the truth poured over her, paralyzing her as the prey of a spider. Looking up at this man, at this creature she was convinced to be the epitome of darkness, Kyla realized what she had been guarding her mind from seeing until now.

Donovan had her. She was alone. And she was going to die.

Kyla spewed at him angrily, "What do you want from me now, you pathetic snake?"

Donovan grinned as he fondled the dagger in his hand. "More than I knew," he told her. "Turns out you are proving to be quite the pretty little asset."

Kyla glared at him, forcing her rage to overpower her fear. "You're wrong," she told him. "I'm useless to you now."

She felt the bitter sting of truth to her words as Donovan stepped closer.

"Perhaps," he told her. "Or perhaps you have misread my intentions."

Kyla tried to read him. "Nathaniel isn't going to come for me," she said. "You're doing this for nothing."

Donovan came to her feet and looked down on her in a way that stopped her from breathing. "This is what I love about your kind," he told her. She could see the glint of his teeth in the moonlight. "You are always so quick to assume."

"What are you talking about?" she snapped.

He grinned at her knowingly. "Whoever said I was after Nathaniel?"

Kyla felt the blood drain suddenly from her face. It took a moment for the implication to set in, but when it finally did, she was sickened by the poison of this fear that had found her.

"No..." she whispered.

That wasn't possible. He couldn't be after Caden.

Donovan's lips stretched even wider across his vampiric teeth, and suddenly she questioned if she was wrong. She knew she wasn't the one he wanted, that he was only using her as bait. To put it in his terms, she was the cheese he had set on the trap. The only question that mattered anymore was the one she'd asked before.

Who was the mouse?

"Game on, Kyla James," Donovan quivered through his grin. And then without another word, sound or moment, he disappeared.

Kyla watched helplessly as he slipped past her, vanishing into the dark of the woods where she wouldn't be able to see him. She stared after him in shock, numb and bewildered for a full three seconds before she finally was able to shake herself from it.

"Donovan!" she screamed as loudly as her voice would let her.

Kyla righted herself and struggled to her feet, realizing only then just how hard she'd hit her head. Her heart was pounding madly, but she shoved this fear back from her. She was too mad right now to be afraid.

Looking all around her in an attempt to find a way through the trees, she realized she had no way of knowing which direction she should go. The dimming light of the moon didn't do much to help her, but it was just enough to keep her from the entrapment of the dark black night.

Kyla didn't know where she was or where Donovan had gone, or even more terrifying, where he was going. But when she thought of it actually being real, what he'd said, that she'd wrongly assumed what he was after, that was enough to push her past her uncertainty and force her to run like hell.

Kyla could find her way out of here, wherever "here" was; she just had to keep moving. Racing through the woods, she could hear nothing but her own breath and the crunching of pine needles beneath her feet. She stopped when she came to a split in the trail, her breathing drastically deepening as the darkness fell in around her. She tried to force away the terror that was threatening to cripple her, but then she heard something.

Spinning around at the noise, Kyla looked frantically in every direction, not sure what she might see. But she didn't see anything.

And again the forest fell silent.

The only sound she could hear was the sound of her own breath, and even that she might have tried harder to quiet if the effort wouldn't have been futile. What point was there in hiding, though, when Donovan already knew she was here? Kyla knew he was watching her, reveling in the fear he was provoking her to. She could feel him.

Then suddenly, she felt something else.

Screaming as she was grabbed from behind, Kyla slashed at Donovan's face with her nails. She managed to break free from his hold and bolt in the opposite direction, but it did her little good. Before she'd even taken three steps, he was in front of her again.

Kyla's eyes widened as she stepped backwards away from him, breathing so hard she thought she might pass out.

"What *are* you?" her voice shook with terror.

Donovan dropped a hand from his face, his fingers coated in blood after touching the place where she'd scratched him. "Your boyfriend didn't tell you?" he asked her tauntingly.

Kyla felt sick at the suggestion, but she didn't say a word.

"That figures," Donovan mumbled. "Nathaniel is as deluded and deceived as you are to think himself any different than me."

"Nathaniel is *nothing* like you," Kyla snarled.

Her instinct to defend him surprised her, but Donovan just laughed and moved closer. With every step he took forward, she took another back.

"How wrong you are, Kyla James," he said. "How delightfully blinded by your own narrow-minded ignorance."

Questioning the validity of Donovan's claim, she felt a different kind of fear choking her now. "I don't believe you," she said. But in the back of her mind, she wondered if he really was lying this time...if Nathaniel might actually be something like this twisted creature before her.

"Unfortunately," Donovan told her, "some things don't have to be believed to be true. Such as your mistrust of my intentions."

Kyla clenched her jaw and stared him down. "What do you want with Caden?" she demanded, keeping her voice flat in hopes that he wouldn't hear her fear.

Donovan stopped moving forward and looked at her curiously. "Who?" he asked.

Kyla blinked as she looked at him. She didn't understand. He had to have been talking about Caden before when...

Suddenly, the fear she had been fighting back latched onto her in a stranglehold as she realized she had just made a deadly mistake. She should never have mentioned Caden's name. Oh, God, why did she do that?

It hit her so quickly that she didn't know what she was seeing, but as soon as it came clear, she fell sick with dread. Coming before her vision as something like a flash, an array of pictures struck her mind; hundreds of images at once of the most gruesome, sickening thoughts she could ever imagine. Visions of Caden lying lifeless before her, his face ashen white as his blood was drained from his body; flashes of Donovan stabbing him through the heart with his black, jagged blade; images of Caden's throat being cut, of the boy she couldn't love more if he were her very own brother screaming in agony as he was tortured slowly. They hit her violently and completely against her will, every conceivable scenario that could end in his death.

Kyla grabbed at her head with both her hands and screamed out in pain, "Stop it! Oh God, please stop it!"

She tried to force her mind from this throbbing horror, but it wasn't in her control. Then at all at once, the thoughts ceased and she could only hear the sound of Donovan's sick, maniacal laughter.

Slowly, Kyla let go of her head. Steadying her breathing, she looked up at him with a new burning in her eyes and a sudden desire to rip out his throat. "I don't care what you are," she breathed to him furiously. "If you touch him, I swear to God I will kill you."

Donovan was amused. "Is that so?" he challenged her mockingly.

Kyla clenched her jaw and stood there, unmoving.

Donovan was quiet for a moment, unsettlingly so, and she couldn't determine what he was going to do. But then in one sudden move, he lunged forward and grabbed her by the neck, hurling her down the embankment beside them before she had the chance to scream.

Caden held his steering wheel in a death grip as he tore up Edlowe Road. He couldn't determine whether his conversation with Val had left him more nauseated or furious, but right now he didn't even care to distinguish between the two. He just had to get back to the house to see his sister. She was the only shot he had now at finding Kyla, and the pressure he felt in his chest told him he didn't have much time.

He didn't know what was going on, only that his spirit was on fire, that something was happening and that he was scared out of his mind at whatever it might be.

Caden couldn't imagine anything that would cause him to feel like this, and even if he could, he certainly didn't want to. It was as he drove up the road in the dark that these thoughts moved through his head, but then he saw something that made him slam on his brakes, sending the Jeep skidding to a halt and very nearly driving it off the embankment to his right.

It was Loni's Civic. And it was crashed onto the side of the road.

Caden didn't wait a second or even bring the Jeep to a complete stop before he sprang out of the cab and sprinted over to the car.

"Kyla!" he shouted.

He saw that the driver's-side door was swung completely open, but no one was inside. He knew if she had wrecked it and called someone to pick her up, she wouldn't have left the door open like that. Maybe somebody else would have, but not Kyla.

He didn't waste a second before he climbed into the car. The first thing he noticed was the blood on the steering wheel, and that in itself was enough to turn his stomach. He fingered it gently with a shaking hand, then he pulled away and saw that it was wet on his skin.

Suddenly he couldn't breathe. Looking around him frantically for any other evidence of what might have happened, any other clue that might tell him something...*anything*, Caden had to force his lungs into submission and stay focused on what was before him. He could be freaked out later; right now he just had to find her.

If he did this…if Nathaniel Blake hurt her…

Caden couldn't finish the thought. Slamming the door of the Civic furiously, he ran back to his Jeep and tore up the road again, shaking as he sped toward Catamount.

Alexa had to have seen this, he thought, and if she did, she had to be able to help him. Caden clenched his jaw to keep his fear at bay. She had to tell him it wasn't too late.

Picking up his phone and calling the house number, he held it to his ear and prayed to God that Alexa was there waiting by it. The last thing he needed was for one of his parents to answer and for him to have to explain himself. Thankfully, this was one instance where his prayers were answered.

Someone picked up on the other end of the line, and when they didn't answer with an immediate "hello," Caden knew it was his sister.

"Where is she?" he asked abruptly.

The line was quiet, but he knew she was there.

"Alexa!"

He could imagine her standing there with the phone pressed to her ear, her skin ghost white and her big brown eyes staring forward.

"Please…" he begged her.

He could hear her breathing on the other end, so he knew she was listening; she just wasn't saying anything.

Caden felt like he was going to cry.

"I found her car," he rambled. "She…she's not…she wasn't in it. She wrecked it, I think and…Val said…they were at Catamount…but I…I don't know where to go…"

He could hear himself talking and he knew he wasn't making sense, but right now Caden was so frightened it was the best he could do. He stopped himself from saying another word and tried to breathe instead.

"Where is she, Alexa?" he asked. Somehow he managed to keep himself calm this time, too. "I need you to tell me which direction I should go…where I should look for her. I know you can see her if you try. You saw her before…"

Alexa had told him that earlier, before he left to find Kyla that night, though she hadn't told him what it was that she saw. When Caden tried to force it out of her, she just shut down like she always did, but she told him enough that he knew she was seeing again.

Caden was about to beat his head against the window when finally, she decided to talk to him.

"I don't know where she is," Alexa said quietly.

He felt his stomach tighten. "Try," he begged her. "Please."

Pulling into the parking lot at the base of the mountain, Caden jumped out of his Jeep with his phone. The trails up here all started off in the same place, and they didn't branch off from one another until about a quarter-mile up into the woods; which meant he had some time. Not a lot of time, but still...time.

Caden was sprinting, praying under his breath that his sister would see something that could help him. "Talk to me," he said as he pushed his way up the trail. He was afraid he was going to lose reception if she didn't hurry up. Even with the satellite coverage they had with their phones, things still got shaky when they got up into the trees like this. "Has something happened to her?" Caden asked harshly. His patience was wearing thin.

Alexa's breathing quickened. "Yes," she said.

Caden had to fight hard to keep himself upright. "Is...is she still..." Unable to force the question, he felt separated from reality, from this mountain...from himself. Somehow nothing seemed real anymore; not the pain shooting through his legs or his nauseating fear. Not even the voice on the other end of the line.

"Yes," Alexa told him. "She's still alive." Her voice was unchanged.

Caden pulled himself to a halt and put his hand on his head, trying to catch his breath when he reached the fork in the trail. He closed his eyes and let the relief of her answer fill him, but he had to force away the emotion he felt with it. "Lex, I have to find her," he choked out. "You have to help me. You have to tell me which way I should go. Right or left. Which is it?"

Alexa fell quiet again in the way that told him she was contemplating something deeply. "I can't do that," she finally said.

Caden tightened his jaw and tried not to get upset. "Why not?" he asked tensely.

He could almost see the look in her eyes as she answered him, "Because I'm not the one who can feel her."

As Kyla lay motionless in the dark on the floor of the forest, she couldn't breathe or blink or cry. Despair filled her when she realized the fall hadn't killed her. That would have been far easier than lying here amidst the rocks and the branches, bleeding to death alone.

A sharp onset of pain shot through the right side of her abdomen.

Looking down, Kyla could see nothing, but when she moved her hand across her stomach she felt a gash at least five inches long that she could only assume had been caused by one of the hundreds of deadfalls that impaled her as she'd tumbled down the embankment.

Kyla wanted to cry, but the hopelessness she felt was powerful over her body's ability to produce tears. She knew Donovan was going to find her here, and that as soon as he did and saw that she was alive, he was going to remedy that quickly.

A noise sounded to her right and her eyes shot open. Holding her lips together tightly, Kyla prepared herself for the worst, for the unthinkable, for the fate she had been fooling herself into believing she could escape. Hot, sticky blood spilled through her fingers where her hand clutched her side. Whatever had pierced her, it had torn through Caden's jacket when it did. But even feeling this laceration and the blood that poured from the wound, she still couldn't find her voice to scream. Even if she could have, she knew there was no one who would hear her.

She was alone here, and she was going to be alone when he killed her.

Her heart froze cold at a new sound that reached her ears. Slow, careful footfalls that crunched against the ground. Loudly. Intentionally.

He wanted her to hear him.

Again the forest fell silent. Kyla sucked in sharply and braced herself as an iron fist came down on her shoulder, setting fire to the pain she was already writhing in. But it wasn't just the pain of a thousand fiery blades ripping through her body. It was the pain of abandonment, the pain of loss...the agony of knowing she was going to die.

Nathaniel wasn't coming for her. He wasn't going to save her this time and it was entirely her fault. That alone made Kyla long for the death she knew awaited her.

She felt her body being dragged back up the embankment and then slammed back to the ground again as Donovan pinned her beneath him.

"*Scream*," he dared her through gritted teeth. "Scream for me, Kyla."

She locked her jaw determinedly and stared him straight in the eye, refusing to give him the satisfaction. Oxygen was becoming more difficult for her to take in, but Kyla forced herself to speak to him anyway.

"You are nothing but a weak, misguided coward," she told him in short, labored gasps. Even in the dark she could see his eyes slant in anger. "I hope you burn," she snarled.

Judging by the response in Donovan's expression, she would have typically thought this unwise on her part, but Kyla figured if she was about to die anyway, she may as well dish it out now.

"No, my dear," he told her. His voice was like poison. "You are wrong." He leaned over her and whispered into her ear, "I am not the one who is dying. I am not the one who is going to burn."

It came over her as a rush of fear that was tied to a hopelessness she had never known; then her conviction carried it to a depth that possibility should never reach, and Kyla was hit by the truth of his words. It was as this truth came over her in full, as the safety net of denial was removed from beneath her that the blackest kind of despair set into her soul.

There was no feeling like it. Donovan could have taken his blade right then and sliced through her heart, and even that wouldn't have hurt like this.

Her eyes were glazed over as she spoke to him. "Why do you care if I live or die?" she whispered. "Who am I that you would even care?"

She could feel his breath spilling through his sharp gleaming teeth. "You are nothing, Kyla James," he sneered at her. "You are nothing but a pawn."

Kyla closed her eyes, unable to keep them open beneath the weight that pressed down on her. She could feel the blood being drained from her body with each passing second, but somehow she couldn't find it in her to care.

Dizzy and hollow and completely detached from her present physical reality, Kyla could feel herself slipping away. Then just before the death overtaking her accomplished its aim, a loud crack sounded through the woods as an oversized boulder was hurled through the air, smashing over three successive pine trees and releasing a rumble on the mountain.

Her eyes shot back open and Donovan looked up, turning to the sound faster than it hit. Kyla's heart was beating again in frenzied pulses, but still she didn't scream. She didn't have the strength left in her to make a sound.

Donovan looked up at whatever was behind her, but she wasn't able to see what he could see. She couldn't even turn her head to look. Kyla watched his eyes expand before her own, but through the dark she couldn't see if it was shock or excitement that played in them. It appeared to her somehow as a horrified thrill, though she didn't know what would bring about this reaction.

Her breath came out strained at the new set of footsteps she heard behind her, and at that point, the pouring of endless blood from her side didn't even stop her heart from being jolted at the sound.

She jerked her head around frantically to see whatever approached, but the sight that met her when she did was more than she could bear.

Taking in short, frantic gasps, she struggled not to cry. Her heart stopped beating altogether for longer than a moment, and when its rhythm picked up again it was moving much too fast.

There in the dark, moving slowly toward her assailant was a blonde-haired boy with fire in his eyes and a blade in his hand...and who human or not was looking more like a man to her with every passing moment.

"Nathaniel..." she tried to choke out his name, but her voice was so strangled it was hardly audible.

Nathaniel moved forward slowly with murderous intent, his gaze fixed and his jaw clenched. Kyla had never seen anything...any man or any creature so ready to kill.

"Get up," Nathaniel ordered the man pinning her to the ground in a low, firm voice.

Donovan stood up off of her, his eyes wild as he faced his adversary. She saw it then so clearly...this was exactly what he wanted. He didn't want Caden and he never had. He was always after Nathaniel. Everything else was just a part of this twisted game he had drawn her into.

"Nathaniel," Donovan greeted him, bowing his head in mock respect. "So good of you to come."

*N*athaniel tightened his grip on the dagger he held, prepared to strike the necessary blow. As he stared at Donovan, a hundred thoughts of dismemberment passed through his head; thoughts of the most painfully imaginative methods of torture ever conceived by a human or inhuman mind.

"Nathaniel..." the sound of Kyla's voice struck a pain in his heart that he wasn't ready to feel as she struggled to speak his name.

He turned from Donovan and looked down on her where she lay broken on the ground, having avoided doing so until now for exactly this reason.

The sight of her was literally too much for him to withstand.

Slowly locking onto her gaze, Nathaniel took in the image of her gashed and bleeding body, and as he did, an agony filled him so violently that he would rather be put through every scenario he'd just envisioned of what he wanted to do to Donovan than to have to see her like this...to know that it was his fault.

Only seconds had passed and he couldn't stand looking at her any longer. Nathaniel had never felt such torturous fury and unquenchable rage. Flashing his eyes back to the monster before him, he clutched his dagger and stepped carefully forward. He and Donovan began to circle each other slowly as Kyla lay there helpless on the ground, unable to move away and unable to speak a word.

Their daggers pointed downward and they kept their eyes locked as they moved their feet sideways, one in front of the other, drawing closer to the center; never blinking, hardly breathing...both prepared for whatever this was going to take.

It was Nathaniel who made the first move.

Lunging suddenly, he propelled himself off a rock and brought his arm out to strike Donovan with his blade, but just as he did, Donovan side-stepped and slashed down on him with his own, cutting him cleanly across his back. Then he grabbed Nathaniel with his other arm, spun him sideways and threw him through the air.

Nathaniel landed on his feet with his dagger still out, his eyes narrowed and his teeth bared. He didn't hesitate for a moment before lunging at Donovan again, but not as he had before. This time he leapt into the air and kick-jumped off the base of a tree, letting out a cry as he came down on him from above.

Just before he could parry the blow, Donovan ducked at the last second and clothes-lined his feet, causing Nathaniel to come up over his head. Nathaniel tumbled forward and landed on his back, the force knocking the dagger from his hand. Before he had time to scramble for it, Donovan grabbed the silver piece of metal and stood at ready, holding his own blade in one hand and Nathaniel's in his other.

"A noble effort, to be sure," Donovan taunted him.

Nathaniel gritted his teeth and stood again. He saw Kyla struggling to sit up, struggling to tell him to leave...both of which were unsuccessful attempts. She didn't have the strength to lift her head, much less move a single muscle or speak loudly enough to be heard.

Nathaniel felt his fury burning him again, and within a matter of seconds, he and Donovan were back to circling each other.

It was the challenger cloaked in black who made the initiative this time, slashing at Nathaniel with both of the blades he held. When he missed, Nathaniel spun sideways in hopes of coming up on him from behind, but unfortunately once again, Donovan was faster than he anticipated.

Cutting his arm with one of the blades, the assailant dropped to his knee and sliced through Nathaniel's calf with the other. Nathaniel clenched his jaw and breathed fiercely through his teeth as he forcefully ignored the sting. He kicked his own dagger out of Donovan's hand, rolled onto the ground away from him and picked it up again as he came back to one knee, facing the unholy spawn before him and fantasizing about the multiple ways he would love to slash his throat.

He would do it, too, just as soon as he was given the chance, and he didn't hesitate to inform him of this either.

"I *will* kill you," Nathaniel promised him. "I want you to know that."

Donovan laughed at him contemptuously. "Your assurance pleases me," he told him. Then he darted forward faster than Nathaniel's eyes could lock in on him and hurled him into a tree.

Nathaniel's back cracked against the base of the pine, splitting it in two as he landed on the ground. Catching his breath, he looked up at Donovan scornfully; then he ran at him again without hesitation, holding nothing back.

Nathaniel knew that the time had passed for human fighting.

His wings burst open as he shifted into Naphil form, sweeping one of them beneath Donovan's feet and knocking his legs out from under him. And while his adversary was still on his back, Nathaniel grabbed him by an arm and swung

306

him around, hammer-throwing his body through the air with all his strength behind him.

As soon as he released Donovan in the ferocity of his anger, panic suddenly struck Nathaniel and he whipped his head back around...his eyes falling to the girl who lay paralyzed on the ground, staring up at him in horror.

Chapter 20

"...if only in your mind."

There had been a lot of instances in the past two weeks that had left Kyla feeling a bit lost on reality. She'd stopped counting after a while, as these instances were becoming more and more frequent since Nathaniel Blake came into her life. But lying on the floor of the forest that night, her hands bloodied, her eyes wide and her pulse completely frozen, she thought everything that had happened up to that point couldn't match with a fraction of what she felt now.

Watching in confused disbelief and a good measure of horror, she stared unblinking at the two massive arcs that had burst from Nathaniel's back...not understanding, definitely not believing, and more convinced than ever that this was a sick, cruel joke. Everything in her mind and everything in her body had ceased movement altogether, and she was holding her consciousness severely in question. But still, Kyla couldn't close her eyes.

The arcs unfolded swiftly, setting off a blast of wind that scattered the pine needles on the ground in every direction. The dark clouds overhead had broken away just enough to let the dimmed moonlight beam down through the trees, illuminating his transfigured shape. Glistening against the black, his wings not only caught the light that fell down on them, but they reflected it, bathing Nathaniel in a bright silver glow. Every feather caught the light at a different angle; some glowing white, some shining silver...all of them too breathlessly beautiful for words.

Kyla had to be hallucinating. There was no other explanation for it. Maybe she'd lost so much blood that she had gone into shock or she had broken out in some kind of fever that was playing these twisted visions before her mind. Whatever the case, she knew there was nothing about what she was seeing now that could actually be real.

Nathaniel Blake did not have silver wings.

Hallucination or not, though, when she saw him break into this angelic form, the fact that she was dying was suddenly the last thing Kyla was concerned with.

It seemed very distant, what she witnessed with her eyes, almost like there was a screen between the physical and the insane, projecting to her sight what she knew she wasn't seeing. She couldn't be seeing it, because she knew she wasn't dead yet. Close to it, most likely, but still not dead. And if she wasn't dead, then that meant she was still here, lying on the cold hard ground somewhere up on the mountain, bleeding to death calmly and hallucinating the whole while.

Yes, that was it. She was hallucinating from the loss of blood. It was perfectly natural to do a thing like that. A lot of people had to see wings burst from people's backs when they were in this sort of condition...or something.

Just as Kyla had almost rationalized it to herself, another shock jolted her when Donovan made a move. In response to Nathaniel's impossible transformation, he morphed into a new form of his own. A far less glorious form...a familiar form.

Another set of wings spanning eight feet at least exploded from Donovan's back. They looked the same, he and Nathaniel, with the exception of the color of their wings.

Donovan's were jet black.

Instead of reflecting the light from above, they repelled it, casting a deathlike shadow of their own to clash against the silver, making war against that which they so utterly despised.

Kyla watched in silent awe, this mirrored reflection of light and dark. Truth had yet to hit her about any of it. As far as she was concerned, she was dreaming, tucked safely away in her bed where she would wake from this soon and laugh at herself for being so frightened by a nightmare.

But it was so real. *Gah*...it was so real.

Still not blinking, Kyla remembered the first night Donovan had come to her, how the thought had struck her so unexplainably...how looking into the face of that sick depraved man, she had somehow seen Nathaniel.

Looking at him now as he lifted up into the air, she recognized his wings. That thing that had flown at her car on Edlowe Road, the hideous black creature with the fire-red eyes...it was *Donovan*?

Kyla was mortified at the realization, but even that didn't faze her now. Keeping her eyes locked on the two sets of wings as they rose in the sky, she held her breath and watched Donovan and Nathaniel collide like eagles. She was awestruck at the sight, and terrified at the same time. There were so many similarities between them in the way they moved and the way they fought, that she questioned what Donovan had told her, whether or not Nathaniel might really be like him...whether he might actually be what Donovan was.

This can't be real, Kyla told herself. But she couldn't force herself to look away.

It was beautiful to a degree she had never known beauty, and as she watched this aerial battle take place, she couldn't help but feel that she was witnessing in the flesh something that she had always known existed, no matter in what realm. And she didn't like the feeling.

Kyla watched breathlessly as they tore through the sky; and though her fear had already crippled her, her gaze was held by silver wings, which were silhouetted like starlight against the black. She flinched violently when Nathaniel hurled Donovan back onto the trail, hard enough that the ground beneath him rumbled.

Nathaniel flew down to deal him another blow, but Donovan moved faster than she expected. Bolting over to her where she lay on the ground before Nathaniel had the chance to stop him, Donovan grabbed Kyla by the throat. His wings towered over her like a darkened canopy and his breath came out in long, drawn wisps. That gleam in his eyes that she knew all too well, it struck his jet-black pupils and danced on

311

her fear, like a foreboding threat of the fate that had been sealed for her.

Donovan was determined; she could see it so clearly. There was nothing this creature would not do in order to hurt Nathaniel.

*C*aden's heart pounded as he stared at the two wooden signs in front of him. They were barely visible in the dark, each with arrows pointing in opposite directions, distinguishing the different trails that broke off from the main one. He still had no idea which of them he should follow.

Caden had come milliseconds away from dialing 911 at least a dozen times already, but every time he started to, he had hung up the phone. Something just wouldn't let him make the call. He didn't know what it was, but something didn't feel right about it.

Alexa's words disturbed him more than he let on when she spoke them, more even than he was admitting to himself now. But despite what he had tried for over a year to ignore, Caden knew what he had to do to get an answer here, and he knew this was not the time to be afraid.

Dropping to his knees in the pine-needled dirt, he hung his head with both of his hands at his sides. Never had he felt so helpless or afraid...and he had known his share of helpless and afraid before. He could feel it all around him; the battle, the war, the existence of the unseen. Everything he had known and tried so hard to run from...not because he'd stopped believing in it, but because he hadn't. He just became terrified of what it was going to cost him, and right now in spite of all he had done to keep that from happening, it appeared to be costing him the very thing he had done everything not to lose.

Closing his eyes, Caden shut off every fear in his mind, every guard he had kept for so long over his heart to block himself from feeling her. It had never left him completely, as was proven tonight when he felt how Nathaniel was upsetting Kyla after he left her with him. But the way it used to be when Caden could feel everything, literally *everything* she was feeling, whether she was hurt or happy or angry or afraid, even when she was nowhere near him…it hadn't been like that in a very long time.

What Caden did next went against everything he had been relying on to protect himself. Dropping to his knees on the floor of that forest, he found himself begging God to give him back what he had rejected, to let him feel her now the way he used to feel her then. Caden didn't know if it worked that way, if it was something he could take back once he'd already given it up; he didn't even know how it happened in the first place. He just knew there wasn't time for him to make a guess on this one. If he went right and she was left, he wouldn't be able to backtrack on the trail and still reach her. It would be too late by then. But then suddenly a shock struck through him with a force so powerful he had to clutch his stomach just to breathe, and he knew it had worked.

The intensity of it was unbearable, but just as quickly as it hit him, the feeling subsided, leaving him doubled over in the dirt and scrambling to understand.

Caden didn't know what this meant, but he knew that feeling. Keeping his eyes closed, he focused on Kyla's heartbeat, trying to feel its rhythm in the loud noise of his confusion. He held his breath in silence in that eternally drawn out moment, waiting to feel it and praying he would. And then just as the pain in his stomach, it came on him suddenly. He heard it and felt it all through him, the steady pounding of the heart he was searching for.

Caden's eyes shot open. He was going right.

*N*athaniel's world stopped moving. His heart, his lungs, his mind…everything in him and around him froze when he saw the depraved Naphil before him grab Kyla by the throat.

Donovan's ebony wings folded in around him as she struggled beneath his grip, as he held a blade in his hand to provoke Nathaniel vindictively forward.

Nathaniel didn't move. He just stared ahead and scrambled to think of anything he could do to get him away from her.

"You have no play here," Donovan said. "Make your choice."

"If you touch her again..." Nathaniel threatened murderously, but he didn't get the chance to finish. Before he could, Donovan backhanded her so hard across the face that her head whipped around to the side.

Nathaniel flinched at the sound, at the sight of her pain. Every muscle in his body tightened as an unrighteous rage flared through him, seeping as blood through his pulsing veins.

Kyla choked as she struggled for breath. With her hands in the dirt, she tried to push herself up and away from Donovan, though she had to know she didn't stand a chance.

Seeing that just about sent Nathaniel over the edge. He was the only chance she had now...and he didn't know how to save her.

"Donovan," Nathaniel's whole body trembled as he breathed his name.

Donovan jerked Kyla up from the ground by her hair and held her up against his chest. Her body was limp, wasted...broken. Donovan kept his blade at ready to be used against her however he deemed fit.

"Surrender yourself," he demanded to Nathaniel. "Vow to serve me and I will release her."

Nathaniel snarled with malice in his eyes, "I know you're not foolish enough to believe I would ever make a vow to you."

Donovan gripped his knife, pressing the flat of its blade hard against the gash in Kyla's stomach. She opened her mouth to scream at the surge of pain, but she didn't have enough strength left in her vocal chords for any sound to come out. Nathaniel could see the agony this caused her. Her mouth stayed open in a silent scream as tears poured down her cheeks, and at that point Nathaniel could only fantasize about taking Donovan's dagger from his hands and ramming the blade through his heart.

Kyla looked like she might pass out from the intensity of the pain. She was fighting it, though, trying to stay strong even as she was being tortured, held there bleeding in the arms of this psychopath.

Nathaniel's breathing was quick and tight, his whole body consumed with a hate he'd never known.

"Bow to me now or watch her die," Donovan threatened. The way he held the knife, he was prepared to ram it straight into her lungs.

Nathaniel felt fire overtake him, a burning he didn't have time to understand. He didn't have a choice anymore and he knew it, though he had tried desperately to think of another way. When Donovan pressed the tip of his blade against Kyla's skin, Nathaniel didn't hesitate for another second. Immediately, he dropped to his knee and bowed his head in submission.

And Donovan let her go.

As Kyla crumpled to the ground like a puppet whose strings had just been cut, Nathaniel winced at the sound. Every instinct he possessed screamed at him to go to her, but he ignored the pull and remained on one knee with his head bowed low.

Donovan walked forward slowly, placing a leather-gloved hand on Nathaniel's shoulder. "You have made a wise decision, my son."

Nathaniel's eyes narrowed when Donovan touched him. "I'm not your son," he breathed to him in disgust.

Faster than Donovan could react, Nathaniel spun around in a maneuver Seth had taught him a year ago, which he had never had the opportunity to use. And in the blink of an eye, he snapped Donovan's neck.

The moment was eternal which fell on him next. In piercing silence, Nathaniel knelt there, clutching the body of the life he'd just taken. Even when reality finally started to settle into him, he couldn't grasp what had actually just happened.

Nathaniel had killed him. It was done. That ever-present threat, the on-going war; all of it was over because Donovan was dead.

As the thought lingered over him, a flash of light came suddenly before Nathaniel's vision…a flash of light he didn't understand. Without explanation, he found himself crouched down before the tree again that he had been kneeling beneath only moments before, watching as Donovan continued to hold his dagger to Kyla's heart.

Blinking hard, Nathaniel scrambled to make sense of what had just happened. He looked all around him, but everything was different, back the way it was before he dropped to his knee.

"What is this?" Nathaniel demanded. "What did you do?"

Donovan, still alive, looked into him with a grin of intent. "I just wanted to see what you were capable of," he said.

Nathaniel felt sick when the truth befell him. "It…it wasn't real?" He struggled to keep himself calm.

Donovan was pleased as he watched defeat fall onto Nathaniel's face. "No, it wasn't," he told him. "However, I am willing to give you one more chance, out of the goodness of my heart. And this time you had better get it right."

Nathaniel felt his fury spike, almost enough to take over this nauseating fear. Images began flashing before his mind of his brothers in London, of all he would be betraying should he surrender to this lunatic.

But then he met Kyla's eyes again and it sealed it in him what he had to do.

Giving up his will and his honor, and breaking beneath the fear of what another choice would mean, Nathaniel dropped to a knee, this time for real, and bowed his head submissively in the way he thought he had before. But then right as Donovan took a step forward, a new flash of light…a different flash of light broke swiftly through the trees.

They were no longer alone.

Nathaniel snapped his head up in shock to look at the one who approached. Of anyone he might have seen there, he did not expect Seth. His leader moved angrily toward them with fire in his eyes, and Nathaniel immediately found himself paralyzed again, only this time by a completely different kind of fear.

*T*hey stood hardly twenty feet apart, Donovan and Seth. Both were eager and ready for the other to make a move, but both resisted the temptation to do so.

A cold, twisted fire knotted in Seth's insides. He wasn't sure how it would feel when he saw Donovan again, but he didn't expect it to feel like this. In the place of rage, there was a violent calm, a disturbing still that controlled him now. Glaring into the hollow amber eyes of this beast disguised as a man, Seth could feel the pulse of evil beating from the place where Donovan's heart used to be.

There was nothing left to him anymore but that...nothing but the dark that had won his life. Anything Donovan had been before, he wasn't that now and he never would be again. What existed in his place was nothing more or less than Seth's greatest enemy, mortal or otherwise.

Narrowing his eyes, Seth focused in on the pale, cold face of the one he used to call brother.

"To what do I owe this pleasure?" Donovan asked him tauntingly. He exposed his sharp glistening teeth in a smile that was thick with depravity.

Seth gripped his dagger firmly, ready to strike. He knew he wasn't permitted to make the first move, but he also wasn't the slightest bit opposed to making the second.

Seth didn't move as he stared Donovan down, and out of the corner of his vision he saw Nathaniel shift back into the form of a man. Bolting over to the girl on the ground, Nathaniel slid to his knees when he came to her side. The sight was more than disturbing, but Seth didn't let it distract him from the eyes of the serpent.

"You have made a mistake," he told Donovan. "I warned you not to pull Nathaniel into your games."

Donovan rolled his eyes as if the whole thing were a joke. "You *would* get bent out of shape over that."

Seth glared at him fiercely. "Whatever you are trying, you are going to fail."

Donovan erupted into laughter, but neither of them advanced. "Surely even you cannot be that blind." His eyes inched slowly to his left, falling on Nathaniel and the girl he'd just grabbed off of the ground. "Don't you see it, Seth? No matter what you do to me, I've already won."

Seth could feel the rage that welled up inside of him, burning at the suggestion; and immediately his eyes flashed to Nathaniel and the girl. It was strange, seeing it happen like this. While Seth had spent more years consumed by the thought of Donovan than he could even keep track of, it was the image of Nathaniel huddled over this girl that wrenched his stomach.

He watched Nathaniel force himself away from her and look down on her face and her body, taking in the extent of the damage that had been done. Seth could see how this was going to end; he could tell just by looking at her. The girl was not going to make it, and it was a good thing, too. He could not afford to have Nathaniel compromised like that. None of them could.

Turning back to Donovan in a slow, careful movement, Seth breathed to him murderously, "*Leave.*"

"Gladly," Donovan agreed with a mocking bow of surrender. "But before I excuse myself from this nice little meeting, I want to leave you with one last thought." He paused dramatically then grinned again. "It is futile, Seth. Whatever you attempt to do, I am going to destroy everything you have. And Nathaniel *will* be mine."

Seth threatened him through gritted teeth. "I would not speak so idly if I were you."

"My words are not idle, I assure you," Donovan said.

Seth could see that he meant it.

"A war is coming that you are in no way prepared to fight, if only due to your arrogance that has blinded you to the sight of it."

Seth clasped his knife more firmly, rethinking his idea of passivity. Orders or not, it was difficult to not want to cut him.

"You will lose everything, Seth," Donovan promised him. "I will stake my life on that."

Then he left them on the mountain and flew off into the night.

Seth turned sharply to face Nathaniel once Donovan was gone. "Do you realize what you have *done*?" His voice shook as he spoke.

"What was I supposed to do?" Nathaniel snapped back at him. "Let him *kill* her?"

Seth could see it in him now as he watched him hold her, as he saw Nathaniel touch her face and heard him speak reassuringly to this little human girl who was so close to death she was practically a corpse.

"It's okay, Kyla," he whispered as he stroked her face. "I'm right here."

Seth's left eye twitched as the truth settled over him, and he was struck with a feeling he hadn't known in eleven years.

The girl looked up at Nathaniel, struggling to catch even the slightest breath. "I'm sorry," she whispered to him.

Seth felt pain strike his heart at the familiarity of the words.

"Don't talk," Nathaniel told her. "Just breathe."

The girl didn't listen.

"You can't save me," she choked out.

Seth could see how her words spread agony across Nathaniel's face. He had never seen anything like what he saw in him now; he had never seen such pain in anything. Waiting to see what he was going to do, Seth held his breath and watched Nathaniel place a hand over the gash in Kyla's stomach, and then another on her forehead.

Locking eyes with the auburn-haired girl, Nathaniel whispered to her softly, "Don't be afraid."

Seth stared forward, unable to move his eyes. The girl named Kyla was breathless as Nathaniel pulled the tattered jacket from her shoulders and away from her body. He touched her carefully…cautiously, appearing to channel all of his power and strength into her tiny, broken body. Seth could almost see how the flood of heat rushed from Nathaniel's heart, into his arms and down through his fingertips. Then he watched Kyla's face as it flooded all through her. He could see it so clearly, but he didn't understand.

Seth had never seen anything like this before.

*N*athaniel knew the risk that he was taking when he put his hands on Kyla's stomach. But his fear over the consequences of this action didn't stop him from taking it. No matter what happened to him, he had to do this. Even with Seth watching him. Even if it cost him everything. He couldn't let her die.

Nathaniel waited with baited breath. With his hands pressed hard against the bloody wound, he looked down into the auburn-haired girl who had changed his entire world, feeling her wounds begin to close beneath his hands. He could see that Kyla felt it. She didn't have to say a word for him to know that, and when he realized it was working, he almost dared to let himself hope that she might survive.

Kyla was trembling from head to toe, her eyes still locked with his out of fear of looking down at her own body. When she finally mustered the courage, she came dangerously close to hyperventilating.

"Wha...what did you do?" she asked Nathaniel in a quivering voice.

Seth seemed eager to hear the answer to that as well. The blood had rushed from his face and he was still standing above them, still watching every move and gesture they made as he tried to find words to speak. It took Nathaniel looking up to meet his gaze before he finally did.

"What have you done?" Seth breathed to him in a horrified whisper.

Nathaniel's face held a look of fierce determination. "I did what I had to do."

He clung to Kyla, refusing to let her go, and Seth stared forward, completely stunned. The anger behind his shock, Nathaniel had expected, but there was a drawn expression on Seth's face that didn't make sense. Something else was going through his head.

Looking down at his hands and at Kyla again, Nathaniel began to question what he thought he understood. Then he turned back to his leader and asked him forthright, "Why didn't you tell me that Nephilim have the ability to heal?"

Seth looked at him slowly, confused and unmoving. "Because Nephilim *don't*."

Nathaniel blinked a few times as he stared at him, not certain what he meant. But before he had time to question him on it, Nathaniel was distracted by a sound from beneath him, so faint and strained he almost didn't hear it.

It was Kyla. She was still hyperventilating. "Nathaniel..." she tried to say. He could feel her body tremble beneath his hands.

Looking back at the girl in his arms, he stroked her face. "It's okay," he tried to reassure her. "Everything is okay."

Her lips trembled as she stared up at him, her eyes bigger than he'd ever seen them.

"Don't be afraid," he said. "You're safe now."

Seth remained firm where he stood above them, overwhelmed with disbelief. "Do you have any comprehension of the chain of events you have just set into motion by your carelessness?" He pointed at Kyla. "By this needless complication?"

Nathaniel glared at him. "She is *not* a needless complication."

"She has nothing to do with this," Seth snarled.

Nathaniel shouted back at him, "She has *everything* to do with this! Why can you not *see* that?!"

Seth was fuming. "*You* caused this to happen, Nathaniel. *You.* Not Donovan."

Nathaniel couldn't think of a time he had ever seen Seth so angry.

"You are to return to London immediately," Seth ordered him, "lest you should forfeit your position in the brotherhood."

Nathaniel shook his head. "Don't do this ..."

Seth looked back at him, emotionless. "You have received your orders. What you choose to do with them will determine what happens next."

Without another word, Seth turned away in a gesture of finality and flew out of sight, leaving Kyla in a panic and Nathaniel staring after him, paralyzed in indecision.

Once Seth was gone, Nathaniel snapped himself out of his paralysis and looked back to the girl he was still holding on the ground. Stroking Kyla's face, he spoke to her softly in another attempt to calm her, but it was no use. She was already in shock.

"I need to get you out of here," he mumbled more to himself than to her. He looked all around him to decide what he should do, but before he came to a conclusion, something happened that changed everything.

Just as Nathaniel bent down over Kyla and grabbed the back part of her leg to lift her up, someone broke through the woods and into the clearing. Someone he didn't expect.

Nathaniel snapped his head up and narrowed his eyes on instinct, bracing himself for another battle; for anything that might be required of him to protect the girl he had already given everything for. He was even ready to kill if that's what it would take.

He just wasn't ready for Caden Howell.

Chapter 21

"...the arms we run to."

Caden ran on autopilot, his lungs burning with such intensity that he couldn't feel the pain that should be shooting through his legs. He allowed no room for doubt or conscious thought; he didn't allow for anything except the determination that propelled his every step forward. He had never known anything to more fiercely take him over, any emotion to so fully grab him that he wasn't even in control of himself.

At least not until he broke through the clearing.

To say that he was stunned wouldn't capture it. There was no feeling to match it, nothing Caden had ever known that had hit him quite like this. Immediately, his gaze fell to the girl who lay shaking on the ground, her clothes torn and bloodied, her body rigid in shock...and the stranger pinning her down who had his hands all over her.

A hundred different thoughts came crashing onto Caden at once, and whether driven by logic or moved by his fear, every one of them quickly blended together into one clearly defined emotion: Rage. Blind rage. Uncontrollable, seething, murderous rage. All of it seeped into him like a cancerous plague. He couldn't escape it; he couldn't even want to. So instead, Caden let it consume him.

Physical heat welled up in his body as the stranger came into focus. It started at his core and then rose to his face; this burning, this fire...this feeling that suddenly made Caden feel capable of murder.

His eyes narrowed in on Nathaniel Blake, his target, who was kneeling over Kyla's body. Nathaniel's bloodied hands were still on her stomach, trembling where they were pressed to her skin. After having torn open her jacket (actually, Caden's jacket that she'd taken earlier from his Jeep) Nathaniel had exposed her red-stained skin, and by it Caden could see that she was still breathing; quite heavily, in fact. She actually looked more afraid than in pain, and on second glance, the source of her fear didn't seem to be directed at Nathaniel so much as it was directed at him.

Caden didn't let that detail register. Right now there was only one thing that did, and that was what he needed to do.

Watching Nathaniel stand up off of the only girl alive that Caden wouldn't hesitate to kill for, he marched forward with intent, his gait methodical and certain. Caden could feel his mind detach itself from his body, as if every step he took were being taken on its own. The level of this detachment should probably concern him, but discretion wasn't high up on his priority list at the moment.

The total dismemberment of Nathaniel Blake was.

In one sweeping movement, Caden grabbed Nathaniel's shirt with both of his hands and shoved him backwards, cracking his back against the base of the pine tree behind him. Nathaniel's eyes were wide, but he didn't resist. He was too startled by the ballsy move to even try and fight back yet.

Caden determined then and there that he wasn't going to let Nathaniel speak. Words were a gift, and one that this monster did not deserve; not after what he had done...not after what he was going to do.

With fire in his eyes, Caden threatened him, "Do not move." He glared into Nathaniel warningly as he stepped backwards away from him and knelt down by Kyla where she lay on the ground.

Nathaniel didn't move.

The night was dark, but the moonlight broke through the trees just enough to let Caden take in her image. Pure revulsion hit him at the sight of her; the kind that came on him like physical nausea and left him so sick he was almost blind. His jacket on her was practically in rags, her face was bruised and there were scrapes across her cheek. He could see by the way her hands clutched the cotton on each side of the broken zipper that there was more underneath the jacket that she was trying to hide, but he was afraid to find out exactly what that was.

As atrocious as she looked, Caden's revulsion didn't come from the sight of her physical body alone; it also came from what he saw in her face, from the hollow of fear that marked her eyes.

He had never seen her look like that.

It ripped him apart, imagining what Nathaniel had done to her, how afraid she must have been...how he must have touched her.

Kyla was shaking, clutching the jacket tightly to her chest and staring up at her best friend in fear and disbelief. Then quickly, so quickly Caden almost missed it, her eyes darted to Nathaniel; not in fear of him, but frantically, as if she were looking to him for help.

Caden didn't understand. He didn't know what that sick freak could have done to her to make her react that way, but something about seeing it made him completely snap. Anger wasn't a strong enough word for it. Rage was far too kind. What he felt in that moment went beyond hatred in its every form. Every sense and emotion he possessed increased on him to a superhuman level, and pure cold focus took him over. It was then he determined, then that he knew: Nathaniel Blake was going to die.

Rising slowly from his knees, Caden turned to face Nathaniel, his dark brown eyes on fire with hate. And they only burned hotter when that animal...that *thing* tried to speak.

"Look..." Nathaniel stepped forward to explain himself.

At the sound of his voice, Caden felt a sudden disconnect from the stranger who stood there, not even caring that he knew his name. Right now he didn't need a name; Caden needed only to exact justice in absolute finality. A name would get in the way of that. It would make this thing seem more human...and Caden *knew* he wasn't human.

"I know what this looks like..." Nathaniel tried to say.

Caden didn't acknowledge his words. He just marched forward calmly and punched him square in the jaw.

His knuckles cracked loudly against the bone, and judging by the force with which he delivered the blow, Caden knew there was a good chance he'd dislocated it. It felt like hitting steel, but he was so flooded with adrenaline that he loved pain. And he certainly wasn't ready to be done with it yet.

Nathaniel staggered to his left on the impact of Caden's fist, his mouth open and his eyes wide. After resetting his jaw himself, he looked back up at Caden in complete disbelief. And then he made a mistake.

Glancing ever so slightly to his left, Nathaniel looked at Kyla, and once he did there was only one thought that entered Caden's mind:

Aww...*hell* no!

Narrowing his eyes and clenching his fists, Caden charged at Nathaniel and hit him at the waist. Then he thrust every one of his 160 pounds into him and tackled him to the ground.

Kyla managed to find her voice by the time Nathaniel's head hit the dirt. It came out in a panicked scream that got caught in her throat, and she also managed to right herself. And while both of these things should have caught Caden's attention, even they couldn't shake him from the objective at hand.

Instead, he pinned Nathaniel's arms down with his knees and hit him again, this time with his left hand, and then back with his right. The more times he hit him, the louder Kyla screamed; but Caden didn't stop.

His knuckles were bleeding and Kyla was still screaming, and while that fact alone should have made him question what was really going on, his mind wasn't thinking clearly enough to deduce that.

Caden got five good hits in; five solid punches before something changed. It was in Nathaniel's eyes that he saw it first. Where they'd held surprise and even fear, they were intent now, set on his face and unforgiving in their focus. It wasn't normal, what it looked like. Caden wouldn't even know how to describe it, but he didn't have long to think on it before Nathaniel reached up and grabbed him by the throat.

His grip was shockingly strong. As big as Nathaniel was and as strong as Caden imagined he'd be, he still wasn't prepared for it. The force he felt coming from Nathaniel's hands wasn't just strong.

It wasn't human.

Standing to his feet as he held Caden by the throat, Nathaniel's eyes slanted in hatred and malice, seeing this boy as an enemy to defeat...a bug to be crushed.

Nathaniel turned his head to one side and spit out blood; then with more force than any man could ever conjure, he slammed the boy into the very tree he'd been held to himself only moments before.

Nathaniel's blood pulsed through his veins as his hatred of Caden Howell grew; this loathing inside of him that began the moment he first learned of who he was. It started when Nathaniel found out that Donovan was afraid of him. It grew when he saw how Kyla cared for him. It pushed him over the edge when Caden assumed he had hurt her, that he would *ever* hurt her...as if something in him knew the monster Nathaniel really was.

That was the force that drove his hand to tighten around Caden's throat; the fact that he saw Nathaniel as the villain and himself as the hero. He was imperfect, but forgiven...not blameless, just redeemed. And for that, Nathaniel despised him.

As he gritted his teeth, a low throaty growl escaped Nathaniel's lips. The sound should have startled him since it was completely involuntary and borderline animalistic, but he was hardly even aware of it. With his left hand clutching tighter at Caden's throat, he pushed hard against the tree with his right, exerting all the energy that flowed through him into the base of it so he wouldn't crush the boy's windpipe. Not that he wouldn't have loved to.

Rationally, Nathaniel knew he needed to let him go. It wasn't unthinkable for Caden to assume what he had, and if their situations had been reversed, Nathaniel probably would have made the same mistake. There was also the faint knowledge in the back of his mind that he still *needed* Caden; that if he killed him now, their chances at defeating Donovan were completely shot. But somehow even knowing this, Nathaniel's grip only grew tighter.

He hadn't meant to do this. Nathaniel hadn't meant for his hate to channel into the physical this way, but after Caden had hit him enough times, he'd snapped. He couldn't help it any more than he could help the way he was choking him now, in the place where logic and rational thought held absolutely no value. Nathaniel wanted him to feel his life slipping away; to feel the bleak weight of hopelessness, his very soul being crushed to the core. He wanted Caden to feel anguish and pain and fear, that he wasn't invincible and he wasn't beyond death; and his longing for these stemmed from one very simple emotion: Jealousy.

Nothing had ever done this to him. Nothing had ever burned him like this or so fully consumed his mind. Not Donovan, not Seth, not a single mission he'd ever been sent on or assignment he'd been given. Nothing.

And through it, every fear Nathaniel ever had of who he really was and what he was capable of was manifesting in the flesh, rising to the surface and proving the words of that serpent to be true. The things Donovan told him, all that Nathaniel had tried so hard to deny, he was fulfilling them now by strangling the life out of this human.

Nathaniel knew that…but he still couldn't let go.

Such an assuming fool, he thought as he looked in Caden's eyes. *Such a waste of a gift.* Caden Howell was nothing, as far as he was concerned. He didn't deserve what he had and he didn't deserve mercy. None of them did.

The deeper Nathaniel looked into him, the more his anger grew; not just toward Caden but toward all of his kind. And as much as he was still pushing his energy into the tree, the balance was faltering and his grip was tightening even further. Just a few more seconds and it would be over. Nathaniel could see it in the way Caden's face was turning colors, by how his eyes were rolling into the back of his head.

These next few moments were critical. He had a decision to make that he was completely incapable of making, because as much as he knew what was right, his discretion had fallen to his weakness, his hatred...his jealousy. And no matter how much he screamed at himself to stop, his hands wouldn't listen to him.

They did, however, listen to the girl behind him.

"Nathaniel!" Kyla screamed. Her voice was shrill and forced, and it was obvious that it took all her strength to push it out.

At that point, Nathaniel should have been too far gone to respond to anything. His primal instinct had taken over, completely shutting him off to the sound of reason.

But that voice could find him anywhere.

No matter how far he fell, how deep he sank, how much darkness tried to claim him, Kyla could always find him. Nathaniel knew that, even if he didn't know how...and he really hated it.

Releasing his grip on the boy he was milliseconds away from choking to death, Nathaniel backed away quickly and put his hands up in front of him.

Oh, God, he thought as he watched Caden collapse to the ground. *Oh, God...*

Caden clutched at his own throat, coughing and gasping for breath. No sooner than he hit the ground, Kyla pulled herself up and crawled over to him. She grabbed onto him frantically and cringed through her own pain, and even as Caden struggled to take in oxygen, his eyes widened at the sight of her.

He scrambled to reach out to her, to touch her, to make sure she was really there; and when Kyla squeezed his hand to let him know that she was, Nathaniel was hit by the crippling weight of defeat.

Watching Caden touch her face, seeing the fear and relief and desperation in her eyes...there was no word to describe what it felt like to him. Out of all Nathaniel had been through that night, this was hardly the thing that should have overcome him. But when Caden grabbed Kyla's arm and pulled her protectively into him, Nathaniel had never felt weaker in his life.

His vision swirled around him in a haze as he watched them. Caden was the one she wanted to protect her. Nathaniel could see that in the way she clung to him, held onto him with a trust he would have killed to have from her. A trust he was certain to never know.

Looking down at his hands, Nathaniel was horrified by what he'd almost done. No...what he *would* have done if Kyla hadn't screamed his name. He wouldn't have let Caden go. As much as he wanted to convince himself otherwise, he knew the truth:

Nathaniel would have killed him.

Backing up further as he watched Kyla bury her face in Caden's chest, Nathaniel was struck by the thought that she had seen what he really was. He felt a knife in his heart when he realized it was over. She would never be able to look at him the same again; and that was assuming she'd be able to look at him at all.

Nathaniel waited there with his hands still out in front of him, expecting her to blurt out to Caden everything that had just happened...everything she had witnessed. But Kyla didn't say a thing. She just let Caden hold her and act like he was the one who had just saved her life.

Nathaniel thought he would have rather had her out him and be done with it than have to stand here and watch the two of them like this. But then something happened that he didn't expect. While Caden held her and reassured her that everything was going to be okay, Kyla looked up at Nathaniel longingly, yearningly...in the last way he ever thought she would.

As her eyes darted toward him and caught him by complete surprise, everything froze in Nathaniel. They pierced him in their desperation, striking his heart and setting him on fire from the inside. A hundred different emotions flooded into him when he saw it...that one single look; and suddenly Nathaniel questioned what he thought he knew.

He and Kyla stayed there like that, reading each other, searching each other; an unspoken message between them that Caden didn't see. It was only a moment that his back was turned on them, but a moment was all it took for Kyla to get her message to Nathaniel:

She was going to protect his secret.

Nathaniel was afraid to recognize it at first, still halfway expecting her to tell Caden that she had seen his wings. But Kyla didn't do it. Even when Caden pulled her to her feet and tried to get her away from there, she looked hesitant to leave at all.

Stepping forward cautiously, Nathaniel tried to brave an apology. "I'm sorry..." he started to say, but Caden wouldn't hear it.

"Stay back," he warned him, placing himself as a barrier between him and Kyla.

Nathaniel swallowed hard. "Caden, I didn't hurt her," he said. "I know you don't believe that..."

"You're damn right I don't believe it!"

Nathaniel clenched his fists to repress his anger, knowing he couldn't strike out at him again. "How did you find her?" Nathaniel asked tensely. "How did you know where she was?"

Caden sneered at him in disgust. "Because I can *feel* her, you bastard!"

Nathaniel's left eye twitched.

"I could feel what you were doing to her," Caden breathed. His words staggered as he struggled to control his rage.

Nathaniel closed his eyes at the accusation, but he didn't lash out or defend himself. "Think what you will," he said. "Just get her somewhere safe."

Caden looked at him warily.

Nathaniel had never felt so defeated. "Don't leave her side," he told the boy firmly. "Not for anything." He wanted to throw up at the thought, but he knew it was the only way for Kyla to be safe. He just wished there was another way.

Caden didn't understand and he didn't respond; he just took Kyla by the arm and guided her toward the trail, not giving her or Nathaniel the chance to speak another word to each other.

It turned Nathaniel's stomach, watching Caden drag her away from him, and even further when Kyla looked back at him helplessly through the trees. She didn't want to go; Nathaniel could see that clearly. But she was also afraid to stay, knowing if she did that Caden was going to find out the truth. Either that or he and Nathaniel might try and kill each other again. That was why leaving was her only option no matter how much Nathaniel may have hated that.

Still, Nathaniel didn't know how he was going to be able to do this.

He knew it was right, letting Caden take her from here, but nothing had ever felt more wrong to him. Clenching his fists at his sides when Kyla was gone, an instinct flared up in him to grab her back from Caden. But Nathaniel knew that would be as foolish as the decision he'd made to hurt him.

He had to get this feeling under control.

Flying up to the watch point that Ethan had marked when he'd been there, Nathaniel landed in a firm crouching position with his hands on the rocky ledge. His wings folded in around him as he squinted into the dark. He knew Kyla was out there, even if he couldn't see her, and he knew she was alright.

There wasn't a chance that Caden wouldn't take care of her.

Turning away, Nathaniel's wings rustled behind him as his whole body trembled, the injustice ripping through him like a knife through his lungs. After all he did to fight for her, to save her, to protect her…he was still the monster and Caden was still the hero. He was still the fallen and that boy was still the saint. He was still the cursed and Caden was still the saved.

The tremor shot through Nathaniel with startling intensity, as much as the thoughts that were plaguing his mind. But it wasn't this that frightened him.

It was the single black feather that had fallen from his wings.

Staring down at it, stunned, Nathaniel couldn't breathe. It clung to the rock for a fraction of a moment, its dark wisps taunting him in unwelcomed truth, and then the wind picked it up and swept it over the mountain.

Oh, God, Nathaniel thought for the third time that night. *What is happening to me?*

Donovan stormed through the long narrow undergrounds of the ritual chambers, his eyes burning with a deeper fire than the torches along the cavern walls. As he made his way to the center of the room, he knocked one of them over angrily. Its flame was snuffed out the moment it hit the cool stone floor.

Balak stood from where he waited, looking frightened as his eyes fell to his leader. "My lord?" he said.

Donovan didn't answer him. He could feel Cerin cowering somewhere in a far back corner of the cave, but aside from the two of them, there were none who had gathered here tonight. It was not a night for the Coven to meet, a fact for which Balak and Cerin were undoubtedly grateful.

"I want him *dead!*" Donovan snarled, throwing over the carefully stacked wood at the center of the room.

As the logs that were meant for a ceremonial fire crashed against the opposite stone wall, Cerin slithered from his corner and ducked behind an oversized boulder at the edge of the cave.

"My lord..." Balak tried again, but again Donovan ignored him.

"I want him to suffer," he breathed venomously, "to see everything he loves and all that ever mattered to him ripped away from before his very eyes. I want to see his face the moment he knows he's lost everything, and then..." Donovan laughed sadistically, "then I am going to kill him."

Balak stepped forward bravely, and also a bit foolishly. "What happened?" he asked.

Donovan felt himself shudder as he stared at the scattered logs on the ground. "He was right there, Balak," he told his second-in-command. "He was standing right in front of me."

"Who was?" Balak asked him.

Donovan turned to him sharply. "Who do you *think*?" he hissed. "Who has *any* of this been about?"

Cerin was still cowering and Balak was still having far too difficult a time figuring this out.

Finally, he gave up trying to understand and just asked him straight out, "Did you kill Nathaniel or not?"

Donovan sneered at him in disgust; then he promptly proceeded to backhand him across the room.

"No, I didn't kill Nathaniel!" he shouted at the top of his voice. "I was never *going* to kill Nathaniel!"

Balak held his face and scrambled back to his feet. "Forgive me, my lord," he said, keeping his head low. "I did not know."

Donovan was repulsed by his ignorance, by these mindless creatures he had been given to work with. Sometimes he thought the humans were of more benefit to him than these idiot Nephilim half-breeds.

It won't be like this for long, he told himself. Soon he would have Nathaniel to take Balak's place.

"M...my lord?" Cerin whimpered from behind the rock.

Donovan grimaced to himself at the sound of his voice. "Speak clearly," he commanded. That was the only way he was going to be able to tolerate this.

The quivering, lizard-like creature with the face of a man poked his head up from behind the boulder. "Are you speaking of Seth?" Cerin asked him.

Donovan's eyes held pity and repulsion as he turned to look back at Balak. "To think," he said, "that the gangly miscreant coward would be the one of the two of you with half a brain..."

Balak kept his head low and Donovan regained control of himself. "Yes, Cerin," he answered. "I was speaking of Seth."

Cerin's eyes darted wildly back and forth. "I beg your pardon, my lord," he said boldly, "but if Seth is the one you are after, then why are you baiting Nathaniel?"

Donovan sighed impatiently. "Because Nathaniel is the way we get to Seth."

Cerin didn't seem to grasp what he meant. "I'm afraid I don't understand, my lord."

Donovan pinched his brow. "Well perhaps you don't *need* to understand! Perhaps you should simply do as you are told and stop asking so many questions!"

Cerin ducked back down again. "Yes, my lord."

With his brow still pinched, Donovan tried to calm himself. That effort was wasted, however, when Cerin chose to speak again.

"Did he interfere with the plan?" he asked in his serpent's voice.

Donovan's brow was still pinched. "No, he did not."

"So the boy...?" Cerin asked.

"He believes Nathaniel is to blame," Donovan verified. But even with this victory, there was still that nagging thought, that lingering irritation that disturbed him. Cerin could see it, too.

"What is it, my lord?"

Donovan turned away, remembering the last image he was left with on the mountain, when Caden and not Nathaniel took Kyla back through the woods.

"There was a slight disruption," Donovan told him. "But it is nothing we can't handle."

"And what would you have us do to handle it?" Cerin asked.

Donovan paused for a moment, closing his eyes and clearing his mind, letting it take him to exactly what could right this wrong. Then suddenly, his eyes opened again. He knew what he had to do.

"Balak..." he said sharply.

Balak snapped his head up. "Yes, my lord?"

"Get me Val," he ordered. "*Now.*"

Balak narrowed his eyes.

*C*old. Disoriented. Dangerously lost. Kyla was completely numb to everything around her. She stumbled blindly in the dark at Caden's heels, hardly aware of where he was taking her, or for that matter where they were. Even if some part of her knew, that part had shut down a while ago. Now she just felt like a wind-up doll.

A wind-up doll that should have been dead.

She was vaguely aware of Caden's having to drag her every step down the trail on the mountain, coaxing her to move forward the entire way. She knew she should probably be afraid, but somehow the emotion couldn't find her; nothing could but her shock.

Moving through the dark, Kyla's fears of Donovan emerging from the trees should have been what incapacitated her, but through what little awareness she still had left, she didn't think that it was. He wasn't the one who was making her numb.

The blonde boy with the wings that she'd left back at the clearing was.

Kyla flinched at the thought of Nathaniel, and Caden felt her do it. "It's okay," he reassured her. "We're getting out of here. He isn't going to hurt you again."

Oh, if Caden only knew...

But that was just the thing; he couldn't know. Kyla couldn't tell him what had really happened without telling him what Nathaniel was. And truth be told, even she didn't know that.

A guardian of light...a silver-winged hero...a creature of terror and beauty whose hands could bring life back to the dead? What could even be said of something like that?

She wanted to tell Caden he was wrong, that Nathaniel had saved her, but she couldn't be honest without exposing his secret. And something told her Nathaniel cared more about protecting that than protecting his honor. Kyla didn't like it, but after all Nathaniel had done for her, she knew she at least owed him that.

Even if the mere thought of him still scared her to death.

When she and Caden got down to the parking lot, Kyla felt him lift her up in order to set her in the passenger's side of his Jeep. Somewhere in the back of her mind, she wanted to help him. At one point she even tried to make the effort to climb in herself, but her legs wouldn't do what she wanted and only ended up causing more trouble for him.

Kyla had never felt so out of control of herself, so lost on time or so completely unaware of her surroundings. Before she knew it, they were driving down Edlowe Road. She didn't remember Caden starting the Jeep or pulling out of the parking lot, and she didn't have any idea how far down the road they had gotten. She just stared forward at the two yellow splashes from his headlights that spilled onto the road.

336

The light held her attention, making her feel momentarily protected from the darkness all around her; but that moment found its end when they passed Skyline Drive.

Snapping out of her semi-catatonic daze, Kyla asked him frantically, "Where are you going?"

He was startled to hear her speak. "To the hospital," he said.

Kyla completely freaked out. "No!" she shouted frantically. "Turn around!"

Her tone alarmed him, but he didn't turn around. "*What*?" he asked. "Why?"

"Please turn around!" she begged him.

Caden was clearly disturbed. She could tell that he was trying to gauge whether or not he could trust anything she said right now, and by the looks of things, he seemed to be settling on no.

"Kyla, I have to take you to the emergency room. I'm sorry, but if a doctor doesn't check you out…"

She didn't wait for him to finish. Instead she grabbed the steering wheel herself and jerked it hard to the right.

The Jeep felt weightless as it lifted up on two wheels, leaving only the left ones clinging to the dirt and gravel beneath them. Kyla grabbed at the door handle to keep from falling over and Caden cursed out loud.

Taking the wheel back from her, he pulled it slowly to the left to keep them from tumbling over the side of the mountain. "Are you out of your mind?!" he screamed at her.

Slamming on his brakes and bringing the Jeep to a halt, he kept his hands on the steering wheel and tried to catch his breath.

"Please," Kyla pled with him. She couldn't force another word than that. "Please…"

Caden finally let himself look at her again, and when he saw how she was shaking, he felt awful for yelling at her, even if she had almost gotten them killed. Studying her face for a long time, he tried again to determine if there was merit to anything she was saying. He had to see that she had a reason for not wanting him to take her to the hospital beyond her just being temporarily insane. Kyla didn't know if he was going to listen to her, but eventually he made up his mind.

"Fine," Caden said. "I'll take you home with me."

Kyla felt gratitude swell up in her chest that she couldn't express to him. He wasn't fazed by her silence this time, just eager to get them out of there.

Caden swung the Jeep around in a half-donut maneuver and drove back up the road toward his house, muttering, "I can't believe I'm doing this," along the way.

Then again, there was a lot about this night that he couldn't believe he'd done.

With her eyes set on the living room window, Alexa clicked the "on" button on the phone in the kitchen. She knew it was late and that this particular phone call might not be pleasant, but she dialed the number anyway. If she were to guess, Matthew was more likely to answer right now than his mother, anyway. Alexa knew he was waiting up for Kyla. He had already called her twice.

Matthew didn't even let the phone ring a second time before he picked it up and asked her, "Anything?"

Alexa kept looking out the oversized window, her eyes on her brother and the girl he was holding by the elbow, guiding her toward his room as they slowly made their way across the yard. "She's safe," Alexa told him. "She's here."

Matthew's relief was evident through a heavy sigh, but still he seemed uneasy. "Is she okay?" he asked.

Alexa paused, but before she could answer him, she heard a sound in the background and the phone went dead. Loni must have heard him; it was the only reason he would have hung up that quickly.

Alexa never thought she would be grateful for that, but right now she was. She would be grateful for anything that kept her from having to answer that question.

Caden was at the sink in his bathroom with shaking hands, running warm water over a washcloth and trying to get a

338

handle in his mind over everything that had just happened. It wasn't real to him; any of it. He didn't think it would be for quite a while.

Walking out of the bathroom, he made his way back over to where Kyla was curled up at the edge of his bed in the fetal position. Incoherent wouldn't begin to describe her present state of being. She was completely checked out, staring forward with glazed-over eyes and looking like her mind was still back on the mountain, replaying over and over whatever had just happened to her.

Caden wished he could stop it. There was nothing he wouldn't have taken on himself if it would offer her reprieve. But he knew it didn't work that way.

Taking the rag gently to her face, he sat beside her and let himself fully take in the image of her body, which even in her present state of shock, Kyla was trying to cover up. Her arms were folded tight across her chest, holding his jacket in place even though it looked about ready to break apart at the seams and fall off of her. It was stained with her blood, and there was a gaping tear in the front right pocket, directly over her abdomen.

"Kyla…" he said cautiously.

She didn't respond.

Caden swallowed hard and tried again. "Kyla, I need to take that jacket off. I think you might be hurt."

Still no response. It was as if she weren't even listening to him, like she could hear his voice but not his words.

Caden didn't want to do it, but he knew he had to. Starting at the zipper that was pulled up tight to her neck, he carefully undid it, moving it down slowly so as not to alarm her. He made it halfway down her chest before she completely freaked out.

Grabbing the zipper and pulling it up tight again, Kyla let out a frightened sort of whimper and balled up even tighter in the fetal position.

"I have to make sure you're not bleeding to death!" Caden argued with a sigh. "You don't want me to take you to the hospital? Then this is the way it's gotta be."

Kyla wrapped her arms tighter around her stomach and shook her head.

"Kyla, please..." he said, trying to unfold her arms. She whimpered again, only this time she sounded much more wounded than frightened.

That was all Caden could take. Sitting there staring at her, holding the bloody, dirt-covered rag in his hands, his eyes softened as they looked on her in pain.

"Kyla, what *happened* to you?" he choked in a whisper.

She didn't answer him. She didn't even look at him. She was too far gone to even blink, much less give him any sort of response.

Caden swallowed back emotion, knowing he couldn't give into that now. He had to stay strong, for her if nothing else. But his determination came to nothing when his eyes fell lower.

It made him ill when he saw it, the ten-inch tear on the left leg of her running pants. Physically ill. In an instant, his mind was filled with images of Nathaniel Blake on top of her in the way Caden had found them in the woods, only worse. A lot worse. The images he saw now were graphic, horrifying...his literal worst fears playing out in his head.

Caden had to resort to anger to keep from throwing up. "What did he do to you?" he asked her tensely. He didn't mean for his anger to come out in his voice, but he was really getting sick of asking her that. "What did he *do* to you, Kyla?"

She looked up at him, terrified, a tremor behind her eyes and still no words from her lips. But even in her silence, he could see that she wanted to answer him.

Caden touched her carefully with a shaky hand, about to cry as he traced the edges of her shoulders. He felt so helpless, imagining Nathaniel hurting her...imagining him touching her.

Kyla flinched and jerked away from him, and it hit his heart fiercely when she did. He swallowed hard and his eyes softened in pain as he looked at her, his every fear confirmed by her reaction.

But even though Caden was certain about what Nathaniel had done, Kyla shook her head.

"No," she finally told him. "No."

It was the only word she could get out, and there was nothing about it that made him believe her.

Caden had never felt so sick or enraged in his nineteen years of life. He wanted to put a hole in his wall, or even better, take the 30-06 his dad kept in the shed out back and put one in Nathaniel Blake's head.

Kyla continued shaking her head, to a point that Caden had to stop her. He was careful when he tried to touch her this time, even more so than he had been before. "It's okay," he tried to say softly. It was hard for him to keep his voice under control, but he did the best he could.

Kyla still clutched her arms to her chest so tightly he was afraid they might lose their circulation. When he saw how she was shaking, Caden went to his closet and grabbed a grey fleece blanket down from the top shelf. She flinched again when he covered her with it, and again he felt the pang of it in his heart.

Kyla buried her face in his pillow, her tiny frame trembling as she hugged the blanket he wrapped around her shoulders. Reaching her fingers out from around the edge of it, she weakly grabbed onto his hand. Caden took the hint.

Swallowing hard and lying down carefully on the bed with her, he put his arm across her chest. His heart crashed against his ribcage, both in agony and love, a torrent ripping through him as he wrapped her in his arms.

Caden closed his eyes when he felt her heartbeat. Now he was trembling, too. He opened his mouth to speak her name, but he realized he couldn't do it. He couldn't control his voice, just like he couldn't control his heart, which even now was screaming at him to never let her go...to never let anything like this happen to her again.

He didn't know how he could have done it; leaving her alone with a total stranger, knowing from the first moment he saw Nathaniel that he couldn't be trusted. Caden would never forgive himself for this.

Sliding his hand slowly up Kyla's arm and even slower back down again, he whispered to her softly, "I'm here, Kyla. You don't have to be afraid anymore."

His own voice was detached from him, like he was speaking what he knew he had to, even if he didn't really believe it.

Kyla's body shook in his arms and his guilt continued to tear at him.

"I'm sorry," Caden choked out to her. "I'm so sorry." Tears brimmed in his eyes as if begging her to forgive him. "I'm not going anywhere," he promised her. "I'm right here, Ky. I swear to you...I am never leaving you again."

Kyla still didn't answer him. He knew she couldn't, but even in her silence, Caden felt her grip on his arm tighten.

Reaching gently forward, he kissed the side of her face where her cheekbone rose to meet her ear. Caden closed his eyes when his lips touched her skin. It was like ice. Even under the blanket, even in his embrace, she was so cold.

Holding her closer in hopes of getting her warm, he whispered to her again, "Kyla..."

He was met with more silence, but his heart didn't slow down.

I love you, he tried to tell her. But his voice never found the words.

"You can sleep," Caden told her instead. "I will take care of you."

Chapter 22

"...nightmares."

It was dark in the ritual room where Donovan waited, anxious for Balak to return with the one he had summoned here. Pacing in the hallowed stone chamber, he watched the torches flicker when he moved back and forth in front of them. He could hear water dripping in the distance in rhythm with the pounding in his head, that ever-steady *thump...thump...thump* that kept him just outside the reach of calm. It prodded him, reminded him with every drip why he had no peace, and that reminder burned his anger even deeper inside of him.

He forced himself to stop pacing and breathe. There was no need to give in to anger right now; he had this under control. Soon there would be a time when he would need it, but for now, it was to his advantage to keep himself even, emotionless, detached.

Val was being brought to him, and she was going to make everything right again.

No sooner than the thought entered Donovan's mind, two figures appeared at the entrance of the cavern. Staying carefully behind Balak, the raven-haired seductress inched forward with caution, something that was highly uncommon for her. Val kept in step with the dark-skinned Naphil towering over her who led their way by torch into the room. If Donovan didn't know better, he would say she was using Balak as a shield.

As if that would actually stop him from harming her.

It was evident in her movements and the way she tried too hard to act sure of herself that she was afraid she had done something wrong. "You called for me, my lord?" Val asked

343

nervously. Punishment was clearly the thought at the front of her mind.

Donovan took in her image by the light of the flame from Balak's torch. Her eyes were still lined in black, as they had been earlier that evening, but they ran slightly at the edges, which suggested she'd been asleep. Not an ideal scenario to wake to, he imagined.

And then there was the one who stood beside her, this pillar of strength and the utmost weakness, naïve enough to believe he could keep his infidelities hidden. Balak was a fool to think Donovan hadn't seen through him and his involvement with Val. The way he tried to mask himself was more than an insult, but Donovan would deal with that in its time.

And this was *not* its time.

There were too many things astir this night that were far more pressing than the grievances of his very temporary second-in-command. Oh yes, Balak was certainly temporary. He just didn't know it yet.

"That will be all, Balak," Donovan dismissed his subordinate with a wave of his hand.

Balak hesitated, lingering for a moment as if uncertain whether or not to leave Val alone with him. Then finally, he ducked his head in submission and exited the cave.

Once he was gone, Donovan turned to the green-eyed beauty who stood uncomfortably waiting for him. He studied her for a long time, basking in her fear; then he pulled something from the pocket of the black trench coat he wore.

"Tell me, Valerie," he said calmly, "would you like one of these?"

Donovan dangled a gold chain with a medallion at the end of it in front of her, and immediately her eyes flashed with desire. It was the symbol of the Alliance, the United Coven; a seal that only those fully inducted and committed to their cause were permitted to wear. Those who were fully committed to him.

Val reached up to touch it, but Donovan jerked it out of her fingers. "Not yet," he said. "Not until this is finished."

She didn't try to hide her irritation this time. "Not until *what* is finished?" she asked.

Donovan looked down at the medallion, toying with it as he spoke to her. "Many things must still be lined up before the coming shift, Valerie, and through everything we have established, there is only one real threat that stands against us."

"You mean the Resitore?" Val asked.

"No," he corrected her. "I mean the awakened."

She had never heard this term before. There were few who had. Not even the awakened themselves knew it.

Val looked at him curiously and Donovan went on. "In the same way I and those of my kind need the ones like you who practice in dark magic," he said, "the Nephilim who operate under a different pretense...mainly those of the Resitore, need the aide of humans as well. But rather than gaining any benefit from witches, their power would be derived from the awakened; the few whose eyes have been opened to the other realm. But the Resitore doesn't know yet how to utilize the power of these few. I'm not even sure they're aware that they need them."

Val's curiosity was growing, but she still looked confused. "Why *do* they need them?"

Donovan dropped the necklace back into his pocket. "Because this battle is not against flesh and blood. Humans are the ones who have access to and the ability to change things in the realm we Nephilim cannot. We can access it in ways that you aren't able to, but we don't have the ability to change it. This is why we align ourselves with those who can engage with the spiritual forces that we aren't able to."

"Why can't you engage them?" Val asked. "Seems like you'd be able to a lot better than we could."

"That isn't the way it works," Donovan said. "If a day ever came where my kind were able to directly interact with those of the other realm...*that* would be a day to be feared. It would take a drastic turning for something like that to come about, and one that we should not under any circumstances wish upon ourselves. As for now, there is a degree of separation. The Nephilim do not align directly with angels and demons; we align with humans who can align with the angels and demons."

"Humans like me," Val said. There was a smugness to her voice that Donovan felt compelled to crush, but for the moment he ignored it.

"Yes," he said flatly. "Humans like you."

Val smirked to herself and he fought back a cringe.

"It is imperative that we eliminate any resistance we are met with that might stand against the power we are raising ourselves to," he continued.

Val looked at him for a long time, trying to figure out what he was saying, and then finally she seemed to get it. "You're talking about Kyla James?" she said. She didn't sound happy about it, either. "Is that why you've had me watching her? Because you're afraid of that worthless little waif?"

Donovan could feel her jealousy as she spewed the words, the hatred that spilled from every one. He had always known Val to despise the girl; it was his predominant reason for placing her and not someone else on the assignment in the first place. He'd just never learned exactly why it was that she felt this way.

Donovan shook his head. "Oh, my dear Valerie, you should know not to judge by sight alone. Trust me when I tell you...*that* one is not to be underestimated."

Val folded her arms across her chest, offended by the idea.

"As it is now, Kyla is no harm to us since she has chosen not to move in the power she has," he told her. "But I have needed your eyes on her to make sure that remains the case."

"So how do I play into this?" Val asked. "What do you need me to do that I haven't already done?"

Donovan could feel her irritation increasing. "My concern is not directly over Kyla any longer, but rather over the one who has recently returned to her."

Val immediately tensed up when she realized who he was talking about. "I already got you what you wanted from Caden," she argued.

Donovan laughed. "Not hardly."

She didn't seem to like that.

"You see," he told her, "the arrival of this particular thorn in my side was very untimely...very inconvenient to our purpose here. So long as that boy is with Kyla James, she is protected."

Val shifted uncomfortably and Donovan focused in on the movement. Slight as it was, it gave him the answer he was looking for and showed him the source of her jealousy.

He began circling her when he saw it, taunting her to prove his discernment over this. "Surely you know how deeply he feels for her?" he asked.

Val kept her arms folded in an unconscious gesture of self-protection. There was hatred in her eyes, burning from the inside out, but she refused him a response.

Donovan was pleased to draw this reaction from her. "So long as the boy is here, he will fight for her. And if he fights hard enough, I fear he may draw her back."

"Draw her back to *what*?" Val asked through gritted teeth.

Donovan wasn't as pleased to answer her this time. "Back to who she really is."

Val looked away from him.

"We cannot have that," he told her. "You must understand."

There was disgust written all over Val's face. "There is nothing special about who Kyla James *is*."

Donovan was tickled by her jealousy. "About this, my dear, you could not be more wrong. That girl is capable of far more than even *she* knows, and it is imperative that we do not give her the opportunity to find out. The power she holds must be contained at all costs, for she presents us with an unnatural kind of threat; one that I have never seen in another."

Val's face contorted into an even deeper disgust. It was obvious she didn't like what he was saying, but that didn't stop Donovan from going on.

"When I first realized Nathaniel had found her," he said, "I was immediately concerned, as you can well imagine. I could only think of what it might do to her...or to him. What it might draw out. But then I began to see the silver lining to this unfortunate predicament, realizing that the very thing I feared was doing something I hadn't anticipated. It was

347

driving an already-driven wedge even further between the two who absolutely must be kept apart. The two we do not want to re-engage in the...*trust*...they once shared."

"So what's the problem?" Val asked, eager for him to move on.

"Our strategy tonight worked flawlessly," Donovan told her. "Rather than Nathaniel and the boy joining forces and working together, they will be lucky if they don't end up killing each other before the end; which was precisely our intention in setting this trap. The problem is, Nathaniel has proven more unpredictable than we had hoped. I had counted on him taking the girl away from the mountain, keeping her from Caden so he could keep her for himself."

"But...?" Val prompted.

"He didn't," Donovan said. "He let Caden take her instead."

Val's face dropped. She wasn't expecting that either.

"That is why I need you, my dear," Donovan told her, stroking her face gently with the back of his hand. "So long as the boy is alive, and so long as Nathaniel Blake isn't working to keep him from her, we are in danger of Kyla waking up."

Val furrowed her eyebrows angrily. "So what do you want me to do? Kill him?"

Donovan grinned, indulging himself in the idea of Caden's death, remembering the images he'd played into Kyla's mind that very night and the pleasure he'd felt when he watched her horror over them. Oh, if only he could.

"While there are few things I would enjoy more than murdering that sniveling little worm with my own two hands, that is not what I am asking you to do."

"Then what?" Val asked. "Do you want me to kill Kyla?"

Donovan shook his head and smiled, brushing her dark, silken hair behind her ears. "So eager for blood..." he cooed. "So eager for death."

Val looked away from him, shaking his hand off of her in the process.

"Unfortunately, there will be none spilled while I am gone," Donovan told her, "and death will have to wait where these two are concerned."

Val looked back at him in question. "Where are you going?"

"I have a short trip to make," he told her. "A business trip, if you will."

She eyed him suspiciously.

"When I return, that is when you will be released to your new assignment."

Val's patience was failing her. "And what is it that you want me to do now?" she asked.

Donovan's eyes fell again to the cavern walls. "I want you to take a hammer to the wedge that exists between those two...and drive it like a stake through Caden's heart."

*I*t was a haunting feeling, being trapped in the dark in a dream you couldn't wake from. The low hollow ache in the pit of your stomach, the sharp sting of fear that made you question if you were awake or asleep.

Right now, Kyla didn't know. She was only aware of the black.

It was all she could feel, all she could see or taste or touch; all that moved in and out of her lungs in the place of the oxygen she craved. Fear stayed on her heels as she was hunted in the dark, chased through the woods that seemed to hold her as a prisoner.

She had escaped these woods before; she knew that as she ran, but even in her escaping them, she had only been drawn back here again in the cruelest way...to the place where truth defied reason and creatures existed that she knew should not exist. To where a man named Donovan waited to kill her, and kill the only one who could save her.

That was what plagued her now. Kyla wasn't afraid of her own demise, but rather that Donovan would succeed in his aim.

She was afraid he was going to kill Nathaniel.

Waking with a start, she gasped for air as hot drenching sweat poured down her face. She sucked in oxygen in uncontrollable breaths, her eyes darting back and forth around her as she tried to make sense of where she was. It took a moment for her vision to adjust to the darkness, but even when it did, she was no less confused. This room was familiar, but Kyla didn't know what she was doing here.

Then she felt the arms that held her.

Flinching when she realized she wasn't alone, her whole body tensed beneath Caden's grip. He had a hand on her forehead and his arm across her chest, and he struggled to hold her still by pulling her back against him.

Even before she remembered, Kyla knew it was him. She didn't even have to look up to see that it was Caden; she would know those arms anywhere. At any other time, they would have comforted her, too, made her feel safe in the midst of the chaos of her mind. But nothing could do that now. Too much had happened for her to ever feel safe again.

"Shh…" Caden's voice was soft, but she heard the fear in it right away. Trying to mask it from her did nothing for him, only showed her how terrified he truly was.

Her mind scrambled to understand what was happening, to find any sort of line that might distinguish between her dreams and awake. But the line was too blurred and her mind was too weak. Fatigue and pain overwhelmed her to the point that she couldn't lift her head, and breathing was another issue altogether. That seemed to be Caden's focus right now; trying to get her to breathe. And that was the last thing Kyla was aware of before she slipped out of consciousness again.

It went on like that for hours, though time wasn't a thing she held much of a grasp on anymore. She would wake off and on into an undistinguished awareness, feeling Caden holding her, hearing the sound of his distant, muffled voice as she moved in and out of sleep. She could never hear what he was saying, but she could feel the peace in it. It was a peace she was afraid of, possibly even as much as she was afraid of the dark; and every time the nightmares took a deadly turn, she would start to breathe harder, moaning and whipping her head back and forth. That was when she would feel his grip on her tighten.

The third time this happened, Caden pressed his hand even harder against her forehead, holding a cold wet rag to her burning skin. She could hear his voice in a whisper; distant at first, but then it came closer. It took her a while to realize he was praying for her.

Kyla couldn't make out the words, but her spirit could feel them, enough that she trembled when he spoke certain things and involuntarily flinched away from him without being able to control it. That happened a lot when Caden prayed.

Had she been conscious enough to give consent, she probably wouldn't have let him do it. Praying wasn't something Kyla was comfortable with anymore. She hadn't been in two years. But being in this place of near-incapacitation, she couldn't resist him; and with the darkness of her nightmares closing in on her like this, she almost questioned if she really even wanted to. Whether she was comfortable with it or not, she knew what happened when Caden prayed. She knew the way things listened to him, and she knew that right now, she needed him...more than she realized and more than she wanted.

"Breathe for me, Kyla," his voice whispered distantly over her.

She wanted it to come closer again, but it seemed to be slipping away. Instead of listening to him, she held her breath, struggling in her lack of oxygen in the exact way Caden didn't want her to.

"Hey," he whispered gently, putting pressure on her chest with his forearm. "In through your nose, out through your mouth," he instructed her. "Don't think, just breathe."

If only that were possible.

Kyla would have given anything to be able to not think right now. She would have killed to erase from her memory what had happened to her that night. It all seemed so unreal to her; being kidnapped and beaten and dragged up a mountain, impaled with a fatal wound in her side and left for dead; realizing that the mysterious, handsome stranger she was falling for wasn't human, and that he was the reason a psychopathic stalker named Donovan ever went after her in the first place; lying in the dirt on the floor of the forest watching a Nephilim death match take place just over her head. And then there was the most painful part of all, when her handsome, heroic rescuer almost killed her best friend.

Kyla moaned and whipped her head to one side, hoping to shake away the memories before they started choking her again. The nightmare drew on, and despite how she longed to, she still didn't wake. She could feel herself burning with fever, though in what reality she felt this, she wasn't sure. Right now, there were two she was operating out of; the world of flesh and blood and the world of her dreams, neither of which she knew how to trust.

It drew on and on and on, until finally a light broke through the dark and swept her away from the demented man with the jet black wings, plunging her into a pool of nothing. Not dark, not light...not anything. And as her fatigued body gave way to the relief of the feeling, Kyla was finally able to rest.

Hours later, her eyes fluttered open to an unexpected warmth. The morning sun spilled over her where she was curled up at the edge of the bed, shining through the glass sliding door at the entrance of the room. Caden wasn't holding her anymore; he hadn't been for a while now. Kyla rubbed her eyes and blinked a few times as she looked around, but she didn't see him anywhere.

Pushing herself up slowly, she cringed. Everything in her ached and for some reason her face felt wet, but she didn't know why. She heard the sound of the bathroom faucet, and a few seconds later Caden walked out with a wet rag in his hand.

He was startled when he saw her alert. He didn't move forward, just stood there for a moment, silent and in pain. Then without a word he walked over to her and sat at the edge of the bed. He pressed the rag to her forehead and used it to cool her face. "I think your fever might be starting to break," he told her.

Fever?

He must have seen the question in her eyes. "It happens sometimes when people go into shock."

Kyla swallowed, though it took effort. Her mouth was so dry.

Seeing how difficult it was for her, Caden picked up a cup of water from the table by his bed and brought it to her lips. She weakly lifted a hand to help him guide the cup to her mouth, and when he set it back down for her, he tossed the rag beside it and looked down, his brow creasing in frustration.

"Kyla..." he said.

She tried to brace herself, but she knew it was futile. There was no way she could prepare herself for this.

Slowly Caden looked back up at her. "What happened to you?"

She fidgeted uncomfortably, her eyes darting around the room. She was trying so hard to shove those images, those memories, those nightmares away from her. She didn't need him to pull her right back to remembering them.

When she didn't speak, Caden's frustration grew, though he was careful to stay calm and not direct it at her. "Please talk to me," he said.

Kyla looked at him; the bags under his eyes, the weariness on his face. It was evident that he hadn't slept a second. He had stayed up with her, no questions asked, and taken care of her. He deserved to know the truth. But how could she tell him a thing like that?

Finally, she found her voice, though it only came out in a whisper. "You wouldn't believe me."

He looked relieved to hear her speak, but hurt by what she said. "When have I ever not believed you?" he asked her.

Kyla pressed her lips together instead of answering him.

"At least give me the chance to try," he said.

She was becoming anxious again and he could tell. Caden put his hand to his face and then pulled it back down again. "Can you just tell me what happened with your car?" he asked. "Why you crashed it into a ditch?"

Kyla flinched visibly, wishing she could have controlled it. *Sure, Caden,* she thought. *A demented creature with red eyes and black wings flew at my windshield.*

"You wouldn't..." she whispered again, but he scowled and cut her off.

"Stop telling me what I won't believe! I mean honestly, have I ever given you a reason to doubt me?"

Kyla looked at him for the first time, though she was terrified of what he might see in her. "No," she said.

"Then please," Caden begged her. "Just *trust* me. Tell me *something*! Tell me what made you crash. Tell me what he *did* to you!"

Kyla shook her head. "He didn't do anything…"

Caden scowled angrily. "Why are you trying to protect him?" he snarled. "Did he threaten you?"

Kyla flashed him a look and spoke very slowly, emphasizing every word, "Nathaniel did not do this to me."

Caden made a face. He despised her protectiveness over him. Putting up his hands, he said, "Fine, if you want to lie to me…if that's where we're at now, then go ahead."

Kyla was getting angry now. Her teeth were clenched as she told him, "I'm not lying to you, Caden." There were few things that angered her faster than false accusations. From anyone else it would be bad enough, but she could not take that coming from him.

That was all Caden could handle. All of the anger that had been bottled up in him all night, he let it out then. "Then what *happened*?!" he screamed at her.

Kyla tensed up and jerked back, her expression staunched. "I have to go," she told him.

Caden laughed at her. It was a tense, angry laugh, as if he weren't taking her seriously, but when she stood up to leave he grabbed her by the wrist and stopped her.

She shot him a glare and he demanded, "Where are you going? Back to *him*?"

She couldn't speak a word without letting him have it, so Kyla bit her tongue and tried to control her anger.

"You want him to finish the job?" Caden shouted. He grabbed at the loose fabric from the tear in the leg of her pants and pulled it so it tore even further. "You want him to finish *this*?"

Kyla gave him the coldest, most hate-filled look she had ever given him. "Is that it?" she asked through her still-clenched teeth. "You think Nathaniel tried to rape me?"

Caden looked like he was about to go out of his mind. She had never seen him look like this.

"You're really gonna tell me he didn't?" he asked in a voice so tense it shook.

Kyla could have slapped him for that. It would have been stupid since she knew she couldn't blame him for drawing the conclusion, but something in her just felt the need to protect Nathaniel, even if only against the accusation. After all he had given for her, all he had sacrificed to keep her alive...

"No, Caden," she said. "Nathaniel did not try to rape me. He didn't touch me."

"Sure didn't look that way to me," Caden retorted.

"Yeah well, even *you* can't always trust your eyes," Kyla muttered.

He looked at her curiously. "What does *that* mean?"

She wrinkled her lips, wishing she hadn't said that. "I have to go," she told him again. She tried to shove past him toward the door, but this time Caden grabbed her by the shoulder.

"Like hell you are," he said. "I'm not letting that bastard anywhere near you."

Kyla glared at him fiercely. "If it weren't for Nathaniel, I'd be dead right now."

Caden tensed his jaw and looked away from her. He still thought she was lying; or maybe he just wanted her to be so that he had an excuse to hate him. She couldn't tell.

"Do you really think I'd be going back to him if he hurt me, Cade?"

"I don't know," he told her honestly. "The way it looks right now, you may have completely lost it for all I know."

"I haven't lost it," she said defensively, crossing her arms in front of her chest.

Caden shook his head in disbelief. "Kyla, I just stayed up all night with you trying to keep you from running out of here screaming bloody murder." He paused to watch her reaction. "Do you even remember? Do you have any idea what you were doing?"

She didn't remember. She only remembered the nightmares.

"Think of how fair this is for me," he said. "Just try for two seconds to think of it from my point of view. I find your car on the side of the road crashed into a ditch with blood on the steering wheel. *Blood*, Kyla. Then I run up into the woods looking for you and find you lying on the ground looking scared as hell and about a minute from death with *him* on top of you."

She fidgeted and looked away from him.

"Oh, and then there's the part where he tried to kill me," he added. "Let's not forget that…or did you already?"

Kyla gave him a scolding look. "You went after him first," she said. "And whatever you think, Nathaniel didn't lay a finger on me."

That was all Caden could take. "Then who *did*?!" he screamed at her. "Damn it, Kyla! Why won't you tell me the truth?"

She closed her eyes, every muscle in her face tensing in response to his raised voice. She wanted him to stop yelling. She wanted all of this to go away.

"I don't know who he was," she rambled off quickly. She didn't know what she was going to say; just that she had to say something. "There was a hitchhiker…on the side of the road. He…he attacked me and pulled me into the woods. And Nathaniel…he found me up there and fought him off." She stopped for a second to see if he believed her. "Nathaniel didn't hurt me, Caden," she emphasized. "He *saved* me."

Kyla felt miserable lying to him, but she figured at least part of the story was true. Unfortunately, Caden didn't.

"A hitchhiker?" he asked.

Her eyes shifted and he grabbed his phone.

"What are you doing?" she asked him. The sudden raise in her pitch gave away her fear.

"Calling it in," Caden said. "If there's a dangerous hitchhiker out there attacking women, the cops are gonna want to know about it."

Kyla grabbed his phone away from him. By the expression on his face, she could see that that was exactly what he expected her to do.

356

"You wanna tell me what really happened now?" he asked her. He was anything but amused.

"I can't."

"Kyla..."

"I can't because I don't know yet," she said. She paused for a moment and bit her lip. "But I'm going to find out."

Caden didn't like that idea. "And how do you plan on doing that?" he asked her.

She told him very pointedly, "I'm going to see Nathaniel."

Caden didn't even hesitate to tell her, "No."

Kyla sighed. "You have to trust me on this, Cade. You *have* to."

He started pacing in front of the bed, not even hiding how angry the thought made him. She could tell he wanted to stop her, but also that a part of him trusted her; the part that knew she wouldn't say this without a reason.

"How are you gonna go see him?" Caden asked her. "Your car's totaled."

Kyla raised her eyebrows a little and looked up at him hesitantly.

"Come *on!*" Caden exclaimed when he realized what she wanted. "You can't be serious!"

"Please," she begged him. "I wouldn't ask if I didn't have to."

Wrinkling his nose and scowling to himself, Caden made his way to his dresser. "I can't believe I'm doing this," he muttered under his breath. Then he handed her the keys to his Jeep.

Smiling for the first time since she was with him at the park last night, Kyla squeezed his arm and kissed him on the cheek. "Thank you," she said excitedly.

Caden looked at her and frowned, and it hit her in full just how much she needed to be thanking him for.

"I mean it," she said gratefully. "For everything."

He didn't respond, just told her flatly, "Get out of here before I change my mind."

Kyla started for the door, but stopped short and turned back to him, biting her lip. "What should I do about Loni's car?" she asked him.

Caden's hands were on his hips and his eyes were on the floor. "I'll take care of it," he told her.

"How?" she asked, surprised by his willingness to help her.

Caden looked back up at her. "You're not the only one who can lie," he said.

It stung, but she knew she deserved it. "Caden…" she started to say.

"I'll help you cover this up," he spoke over her, "but I want the truth, Kyla. All of it."

She gave him a brief, tense smile and then ducked out the door, dashing toward his Jeep with his keys in her hand.

Not a chance in hell, she thought.

Chapter 23

"…they burn like fire."

Caden sat on his bed after Kyla left, his face in his hands and his elbows on his legs. He was trying to figure out what to do, trying to decide if he was insane to let her leave like he had, but nothing made sense to him anymore. Not a single thing he did or heard or saw; nothing he chose to believe or chose to deny.

He felt like he was going out of his mind.

Caden had never known a feeling like this, where he was literally afraid that every decision he made was going to be the wrong one. He couldn't help but feel that somehow this was his fault, and if he could just get his head straight he could find a way to make it right. He was also starting to feel that if he didn't, something a whole lot worse was going to happen.

There had obviously been no hitchhiker last night; he'd called Kyla on that lie pretty fast, but it was just as difficult for him to believe she would run back to her new boyfriend if he really was the one who beat her up. Part of him just wanted Nathaniel to be so he'd have an excuse to kill him.

Thinking back and remembering Kyla's face on the mountain, the way she had looked at Nathaniel and the way he'd looked back at her; remembering in more detail the way Nathaniel had appeared when Caden saw him, (as if he'd been holding her, not attacking her) Caden's stomach turned. Nathaniel hadn't looked like a rapist or a killer; he'd looked like someone whose heart had just gotten ripped out of his chest.

He had looked the way Caden felt right now.

The realization (or maybe just his finally admitting it) made him want to break something. He wanted to direct that anger at Nathaniel, but he knew it wasn't him he was mad at. Caden was mad at himself for ever being stupid enough to leave Kyla in the first place, for ever listening to that damn voice in his head that told him it was the only way to bring her back.

He forced himself to shake off the thought. There was more at hand here than the state of Kyla's spirit. Right now, there was someone out there who wanted to harm her body, someone else who was fighting to protect her...and another person who had to know about it.

With the thought of his sister coming into his head, Caden stood from his bed, and with a renewed determination he marched toward the house to find her.

He didn't care what he had to do anymore. Alexa was going to tell him the truth.

Kyla drove Caden's Jeep far too quickly down the mountain. He wouldn't have been happy with her about it, but luckily he wasn't there to tell her to slow down. Speed limit or not, she had no interest in slowing down. The only thing she was concerned with was getting home, getting cleaned off and getting to the Blake mansion before it was too late.

Kyla didn't know what Nathaniel was going to do. It was hard to think about it logically, considering all that had happened to them, but right now her mind was taking her back to where the man named Seth (she shuddered at the thought of calling him a man) had ordered him back to London, threatening him severely if he didn't comply with those orders.

It was also taking her back to Nathaniel's face when Caden dragged her away from him; how torn he looked, wanting to talk to her...desperate to explain.

Surely he wouldn't leave without seeing her again.

Kyla bit her lip and pressed her foot harder against the gas pedal. As much as she wanted to believe that, she just wasn't sure.

After stealthily making her way through the back door of the condo and up to the shower without being seen, Kyla rinsed off quickly and avoided the mirror with the horrifying reflection that no doubt awaited her as she slipped into her room to grab some clean clothes.

It took her three minutes to get dressed, braid her soaking wet hair and get back out the door without waking Matthew, who had fallen asleep on the couch. The thought of him staying up waiting for her stabbed a new pain into her chest, but she couldn't think of that now. She would deal with her little brother later; right now she had a far more time-sensitive issue on her hands.

Pulling up Falcon's Rest, Kyla parked across the street, not wanting to deal with Nathaniel's uncle (assuming he even had an uncle) if he were home. For all she knew, that could have been a lie too, but on the off chance that it wasn't, she didn't want to risk it.

Walking hurriedly across the street and up to the driveway, Kyla took a deep breath when the front door came into view. She didn't know if she had the courage to do this, especially without knowing if Nathaniel was even there. It certainly didn't look like anyone was home.

But then she felt someone behind her.

Spinning around sharply, her eyes fell on the tall handsome blonde who stood at the edge of the driveway; gorgeous as ever, too perfect for words, searching her face as he analyzed her reaction. The sight of him still managed to leave her stunned, but even through her awe at Nathaniel's beauty, she could see straight through him.

He was so scared.

Kyla felt an instant pull to be near him, though she knew that she shouldn't, and she saw the same thing in him as well. It was so in rhythm, what they both felt. She didn't even need words from him to verify that to her.

They were silent, wordless, weightless as they stood there; the atmosphere around them changing with every quickly-passing moment. Kyla didn't understand the feeling that hung there; she only knew it wasn't normal, and that she should probably say something to knock them out of it before she did something stupid.

Not that she wouldn't love doing something stupid right now.

Nothing would feel better than to fall to this magnetism between them, which in spite of everything that had happened had only grown stronger.

Kyla wouldn't have thought that possible. She had expected things to be different when she saw Nathaniel again, but to think that what she'd felt for him before would only be intensified, well...she hadn't counted on that.

"Nathaniel..." she said, but she had no words.

He stepped up to her, touching her face and moving his hands down to her shoulders. He swallowed hard as he looked down on her body, more tormented than she had ever seen him. "Are you alright?" he asked her desperately. The jacket she wore was covering her scars, but Nathaniel knew they were there.

"Yes," she answered him in a shaky voice. "But I shouldn't be."

Nathaniel swallowed again, his pained expression taking on a stronger edge of fear.

"What happened, Nathaniel?" she asked him. "How did you..."

"Did you stay with Caden?" he asked her abruptly. It was clear that he didn't want her to finish that question. Kyla could imagine why, but it still frustrated her.

She looked down and nodded, and with that the magnetism between them was quenched. Even the mention of her best friend created an automatic rift between them. Now more than ever.

"Good," Nathaniel said tensely. She could see he didn't mean that. "Is he okay?" he asked her.

Kyla frowned when she thought about it. "He's angry," she said. "He's confused out of his mind and threatening to go to the police, but other than that he's fine."

Nathaniel looked guilty, ashamed. "I'm sorry," he said. She knew he meant it, too.

Thinking back on the image of Nathaniel choking him, Kyla shook her head and tried to block it out. That was the last thing she wanted to remember right now. She came here for answers, not to rebuke him; and judging by what she heard in his voice, Nathaniel seemed to be beating himself up about it enough already.

"Nathaniel…"

He must have known what she was going to ask by the tone she used, because he told her, "We should talk inside. It isn't safe out here."

Kyla looked around her, expecting someone to jump out at them from the woods across the street.

"Come with me," he said. He put his hand lightly on her back and guided her toward the door. "We don't have much time, but we have a little. My uncle is supposed to fly in today and I'm not sure what time his plane lands. His caretaker, Miguel, the one you met…he thinks I'm already gone."

Nathaniel reached for the door and Kyla stopped him short with a question. "Why aren't you?" she asked him.

Nathaniel held the door but he didn't walk through it. "You know why," he told her simply. Then he motioned for her to follow him into the estate.

*W*hen Nathaniel and Kyla got up to his bedroom, he let her in and turned back to close the door. After locking it behind him, he rested his left hand against the frame and kept his head down. He could feel Kyla's eyes burning into him where she sat uncomfortably at the edge of his bed. He didn't want to turn around…to face her. He didn't want to answer her questions. But with the moment of truth upon him that he'd been dreading for days, Nathaniel knew he couldn't avoid it anymore. Sooner or later, this had to happen, and considering that Kyla had already seen what she had, sooner was going to be better than later in this instance.

She was shaking; Nathaniel saw that when he finally turned back to her. But no matter how afraid she might be, Kyla had to trust him to at least some measure if she was willing to be here in his room alone with him like this. If she thought he was dangerous to her, she wouldn't have come back.

Moving cautiously toward the girl on his bed, Nathaniel tried to keep his distance; but he was no more able to stay away from her than he was able to control the compulsion he felt to be near her. With every step he took, he read her face and determined that the second she became afraid again, that was as far as he was going to go, as near to her as he was allowed to be. But Kyla's expression didn't change.

Nathaniel tried to tell himself that he was reading her wrong, but the further he looked into her, the clearer it became: She wanted him closer.

Even if she didn't know his secrets, even if he hadn't told her how it was that she hadn't bled to death on the mountain...even if he wasn't human. He still wasn't close enough for her yet.

Nathaniel stood over the edge of his bed, half-expecting her to come to her senses and beeline for the door. But Kyla didn't move an inch.

He didn't understand.

The two of them were held there wordlessly for a longer time than either was aware, reading each other like they always did, trying to gauge the other's thoughts through the windows of their eyes. But as eager as Kyla had been outside to learn the truth, she didn't seem very interested in words right now. Something else was on her mind, and whatever it was, she wasn't taking her eyes off of him.

Nathaniel's heartbeat stumbled when she reached out to him slowly, her fingers pulling at the bottom of his shirt. It sent a chill up his arm when she bit her lip and began toying with the edge of the fabric. He didn't know what she was doing, but whatever it was, he was nervous. Her hands were still trembling as she pulled at his shirt slowly...carefully, as if she didn't want to alarm him. Then slipping both her hands beneath his shirt, she moved up his torso, pushing the navy blue fabric up along with them.

There was no word to describe the feeling that came on Nathaniel as her fingers slid up his skin. Like a wave of heat and a shock of fire, he could hardly even breathe. She didn't know what it did to him when she touched him like that. She couldn't even imagine.

His stomach muscles tensed at her softest touch, but he wasn't about to fight it. Instead he pulled his shirt over his head like it was on fire and threw it to the floor, more than eager to help her in this endeavor, whatever her aim might be.

Kyla jerked back her hand at the boldness of the gesture, her eyes growing wider when they fell on his chest. She wasn't expecting him to do that. Nathaniel wasn't expecting it either.

Biting her lip as she stared at him, Kyla's eyes glazed over in a way he wasn't familiar with, and he questioned for a moment if she might be afraid of him.

"Answer me one question," she whispered to him in a low voice.

Despite the thousand things she could ask that Nathaniel should be terrified of, he found himself telling her, "Anything."

Kyla unzipped her jacket and his heart pounded harder. She tossed it to the floor where he had thrown his shirt; then slowly she pulled up the white tank top she wore beneath it.

"Why am I not dead?" she asked him.

Nathaniel froze when he saw her stomach.

The scars it held that hadn't healed beneath his hands sent daggers of guilt ripping through him. He was pained as he reached out to touch her, desperate to fix what he had broken. But try as he did to heal her scars, it didn't do a thing.

Nathaniel's face fell in disappointment. Kyla must have seen it in his eyes, because she reached out to touch him and tell him it was okay.

"How is it okay?" he asked her. "*I* did this to you."

Kyla looked at him, bewildered, her eyes filled with awe and grace. "Nathaniel, you saved my life," she said.

He shook his head and choked up on the emotion that he couldn't keep away. Leaning down over her, he kissed her stomach gently, tracing the side of it with his hand as he steadied himself with his other. He could feel her heart pound when his lips met her skin, and he looked up at her curiously, into her face.

Her expression was different now; a great deal different. The gratitude in her eyes had been replaced by something else. Nathaniel trembled in response to the look she gave him.

What was she thinking, looking at him like that? Did she really not have any idea what he could do to her?

Kyla reached out to touch him again, this time placing her hand just over his heart.

Now it was his breath that staggered. Nathaniel couldn't figure out what she was trying to do, and at that point he almost didn't care. He wasn't about to stop her or question a thing...at least until she took him by the shoulders and turned him carefully so that his back was facing her.

That was when he realized what she was after.

She wanted to see his wings.

He could see that she was afraid...almost as afraid as he was, and as he looked into her eyes and read into the depths of her, he allowed Kyla to turn his back so she could see it. Nathaniel wanted her to know that he trusted her with himself, which was more than he could say about anyone. He had never made himself so vulnerable before, but something in him just had to give her that much. She wanted to see his back? He would let her. She wanted to cut him herself and watch the wound close up? He would put the knife in her hands. There was nothing he wouldn't do if it would earn her trust.

Kyla was surprised when he didn't resist her, but her initial surprise was nothing compared to what hit her when she saw his back.

No doubt, she had thought she would find something of a scar where his wings should have been, or at least some trace of evidence as to what she had seen on the mountain. Maybe she thought if she found that, she could convince herself it was real, that what she had witnessed hadn't been imagined; but Nathaniel knew there was nothing there. There never was.

It defied everything about the physical world, the transformation from man to Naphil. There was no explanation for anything of such sheer size and diameter releasing and retracting the way his wings did. But somehow, even in its impossibility, the shift still happened every time.

It took a moment for Kyla to find the courage to trace her fingers along his back.

"How does it happen?" she asked him in a quiet, unsure voice.

"I wouldn't know how to explain it," he told her. "I'm not even sure I understand it myself."

She gingerly moved her fingers along his skin, appearing more fascinated than mortified.

Nathaniel turned around to look at her, his eyes imploring of her face, and it was as he searched her that his own fear was realized, no matter how foolish it might have been. Through all that had happened, he found himself terrified that she was going to run from him again, just as she had before. He had seen the disgust in her eyes as she looked on him then, when she had first learned he wasn't human...as she told him to stay away from her. Nathaniel was afraid of that now, that he would be met with the same. But he wasn't prepared for what he saw instead.

"Does it hurt?" she asked him softly. Her brow creased with worry that he might say yes.

Nathaniel swallowed hard. "Not anymore."

Kyla closed her eyes.

As she dropped her hands from his back, he was pounded by uncertainty as he searched her again. "Why aren't you afraid of me anymore?" he asked her.

The question seemed to hurt her, but he wasn't sure why. Something that looked like guilt played briefly across her face, and then before she could stop herself, Kyla asked him emotionally, "How could I be afraid of the most beautiful thing I've ever seen?"

Nathaniel stared at her, stunned.

"You saved my life," she told him again. "You risked everything for me."

Something about the way she said it hit him harder than anything should, and it triggered something in him that he didn't know he could feel.

He also didn't know how he could control it.

It was purely impulse, what Nathaniel did next. Pressing his brow to hers, he took Kyla's face in his hands and then pulled her back carefully. When he kissed her forehead, her whole body shook, but she didn't resist him. Even if she tried to, Nathaniel wasn't sure he would let her.

"I would do it again," he breathed to her. And he would have, too.

Kyla pulled back a little, just enough to be able to see his eyes. "*Why?*" she asked him. "Why did you do it?"

The question tore him up. "I couldn't lose you," he said, stroking her hair back from her face. "Not you."

Her lips quivered at his touch. "Nathaniel..."

He didn't let her finish. Instead he kissed the side of her face, moving inch by inch down her jaw-line and stopping only when he reached her mouth. He was yearning, torn between what he knew he should do and what he absolutely shouldn't. With bated breath, he waited there, his lips hardly half an inch from hers. His pulse felt to stop altogether, and then as if to seal it, Kyla's eyes flickered up to him for a fraction of a second, staring into his where they were set on her face.

That was all it took for him, just one flash of a look and he was back on her mouth. And it felt so incredible he couldn't even regret it.

It had started so carefully, sweetly almost. But that hadn't lasted. No sooner than Nathaniel kissed her did the current take him under, that electricity that surged through him every time Kyla so much as looked at him. And this time it spiked an aggression in him that was borderline frightening.

Overwhelmed by the power of the kiss, Nathaniel's pulse surged as he held her, to a degree that made him think he wouldn't be able to stop. It was harder than the one on the mountain, deeper and more intense; like a magnified version of what that had been. Nathaniel realized he couldn't slow down, even though he knew he should. No, not just should...he *had* to. But that logic failed him as he kissed her harder, sliding both of his hands to the back of her head.

He hadn't meant to do it. He hadn't meant to grab her like that and move on her with such force that she could hardly catch her breath. But that hadn't changed what he actually did. Nathaniel didn't feel even the slightest bit in control of himself, and for a moment he was afraid he might be forcing her. But Kyla answered that question for him by knocking him onto his back.

She ran her hands up his chest and he felt a tremor through his body. Closing his eyes, he leaned his head back and moaned, his strength giving way to desire.

If she kept this up, Nathaniel didn't know what he was going to do to her.

Slipping his hands beneath her shirt and around to her back, he pulled her against his chest, feeling that nothing was close enough for him. He could feel the struggle inside him, how he was trying to hold back and yet desperate to give in. Nathaniel wanted to protect her, to fight it, but he also wanted her more than he had ever wanted anything in his life.

Sliding his hands down her back again, he breathed to her, "Kyla..." never having felt so divided against himself.

She didn't respond. Apparently words were of little value to her right now.

Grabbing her by her waist, Nathaniel flipped her over so that she was underneath him. Her eyes were wild with excitement, and it was clear by what they showed that she wasn't about to stop him. When she saw how hard he was breathing, she looked like she was just about driven out of her mind. She watched his chest heave as it made a labored effort to get oxygen to his lungs, and as she did, he could have sworn he saw her eyes changing colors.

Nathaniel smiled at her curiously. "You know what your eyes do when you're with me, right?" he asked her. "The way they change?"

Kyla swallowed nervously, her gaze still fixed on his chest. "They do?"

He kissed her lips softly. "Mmm hmm," he said. "Sometimes they're blue. That's usually when you're happy. And when you start to look into me...to *see* me, they change to green." He kissed her again, twice as long this time. "When you're angry, they turn grey..." he said, bringing his lips for a third time back to hers, but instead of kissing her again, he barely teased the edge of them. "But I've never seen them brown before," he whispered. "Not until now."

Kyla's cheeks flushed in embarrassment and Nathaniel smiled again.

"So tell me, Kyla James," he said smoothly. "What exactly is going through your mind?"

She didn't answer him. Instead she grabbed him by the shoulders and pulled him down on top of her.

When she moved her hands under his arms and dug her nails into his back, Nathaniel could almost hear his heart crash into his ribcage. It was frightening, the desire that tore through him; powerful over his mind and his lungs and everything in him that he used to control. And he honestly didn't know what to do about it anymore.

He had been tempted by human women before, despite how Caleb teased him about it, and every time he had been able to shut that temptation down, switching over into the robotic frame of mind that kept him alive. But what Nathaniel felt for Kyla didn't even compare.

He didn't understand it; she was just a girl. Just one little human girl...who happened to be a seer. And who happened to burn a fire in his blood like nothing ever had.

Nathaniel didn't see it coming. He was so caught up in the way she looked, the way she felt...the way she moved that he couldn't have anticipated it even if he'd been looking for it. So when an unexpected conviction came crashing down on him hard and fast, he jerked back from her suddenly and pushed her off.

370

"No!" he groaned as he stood up off the bed. He wasn't sure if he was talking to Kyla or himself, and judging by her expression, she didn't seem to know either. He only knew that it was the hardest thing he had ever had to do.

Kyla sat up quickly. "I'm...sorry?"

Running his fingers through his hair in aggravation, Nathaniel walked toward the door, but he didn't walk through it; he just stopped somewhere in between and started pacing. He didn't want to leave, but he knew he couldn't stay. He didn't trust himself to. Pressing his fingers to his brow, he bore them so hard into his skull he was surprised they didn't leave a dent in it.

It was clear to her that he wasn't doing well, but Kyla seemed to be having a difficult time figuring out why.

"I can't do this," he told her. His voice came across a lot harsher than he meant for it to, and she immediately took it wrong.

Cowering back from him and looking very much like a small frightened animal, she stammered, "I didn't...I didn't mean..."

Nathaniel shook his head. "No," he said. "Kyla, no..." He hated that she thought she'd done something wrong. "You just...you can't do this," he told her. He knew he sounded like an idiot, but even though he wanted to explain himself, he didn't know how.

"*I* can't or *you* can't?" she snapped defensively.

"*We* can't!" he exclaimed. He was so frustrated he was about to rip his hair out.

Kyla's shoulders were tight as she hugged her knees. He could see that she was hurt and trying hard to look angry. "Why not?" she asked him.

Nathaniel winced and looked away from her, unable to meet her eyes. It was painful for him to answer that question. "Because you don't even know what I *am*."

She held a look of awe as she stared at him. "Yes I do," she said.

Nathaniel looked at her, surprised.

"You're an angel," Kyla told him softly.

The stab of the assumption hit him right in the chest. Furrowing his brow, he dropped his eyes to the ground.

"Not exactly," he told her.

Chapter 24

"...and the truth shall set you free."

I t was clear that Kyla didn't understand. It was also clear
that her lack of understanding was worrying her, but as
much as Nathaniel wanted to explain, he couldn't. After the
silence that fell on them became uncomfortable, he brought
his eyes up slowly to meet her and saw that her face had lost
even more color than before.

"But...I saw your wings," she argued. "I saw you *fly*."

Nathaniel cringed. "I know."

It took her another few seconds before she could even
attempt to articulate herself. "Then...how...?"

Nathaniel felt sick. After everything they had been
through, had it really come down to this? Could he really tell
Kyla the truth?

As it turned out, he could.

"Have you ever heard of the Nephilim?" he asked her.

She swallowed hard, looking about as sick as he felt;
possibly even sicker. "I...maybe?" she stammered. "What are
they?"

Nathaniel wouldn't meet her eyes. This would be so much
easier if she knew more about history. "In essence," he told
her, "they are beings. Physical beings. Half human...half
angel."

Kyla wasn't blinking. "*Half* angel?" she asked. "How is that
even possible?"

Nathaniel shifted anxiously. "My mother was human," he
said. "My father...wasn't."

Kyla stared at him, still not blinking, and he started to
wonder if this should worry him. Pressing her hands so hard

against her knees that her fingers were turning colors, she was rigid with disbelief.

That couldn't be good.

Moving back over to her slowly, Nathaniel set his hand on hers to try and get her to take it easy, fearful that if she didn't loosen her grip she might cut off her circulation. Kyla looked up at him with fearful eyes, and it took everything in him not to kiss her again.

Holding her hand in his, Nathaniel rubbed it gently and pressed his lips to her fingers instead. On their contact, he felt a familiar heat move into him, and he could see that she felt it, too.

"Is that why?" she asked him. "Is that why it feels like that when you touch me? Because you're not..."

She didn't say "human." Nathaniel was grateful for that, but still the word hung over them.

"I don't think so," he told her. "It doesn't feel like that when I touch anyone else."

Kyla swallowed nervously, her eyes still locked on his face. "So your father," she said carefully, "he was...or is...an *angel*?"

Nathaniel made a face at the thought of his father. That was one thing he made a point not to think about, more even than he made a point not to think about his mother. "That's one way to put it," he muttered.

"What would be another way?" she asked him.

Nathaniel set her hand carefully back on her leg. Turning away from her, he stared at the opposing wall. "My father was a Watcher," he said. "Not of the original 200 who were imprisoned until the final judgment, but one of the new wave of Watchers that came to the earth in preparation for the coming age. I never knew him, and I know very little about him..."

He knew he was moving too fast when Kyla shook her head a little. "New wave?" she asked him.

Nathaniel sighed. This was not going to be easy.

"The original 200 Watchers were here before the flood," he explained. "They bred the Nephilim history knows of; the giants that were called as "heroes of old"...the "men of renown." Cursed beings that gave way to such evil that God sent His judgment to the earth in the form of a great flood to destroy all living creatures."

"Yeah, I know the story," Kyla muttered irritably. "That's what felt boards in Sunday school are for." She didn't even try to hide her bitterness on the remark.

"Sorry," Nathaniel said curtly. "I never went to Sunday school."

She pursed her lips in the tense way she always did when she was trying not to give him a snide remark. Nathaniel went on before they started to argue. "The new wave of Watchers came not too long ago," he told her. "They returned to fulfill the prophecy that was written in the gospel of Matthew."

"What prophecy?" Kyla asked. Her face looked so sour Nathaniel would have thought someone had just shoved a lime into her mouth.

"Chapter Twenty-Four, Verse Thirty-Seven," he answered. *"As it was in the days of Noah, so it will be at the coming of the Son of Man."*

Kyla's eyes held an emptiness behind them that rivaled despair, like she was remembering something she had long forgotten, or maybe something she just really didn't want to remember.

"I don't believe in that stuff anymore," she said quietly. "I don't believe in things like you."

Nathaniel gave her a look like he didn't believe her. "Yes you do," he said. The bluntness of the remark surprised her. "And you can keep lying to yourself all you want about it, but the longer it takes for you to admit what you already know, the longer all of us are going to be in danger."

Kyla flashed him a look. "*What* did you just say?"

Nathaniel sighed again and stood up off the bed, taking a few steps toward the door. He waited a moment before he stopped to look back at her, wanting to be careful about what he said next.

"Do you really think any of this was a mistake?" he asked her. "That it was just chance that let me find you?

Coincidence that made you stumble across the path of the very thing you've been running from?"

"I haven't been running from *this!*" Kyla insisted. "I swear I never knew the Nephilim were real! Hell, I hardly even knew what they *were!*"

"No," Nathaniel said, "but you know more of reality than you've been letting on."

Kyla stared him down. He knew she would never admit that, but her eyes gave her away.

"I'm not trying to start an argument with you," he told her. "I am just trying to help you to see."

"And what is it, exactly, that you want me to see?" she snapped. "That I was somehow *meant* to find you? That it was fate that threw me smack in the middle of a present-day Nephilim battle to the death? Honestly Nathaniel, do you really buy that?"

He smirked a little at the irony. "Trust me," he told her. "I've lived my entire life in opposition to the idea of fate."

"So what changed?" she asked defensively.

The question frustrated him, if for no other reason than that it should have been obvious to her. "*You* did!"

Kyla looked skeptical. That frustrated him, too.

"You changed everything for me, Kyla. Everything I believed in...everything I am doing this for."

Nathaniel realized he sounded angry again. Sighing, he looked at her helplessly, dreading his next words.

"That's why I have to leave," he said.

*K*yla took the blow, but she didn't respond to it. She just sat there   feeling distinctly as if she'd been kicked in the stomach, holding her breath and trying not to react.

It surprised her how much it hurt when Nathaniel dropped that on her, and she knew it wasn't just because she didn't expect it. She was stunned as she looked at him, and for a fleeting moment she questioned if he'd really just said that.

"You have to understand," he tried to explain, "I have to set this right."

376

A new pain stabbed into Kyla's chest when she realized he meant it, that he really was leaving her. She turned away from him in an attempt to hide her emotion, though there was nothing in her that wanted to.

She knew she had no right to be hurt by this. Nathaniel Blake had lied to her; he had broken her trust and deceived her. He had endangered her beyond all reason and pretended to be human when he was anything but. And yet all she could see was everything he had done, everything he had risked to keep her alive.

Human or not, Kyla couldn't deny that...just like she couldn't deny how it was ripping her apart.

Nathaniel looked tortured. "I have to set this right," he repeated himself. "It's the only way I can stop Donovan from accomplishing what he's after with you."

Kyla smirked as if he'd told some kind of joke. "Donovan was using me as bait for *you*," she said. "He wants nothing with me."

Emotion played briefly across Nathaniel's face, though it was hard for her to tell which one. It looked like pain, but also disbelief. "Do you really believe that?" he asked her.

Kyla squared her jaw, but she didn't answer him. As an impulse reaction, Nathaniel stepped closer to touch her, but he stopped himself and looked down instead. "You're wrong," he told her.

Kyla frowned stubbornly and kept her eyes on the edge of the bed. She didn't like being told she was wrong.

"We can't win this," Nathaniel said. "None of us can win until you open your eyes."

"My eyes aren't closed," Kyla spoke through gritted teeth.

Nathaniel disagreed. "Your eyes haven't been open in a very long time."

She denied it in her mind. *He's wrong*, she told herself. *He doesn't know what he's talking about.* But in that irritating place inside of her that always contradicted what she wanted to be true, Kyla knew that was a lie.

"He wants you asleep, Kyla. Don't you understand that? So long as you stay asleep, he doesn't have to be afraid of you."

She scoffed at the idea. "Why would Donovan be afraid of *me*?"

Despite how insane he sounded, Nathaniel's sincerity ran deep behind his eyes. His voice was quiet and bewildered and thick with conviction. "Do you really not know who you are?"

Kyla looked at him painfully. "What are you talking about?" she asked. She didn't understand.

Nathaniel furrowed his brow as his eyes fell back to the wall. Something told her he hadn't meant to say that.

"You shouldn't have left Caden," he blurted out suddenly.

Kyla blinked twice and stared at him, lost on what could possibly have provoked him to say that. "*What?*" she finally asked.

He spouted off almost harshly this time, "You shouldn't have come back here."

Kyla pulled back a little, surprised by his tone. "What are you *talking* about?"

Nathaniel looked agitated now, as if he didn't like what he was saying and he had to let himself get angry to be able to say it. "I don't know what's so difficult about that," he muttered.

"Gee, I don't know," Kyla snapped. "Maybe the fact that ten hours ago you tried to *kill* him?"

Nathaniel furrowed his brow. "I did *not* try to kill him!"

She got up off the bed and glared at him accusingly, folding her arms across her chest.

"I didn't!" he insisted. "If I'd tried to kill him, you'd be *burying* him right now!"

It got him slapped across the face, too. Hard.

Kyla's eyes burned into him like lasers as Nathaniel tried to recover from his shock. Saying a thing like that, he should have expected it, but clearly he hadn't.

"Don't you *ever* say anything like that to me again," Kyla threatened him.

He exhaled slowly to keep himself calm, but it didn't look easy for him to let it go. "I'm sorry," he told her. "I'm just being honest here."

"Honest?" Kyla scoffed. "Since when? You haven't been honest with me about a single thing from day one!"

It didn't look easy for him to let that one go, either. "I'm just saying," he spoke slowly, "I didn't try to kill him. He attacked *me* if you didn't notice. I was only defending myself."

"Because he thought you *raped* me!" Kyla screamed at him.

Nathaniel's expression changed. "He told you that?"

"Yes, he told me that!" she exclaimed. "And I couldn't even explain it to him. I couldn't tell him the truth because I hardly knew it myself. And now that I do, I *know* I can't tell him because he'd think I was out of my mind!"

Through her high-pitched ranting, Nathaniel looked concerned, which made Kyla question what she must have looked like.

"*Gah*...this is insane!"she ranted. "I'm lying to my best friend for you now. I'm *lying* to him! Do you have any idea how hard that is for me?"

Nathaniel's voice was monotone. "I wouldn't worry about it," he said. "I'm sure he's lied to you, too."

Kyla's eyes were filled with fire, and she thought seriously about hitting him again. "How *dare* you?" she said in disgust.

Nathaniel didn't apologize. "Did he ever tell you why he left?" he asked her. "Why he didn't bother to call you in...how long was it?"

Kyla laughed in disbelief, but it wasn't an amused laugh. "You really can't let that go, can you?" she asked him. "Tell me, Nathaniel, if you resent him so much, then why do you want me to stay with him?"

"I *don't* want you to stay with him!" he answered a little too strongly and a little too fast. Nathaniel stopped when he realized he was giving himself away. He closed his eyes for a second so he could control himself. "I just need you safe," he said, "and whatever I think of him personally, I know he can protect you when I can't."

Kyla didn't understand. "How could Caden protect me from *Donovan*?" she asked him. "He's only human."

Nathaniel made a face that easily matched her disgust. "Yes, he is. And it might surprise you to know what some humans are capable of."

This wasn't helping her, his speaking so cryptically. Now more than ever, she needed straight answers from him.

"I can't bring him into this," she said. The mere thought of it made her shudder as she remembered the images Donovan had played through her mind on the mountain. "I can't let Donovan hurt him the way he wants to."

Nathaniel's expression was still bitter. "If the two of them were ever brought face to face, it isn't Caden I would worry about in that situation," he told her.

Kyla looked at him like he was crazy. "What is *that* supposed to mean?"

He wasn't going to explain; his face told her that much. "Do you really think I would trust him with you if I didn't know you would be safe with him?" he asked her.

"I don't know," she lied. "Maybe you've already gotten what you wanted out of me and are trying to pass me off to someone else so you don't have to protect me anymore."

That upset him. A lot. Nathaniel kept his mouth shut tight and started breathing harder like he was trying to hold back what he really wanted to say.

"I never *had* to protect you," he told her coldly. "I could have just let him kill you."

Kyla was stunned at the remark. To say she was angry didn't cut it. Defensive didn't either. There really wasn't a single word she could think of that did.

"You want to know what I *had* to do?" Nathaniel asked her. "I *had* to stay away from you. Those were my orders, Kyla. But I didn't listen to them because you meant too much to me. And I would rather have let Donovan kill me than to let him have you."

Nathaniel stopped when he realized what he'd said and he put his hand back to his face. "I'm not sure you know...that you could ever understand what I've given for you," he told her.

Kyla was frozen, so tense she was balling her fists. Conflict tore through her that she couldn't control, pulling her one way and then jerking her back the other until she had no idea what she should actually believe.

Nathaniel looked at her again in a move of blatant vulnerability. "So tell me," he said. "Is that really what you think? Do you really believe I'm just trying to *pass you off?*"

She wanted to tell him she didn't. She wanted to say she was sorry. She wanted to pin him back down on his bed and attack him again, only this time without letting him stop her. But instead, Kyla just shrugged her shoulders and said, "You're the one who's leaving."

She could have sworn she saw a few degrees of color drop from Nathaniel's face.

It hurt her more than it even hurt him, speaking word after word that she didn't mean. But Kyla didn't know how not to. It was self-preservation, her only defense. Call it what she may, she couldn't let it go. And yet at the thought of him actually leaving, knowing this might be the last time she ever saw him and the last chance she might have to tell him the truth, she felt like a vial of acid had just been poured into her stomach. No matter how she tried to beat it into her head that she should want him gone, the only thing she really wanted was to cling to him now and refuse to let him go.

Making his way slowly across the room and back over to where she stood, Nathaniel looked into her deeply.

She didn't know if he saw the truth in her eyes. Part of her wanted him to and part of her was terrified of it, but whether he did or not, she knew he wasn't lying in what he said to her next.

"Kyla, I don't want to leave you. Whether you believe me or not, that's the last thing I want."

Her eyes softened at his sudden transparency, but she didn't want to let him in. She had to stay cold, but she also knew she couldn't let him leave like this or she would never forgive herself.

"Nathaniel…"

She didn't get the chance to finish. From outside, they both heard a car pull into the driveway of the mansion. Nathaniel's head snapped up at the sound of it and he darted smoothly to the window, cursing under his breath when he saw who was out there.

"It's my uncle," he said, grabbing his shirt from off the floor and slipping it over his head. "We have to go."

Kyla picked up her jacket and started for the door, but he stopped her. "This way," he said, motioning for her to join him at the window.

The two of them stayed back behind the dark tapestry curtains, peering out at the venom red SRT 10 Viper that had pulled into the driveway. Its silver racing stripes gleamed against the sunlight that beat down on the hood, taunting Kyla in their pristine glory. Her mouth fell open as she watched the balding fifty-year-old man she assumed to be Nathaniel's uncle and his estate caretaker, Miguel, emerge from the vehicle; but she quickly forced it shut again and shoved away her envy. This was hardly the time for drooling over extremely fast cars owned by extremely wealthy men. She could do that later. For now, Nathaniel was pulling her out the window and onto the balcony off of his bedroom.

Waiting until his uncle and Miguel were inside and had closed the massive double-doors at the entrance behind them, Nathaniel took Kyla's hand and helped her out onto the balcony.

It was small and guarded by an intricate wrought-iron railing. It barely fit the two of them, but that hardly mattered since Nathaniel quickly scaled the railing and swung himself over the edge of it the second he set foot out there.

Kyla gasped and sprang forward, looking down at him in shock where he'd landed soundly on his feet. There were cement steps below the balcony that led to the driveway, and she wasn't about to attempt jumping down on them. She'd break her ankle for sure. So when Nathaniel turned back to her and motioned for her to climb over the rail, she looked at him like he was out of his mind.

"You're kidding, right?" she said.

He held out his hand and motioned for her again. "Just climb over," he said. "I'll help you down."

She looked back into the bedroom and frowned. She knew she would never be able to get through the house without being seen, so she scowled and straddled the railing instead. "This is unbelievable," she muttered under her breath. Looking down at Nathaniel, she added, "You drop me and I'll kill you."

Nathaniel gave her a smirk. "Please," he said.

Kyla bit her lip and grabbed onto the bars from the outside, lowering herself as best she could, but also knowing she wouldn't be able to hold on for long. As strong as her legs were from all the running she did, her arm strength was practically nonexistent. Fortunately it didn't matter, because as soon as her grip started to weaken, Nathaniel placed his hands beneath her feet and let them act as a stepping block for her.

"Let go," he told her.

Kyla thought about arguing, but decided against it, figuring she had better choose her battles right now. Letting go of the bars, she braced herself for the impact, but instead Nathaniel caught her by the waist and set her softly on the ground.

She flashed him a wide-eyed look, but he didn't waste a second. He took her by the hand and ran with her along the edge of the house, out across Falcon's Rest and into the woods across the street.

Kyla had to hurry to keep up with him. She still glanced over her shoulder every once in a while, certain that his uncle or the caretaker would spot them. But they made it to cover before anyone did.

When they made it into the trees, she looked up at Nathaniel and smiled in relief, feeling somehow like they'd just achieved some sort of victory. But when she saw the sadness in his face that he was trying to hide, her smile sank and her heart along with it.

She wasn't ready for this.

Nathaniel reached carefully for her hand and slid his fingers in between hers. It was a simple gesture, one that from the outside might not seem very significant, but it did something to her that hit straight at her heart.

She wanted to tell him to stop before he spoke another word, thinking that maybe if he didn't say it then he wouldn't have to do it; but Kyla knew in the end that he wouldn't change his mind.

Squeezing her hand gently, he told her with all conviction, "I *will* come back for you, Kyla James..." She held her breath as he held her hand, aching at the thought of him letting it go. "...and heaven help anyone who tries to stop me."

It took a moment for her to find her breath again. She believed what she saw in Nathaniel's eyes, though their truth was almost too much for her to bear. But even still, when he set her hand back at her side and turned away from her to leave, she felt something lurch up inside of her that she couldn't explain.

She couldn't help but feel that he might be wrong about this.

*C*aden marched across the backyard and into the house, cold and determined and mad as hell. He knew it wasn't his little sister he was mad at, that his frustration with Alexa in this instance was probably unmerited, but right now he didn't care. Too much had been bottled up inside of him, and taking a few shots at Nathaniel Blake last night hadn't done enough to ease that. Not hardly. Caden doubted anything would, short of Nathaniel's death. But considering how well his attempt at that *hadn't* gone last night, he had been forced to settle on something a little less rash and a lot more effective: Finding out the truth.

Throwing open the glass-paneled French doors that opened to his parents' living room, Caden asked his mother without missing a beat, "Where's Alexa?"

Melissa Howell looked up from where she was attempting to wrestle Jackson and Jaime into their chairs at the kitchen table. "Well, don't you sound grumpy?" she asked in her drippy-sweet Southern drawl. Looking at him a little more closely, she added, "You don't look like you slept a wink."

"Imagine that," he grumbled under his breath. Melissa went back to wrangling Jaime into his booster chair and Caden fidgeted impatiently. "Where is she, Mom?" he asked again.

384

Melissa sighed. "I don't know, sweetie. She's probably in her room. Why?"

Caden didn't stick around to answer her. He didn't have the patience to explain himself right now. Crossing the living room, he marched down the hallway with intent, not even bothering to knock on Alexa's door before he threw it open.

That in itself wasn't like him. Caden had always respected his sister, always used discretion and walked on eggshells around her. But he was done playing cautious and worrying about her feelings. There was only one thing that concerned him right now, and it was not whether or not he upset her.

Alexa was sitting in her window seat. She didn't look up when her brother came in or acknowledge him at all.

Caden shut the door behind him and stood there with his arms folded. "I want to know everything," he told her.

The corners of Alexa's mouth tightened, but she didn't turn to look at him.

"I want to know what you've seen," he said. "All of it." Caden stopped for a second to let her respond, but she didn't. "I'm serious, Lex. I'm not messing around here."

He was met again by silence and about ready to hit something. He didn't have time for this.

"Alexa!" Caden snapped harshly enough that she finally responded.

"I can't do that," she told him. She kept her eyes on the window.

Caden tensed his jaw. "Why not?"

"It isn't time," she said.

Caden closed his eyes, fighting off the urge to cuss out his eight-year-old sister. "Make it time," he told her through gritted teeth, "or I'm gonna do something stupider than I already have."

That caught her attention. Looking up in alarm, Alexa asked him, "What did you do?" She seemed afraid.

Caden jutted out his chin, trying to appear confident when he really just felt guilty; not because he regretted what he did, but because he knew it was an idiot move to begin with. "I attacked him," he told her.

Alexa stared at him blankly. It took a second for that to sink in, but when it finally did, he saw the blood fall from her face. "You attacked...Nathaniel?"

He felt defensive at her tone. "He hurt her, Lex! He tried...he..." Caden couldn't bring himself to explain. He didn't want to say the words because he didn't want to have to admit them, and he also knew this wasn't a thing he should be telling a little girl. Sometimes he forgot how young his sister was since she never acted her age.

Alexa looked confused. "You saw him hurt her?"

"He was right there when I found her," Caden insisted. "He was freaking on top of her! And she was so beat up..." He swallowed hard, not wanting to remember. "I've never seen her so messed up before."

Alexa looked terrified. Caden didn't know why.

"Kyla said he didn't do it," he went on, "but I think he did something to screw with her head."

The blood drained even further from Alexa's face. "No..."

He didn't like the sound of that. "What?" he asked her irritably.

Alexa shook her head. "You didn't..."

"Yes, I did!" he snapped. "Now would you please tell me what's going on?"

Alexa looked nervous, paranoid even. "Caden, you have to listen to me," she said.

"No," he replied stubbornly.

That surprised her. "No" wasn't a word that Alexa heard very often from her brother.

"Not until you tell me the truth," he said.

"Caden..."

He wasn't about to bend on his ultimatum. "I'm not gonna listen to you until..."

"Caden!" Alexa raised her voice to him.

He stopped and stared at her. He had never heard his sister raise her voice over anything.

"You have to listen to me!" she re-emphasized.

Caden was worried enough by her tone that he decided to shut up and stop arguing with her. He stood there staunchly, waiting for her to say whatever she needed to say, but he wasn't sure he would want to hear it.

"Nathaniel isn't the one who hurt her," Alexa said.

Nausea hit him on her words. As much as Caden had denied the prodding feeling he'd had all night as he'd pieced together the details of what had happened, as much as Kyla had insisted exactly that (and in his stubbornness he'd refused to listen to her) the truth of this possibility was finally able to reach him.

"But I saw..."

Alexa cut him off. "He didn't do it. And I know you want me to tell you who did, but I can't. You have to trust me, Caden. You have to stay away from this. Don't ask any more questions or more people will get hurt."

"Stay away?" he all but shouted at her. "How am I supposed to stay away from this? She's my best friend! What if he tries to hurt her again? What am I supposed to do then, just sit back and watch?"

"He didn't," Alexa insisted.

Caden tensed his jaw. "How do you know that?"

She hesitated. There was something she wasn't telling him; a secret she was keeping for Nathaniel. Caden wasn't sure anything could have upset him more.

"Alexa, you're my sister for God's sake!" he yelled at her, not even caring anymore if anyone heard him. "Tell me the truth!"

He felt so desperate, so helpless, so betrayed...Caden didn't know what he might do to get the truth out of her if she stayed quiet much longer. Fortunately for both of them, Alexa decided to speak.

"There are some forces that can't be stopped," she told him, "and others that can, but only at the highest cost."

"What are you talking about?" he asked her.

"I'm talking about what's behind all this," she said. "The thing that brought Nathaniel and Kyla together."

Caden flinched at the suggestion and balled his fists up at his sides. He wanted to call her a liar, but there was no point in that. He already knew she wasn't lying.

"So which is it with them?" he asked tensely. "Stoppable or not?"

Alexa wouldn't meet his eyes. "I don't know," she told him, casting her gaze cast back through her bedroom window.

This time, Caden couldn't tell if she was lying.

Chapter 25

"...Aria."

Sitting on a bench off a busy street in London, Caleb Holcomb took a sip of his espresso and made a face. He looked back at the man with the cart he'd just bought it off of and then chucked the whole thing into a nearby trashcan. Caleb stood up off the bench and told himself he needed to stop procrastinating and get home. He just really didn't want to. The place was so empty and bleak now, and he knew the sooner he went back there, the sooner he would have to be on watch with Ethan.

Caleb grimaced again, both at the lingering taste of burnt espresso and the thought of another night on watch at the tower.

Since Nathaniel left, everything had been so mind-numbingly uneventful here that Caleb wasn't sure how much longer he'd be able to handle it. He couldn't take the monotonous watches with Ethan, Justin's ever-cocky attitude and that drab, useless flat he came back to every morning. He hadn't even been able to see Samantha again since that day at the café, not even at half-glance by coincidence.

Caleb would be lying if he said he hadn't gone out of his way to pass several of the places she was known to frequent; *Apostrophe*, her favorite coffee place on Baker Street, the Italian Gardens at Hyde Park where she liked to sit and watch the fountains. He'd even taken to meandering around the campus on the off-chance that she might be drawn there. But Samantha hadn't been at any of those places; not once. It was almost as if she had disappeared.

Caleb knew there was still a connection between her, her sorority and Donovan, something deeper than the narrow-minded view of the Resitore on what the Coven was really up to. It might not be as direct as they'd thought, but he could feel it. Every time he was with her he had felt it, the deeper power Samantha was tied to. And he saw it in the eyes of the other girls as well, especially the bitchy blonde named Mara. They all had that same slanted look he could spot from a mile away, which told him so much more than any physical evidence could; more even than the strange symbol they wore on the medallions around their necks.

Caleb's intuition was of far greater value than these, and that was why he was frustrated; because Seth didn't recognize it. His leader didn't trust him and he knew it, which made it all the more frustrating that he was bound by his orders, forced to listen to the perpetually flawed reasoning Seth gave.

So what if Samantha and her sorority witch sisters were up to something? That didn't mean it had anything to do with them. And so what if that necklace of hers, that symbol they wore, *could* be tied to some mysterious coven running deep underground at Oxford? Apparently that wasn't conducive to their purpose here, and it didn't concern the Resitore.

Caleb sneered at Seth's logic, hating that he didn't have the pull that Nathaniel did, where he could suggest something to Seth and actually have him listen. But the fact was, he didn't, and he had to accept that. Right or wrong, foolish or not, he knew for the moment Samantha Ross was out of his life.

Caleb sighed and looked out at the street, his eyes falling to a group of twenty-something Americans with cameras and maps who appeared to be looking for the Westminster Abbey. He could have helped them find it, but that would deprive him of watching them bumble around helplessly, entirely unaware of how foolish they looked.

Maybe Caleb was overreacting to this. Maybe he wouldn't be so irritated by Seth's closing the book on this assignment if he just had something else to do. Preferably something better than sitting here watching the pathetic masses of tourists that passed him by. It was just hard for him, putting all of that time and effort into something, only to have it come up as useless in the end. This wasn't what he'd signed on for. When Seth recruited him to the brotherhood, he made it sound like he would be helping to save the world, not being put in time-out in a watchtower, accomplishing next to nothing.

Caleb turned away from the stupid Americans, about to give up and go back to the flat. But then just as he determined nothing was going to happen that day, something actually did. As clearly as if the man walking past him had spoken the words, he heard his leader's voice in his mind, ordering him to a meeting in the cemetery. Sharply. Urgently.

Something had happened.

Caleb didn't waste a second getting down there. This had to be important for them to meet like this before night had even fallen, and whatever was going on, he was anxious and ready to do something about it. Or at least that was what he thought.

The sky was fading to dusk as he arrived. Approaching the three trench-coated figures that stood amidst the oversized headstones, Caleb's initial excitement was quickly replaced with another feeling. He became worried when he saw the expression on Seth's face...and when he saw how Ethan and Justin had fallen silent as they waited for his approach.

"What's going on?" he asked no one in particular.

Nobody answered him.

There was a tension thick in the air that left him unsettled. Whatever this was about, Caleb didn't trust it.

"It's Nathaniel," Seth finally responded. "He may have been compromised."

Caleb felt like he'd just gotten stabbed. "*What*? How?"

His leader's jaw was tight and neither Ethan nor Justin said a word.

"He may not be coming back to London," Seth tried to speak in a detached tone, but it hardly lacked emotion.

Caleb tried to keep himself calm. "*Why?*"

He could see that Seth was more upset than he was letting himself show.

"Is it Donovan?" Caleb tried again. "Did something else happen?"

Seth shot a look at him, and Caleb felt the blood rush from his face when he realized what he'd said.

"Something *else*?"

Caleb's eyes were huge. "Did *something* happen?" he tried to correct himself. But he knew his enunciation wasn't going to get him out of this one.

"Start talking," Seth ordered him. "Right now."

Caleb panicked, knowing he had no choice at that point but to tell him the truth. Keeping valuable information from his leader was one thing, but disobeying a direct order was something he was not going to mess with.

"Nathaniel fought him," Caleb gave in, cringing as he spoke. "Donovan attacked a human to bait him and he didn't have a choice but to intervene."

Seth's eyes burned with fury. It took a moment for him to find the words he was looking for, and even then Caleb wasn't sure he found the ones that he was really thinking. "How could you keep this from me, Caleb?"

"Nathaniel made me promise." He felt so juvenile saying it like that, but he didn't know what to tell him other than the truth.

That was when Justin chose to speak up. "He's gone rogue, Seth. You know the protocol of the brotherhood for a situation like this."

Caleb flashed the newest among them a look. "Are you out of your mind?" he practically shouted. "Nathaniel has *not* gone rogue!"

"Oh really?" Justin challenged. "Then how do you explain his stunt on the mountain? How do you explain the fact that he isn't here?"

Caleb looked to Seth to explain, but his eyes were cast down. Caleb didn't know what Justin was talking about, but he didn't have to ask him.

"He broke the rules, Caleb," Justin happily informed him. "Fighting Donovan would be enough in itself, but jeopardizing every one of us for the sake of a human…"

Caleb's expression changed quickly and he cut him off. "Is she okay?"

Seth looked up slowly and glared at him. "Yes," he sneered. "Thanks to Nathaniel's disregard for every rule we have, I am sure the human girl is fine."

"Why are you so upset about this?" Caleb asked. "Isn't it some major part of our purpose to protect humans from Donovan and all the other evil psychopaths who are like him?"

"Watch it," Seth warned him, but Caleb was too mad to care about propriety.

"Protect them, yes," Seth agreed. "But we *never* cross that line, and this is exactly why."

"Nathaniel hasn't crossed any lines!" Caleb shouted. "He just saved a girl's *life*!"

Seth's anger was burning now, to a degree that his face was actually getting red. "This isn't like what you have dealt with on your assignments, Caleb. Nathaniel isn't keeping himself emotionally detached."

Caleb pressed his lips together, wishing he could throw it at Seth how naïve he was to assume he hadn't done the same thing. But Caleb knew he couldn't do that and not have it end in disaster.

"He compromised everything," Seth mumbled. "Everything."

Caleb watched his leader in awe as he listened to him. He was completely losing it. Every one of them could see it, but none of them addressed it, and as Seth paced back and forth, he was all but ripping his hair out.

"Don't you understand?" Seth asked. "Donovan knew we were coming. He knows our strategies before we implement them. He was *waiting* for Nathaniel to fall into this trap!"

"How?" Caleb asked. It didn't add up.

"I don't *know* how!" Seth answered through clenched teeth. "But I have my suspicions…and I am *going* to find out."

Caleb felt lost. He couldn't determine if Seth was wigging out over Nathaniel fighting Donovan or over some mystery informant who may or may not have disclosed this information to him. He wished Ethan would get a backbone for once and help him out here, because he did not know how to deal with this. Seth was clearly not in his right mind, and this smug piece of crap, Justin wasn't about to help him fix it. All he was doing was making it worse.

Caleb watched dumbfounded and speechless as their leader turned and left them in the cemetery still waiting to be dismissed. Seth didn't even bring an end to the meeting, he just disappeared.

As soon as he was gone, Caleb exchanged a worried look with Ethan, but avoided Justin's gaze.

This was bad. Really bad.

*I*t was muggy in London when Nathaniel returned, overcast and drizzling in the most miserable kind of way. It did a number on his mind, arriving in the day when his body was telling him it was supposed to be night. The time change was something he was going to have to get used to.

Landing carefully on the Hampstead Heath Bridge, (which he made sure was absent of meandering tourists) Nathaniel frowned to himself when he realized how human he was beginning to sound, even if only in his head. He shook away the thought and moved out from the trees that canopied him as he transfigured back into the form of a man. No one saw him do it. No one ever did.

Quickly crossing the bridge just as an elderly couple holding hands started to make their way onto it, Nathaniel dropped his eyes to the ground and discreetly left the area. Right now there was only one thing before him, and that was finding Seth. It wouldn't be easy, especially not in the middle of the day like this, but he knew he had to do it.

The interaction between members of the brotherhood was never casual on a personal level. Nathaniel and Caleb were a rare exception in that since their cover required it of them to remain so close. For everyone else, it was uncommon that they ever even saw each other outside their designated protocol, which entailed the meetings Seth called them to and the assignments he placed them on. But getting a hold of those who were placed in charge over them, well, that was another story.

Had it been anyone else looking, they probably wouldn't have been able to find Seth, but Nathaniel had a different sort of discernment than the rest of his brothers. All of the Nephilim could discern in a general sense, the presence of the others of their kind; but Nathaniel's discernment in this (much like his discernment in everything else) was heightened over that of his brothers.

It wasn't so clear that he could tell who was near him, but rather just clear enough that he could feel an overall change in the atmosphere when one of them was close. Nathaniel knew it was a long shot, but if he felt it out and searched enough, there was at least a chance that he might be able to find Seth. And right now, any chance was worth taking when he considered the alternative.

Nathaniel's pace was quick and his stride was long as he made his way to the entrance of Highgate. He didn't glance up at the towering stone pillars that stood as sentries before him, just kept his head down and moved through the dank, familiar tunnel.

An American tourist with a red backpack and a camera snapped pictures up ahead of him as she fumbled her umbrella in the rain, which had just started up again. She was standing just outside the cemetery, her short dark hair in pigtails, and thick-rimmed glasses that kept sliding down her nose and forcing her to push them back up with her index finger. She was awkward and uncoordinated and almost hit Nathaniel with her umbrella when he passed her by, but he didn't miss a step. Apparently the tourist girl found this odd because she stared after him as he walked through the tunnel. Or maybe she was staring at him for another reason. Either way, Nathaniel didn't bother with her. He just needed to get into the cemetery and hope that for some unlikely reason, Seth was somewhere close.

There were a surprising number of tourists out here today, even in the rain, but then it *was* London after all. Precipitation of any sort was just to be expected, and certainly not a thing to hinder the travelers from seeing the historical Highgate Cemetery. It might, however, be enough to keep Seth from calling a meeting here...assuming they hadn't already come and gone.

Nathaniel made a face as he scanned over the moss-covered headstones and the people that wound through them. There wasn't a chance Seth was here anymore. The brothers had no doubt already met last night, and Seth wouldn't risk returning in the day like this; not when he suspected one of his own to have become disloyal to the brotherhood.

Dropping his head, Nathaniel was at a loss for what to do. He could always go back to his and Caleb's flat, but Caleb wouldn't be able to help him right now. Caleb was the last of the brothers that Seth would trust with his location, especially under these circumstances.

Nathaniel's face was still contorted in a grimace when a voice asked from beside him, "Beautiful, isn't it?"

Nathaniel looked up to see the red-backpacked tourist who had almost taken him out with her umbrella a few moments ago.

"I beg your pardon?" he asked.

The girl motioned toward the stone angel with sweeping wings that Nathaniel stood beside. "The statue," she told him.

He glanced at it, unimpressed. Nathaniel had to have seen that statue a thousand times. "Yeah, it's really something," he agreed insincerely.

The girl had her camera hanging from the strap around her neck now. "Sorry about almost hitting you back there," she apologized. "I can kind of be a klutz sometimes."

That, Nathaniel didn't find hard to believe.

"It's fine," he mumbled. He was eyeing a spot up ahead that he might be able to move toward to get away from this girl as she continued to study the statue.

"You know, I think out of everything in this place, this one fascinates me the most."

Nathaniel looked away from his escape route and back at the girl like she was either crazy or stupid. "You're serious?" he asked her. Surely out of everything in Highgate Cemetery, this one simple statue was not that impressive.

"I don't know what it is," the girl shrugged, still studying it in detail. "I guess I've just always been fascinated by angels."

Nathaniel's expression grew tighter. *Leave it alone*, he told himself. But he found himself asking her anyway, "What do you find so fascinating about them?" He tried not to sound defensive and failed at it pretty hard. Either way, the bumbling tourist didn't seem to notice.

"Everything," she sighed. "I mean, just imagine what it would be like…"

Nathaniel wasn't sure what she meant. "What *what* would be like?" he asked her.

She gave him a sweetly naïve smile. "What it would be like to fly."

Nathaniel looked away from her resentfully and fixed his gaze on the statue so he wouldn't have to see her face. This girl didn't have a clue. None of them did. Humans were perpetually blinded by their ignorance, desiring what they could never have and forsaking what they could…what they could so easily have access to if they would only choose it.

"Yeah, really great," Nathaniel mumbled.

The girl kept talking, but he stopped listening after that. Her voice faded quickly to the back of his awareness as he stared at that statue, seeing it now in an entirely new light. A bitter light…a jealous light.

To be fully human, or even fully angel…to be fully *something* and not a half of a being, Nathaniel would have given anything for that. But it was a foolish hope, more naïve than the girl still rambling on beside him.

He was never going to be anything other than what he was.

Suddenly, Nathaniel's head snapped up when something caught his attention. It was the feeling that hit him first, like a cool breeze blowing past his face, despite that there wasn't one out here. He wasn't sure where it came from, or what this compulsion was that it brought along with it, but it quickly forced his eyes away from the angel. Nathaniel didn't know what he was looking for, but he could no more stop himself from looking for it than he could deny what he'd felt.

That was when he saw the woman who stood twenty, maybe thirty feet away from him, cloaked in deep purple velvet with a hood pulled over her head. The cloak had an intricate satin latch at the neck, and her dark brown hair spilled out from inside it, cascading in loose ringlets down her heart-shaped face.

He staggered backwards at the sight of her; particularly at the sight of her eyes, which were so intensely green and piercing that he lost his breath when he saw them.

There was only one thought in Nathaniel's head as he looked on this woman: Her beauty was not natural. The perfection to her every detail, from her silken skin to the iridescent glow that left her strangely illuminated, there was nothing normal-looking about her. And equally as strange, the sight of her was so peculiar and her features so striking that Nathaniel would have expected every eye in the cemetery to be fixed in her direction; yet not a single one was. The only eyes but his that were fixed anywhere were hers...and they were set directly on him.

For a full five seconds their gaze was locked. The woman looked into Nathaniel knowingly as she continued to walk forward, but he thought there was too much grace in the movement for it to be considered as that. It was more floating than walking, if such a thing were possible. Whatever this woman was doing, it left him completely mesmerized. He was hypnotized as he watched her, as if placed under some kind of spell. And then without another glance or gesture, the beautiful woman turned away from him and disappeared through the headstones.

Nathaniel kept his eyes set on her as she left. He didn't hesitate, just moved forward on compulsion and followed her through the cemetery, not even bothering to say goodbye to the ever-chatty tourist girl who was still talking beside him about God only knew what. Logically he knew it was a mistake to follow this woman, that she was likely set there as a trap for him. She might even be one of the sorority witches that he suspected of targeting Caleb, but that still didn't stop his feet from taking him to her.

Ducking in and out of the headstones and statues that spotted the area around him, Nathaniel moved in the direction that the woman had gone. Rational thought hadn't fully kicked in for him yet, and what little actually had wasn't telling him what it needed to. Instead of telling him to turn on his heels and run in the opposite direction, it was trying to make him justify this foolish endeavor by convincing him he needed to find out what was going on here, if someone was following him or baiting him in any way. But it wasn't his rationale that kept Nathaniel moving forward; it was that hypnotic trance that held him, that even now was taking over every one of his senses.

Picking up his pace, he followed the woman down a dirt path lined with tiny white flowers; the one that wound through the above-ground tombs known as the "Circle of Lebanon." Then suddenly, so suddenly it jolted him, the woman stopped on the path and turned around to face him.

Nathaniel froze as he looked at her. He was instantly alarmed by the expression on her face and the fierceness to her eyes, but he didn't have time to speak before she spoke to him first.

"You are in danger," she told him.

Nathaniel was hit with a chill on her words, and immediately he knew this woman was not a witch. What he felt in her presence, he had only ever felt before in trace amounts. He recognized it, though, even in the intensity of its concentration, but he didn't understand why it was so strong around her.

"Who are you?" he asked her abruptly.

The woman didn't answer his question. "Everything has changed, Nathaniel," she told him instead. "You are no longer safe in London."

Nathaniel tensed up when she said his name. It should have surprised him more to hear her say it like that, but he felt it as he watched her, even from a distance; he felt that she already knew him.

"Who *are* you?" Nathaniel asked her more firmly, but again he was ignored.

The woman looked nervous, like she shouldn't be talking to him. "There is more at stake than you know," she told him. "More than any of you could possibly realize."

She didn't mention them by name, but somehow Nathaniel knew she was talking about his brothers, and as soon as that clicked, he immediately felt threatened.

"I will ask you one more time," he spoke to her slow and measured. "Who *are* you?"

The woman paused long enough to look at him. "My name is Aria," she finally told him. "And I have been sent here to help you."

Watching her eyes move back and forth, Nathaniel thought there was something off about this woman; this...*Aria*. She didn't seem to be looking at what was physically around them, but rather at something that wasn't, almost as if she were looking into an entirely different place.

"If you were sent to me," Nathaniel said, "then why are you acting like you're not supposed to be here?"

Aria stayed on his eyes after that, her expression completely unreadable. She was difficult for Nathaniel to see into, if not impossible, because her face didn't match with normal human expressions.

"Because I'm not," she told him bluntly.

Nathaniel felt another chill rush over him, and it certainly wasn't a result of the muggy rain. Studying her intently, he probed this woman's spirit, and as he did, the realization of what Aria was fell over him hard.

Everything did a one-eighty for him then as the pieces fell into place. He began to see what was happening, what had *been* happening from the start of this; and the magnitude of that realization was almost too much for him to take.

"Why have you come to me?"Nathaniel asked her. He was unable to keep the tremor out of his voice. "When do our kinds ever cross paths?"

Aria's look was firm. "When it becomes necessary," she said.

Nathaniel's voice was cutting. "And what would one like you have to do with any of this?" he snapped. "What would an *angel* have to do with what is happening here?"

Aria glared at him coldly, as close to offended as he imagined this one could look, but still she was calm as she spoke. "Do you really believe it was coincidence that brought you to Woodland Park?" she asked him.

Nathaniel tensed his shoulders.

"Do you really think it was chance that brought this girl into your life?"

Nathaniel didn't like what Aria knew, almost as much as he didn't like what she was suggesting; and not only because her words sounded so much like his own. His mind raced frantically, trying to understand what this could mean.

"Do you really believe that any of this," she asked him, "that any single part of this has happened by mistake?"

Nathaniel kept his jaw set. "What are you saying? That *you* made this happen?"

The woman (who really wasn't a woman at all) fell silent.

"*Why?*" he sneered at her.

Aria didn't answer him directly, but her eyes burned into him with conviction. "To fight for the future, you must go back to your past. You cannot keep hiding from it and expect to stay alive. If you don't stop running, you will never find the key that will win this battle, and then everything you have fought for, everything you have done will be completely in vain."

The angel wasn't being clear, and very intentionally so, but Nathaniel could feel the power on the words she was speaking. That alone was enough to push his anger to a whole new level.

It would be a gross under-exaggeration to say he didn't like this. The thought of going back to anything about his life before, even if only to remember, it sickened him...weakened him. Nathaniel knew he couldn't do it.

"What does that have to do with the battle?" he demanded.

Aria looked him straight on. "That *is* the battle. You cannot separate them, one from the other."

Nathaniel shifted uncomfortably. He didn't like this at all.

"The battle is like a tree," Aria explained. "Its branches grow off of one another, reaching and extending beyond what you can see. They grow and grow as you stand at its base, trying to cut it down with an axe. But you can't kill the tree with an axe, Nathaniel. You can't cut it off at the base.

To kill a tree, you have to find the root. Only then can it fully be destroyed."

He was glaring at her now. "And I'm supposed to know what that means?"

"Find the root, Nathaniel," she said. "It is there you will find the key. And do not wait for Seth to guide you in this. His interests are not your own."

Before Nathaniel could ask her what she was talking about, Aria flashed her eyes up behind him sharply enough that he turned to see if someone was coming. But as soon as he turned back to her, she was gone, leaving him with nothing but a memory of her presence and a disturbing question about his leader lingering in his mind.

Nathaniel could imagine what this angel had meant about Seth's interests not being his own, at least in a general sense. That much had been made clear on their last encounter on the mountain, though what Aria specifically meant, he couldn't be certain. What disturbed Nathaniel about it was that she knew even that much. What disturbed him was that she had come to him at all.

Stepping forward to leave the tomb-laden "Circle of Lebanon," Nathaniel began to move in the direction he had come. But then he heard a noise behind him and stopped in his tracks. Spinning around sharply, he faced the frightened-looking girl who had followed him here.

It was the American. He should have known.

The girl was soaking wet now, and appeared to have had an unfortunate mishap with her umbrella in the last few minutes since he'd seen her. She looked like a deer caught in a pair of headlights when he snapped at her, "What do you want?" Nathaniel's voice had lost its edge of dry politeness, and the girl looked genuinely afraid.

Inching cautiously forward, she tripped over her words and very nearly her own feet. "I'm sorry," she apologized. "You just left so fast and I...I saw you walking back here like you were following someone, but when I looked, there wasn't anyone here and..."

Nathaniel cut her off mid-ramble. "I wasn't following anyone."

The tourist girl nodded, eager to agree with anything he said right now if it meant that she could get away from him. She glanced around her nervously and Nathaniel almost felt bad for frightening her. Almost.

"I apologize for leaving so rudely before," he told her. "Now if you don't mind, I really must be going."

"Of course," she agreed quickly.

He turned to leave, thinking the girl would high-tail it in the opposite direction, but instead she called out to him, "Wait!"

Confused and slightly irritated, Nathaniel turned back to look at her. "Yes?" he asked.

The girl bent down onto the path, fumbling her backpack, her camera and her now-broken umbrella as she picked up a small metal object that had fallen beneath a tree root that was protruding from the ground. The root was old, moss-covered and twisted; not unlike everything else in this cemetery. But it wasn't this that held Nathaniel's attention.

It was the two-inch brass key that the girl held in her hand.

"You dropped this," she told him, holding the key out so he would take it.

Nathaniel hesitated, looking at her warily; then he took a step forward and let her drop it into his palm. It was simple by design, old and rusted like he would expect of any key that looked like that. But holding it now, he knew there was nothing simple about it.

His eyes glanced down to the root from which the girl had pulled it, mumbling under his breath, "Little obvious, Aria, don't you think?"

The American tilted her head in confusion. "Who's Aria?"

Nathaniel ignored her, continuing to stare down at the brass object in his hand. This could mean anything, he realized, though he didn't like the thought. Looking back up, he hoped in vain that he might see Aria approaching him again, coming back to explain what this was supposed to mean, but his eyes only fell on a very confused-looking tourist he had no time to deal with any longer. Pocketing the key, Nathaniel left without answering her question.

He had to get out of here. He had to find Seth.

*I*t was dark in Rome that night. Seth's eyes were set as he moved thoughtlessly through the alleys and streets, driven by anger and instinct and inhuman rage. But despite the turmoil he felt, he managed on the outside to remain completely calm. He knew what he had come here to do and he was not leaving until that purpose had been accomplished.

Following the instructions of the young Naphil, Shebna, whom he had paid another visit to earlier, he made his way to the Aqueducts in the dark. It didn't take much for Seth to frighten this young one into providing him with Eli's whereabouts, something he was not willing to do when he had attempted to locate him before. The situation wasn't as dire then and he hadn't been nearly desperate enough.

He was desperate enough now.

As Seth approached the Aqueducts, he prepared himself to do whatever it took, knowing that at that point he had nothing to lose. He didn't have a reason to show discretion or adhere to the rules and he wasn't about to hold back. Failure was not an acceptable outcome...not this time.

Shebna had told him, however reluctantly, that they had a meeting tonight, and that Eli typically stayed behind after everyone left. He had also alluded to Eli having a difficult time coping with what was required of the Nephilim of the Resitore...nothing that went against Seth's theories about him. Due to his being the newest inducted member, and due to his recent defection from Donovan's league, Shebna told him that Eli often dealt with extreme mental trauma.

Apparently it took him longer than the others to adjust to a change in setting or environment, and to shift in and out of a role of humanity. He required time alone to set his mind straight, and this was why Seth approached the Aqueducts now and not before. He had waited for the others to leave so that he could meet with Eli alone, so that none could interfere with what he knew must take place.

As Seth moved closer, he saw the one he assumed to be Eli sitting on the ground with his back against a towering stone arch. His head was down and his hand was on his brow, and he looked upset, to say the least. Seth approached him slowly, and as soon as Eli saw him, he scrambled to his feet.

"Who are you?" he asked.

Seth could see that he was only a boy, maybe a year or two older than Nathaniel, with dark curly hair and frightened eyes. Seth remained somber and quiet as he stared forward, a distinct mark of rage in his countenance that caused Eli to back up from him.

"I know what you are doing," Seth told him. "I know what you have done."

"I don't know what you are talking about," Eli rambled quickly. "I don't even know who you are."

Seth grabbed him with force and slammed him face first into the stone of the Aqueducts.

"Do *not* lie to me!"

Eli was shaking as he spun again to face him. "Who *are* you?" his voice trembled. "What do you want from me?"

Seth nailed him in the face with an iron fist, causing him to spit up blood. "Do not think me a fool," he breathed. "You may be able to deceive Malachi and Samuel and the lesser ones who follow them, but you have not deceived me. I know your defection was a lie," he spoke viciously, "that all you have done has been rooted in the deception Donovan takes in like oxygen. I know you have compromised us all by telling him the location of the London faction, and I swear to you, if you do not start talking, I am going to make you beg me for death."

"No..." Eli tried to deny it, but Seth didn't give him the chance.

Grabbing him with both hands, he threw him to the ground, and when Eli attempted to crawl away, Seth took his foot and planted it at the center of his back, kicking him down again and standing above him as he pinned him to the ground.

Setting his foot on Eli's throat, he said, "I am going to give you one chance to tell me the truth before I crush your windpipe."

Eli's eyes were thick with fear. "I already *told* you..." he tried to say.

Seth felt the heat of his anger surge, but instead of bringing his foot down harder on the boy's neck, he grabbed him by his ankle and swung him around like a mace, hurling him through the air so his body cracked into a mid-level wall of an aqueduct. The stone crumbled on the impact and Eli's body landed hard.

He was bleeding badly by that point, but Seth wasn't fazed. Nor was he finished.

Opening his wings, he flew up onto the Aqueducts and positioned himself above Eli as he tried to stand. Cursing Seth beneath his breath, Eli told him, "You're crazy," to which Seth responded by grabbing Eli's hair, holding his head up and screaming into his ear.

"What have you told him?!"

Eli clenched his teeth together, his breath coming out far too quickly. He had obviously learned enough of Seth by that point to know reasoning with him was not going to get him anywhere. So he kept his mouth shut.

"You compromised our location," Seth accused him. "You compromised Nathaniel." The reality of it all was spinning faster in his mind.

"You're wrong," Eli snarled.

Seth kicked him in the stomach so his body flipped upright again, then he grabbed him by the throat and began to choke him, holding him up so that his feet didn't even touch the ground.

"What is his plan, Eli? What is Donovan's plan?"

Eli was choking, squirming, trying to break free from Seth's hold, but all to no avail. It was obvious to Seth that this one was one of the Nephilim whose abilities lay more in the realm of mental power than physical strength. Eli was no match for him.

"I know you are the informant," Seth told him. "I know you told Donovan everything…that this is all a maneuver to destroy us from the inside out."

Eli gargled beneath his grip, trying to suck in oxygen.

"I know that you know his plan," Seth said. His fury was growing at an exponential rate, and with every second that passed, Eli came one second closer to choking to death. But just before he did, he burst into Naphil form with his last bit of strength and flew onto the top of the Aqueducts, kneeling on the stone and clutching at his throat, gasping in an attempt to fill his lungs with air.

Seth flew up meet him there, landing in front of Eli so they were again face to face. He pulled his dagger from the sheath that was strapped to his back and gave Eli a taunting look, provoking him to try something. What happened next, however, Seth did not see coming.

He first noticed Eli's breathing pattern shift, which shouldn't have been all that noteworthy given the level of stress he was under. But there was something about it that didn't feel right. He looked panicked, his eyes darting like a lizard's all around him, as if he were trying to find a way he could escape the crazed Naphil who was about to kill him.

Like a cornered animal. Like someone who was guilty.

"Leave," Eli said. Seth stopped when he heard the inflection in his voice. It was different than it had been before. "You are not welcome here, Seth."

Seth froze in his tracks. "How do you know my name?"

Eli's breathing pattern shifted again, as did his voice. "You think I don't know who you are?" he asked mockingly. "You think I can't *see* you?"

Eli's eyes darted up and down, and then in his own voice he begged pleadingly, "Don't…you can't…please. Don't do this."

Seth was disturbed, to say the least, and not entirely sure of what he was witnessing. He would call it schizophrenia, if he believed such a thing existed, but he knew enough to know that this particular mental illness was nothing more than the medical explanation for a spiritual phenomenon. It made sense that Eli would succumb to this, considering the level of darkness he had undoubtedly partaken in, but there was one small problem with that theory: Nephilim did not become possessed by demons.

There were lines that were drawn between their worlds, and those lines were never crossed. That was why they needed the humans, both the Nephilim who strove for right and those that lived for the dark. But right now, Seth wasn't sure what was happening. Against everything he knew was possible, he watched that line blur before his eyes as Eli's countenance changed yet again.

Seth spoke to him then without speaking to him at all, as if he could see the very demon on his back. "Who are you?" he demanded. "What is your name?"

Eli started choking in deep, throaty laughter and Seth held his knife up to threaten him. "Your name," he said. "Now."

The demon that had come over Eli in such a way as to shift even his countenance spoke to him fiercely. "My name is Talon," it said. "But I am not alone."

Seth's gaze was set. "You have no place here, Talon."

The demon chortled. "Do not speak to me as one with authority. You know you can do nothing to me."

Seth glared into the eyes of the creature before him.

"I know who you are, Seth," it used Eli's vocal chords to taunt him. "I know what you are afraid of."

Seth stepped forward and Eli flinched in fear, though his eyes didn't match his outward demeanor.

"You do not know me," Seth growled.

A devious smirk appeared on Eli's face, along with beads of sweat on his forehead.

"Oh, but I do," Talon spoke again. "I know what you did. I know what it is that haunts you."

Quicker than he knew what was hitting him, Seth was flooded with recall of a memory he had tried for eleven years to forget. The image of a forest…of a trail…of a boy hiding in a hollow tree and a woman with strawberry blonde hair and blood at her throat. Motionless. Lifeless. Screaming in her silence that he had been too late.

Grabbing Eli by the shoulders, Seth held his blade up to kill him, if for no other reason than to keep this demon from speaking another word. But just before he could, he heard a voice sound to him from below the Aqueducts.

"Seth…release him."

Seth's eyes narrowed when he recognized Malachi's voice. Turning sharply, he flashed him a look, still not letting go of Eli. "Are you in on this, too, Malachi?"

408

"You are testing my patience," said the white-haired Naphil who stood on the ground beneath him. "Release him, come down here to me now or suffer the consequences."

Seth debated direct disobedience, but decided instead to listen to the one who was still technically his superior. When he flew to the base of the Aqueducts to stand before Malachi, Seth crouched down as he landed and then rose again, his eyes burning fiercely with anger.

Eli was still at the top of the Aqueducts, clawing at his head, talking to himself and shaking uncontrollably. Seth ignored the highly disturbed Naphil and focused instead on his leader.

"You knew this would happen," he accused Malachi. "You had to have seen that there would be a human girl."

Malachi cocked his head to one side, trying to read him. "What human girl?"

"Don't lie to me, Malachi," Seth snarled. "I know the sight you hold."

Seth was convinced as he made the accusation that he was right, but when he looked into the withered face before him, his doubt began to edge to the surface, replacing his confidence in the statement he'd just made. Was it really possible that Malachi hadn't seen this?

"*What* human?" Malachi reiterated.

Seth started breathing harder. "I have done everything to protect Nathaniel from this," he muttered to himself, unwilling to admit the possibility. *"Everything..."* His surroundings were beginning to blur and his senses distorting into a haze without color. The more he focused in on any one thing, the less sense it made to him...the less sense any of this made.

Malachi looked disturbed. "Tell me what has happened," he said.

Seth could feel his own stance being weakened as the thoughts filled his mind of the way he'd left Nathaniel. The look on his face, the determination in his eyes...the displaced sense of purpose that had blinded him to this trap. It was exactly what Donovan wanted; it had to be. It was why he had attacked the girl, setting Nathaniel in a position where he would have to fight to defend her, drawing out of him emotions that Nathaniel had never known, that he didn't have the experience to know how to control.

Nathaniel did not know how dangerous it was for him to become entangled with a human. Maybe he knew it in his head, but he didn't understand what could be altered as a result. Even if he thought he knew the cost, he didn't; because to feel the cost of everything, you had to have something to lose.

Nathaniel had never known that.

Seth's voice was quiet now, broken. "I told you he wasn't ready, Malachi. Why did you not trust me?"

Somewhere above them, Eli was yelping like a dog in pain, but neither of them looked up to see why.

"Who is this girl?" Malachi asked. "And how exactly has Nathaniel become involved with her?"

Seth shook his head. "I don't know. I don't know what he has done...just that he claims her to be one of the awakened."

Malachi's countenance shifted. "They have a presence there? In Manitou Springs?"

"He insists they do," Seth grimaced.

"You don't believe him," Malachi said.

"No, I don't."

Malachi studied him before he spoke again, ignoring the deranged mutterings from atop the Aqueducts the whole while. "You cannot shelter him any longer in hopes of keeping him from making your mistakes."

The blood dropped from Seth's face at what Malachi was suggesting. "*Don't...*" he warned him.

Malachi didn't stop. "You have to let it go, Seth. You have to let *her* go."

Seth knew he wasn't talking about the girl. Feeling a fire flare up in him that he feared he wouldn't be able to control, he breathed to him heatedly, "Malachi..."

"Rachel is gone," Malachi cut him off. "You have to accept that you cannot change the past."

Seth was all but murderous in his tone. "Do *not* speak her name..." he threatened.

410

Malachi looked into him with sorrow behind his eyes. "You must release your anger, my son. If you don't, I fear it will destroy you."

Seth could feel heat on his face where his anger continued to burn. "He took everything from me, Malachi," his voice shook as he spoke. "He took everything..."

Malachi continued in his calm. "You have to let it go, Seth. If your own life doesn't matter to you enough, then you need to do it for those of the brotherhood who are in your charge." He paused to ensure that his words would sink in. "You need to do it for Nathaniel...for the promise you made his mother."

Seth's entire body quavered. "Don't you understand? Donovan will not stop until he has him, until he has everything. He won't stop until he has destroyed the brotherhood and taken all that I have." Seth pointed up at Eli, who was still cowering at the top of the Aqueducts. "And because of *that* worthless traitor you are protecting, you are surrendering to this evil!"

Malachi frowned, but Seth didn't stop.

"This is going to cost you blood, Malachi..."

That was the end of Malachi's patience. "Get in line," he warned Seth, "or I will be forced to take drastic measures. We cannot afford this sort of reckless behavior when there is a war coming."

Seth scoffed at the decrepit Naphil before him who used to stand as a pillar of strength. "You don't even see it, do you?" Seth shook his head, pitying Malachi's ignorance. "The war has already begun."

Epilogue

I t was dark as Donovan approached the nightclub in downtown London his source had directed him to. A strange place, to be sure, but no stranger than the rest of this city. The clouds hung thick tonight, masking any potential the stars had for shining through. They usually did here.

Donovan fit into this crowd well, enough that his approach was unquestioned. Heavy liner on his eyes, his jet black hair hanging down in his face, and in place of the trench coat he normally wore, he donned a pair of tight black leather pants and a white v-neck shirt with a chain tucked down inside of it.

Watching the entrance of the club and a group of young ladies who had obviously been drinking, he saw the girls fall over each other as they stepped onto the street, tripping over their own feet and laughing as if it were the most hilarious thing in the world.

Donovan made a face. Though intoxication did have its benefits when it came to taking advantage of human women, there was far too much about it that he found revolting; such as the complete lack of awareness these girls possessed over how hideous they looked. It was pathetic. Almost as pathetic as their existence.

Stepping casually to the side of the building, Donovan waited for the drunken fools to pass him. He leaned against the wall and hoped he had timed his arrival accurately.

As it turned out, he had.

As soon as the first group of college-aged women turned the corner, another emerged from the entrance of the club. Donovan's attention was immediately drawn to the tall, slender blonde with the skin-tight jeans and spike-heeled boots. She walked confidently, laughing with her friends on each side of her; the one to her right an unfortunate-looking redhead who grinned stupidly and unaware, the one to her left a great deal more attractive and discerning in appearance as she eyed his approach.

Donovan smiled in satisfaction at the sight of them.

"Excuse me, Miss Whitlow?" he said, stepping out in front of them so they would stop.

The blonde seemed startled to hear her own name. "Do I know you?" she asked rudely.

"Not yet," he replied.

The pretty, dark-skinned, discerning one seemed wary of him, and even the redhead gave him a curious look; but it was clear that the blonde called the shots in this trio because neither of them voiced their opinion on the matter.

He had counted on that.

Donovan kept his voice unthreatening. "I was wondering if I might have a minute of your time?" he asked.

The blonde eyed him up and down as if debating whether or not to give in. "Alright," she agreed. She was curious. Donovan could hear it in her voice.

"I don't know, Mara..." the girl on her left interjected.

"It's fine," Mara cut her off. "Get back to the house. I'll meet you there."

Neither the pretty one nor the redhead seemed too eager to go along with this plan, but they seemed even less eager to oppose her. So reluctantly, they left.

"Can I buy you a cup of coffee?" Donovan offered once they were gone.

Mara folded her arms. "I would rather you just tell me what this is about."

He was amused by her impertinence. "Very well," he agreed. He motioned toward the side of the building and she followed him without question, which told him she was either

414

foolishly trusting or naively sure of herself. His guess was the latter.

Mara stopped at the entrance of the alleyway that ran behind the club. She turned and looked at him expectantly with her arms still folded.

"So what exactly is this about?" she asked him. "And for that matter, who are you?"

Donovan was calm, despite her rudeness. "One question at a time, my dear."

She sneered at him in resentment and said, "Very well then. Let's start with you telling me who you are."

Donovan placed a hand by her head on the brick wall behind her, leaning over her daringly and grinning with intent. Her breathing faltered a little at his nearness, and he saw the question in her eyes of whether or not he was going to hurt her. Mara wasn't quite afraid yet, but she was getting there. At the very least, his assuredness seemed to be throwing her off. There was more intrigue behind it than fear, which Donovan would have found strange if he didn't know who this girl was.

From what he had heard of Mara Whitlow, she was not one to scare easily.

Pulling at the long gold chain he had tucked down in his shirt, Donovan let the medallion fall out into view. He dangled it against his fingers and watched her eyes dart to it immediately. Then slowly they came back to him.

"Where did you get that?" Mara asked him. She was startled now, and he could feel her questioning if he might have gotten it from one of her girls.

Donovan eyed the medallion in nonchalance, at the symbol on its face that he'd designed himself. "Why?" he asked her. "Do you like it?"

She narrowed her eyes, knowing that he was teasing her.

"Where did you get it?" she asked him more tensely this time.

He dropped the chain and let it fall against his chest then flashed his eyes fiercely into hers. Mara flinched and pulled back when he did this.

"This symbol is mine," Donovan told her, dropping his playful tone. "Those who wear it are subject to me, and *from* these I expect to be shown the respect I am due."

The girl was on her knees before he'd even finished speaking, kneeling on the cold dirty asphalt in her designer jeans. She kept her head low as she apologized profusely. "Forgive me, my lord," Mara rambled out the words. "I didn't know."

Donovan rolled his eyes and jerked her up off the ground by her arm. "Get up," he told her. "You're only going to draw attention to us, acting like that."

The otherwise pompous and arrogant girl kept her head bowed low. "I'm sorry, my lord," she apologized again. "I just...I wasn't expecting..."

Donovan put a finger beneath her chin and lifted her head so she would look at him. She was practically trembling.

"I know this visit was unannounced," he told her, "and for that I apologize. It was not my intention to frighten you."

"Then what is your intention?" Mara asked him. He quite enjoyed the fear in her eyes, knowing how rare the sight must be.

"I need your help, darling," he answered her. She about melted at the tone he used, and for a moment he thought he might have to catch her.

Staggering a little, she told him, "I am at your disposal, my lord. Ask whatever you want of me; I will give it."

Donovan smiled, pleased with the ideas that were dancing through her twisted little mind. "And I will most certainly take advantage of that," he assured her. "But first, there is someone I must locate. Someone in your charge."

She looked at him curiously. "Who, my lord?"

He dropped his hand from where he'd kept it at her face. "A young lady by the name of Samantha Ross."

Mara's expression shifted to somewhat of a scowl. "Samantha has been demoted," she told him, as if this might somehow change his mind on inquiring of her.

Donovan was curious. "And why is it, may I ask, that she was demoted?"

416

Mara looked agitated, enough that she re-folded her arms. "Direct disobedience to the rules of the sisterhood," she told him. "There was a boy she was seeing that we didn't approve of; someone one of our sisters had a very bad sense about. I ordered Samantha to stay away from him in case he might jeopardize us, but she didn't listen. She claims she fell in love with him…"

Donovan grinned as he said the name, "Caleb Holcomb."

Mara stared at him, obviously caught off guard. "Yes," she verified. "How did you…"

"Like I said, I really must find Samantha. I assure you, your assistance in this matter will not go unrewarded."

Mara's curiosity was getting the best of her. Donovan could see how she was struggling with whether or not to press him for more details.

"I don't know where she is," Mara told him, "but I can find out."

Donovan leaned against the wall patiently, keeping his eyes fixed on her as she pulled a cell phone from her purse and started typing out a text message. In a matter of seconds, her phone blinged with a response. Those "sorority" girls must have known better than to keep her waiting.

Mara dropped her phone back in her purse and looked out into the street, irritated. "Hyde Park," she told him. "Samantha goes there and sits by the fountains when she's feeling particularly sorry for herself."

Donovan took her hand and kissed it dramatically, trying to redirect her eyes back to his face. "My deepest thanks to you, Miss Whitlow."

Mara pressed her lips together, clearly not satisfied.

Donovan knew how to remedy that. "Now where might I find you when I am done with her?" he asked.

Mara's eyes slipped back to him, the corner of her lips turning up in a smile.

Within a matter of minutes, Donovan was moving through Hyde Park without the slightest precaution. The darkness was hardly a reason for him to hesitate. It was his assurance, his source, his shield. And the fact that he found Samantha

Ross here in the grasp of its vulnerability only made him feel that much more powerful.

There weren't many in the park tonight, just as he didn't expect there to be. So seeing the pretty little girl sitting on a bench against an ornate railing, hugging her knees to her chest and looking lost was a strange picture, he had to admit. But it intrigued him, too. This one must not be as helpless as she appeared, to be out here alone like this in the dark. Witches rarely were.

As Donovan approached her from behind, Samantha lifted her head and turned to him, looking more curious than afraid.

"Samantha Ross?" he asked her.

She eyed him suspiciously. "Yes?"

Donovan moved out in front of her, taking in the image of her tiny frame. She was so small she almost looked like a child, especially with the way she held herself; but there was something about the way she looked at him that threw off that feeling. For a reason he wasn't sure of, she didn't hold the slightest bit of hesitation in his presence.

As he tried to get a feel for her, Donovan began to see that this girl was more numb than afraid. There was a glazed over look in her eyes that suggested she didn't care one way or another what happened to her. Perhaps Samantha had taken it harder than she should have, this demotion Mara had spoken to him of. But looking into her further, Donovan saw that that wasn't it. It was about more than that...a great deal more.

The others had done something to her. Whether physical or mental he didn't know, but it was clear to him that she had endured a great deal of abuse. Donovan knew that look all too well.

Imagine what Mara would have done to her if she had known what Caleb Holcomb really was. He shook his head at the thought.

"The timing is far from ideal," Donovan told her, "but you've picked out a nice location, I'll give you that."

Samantha wasn't entirely responsive, but she wasn't shut off to him either. She simply looked away from him and turned back to the fountains. Something about the water appeared to calm her; he could tell that when she defaulted to looking at it instead of him. Donovan wasn't used to that sort of thing. Humans were usually spellbound by his appearance.

"Do you mind if I sit with you for a while?" he asked her.

She looked at him again, more closely this time, and when she seemed satisfied with whatever she was looking for in him, she motioned her eyes to the bench to let him know it was okay.

Donovan sat beside her and rested his forearms against his legs. He looked out at the water with her for a moment, though he was hardly as interested in these fountains as she seemed to be. Small talk wasn't going to work with her, that much was obvious. So he didn't waste his time with it. Samantha wasn't going to respond to it anyway, so there really wasn't much of a point; especially not when he had a gorgeous blonde waiting for him back in the city.

"Are you aware that you have been used?" Donovan asked her point blank.

That, Samantha responded to. Turning to him sharply she asked, "What are you talking about?"

"A friend of yours," he told her. "Someone you trust...he is not what he seems."

She looked offended at the suggestion. "Which friend?" she asked. "What are you talking about?"

He turned to look at her. "Caleb Holcomb."

Donovan watched as her face went white.

"How do you know about Caleb?" she asked him slowly.

He ignored the question. "You have been compromised, Samantha. You and your...*sorority*."

His enunciation of the word drained the color in her face even further.

"Caleb and his brothers are working against you," he told her. "They are working to destroy everything you have all spent such a strenuous effort setting up, and they have used you to do it."

Samantha's face was flushing now to a distinct shade of red. "No..." she said in disbelief. "Caleb wouldn't..."

"He would," Donovan interrupted. "And he has. Do not be fooled by the boy's simple charms. He has been using you from the first moment you sought after him."

"How do you know this?" she demanded.

She was angry. This was good.

Donovan didn't bother withdrawing the gold chain from inside his shirt again; it wouldn't be necessary in this case. Instead he remained emotionless. "I am someone who supports your vision, Samantha. Someone who can help you."

"Help me how?" she asked defensively.

He could see that she was not prone to trust, especially not after what had been done to her as a result of her demotion. And yet it was through her feeling threatened by his suggestion that Samantha's apathy quickly faded, a spark of fire taking its place in her eyes. He could see it then, the fierceness in her that gave her a stubborn strength.

Caleb must have had quite a time with her.

Donovan leaned closer to her, but she didn't back away. "Help me," he whispered, tracing his fingers along her collarbone where he knew a gold necklace used to hang, "and I will ensure that you regain your rightful place in the Coven."

"My rightful place?" she questioned.

He grinned at her sadistically. "I will have Mara Whitlow crawling after you like a dog," he promised her.

That seemed to catch Samantha's interest enough to make her listen.

"Help me to destroy those who are seeking to destroy you," Donovan said, "and I will show you a power you have never known."

420

This story isn't over.

THE CHRONICLES continue with:

Book Two of
THE AWAKENED CHRONICLES

To find out more, go to:
TheAwakenedChronicles.com

A VERY SPECIAL
Thank You...

TO MY DADDY:
For every Woodland Park adventure you took me on, and for giving me the idea to write about the Nephilim in the first place.

TO MOM:
For pushing me to keep writing every chapter by threatening me if I didn't put the next one in your hands.

TO MY OLDER BROTHER, AUSTIN:
Without you, the fight scenes in this book would completely suck.

TO MY LITTLE BROTHER, CAMERON:
I could never thank you enough for the music you write for *The Awakened*, or for the music that has yet to be written. (You also look metal on the cover. Just saying.)

TO CATHY, MY EDITOR:
For your brilliance and patience, and for the fact that without you, the final manuscript would have been atrocious. I will miss you every day for the rest of my life.

TO PAPA LOU:
For believing I would write a story that had the power to change something.

TO SLEEPING GIANT:

Your music has shaped so much of *The Awakened*. It broke through to my soul when nothing else could and reminded me of what I fight for. The heartbeat of God is in your songs, and your cry has not fallen on deaf ears. I stand with you and fight this fight; you with the sound that has been given you and I with the words that are given me. And I know that together, we will see a generation know life again.

And finally...

TO THE ONE WHO HOLDS MY HEART:

That the word that goes out from your mouth will not return to you empty, but will accomplish what you desire and achieve the purpose for which you have sent it.

"Somehow it feels as betrayal to me, not to write the words I hear screaming on the inside. But it also takes a hope unseen, a frightening trust to make them fully live. To accurately portray the words of the soul, sometimes you have to lose your own, even if only for a moment…and trust the One who brought you here to bring you back to life again."

ABIGAIL BLACK

Visit the Official Author's Website:

AbigailBlack.com

ABOUT THE AUTHOR:
Abigail Black

From the day her third grade teacher told her to remember her when she published her first novel, Abigail Black has always known what she wanted to do with her life. Writing stories since she learned to write complete sentences, she has dedicated herself to following this path she has always believed she was meant to follow.

Surrounded by the majestic Rocky Mountains of Colorado, Black is never short on inspiration where she lives, and often travels to the locations she writes about in her stories so she can bring an element of reality and depth to them that pulls her readers in.

With a wild imagination and a vision for life that few to none carry, Black has woven a story that many have already claimed has "changed their life" in *The Awakened*, book one of the *The Awakened Chronicles*. It isn't an uncommon thing for her readers to contact her after finishing this book in only a day or two, professing that they will "never be the same again."

With a haunting way of playing into her actual life, Black's stories carry an almost prophetic edge to them that not only affects her, but just about anyone who reads them as well. In fact, many of her readers come away convinced that these stories were written about them. Part of this is due to the realism of Black's characters and the challenges they face. No matter how obscure the storyline, every moment of every scene is interfaced with truth, drawing parallels between fiction and actual life; because in one way or another, Black's own life experiences have been written into every one.

When asked about the undercurrent to these books that draws out from the readers the long-dormant places inside of them that are suddenly brought to life, Black can't explain it. "I never meant to make people dream about this story," she says. "I never meant for them to start writing songs about it or to identify so deeply with the characters that they begin to see everything about it playing out in their actual lives. I never meant for it to become so *real* to them."

However unprepared she was for this reaction, though, Black also can't deny the countless testimonies she has been given of exactly that. Whatever the reason may be for this obscure sort of phenomenon, she knows there's a good chance it has something to do with what she has always believed…that she is supposed to write these stories.

VISIT HER OFFICIAL WEBSITE:

AbigailBlack.com